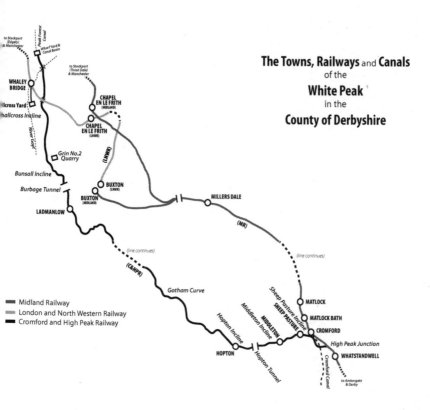

The Towns, Railways and Canals
of the
White Peak
in the
County of Derbyshire

to Stockport
(Edgely)
& Manchester

Peak Forest Canal

Wharf Yard & Canal Basin

WHALEY BRIDGE

to Stockport
(Tiviot Dale)
& Manchester

lcross Yard

CHAPEL EN LE FRITH (MIDLAND)

hallcross Incline

CHAPEL EN LE FRITH (LNWR)

River Goyt

Grin No.2 Quarry

(LNWR)

Bunsall Incline

BUXTON (LNWR)

Burbage Tunnel

BUXTON (MIDLAND)

MILLERS DALE

LADMANLOW

(MR)

(line continues)

(line continues)

(C&HPR)

Gotham Curve

Sheep Pasture Incline

MATLOCK

Hopton Incline

Middleton Incline

MIDDLETON

SHEEP PASTURE

MATLOCK BATH

CROMFORD

High Peak Junction

HOPTON

Hopton Tunnel

WHATSTANDWELL

Cromford Canal

to Ambergate & Derby

■ Midland Railway
■ London and North Western Railway
■ Cromford and High Peak Railway

FATAL
CONNECTIONS

David J. Boulton

Published by

MELROSE BOOKS

An Imprint of Melrose Press Limited
St Thomas Place, Ely
Cambridgeshire
CB7 4GG, UK
www.melrosebooks.co.uk

FIRST EDITION

Copyright © David J. Boulton 2016

The Author asserts his moral right to
be identified as the author of this work

Cover by Hannah Belcher

ISBN 978-1-910792-23-0
epub 978-1-910792-24-7
mobi 978-1-910792-25-4

Printed and bound in Great Britain by:
Gomer Press Ltd
Llandysul Enterprise Park
Llandysul
Ceredigion
SA44 4JL

FSC
www.fsc.org
MIX
Paper from
responsible sources
FSC® C114687

Contents

PART 3

Part 1

Chapter 1

Ladmanlow, 17th December, 1875

Up in the White Peak, a cold, clammy mist hung in the air. It wasn't quite impenetrable, but it distorted reality. So, when the two trains, heading toward each other on the same stretch of single track, emerged suddenly from the gloom, it offered very little warning for the crews.

"Hey – look!" the fireman saw an elusive shadow in the murk ahead.

The driver stared intently along the length of the boiler, past the tall chimney, and saw the silhouette as it materialised a moment later.

"Jump, lad! Jump – we're going to hit!" To his relief, the driver saw his young mate leap from the footplate. In a vain attempt to stop his engine, he closed the regulator and slammed the reverser across before he, too, leaped for his life.

Quite how the Cromford & High Peak Railway's slack operating procedures allowed this shocking accident to occur would later be investigated by official enquiry. The Railway Inspectorate of the Board of Trade would preside over the incident the following year. The immediate consequence, at five-and-twenty to nine on the morning of Friday, 17th December, 1875, was a catastrophic collision.

As the driver and fireman lay winded by the trackside, they heard an almighty tearing and rending of tortured metal. Their engine reared up, pushing the tender of the other locomotive aside and crashing into its cab before overturning it. The two engines came to rest; the hellish sound of their head-on coming

1

together was followed by the clanking of abused trucks as they pushed up, one upon another. For a few moments after the horrific clamour, only the gentle hissing of escaping steam was heard. Then the air was rent by cries of pain.

"Come on lad, let's see what we can do," the two men clambered to their feet and ran past derailed trucks toward the stricken locos.

Since their own train was simply carrying out an extended shunting movement, it had no guard; but the other was doing something more important. Travelling the whole length of the line, from Whaley Bridge to Cromford, it was known as a 'Fly'. In the guard's van – the only seating the railway could offer – were a handful of passengers. None were hurt, so the guard left them to their own devices and ran forward to the entangled engines.

The cries were coming from the driver of the Fly. The torn, bloody body of his dead fireman was wrapped round a driving wheel of the overturned engine. Reeling from the shock, the three uninjured railwaymen did what they could to help the driver, who lay half-in and half-out of his cab, a broken leg rendering him immobile.

The fearful sound of the crash was carried with distressing clarity on the damp air. Shocked railway workers in the nearby marshalling yard at Ladmanlow were in no doubt as to its cause. Indeed, as they hurried to see what they could do to help, one or two were considering whether their own negligence may have played a part.

Sergeant Samuel Spray of the railway police was well down the line, in the opposite direction, at the time of the accident, but its distant boom alerted him. The investigations, which had occupied him over the previous few days, were almost complete. He had been hoping to walk to Whaley Bridge without attracting attention. However, weary as he was, he hurried toward the source of the sound. There was no sign of damage at the rear of the train, but as he walked on, derailed trucks forewarned of what lay ahead.

Out of the mist a wagon loomed, as if suspended from above. It had obviously been forced over the next in line, which was almost at right angles to the track. As he drew closer to the head of the train, Spray found himself scrambling over piles of limestone disgorged by the laden trucks as they had driven into ever-increasing chaos. By the time he arrived at the point of impact, there was quite a gathering – mostly railway servants, but others too. The compact, self-contained man, wearing a low-crowned bowler and dark greatcoat, passed by discreetly.

One casualty was being carried away on a makeshift stretcher: a driver, if his overalls were anything to go by, thought Spray. Two dead bodies were laid out beside the track. He was looking them over when someone brought a piece of canvas. Before the decedents could be decorously covered, he noted that one had clearly been lacerated and crushed, with sticky blood seeping from fatal wounds, whilst the other was relatively undamaged.

"Did you help get the bodies out of the train?" he asked the man with the shroud.

"This 'un, yes – an' a right job it were. He'd been trapped around a wheel, y'see – an' crushed."

"And this one?" asked the sergeant, whilst helping cover the second victim. He noticed that the body was stiff and cold, and had a bluish tinge to the face.

"Nah – we'd spent so much time getting this poor feller out, some of the others must have done him."

The dissimilarity between the two corpses didn't seem to be arousing any suspicion amongst the rescuers; after all, fatalities were to be expected at the site of such a crash. Spray asked around, but no one admitted to finding the undamaged body in the wrecked train. Each believed that someone else had done so. To the detective, a veteran of active military service, death was commonplace in all of its presentations. A thin line of bruising around the neck of the otherwise-undamaged body left him in no doubt: this victim had been garrotted, but how long ago it was impossible to say.

Spray melted into the mist as he resumed his trek along the track to Whaley Bridge. His presence at the accident had gone unremarked, and his departure was unnoticed. He'd made the journey several times in the past week, mostly as a clandestine passenger on a mineral wagon. The accident had put an end to traffic on the line, so he had to walk the five miles. Deep in thought, he nearly missed the object. Whilst the fog was lifting, there was still no sun to be seen, but its rays suffused the mist, providing a surprisingly intense light. Out of the corner of his eye, colours of red, white and blue caught his attention.

"What the deuce is that?" during the long hours all alone, keeping watch in the quarry, he'd taken to muttering to himself. "Let's take a look," he turned and took a couple of paces back. Seen from a different angle, the thing almost disappeared into the undergrowth that spilled out onto the permanent way. He stooped and picked it up: it was a soaking wet, battered and muddy hat. At the time, he couldn't recall anyone, other than the two corpses, hatless at the scene of the accident. Though he hadn't been paying much attention to headgear.

"None of them'd wear this anyway," he said to himself. In his hand was what had once been a high-crowned bowler in pale grey with a band of red, white and blue. The words *Happy Holidays* were embroidered in gold-coloured thread. "Hmm... been here a day or two, by the looks of it," he muttered. With the hat in his hand, he walked on.

Chapter 2

Crewe, 10th December, 1875

Crewe Junction was a busy place. Its myriad passengers arrived and departed on the frequent trains, but the platforms forever teemed with people. In amongst the throng, railway servants helped, and occasionally hindered, this ocean of humanity. Whilst the platform staff were visible, many others worked unseen behind mysterious doors, and in obscure corners, found all over the station.

The LNWR Constabulary (Northern Division) occupied just one such place. It would be pretentious to describe them as offices. It consisted of just two rooms, one larger than the other, in what had once been storage for parcels. The solitary fireplace was in the back room; with the door between the two closed, the larger was a chilly place.

Superintendent Charles Wayland occupied the smaller, cosier room. A former lieutenant colonel in the Land Transport Corps, he had seen service in the Crimea some twenty years earlier. A near-fatal leg injury put paid to his command of a temporary military railway. On relinquishing his commission, he sought employment in the railway police service. With the burgeoning network of lines providing an attractive target for the criminal fraternity, the London & North Western created a uniformed constabulary. The superintendent wore his attire with military élan, diminished only slightly by his limp. His position was an isolated one in the small establishment he now commanded, consisting as it did of four constables, a sergeant and himself. He found it expedient to be on more intimate terms with his sergeant than would have been thought proper in military circles. Of course, proprieties had to be observed, but as long as foreheads were knuckled, and he didn't see any fraternising between the ranks, he was content.

"Sergeant!"

"Sir?"

"In here, if you please," the former colonel was quite sensible to the incongruity of calling his meagre accommodation an 'office', so in *here* it was. The door closed, with superintendent and sergeant on the warm side, and the rest of the small force on the cold one.

"Take a seat," the senior man gestured towards a small, hard chair. He sat in greater comfort on his padded one, behind a desk covered in correspondence and sheets of figures. "Here's a fine to-do."

"Sir?"

Two pieces of paper passed from one man to the other. With this transfer, a subtle alteration in the balance of status that lay between the two took place. Investigations usually started in this way.

Wayland was a successful leader of men, and a keeper of the peace, but he was no detective. Seated opposite him was Sergeant Sam Spray, who most certainly was. At the age of sixteen, to the dismay of the God-fearing people who reared him, Spray had succumbed to the blandishments of a recruiting officer and joined the 95th Regiment of Foot. He'd developed a strong sense of self-preservation which helped him survive the rigours of army life. The privations of a nonconformist childhood and those of the military weren't so very different.

The papers he received from Wayland were two letters. One was from the head of commercial traffic on the London & North Western Railway (LNWR); the other from the owner of a small quarry near Ladmanlow. They each told a similar story: despite working the same hours and running the same number of trains as previously, income had fallen. The first letter, from the quarry owner, was more precise: he was losing forty tons (four wagonloads) a week. This was sufficient to be of serious concern to a smallish undertaking like Cross & Blackwood, whose letter, Spray noted, was dated several months before the one from the LNWR. Clearly, the proportionally smaller loss to the bigger organisation had taken longer to surface. It was, however, the second letter that had spurred the superintendent into action.

"Well, sergeant, do you think you can make something of this?" there was a few moments of silence. Wayland waited.

"Yes, sir, I believe I can. I take it you will be wanting prompt action?"

"Of course," Wayland was curious to know what action his subordinate proposed, but he made no enquiry. Experience had taught him that a request for information would be met with meaningless generalities.

"May I have permission, sir, to proceed in civilian clothing, and to have access to sufficient funds to travel and live away at the department's expense?"

Crumbs of information were coming in Wayland's direction. He collected them carefully, "Travelling expenses? Will your warrant card not suffice in the company's territory?"

The question was ignored, "I also think it would be prudent if you were to tell people that I am to be on leave for the next fortnight, sir."

The superintendent's choler rose at the notion of his sergeant taking a holiday at departmental expense.

Spray pressed on: "You have no doubt already realised, sir, that this fraud must originate from within the company.

If any news of my investigation concerning company staff should escape from this department, it might make things very difficult."

When collected together, a rather deflated Wayland's crumbs amounted to this: his sergeant would proceed, incognito, to the Peak District, to investigate the company losses.

Rather him than me, Wayland thought. As a man of the Cheshire plains, he had misgivings about any terrain more than 100-feet above sea level. It was a distaste accentuated in the Crimea, by an encounter with a runaway truck careering down from the Sevastopol plateau to the coast.

"Very well," he conceded.

"I propose billeting myself in Whaley Bridge, sir."

At the mention of that small mill-town, Wayland had a suggestion: "May I recommend you take lodgings with Mrs Oldroyd? We like to do what we can for the families of railwaymen. Her husband died a while ago whilst in our employ." He wrote down the address and handed the note to Spray, "You will leave tomorrow."

Chapter 3

Blackpool and Whaley Bridge, Autumn, 1875

On Saturday, 17th November, 1875, a short item concerning the Cromford & High Peak Railway appeared in the *Derbyshire Times,* in the section devoted to odd snippets and obscure pieces of company news. It attracted little attention from a readership fed on local scandals, church fetes and the like.

Proposed Railway Company Acquisition.

It has come to our notice that moves are afoot for the London & North Western company to take ownership of the Cromford & High Peak Railway. The former has controlled the latter under a lease since the management of the latter got into difficulties some years ago. It is understood that there is resistance to the move on the part of some interested parties, but we are reliably informed that this will be overcome.

The piece was carefully cut from a copy of the paper, tucked into an envelope and, along with a covering letter, entrusted to the Royal Mail. Having traversed the White Peak, and then the Fylde overnight, it arrived next day at an accommodation address in Blackpool, where it remained for several days.

Eddie Markham was a bit of a lad. Despite the gambling and the ladies, he survived by being quick on his feet. He had friends – well, that was what he called them – but they were

9

keener to see the back of him when he departed than his lean, moustachioed face when he arrived. His shifty eyes darted about like those of a hunted animal nervous of predators, and – in reality – that was what he was. Not that he'd admit it; what with his swagger and his fancy clothes, he reckoned to cut a dash. It was the flash hat, really; the rest of his ensemble might have been smart once, but the frayed cuffs and worn elbows gave him a shabby air.

Right now he owed money – enough to make his creditors dangerous – so he was lying low, and the letter rested, undisturbed, in the rack at Mr Griffiths's shop. He managed to rearrange his debt so that, for a few days at least, it was safe to emerge and stroll nonchalantly along Talbot Road to enquire after his mail. He collected a letter with a Cromford date stamp of November 18th.

"Bit posh fer the likes of you, in't it?" said the boy behind the counter as he held out the letter.

"Cheeky bugger," replied Eddie, clipping him round the ear as he took it. "Don't know why old Griffiths keeps you on."

The boy had a point: the letter was a cut above Eddie's usual mail. For a moment, he struggled with the embossed lettering, which read: *Barford & Smythe, Solicitors.*

When he tore the envelope open, it all came back: his aunt's will, the disappointment, the injustice. A newspaper cutting fluttered to the pavement, unnoticed, as he perused the letter. *Dear Mr Markham, I would be obliged...* it droned on, ending with Nathaniel Jones's signature. Eddie noticed a reference to the clipping and spied the escaping newsprint, chasing after it. The small piece of *Derbyshire Times* had reached its destination.

It had been a godsend, really. *I have a proposition arising from the information enclosed that might be to our mutual advantage, and would be pleased to receive you at your earliest convenience to discuss the matter.* Eddie resisted, with some difficulty, the urge to gamble with the modest amount of cash enclosed for his train fare. The old humbug had only sent enough for a third class ticket, for only part of the journey. Even the obsessive gambler in him couldn't see it as a big enough stake to make it worth joining a card school. The rest of the journey, from Whaley Bridge to Cromford, was covered by his gold pass for the Cromford & High Peak Railway.

Old Mrs Markham's family had been a disappointment. Her husband died long before she did, and her sole living relative was a wayward nephew. Cats were her only solace. By the time she passed away they were the only things she loved. Well, perhaps she was fond of her companion, too. Certainly, in her last years she couldn't have managed herself or the cats without the woman's help. So it seemed entirely rational to leave her all the money, with the proviso that she kept the cats comfortable till the end of their lives.

When making her will, Mrs Markham forgot about the railway shares. They were worthless, never paid a penny, so she couldn't understand why her brother-in-law had ever bothered with them. Still, she had to admit that it was his money she was bequeathing. It was that nice Mr Jones who reminded her about the shares. She was happy to allow them to go to her nephew, Edward.

"Well, he wouldn't gamble them or spend them on women, would he?" she'd remarked.

The one benefit they did confer was a free gold pass for all journeys on the C&HP. She wasn't to know it would languish at the offices of her solicitor until he found it expedient to pass it on to its rightful owner.

The deferral of his debt would keep Eddie safe only for a day or two. He joined the first train from Blackpool to Manchester, changed to another to get to Stockport Edgeley, and arrived at Whaley Bridge. Not only had it been a tedious journey so far – third class, hard seats and late-autumn draughts – but he was unable to continue to Cromford that night. *Bradshaw* stated, correctly, that it was possible to travel from Whaley Bridge to Cromford, but hadn't been helpful about train times. (The publication was less at fault than the C&HP, whose approach to the timetable was casual to the point of total disregard.) Arriving at Whaley Bridge, he had discovered that there was only one train a day, and that left early in the morning. For now, he had two choices. He could continue to Buxton, and then catch a Midland Railway service to Cromford, or he could find a bed for the night.

He'd managed to get a bite to eat on Edgeley Station. By the time his train was heading for the Goyt Valley and the Peak, he was searching his pockets for a toothpick. A bit of ham was irritating, but the best thing he could find was a business card that had spent some time in his coat. Its corners were now bent and it was rather grubby, but would have to do. With the ham dislodged, something on the card caught his eye as he leant toward the window to throw it out. The words *Whaley Bridge* were clearly visible. Struck by the coincidence, he took a closer look.

It was a lady's business card. *Where the devil did that come from?* he wondered. After a few moments, he began to recall assisting a woman at a dance in Blackpool the previous summer. She'd been rushing out in a crowd when her bag was knocked from her arm, and he'd helped pick up her scattered belongings. She had handed him the card, and said that if ever he was in her area and needed somewhere to stay... He looked at the card. It read: *Comfortable lodgings by the night or the week. Mrs Elizabeth Oldroyd, 37 Old Mill End, Whaley Bridge.* The twist of fate being too startling to ignore, he disembarked at the station, asked the porter for directions, and set off at once.

"Yes, I do have a single room vacant, sir." He mentioned the early train to Cromford, "Of course, sir, early breakfast can be provided – at a small extra charge." The total cost was computed. "It would be most acceptable if payment could be in advance," Mrs Oldroyd hadn't survived in business without learning who to charge up front.

Eddie's train journey to Cromford the next morning was an unusual one. The C&HP was a mineral line, so no platforms or passenger stations were provided. The most the railway could offer human cargo were a couple of hard, wooden benches in the guard's van. Not only was the journey uncomfortable, it was repeatedly interrupted. Each time the train arrived at an incline, it was winched up by horse-driven capstan, or steam winding-engine, and the beleaguered passengers were obliged to alight and walk alongside.

Eddie wondered, as he trudged up the first incline, if his boots – ill-suited to this kind of activity and well past their prime – would survive the day. At the top, he clambered into a converted brakevan and enquired if this was the only incline. There were several more before the limestone plateau of the White Peak was reached, and then there were some downhill ones at the other end. He was tired and irritated by the journey after less than an hour and – worse – there was no peace because his attention was sought by a fellow passenger.

"See here: a most remarkable landscape, don't you think?" Eddie was only thinking of the discomfort of being jolted about on the hard bench. "The railway was to have been a canal, don't y'know, but there was not enough water up here to keep it full! What d'ye think of that?"

Eddie resolved not to think of it, and conveyed his lack of interest to the other man by the blank expression on his face. A rather fraught silence reigned.

The train stopped frequently to pick up full wagons and leave empty ones, causing Eddie to become anxious about being late for his appointment. He asked the guard what time he supposed they would arrive, remarking that, "Things move uncommon slow up here." The guard, who on this line was known as the 'Flyman', advised him that, to save time, he should alight at Black Rock and walk down Cromford Hill into the village.

It was a rather jaded traveller who presented himself at the offices of Barford & Smythe, situated in a modest side street off the Derby Road. A servant led him into a private room, and announced him to a pompous, rotund individual who was neither Barford nor Smythe, as both had passed on some time ago.

Despite his well-filled waistcoat impeding its retrieval, Jones extracted his gold hunter, flipped open the cover ostentatiously, and gave a grunt of disapproval.

"Good day to you, Mr Markham, my name is Jones, Nathaniel Jones," the pair shook hands.

Eddie found himself seated on the most uncomfortable chair in the room. Social niceties were dispensed with and the matter in hand was addressed without delay.

"Mr Jones, I am here to uncover the mystery of your letter," Eddie offered.

"You will remember that when we last had contact, it was over the matter of your aunt's will," Jones began.

Eddie remembered very well, and still smarted at the injustice of it.

"I will reiterate the circumstances," there didn't seem to be any way Eddie could stop him, so he continued: "Your late aunt left her entire estate to her lady's companion, on the understanding that six, er, feline creatures were cared for by said companion for the rest of their – presumably nine – lives."

Jones paused in order to smile at his own quip, then went on, "Your sole interest in the estate was as residual legatee of a substantial block of shares in the Cromford & High Peak Railway." Eddie already knew that much, and a fat lot of use it had been to him, as they paid no dividend. "The companion – and presumably, the cats – died some time ago, and you will remember that I wrote to you at the time to clarify the matter."

"Pardon me, Mr Jones, but I can't see why I've had to endure two days of uncomfortable travel, just to be told what I already know."

"If I may say so, sir, you have failed to appreciate the importance of the news in the cutting I sent. I take it you did, in fact, read it," a smirk flitted across Jones's face. "Ah, I see: you did not."

In truth, Eddie had glanced briefly at the piece of newsprint, but its contents hadn't seemed important; such matters bored him.

"If, sir, you would be kind enough to pay attention, I will explain," the older man's haughty tone was beginning to grate. "There were a number of investors in the original company in 1830, who received nothing for their pains. Indeed, they were fortunate not to have been bankrupted. They were saved when the LNWR took control. A small emolument was paid. In their wisdom, the rump of the original board of directors decided to retain a company secretary and a legal advisor to keep an eye on their residual interest. The firm of Barford & Smythe was entrusted with the latter purpose, and I am its representative. Most of the original investors have passed on," he remarked, his grave tone at variance with the avarice in his eyes, "and their successors have little interest or knowledge of the shares."

Eddie, bored by the interminable details of a moribund company's affairs, noted the other man's expression and showed more interest.

"The railway has, surprisingly, been turning over a profit of late, and the LNWR have proposed that, to regularise the position, they should pay out the surviving shareholders and assume ownership of the company and its assets."

Eddie's interest, which had already overtaken his boredom, was suddenly reinforced by greed.

"The shares would not, of course, be paid out at face value, but, nevertheless, a tidy sum could be realised by yourself," Eddie's palms began to sweat and his pulse raced.

"I see, and would you care to give a value to that tidy sum?" Eddie's question was ignored.

"There is, however, a problem. One original shareholder is still alive. He is a wealthy man, though elderly and physically infirm. He has given authority to the company secretary to oppose, on his behalf, the sale of the company."

"Why on earth would he do that?"

"I have pondered that matter myself. As a child, the secretary was a protégé of the family, and has remained close ever since. Indeed, that is how he came by his position. So vehement is he regarding the sale, that it is my belief that the opposition is entirely his doing. It occurred to me that, if pressure were to be put on the secretary, this impediment could be, er, dealt with."

So, that's it, thought Eddie, realising at last why he'd been brought all that way. Lurking in the verbiage was the suggestion that the pressure in question was to be applied by him. The matter was discussed further – names, addresses and social habits were divulged. The meeting closed on the understanding that the 'tidy sum' would be forthcoming, if Eddie arranged matters so that there were no further objections.

Chapter 4

Crewe, 18th December, 1875

"Really, sergeant, I can't see a reason for all the rush. Surely Monday morning would have done?" Wayland's expostulation was ignored. News of the previous day's events had clearly failed to reach the railway constabulary offices in Crewe.

"Under the circumstances, sir, with an additional matter to consider, I felt it was important that you were made aware of how things stand. Particularly as they may require your intervention."

At this, Wayland felt his irritation evaporating. He would never admit it, but he was flattered that his subordinate had, for once, found something useful for him to do. The usual pattern was for Spray to present him with a fait accompli, leaving him feeling redundant.

"Here are my findings so far sir," he passed a document to his superintendent.

It was brief and in truth, not very tidy. Spray had completed it in haste the night before, and it showed. Wayland started to read.

Having received instruction to investigate loss of revenue by both the C&HP and the quarry company of Cross & Blackwood, I proceeded to Whaley Bridge in civilian clothes and took a room at 37 Old Mill End.

It was midday by the time Spray boarded a Stockport-bound train, after changing out of his uniform, and tying up the odd loose end. With no clear idea when he'd be back, things ought to be left tidy. He managed, without actually saying so, to leave the impression that some urgent personal matter occasioned his absence. It was a close shave when Constable Archer asked if there was anything he could help with. He was saved by one of the others barging past and knocking some papers onto the floor.

First things first: a bed for the night. As he made his way to Old Mill End, he got to wondering why 'the Whale' – darn it, one day the super would overhear this nickname – had selected Mrs Oldroyd. In his experience, landladies were all the same – grasping, dictatorial and bewhiskered. After climbing a long hill he was out of breath by the time he arrived at No. 37. He knocked on the door and waited.

"Good evening, sir, can I help you?" The firm voice, pretty, young face and steady grey eyes were at such variance with the stereotype he'd imagined, that he chided himself.

"Good evening, ma'am. My name's Spray, and I'm looking for a billet. A week to start with, and possibly more."

The warmth which seemed to lurk at the corners of her mouth spread into a welcoming smile, "Of course, sir; if you would like to step inside we can discuss terms."

These were entirely acceptable and, although it wasn't mentioned, seemed to include a dish of tea. Seated in comfortable chairs in the front parlour, the two made polite conversation.

"Have you come far, Mr Spray?"

Spray mentioned Stockport and it was true, as far as it went. The omission of Crewe left him uncomfortable in the face of this patently open and honest woman.

"Will it be acceptable if I keep rather irregular hours? My, er, business is of a somewhat unpredictable nature," the need for discretion felt more awkward than he'd expected.

"Of course, Mr Spray: you can have a latch-key. Breakfast might be difficult if you are to be out early. Perhaps I could put something up the night before, for you to take with you?" Her look wasn't penetrating, but Spray couldn't escape the feeling that this composed and attractive young woman could see right through his prevarications and half-truths.

"Thank you. That would be most acceptable. I'll be out early tomorrow."

I proceeded the next day to Grin No. 2 Quarry to carry out observations.

Spray had set out from Mrs Oldroyd's around half past five. She had been true to her word, and stuffed into his poacher's pocket were enough victuals to last all day. He'd estimated it would be a two-hour walk to Grin No. 2 Quarry, but twenty minutes into the journey he had a change of plan.

The winding engine at the top was already at work by the time he arrived at the foot of Shallcross Incline. As he puffed his way up the hill he found he was keeping pace with a trio of empties rising sedately alongside him. Descending on a parallel track was a counterweight of two loaded wagons. The trucks moved in ghostly silence. Bustling about at the top was a small engine forming up a short train. As Spray walked on, it slowly overtook him as it gained speed. Why not ride? The running jump to climb onto the last mineral wagon had seemed like a good idea, but he wasn't so sure as he dangled from it, feet scrabbling for purchase. In the end, he made it onto a buffer, and perched there until the line of trucks started bunching up on the engine as it braked gently for Grin No. 1. So far, in the gloom of early morning, no one had paid him any attention, but the day was getting lighter. After clambering over a drystone wall and fighting with a patch of brambles, a struggle through a stretch of undergrowth brought him to the edge of Grin No. 2. He peered down from the lip of an irregular amphitheatre to the workings below.

Well, I got that right, he thought. Good fortune had brought him to the worked-out side of the quarry. Explosions were taking place across the abyss, sending rocks tumbling unceremoniously to the bottom. He was grateful not to be joining the boulders of limestone in their headlong rush.

The empty trucks lined up below him were dragged, one at time, by a horse to a loading point, where small wagons on a narrow track were manhandled until they could tip their loads and move on. After a while the scene began to pall, and Mrs Oldroyd's sustenance came to Spray's mind. She had certainly done him proud. A breakfast of fresh bread, strong, hard cheese and sharp pickle had been consumed. Then Mrs Oldroyd's provisions made way to thoughts of Mrs Oldroyd herself. It was something with which to while away the long vigil.

There was a half hour in-between wagons being loaded and his making notes, so he used the interval to recall her face, with its high cheek bones and pale skin, framed with dark brown hair. After a while the steady, dependable, even dull man – as he saw himself – was chasing flights of fancy. Perhaps a discreet meal together? Or a quiet walk in winter sunshine? Breaking off to note another full truck as it was hauled away, his imagination returned with an intensity that alarmed him. He struggled to establish his former equilibrium.

A record was made of the number of loaded wagons leaving the quarry over a four-day period.

Although she was formally Mrs Elizabeth Oldroyd, Spray's landlady never thought of herself as anything other than Lizzie, her mother's pet name for her. 'Lizzie, it's your bedtime!' had become, 'Lizzie, could you help me with the dinner?' Later, when her mother finally took to her sick-bed, it was: 'Thank you, Lizzie my dear, I don't know how we'd manage without you.'

After his wife's death, Isaac Bennett, Lizzie's father, had assumed the responsibilities she would have shouldered, and took it upon himself to do something about his daughter's mistaken sense of duty. 'We can't go on like this, Lizzie. I'm not having a sacrificial spinster for a daughter,' he was adamant, 'You needn't fuss over me, you're not your ma; you should be someone else's wife and mother.'

As a white-collar railway clerk, Albert Oldroyd was considered respectable. More so than Mr Bennett, who was a guard, but both were railwaymen, and Albert allowed himself to be brought home for inspection. Lizzie provided tea, bread-and-butter, and a Victoria sponge, after which Albert admired her sketching. She was self-taught, and was insecure about the results of her labours with chalk and paper. Her self-assurance blossomed under Albert's flattering remarks, and when the talk moved on to books, the afternoon took on a convivial air.

At the time, he didn't comment on the literary reference from Jane Austen in the name Isaac and his wife had given their daughter. He later suggested – jokingly – that one reason for agreeing to his marriage proposal might be to divest herself of it. But she never thought of herself as Mrs Oldroyd: even after she had married the pale, slim, gentle man ten years her elder.

Perhaps it was the lack of passion, or perhaps the *otherness,* that defined their marriage. Whatever the cause, she'd found it hard to grieve when Albert's pale complexion became the waxy pallor of consumption.

During her marriage, Lizzie had not been short of money. Her frugal housekeeping meant she never had to ask her husband for more than her allowance – although he made it plain that she was welcome to do so. The will, when it was read, was a surprise. She'd assumed from his talk that Albert owned No. 37, an unusual thing in itself, even though he'd been the chief clerk in his office.

He'd let it be known during his last illness that the property would be hers. And so it was, but the half share in the house owned by his brother, Arthur, stayed with him. Not that he was any trouble. 'Treat it as your own my dear,' he had assured her, and later, 'Perhaps it would help if I took one of the rooms on regular basis.' With his regular payments, Lizzie realised she could make a secure, if modest, living by letting out the other spare bedrooms.

Even when she didn't like her guests, there was pleasure in finding a pigeonhole for each one, and deciding when to demand payment in advance. Not from Mr Spray, though. She gave little thought to his irregular hours, and felt that the straightforward man, whose shyness couldn't mask his inner confidence and transparent honesty, would pay at the end of the week. She was sure of it. It wasn't doubt that led her through the assessment several times over; she enjoyed appraising her new guest.

The number of departures recorded was compared with the records kept by the tallyman at the quarry.

It was Wednesday: Spray's fourth visit to Grin No. 2. By the end of the first, he had established the departure pattern.

Between twelve and sixteen wagons were loaded daily and drawn away next morning. Since he'd worked out how to avoid the brambles, he'd had no difficulty in making his way across country from Grin No. 1 to No. 2. He would arrive in time to see the ingoing empties and their exchange for the wagons loaded the previous day. His journey was satisfyingly neat: he hitched a lift each morning on the same movement that worked into both Grin quarries. It delivered him in perfect time to start his day's observations. He had seen enough: Wednesday was to be his final day. He had one final task to carry out in order to complete his investigation. His mind wandered back to the previous evening.

"Might I have a word with you, Mrs Oldroyd?" Lizzie emerged from the kitchen, hastily taking off her apron. "I shall be away from Whaley Bridge for two nights and back on Friday," he began to take money from his purse. "Will it be all right if I leave my things?"

"Of course, Mr Spray, and it will be perfectly in order to settle up when you've concluded your business."

Spray shivered. Night was falling and the quarry was shutting down. His greatcoat had done its best but the steady rain had soaked through. It now weighed heavy and let in the cold night air. Still he waited. The light in the tallyman's hut continued to burn whilst fragments of voices floated upward to his vantage point. The quarrymen were bidding each other goodnight. Still, the light glowed. Finally, darkness fell. He waited another hour and then set off. In daylight he might have chanced a descent down the quarry face, but in the dark it seemed prudent to retrace his steps. On previous forays into the quarry he'd been less cautious. This time he wasn't just noting the destinations from the dockets attached to the trucks, he had something more risky in mind.

Fingers stiff with cold made picking the lock of the tally-man's hut tricky. In his head Spray could hear his superintendent's disapproving voice: 'Skeleton keys? Really sergeant, most improper, not at all the sort of thing to reflect well on the service. I'm surprised at you.'

All in all, a bit of ignorance up above wasn't a bad thing. The Whale had been happy enough when Spray and Archer had caught the original owner of the keys. He hadn't enquired too closely as to how the screwsman made his illicit entries. It was all a matter of 'feel', that's what the rogue had said. He'd been willing enough to tutor the detectives in return for having one or two misdemeanours overlooked. 'Just tickle around until you get a bit of resistance. Gently, mind.'

Spray tucked his hands into his armpits beneath his coat. His numbed fingers had dropped the darn keys once already. Finally he was inside. He couldn't see a thing at first but eventually he found the tallyman's lantern. It was a gamble he had to take – that the quarry would be deserted at this time of night. Once or twice during the day, the man had come outside with a big, leather-bound ledger, and there it was. He crouched down on the floor, taking care to shade the light from the blackness beyond the window. It didn't take long to scribble down all the destinations, though he almost knocked over the paraffin lamp in his haste. Spray put the ledger back in place and doused the light. Outside he fumbled about, trying to re-lock the door. The old reprobate must have gained some recompense for the loss of his dubs by missing out this part of the lesson. Finally, with a satisfying click, it was done.

During this period all wagons were despatched to Cromford goods yard, where there is connection to both the Midland Main Line and the Cromford Canal. Examination of all the destinations showed that each of four unrecorded wagons of limestone was destined for the same customer, and the cargoes were to be transferred to narrowboats on the canal system.

The Crimea had never been as cold as this. True, he was twenty years younger then, but trying to sleep in a lineside hut had left Spray stiff, hungry and chilled to the bone. Lizzie's victuals were lasting well, though the mere thought of her pet name felt dangerously familiar. Not that he'd been invited to use it; he'd learned it when a neighbour called to her through the kitchen door. He had no idea what she thought of his comings and goings, and he'd been apprehensive about asking for an extra supply of food, but she had made no enquiry and had packed enough bread and cheese to last him a good two days. Now, with something solid in his stomach, he set off for Ladmanlow sidings, where the through trains for Cromford yard were assembled. He made it by five o'clock, and already a fire was being made up in one of the engines standing ready for its day's work. With his eyes focussed on the fire hole, the steam raiser would need a moment to adjust to the gloom of the yard. As the man jumped down and headed for the next loco, Spray slipped stealthily between two trucks making up the early morning goods.

It is a paradox of the White Peak that its high rainfall is accompanied by a lack of accessible water. So porous is the limestone that rainwater vanishes, only to reappear as springs in the lower ground at its periphery. Locomotives, winding engines and people marooned on the plateau all needed water, so the C&HP laboriously trundled it back uphill to supply them. Spray found himself hiding next to a tanker. He scrambled through the open coal-hole into the empty hopper of the old tender of a scrapped engine, reused by the thrifty company for transporting water. He waited there, out of sight. Knocking the water container produced a hollow 'bong'. Just as well it was empty, he thought. It must be going to Cromford yard to be filled up. He must get out before then; he was pretty well hidden from the track side, but he'd be rumbled by whoever clambered up top to manage the refill.

A gentle bump woke him as a locomotive buffered up to the line of wagons. He must have dozed off, despite the cold. He could hear muffled voices. It sounded like a guard and driver were conferring about the weight of the train and its stopping points. Spray wished he could hear the detail; it might help with the problem of leaving unseen. Finally, with a violent jerk and a lot of clanking as the couplings tightened, they were moving.

I made my way to Cromford yard by way of the C&HP.

Even though Spray had looked at a map before he left Crewe, and made a few discreet enquiries at his lodging, he didn't know much about the Cromford end of the line. Thirty or so miles, three inclines and a tunnel was about the extent of his knowledge. He was shaken out of his drowse by the jerks and rattles of the goods train coming to rest. The descent was going to be a bit chancy: splitting the train between his hiding place and the next wagon would reveal him through the coal hole. Slowly the line of trucks was pushed up to the top of the incline, where they were separated from the rest, three at a time. Then they were attached to a cable for the descent.

As the water tankers got nearer to the head of the queue, he could feel his pulse racing. He daren't look out to see what was happening; trapped in his coal bunker he had to sit tight and hope. Then, silently, the sandwich of a tanker each end, and Spray's prison in between, set off sedately down Hopton Incline. He'd made it, undiscovered. This was his chance. Straining to get its heavy train, now in one piece again, on the move, the locomotive was making a lot of smoke. The fumes, spilling into the damp air, were suddenly constricted as it entered Hopton Tunnel. The great clouds of smoke were forced back, bursting from the tunnel mouth and smothering everything nearby. The guard wouldn't see him in the murk, but, unfortunately, Spray couldn't see where he was, either.

How long he'd lain unconscious he'd no idea. To start with, he could think of nothing except the throbbing pain in his head. Then he knew he had to get away from the line side. Why, and where to, wasn't the point – just move. Standing didn't seem an option, so he crawled, despite a painful shoulder. His view uphill wasn't clear, either, he just knew it was the thing to do. Well, two things: away and uphill. By the time he'd made it to the undergrowth near the lip of the cutting, he'd achieved a third. He was at the entrance of a tunnel.

Lying in its cover, he could see the stonework around the opening and the rails disappearing into darkness. That was enough thinking for now. He drifted into a trance for a few minutes. When he surfaced again things had improved marginally. It had stopped raining. He tried to stop the wet still creeping down his neck, but that hurt his shoulder. Worse, his hand returned from his neck with blood on it. Still, his head wasn't so bad now.

That was it, an investigation and an illicit journey, and then it all came flooding back. He'd climbed down the rungs of a ladder on the side of the tanker and was just jumping onto the track side when... bang! He must have left it too late and been flung against the tunnel entrance. He made a voyage of inspection round his person. The painful shoulder could be made to move if necessary, so at least there was nothing broken. The blood on his neck had come from his head, but there wasn't much of it, and the wound was more bruise than laceration. He must have been protected by his hat. His hat! Where had that gone? It certainly wasn't on his head.

At the earliest opportunity, an investigation of Cromford yard was undertaken. A record of traffic was kept by the yard foreman. It was compared with the record kept at Grin No. 2 Quarry.

A spring bubbling out from the limestone cutting transformed the bedraggled Spray. Rinsing the blood from his hair and wiping the thin trickle from his neck left very little to be seen of his encounter with the masonry of the tunnel mouth. Even his bowler, once he'd found it and punched out the dent, didn't look too bad on cursory inspection. It certainly hid the egg-like lump that was developing on the side of his head.

By now it was dark, and work must have finished in the yard at Cromford goods. Standing at the basin by Mill Wharf, Spray heard, rather than saw, the railwaymen come along the towpath toward Cromford and home. It had been late afternoon by the time he'd found his way from Hopton Tunnel into Middleton. The watery sun, having struggled all day, had finally broken through the mist and low cloud, and was making a brief appearance before setting.

Spray's body yearned for warmth and comfort, and he needed time to plan the night's doings. The Rising Sun pub had looked irresistible. "Bit better now, tha knows," said the publican, opening the conversation.

"You've the right of it," Spray replied. "It's been a miserable day, but I s'pose you get used to it, living here."

"Oh aye, yer do that. What'll you have?"

With a pint in his hand Spray stood with his back to the fire and began steaming as his sodden coat warmed up.

"Not from round here, I'm guessing?" enquired the landlord.

"Just passing through."

"Yer'll not get far afore nightfall."

"I thought I might make Cromford."

"Oh aye, 'appen you might."

Warmed through and well fed, Spray felt refreshed, renewed and ready to embark on his night's work. Arkwright Mill was at his back, and any moon there might have been was hidden behind the low cloud that had reformed since opening for a brief appearance of late-afternoon sun. He stumbled, and righting himself, tripped again. Ropes, stretched like tripwires across the towpath, moored narrowboats close to the canal bank. He surprised both himself and a heavy horse tethered for the night, by walking into its warm flank.

"Evening," said a boatman, on his way to the village for a drink. More used to life on the cut, he seemed to be making better progress than Spray.

Once he'd left the moored boats the going became easier, but he missed the comforting glimmers of light escaping from the little cabins in the stern of each one. Stumbling, Spray only just avoided falling into the cut. *Damn it, what's that?* At least he'd only caught his shoulder this time as the towpath wriggled round to pass under a bridge. Concealed by the night, Spray stared over the canal toward Cromford goods yard. The dark mass of buildings formed a single, blurred image. Tiny chinks of light showed along the cut where boats were moored up at the wharf for the next day's cargoes. Images of Lizzie crept, unbidden, into his mind as he watched and waited. There was nothing much to worry him across the water, in the yard. He was more disturbed by his inability to banish thoughts of his landlady. Such was the effect of a chaste conversation and two cups of tea.

He was startled by the noise of his own boots on the planks of the bridge. It seemed the whole of Cromford, half a mile away, must have heard them. Once safely on the other side, nothing stirred as he waited anxiously for the alarm to be raised. Reassured, he set off to investigate. A full moon had risen but was hidden by cloud, as had the sun for most of the day. The cloud was thinner now, allowing the faintest glimmer of moonlight to seep through.

From a different angle, the single mass of buildings began to resolve into separate silhouettes, and he could distinguish the characteristic outline of a locomotive. He was close enough by now to hear its faint creaks and groans as it cooled after the day's work.

"It's got to be hereabouts," he whispered to himself.

Picking his way across the tracks toward a building behind the resting engine, he passed a high, arched opening with gates closed over a pair of rails. Must be a workshop – that's more promising. To the side of the taller building ran a line of doors and windows. The thinning cloud broke momentarily and he froze, vulnerable to discovery in the moonlight. As if by magic the words, *Yard Office,* appeared. The letters were faded and some were missing, but before the moon vanished he'd found what he wanted.

It took only a few moments for the lock to give way to his skeleton keys. It opened with a satisfying click. As a trial run, his exploits at Grin No. 2 had its limitations. He was inside the yard office, that much was true, but what was revealed bore no resemblance to the tallyman's hut at the quarry. That had been little more than a shelter with a small stack of ledgers all devoted to the same subject. Here, as he fumbled to light a lantern, two desks with numerous pigeonholes, and shelves stacked with papers, flickered into view. It was a daunting sight for a man of the outdoors, happier on his feet than sitting down.

More than two, fruitless hours had passed when the rattle of boots on the canal bridge broke the silence. The noise came from the other side of the yard, and was muffled by the engine close to the office door, but there was no doubt what it was. Adrenaline flowed, and Spray, roused from the numbing boredom of paperwork, felt alert again. He doused the light, and trying to get behind the door in the darkness, blundered painfully into something sharp. *Damnation! And it would be that same shoulder again!'*

As he waited, on tenterhooks, he realized that the men walking into the village earlier hadn't been going home; they were going to spend an evening in a Cromford pub. Somewhere in the darkness behind the yard there must be railwaymen's cottages. Suddenly, there were voices, indistinct and slurred by alcohol, but getting closer. The men's words became clearer, and Spray heard an oath that suggested a stumble over a rail. Then silence fell. They must have found their way round the back of the building. Spray continued to wait.

There was no more activity outside and the suspense ebbed away. With the lantern relit and his shoulder still aching he examined what he'd bumped against. It was a small shelf, upon which was a leather-bound ledger with the words *Day Book* picked out in faded lettering. The shelf was placed just inside the door, so the yard foreman could easily reach in and grab it. The irony of a fortuitous collision, revealing what two hours of labour had failed to find, was not lost on him.

As the quarry record understated the number of wagons despatched since Saturday by four, and as the record at Cromford goods agreed with the one at the quarry, I deduced that there were four unrecorded wagons in the yard.

Even after dousing the lantern and waiting for his eyes to adjust to the gloom, Spray could barely see the loco standing patiently outside. Whilst he'd been in the office, the fog had returned. The faint glow of moonlight was now obscured, and crossing the yard was a matter of feeling carefully for each step. There were no more chinks of light escaping from the boats, either; boatmen and their families were early to bed. It would be quite easy to fall into the canal. Risky though it was, he had to check what was on the wharf siding. If they were the same wagons that he'd noted in the quarry, and their presence had gone unrecorded in both places, he could complete the picture.

There was movement on one of the boats: a quiet curse was followed by a splash and then the click of a cabin hatch sliding shut. The cut was more than just a thoroughfare; it also took care of the slops. A few more paces and Spray all but walked into a wagon standing between him and the canal. He was reasonably safe from discovery – even if another boatman needed to empty a slop bucket – as long as he remained on that side and did nothing to attract attention.

The truck's planking was battered and Spray found nothing but splinters as he ran his hand along it. *I'm on the wrong side, darn it.* By now, he'd established that there were four in line. *That's promising, got to go round and check, though.* He knew he'd have to chance it. With the lantern burning as low as it would without smoking, he did his best to use his body to shield its light from the boats, only a few yards away. He went in search of the wagons' labels. *GRIN No. 2 to CROMFORD (HIGH PEAK)* appeared in the shaded light, printed on brown card and fixed to the truck's wooden side. *Nearly there. Ah, that's it.* Lifting the corner of the label, there was a chalk mark just where he'd made it, before the wagon had left for the wharf.

The presence of all four unrecorded wagons was established at the wharf. One had already been unloaded, and other boats were awaiting their cargoes.

Spray was losing count of time. With only a couple of sleepers, and a short length of rail to follow, he plodded on. Even the rail across the other side of the four-foot was out of sight in the fog. It was worse now up in the Peak than down in the valley. Only the hollow sound of his own footsteps alerted him to his entry into Hopton Tunnel. For the rest of the time, they were muffled in the moist atmosphere.

Tired, cold and damp, he was getting disorientated as step followed step, and hour followed hour. In the gloom he couldn't even see his pocket watch. To his numbed mind, the distant sounds up ahead didn't mean anything at first. After a while, though, the clanking of trucks being alternately pushed up together, and then stretched out again, brought Spray back to reality. An engine puffed away in short bursts on a quarry siding, adding to the din.

By the time he'd come up to the rearmost wagon, the locomotive had drawn the train onto the main line. There it stood, waiting for the fireman who'd been left at the ground frame. After resetting the points, the fireman walked forward to rejoin his driver.

Spray took his chance and clambered aboard. Impeded by

the fog, they were moving little faster than walking pace. At least, perched on a buffer, he didn't have to continue taking one weary step after another. Leaning forward over the top plank onto the tarpaulin protecting the limestone beneath, Spray even managed to doze.

He was woken as another shunt drew even more wagons from the next quarry. By now the fog was thinning, and the faintest light could be seen over his shoulder to the east. With the marginal improvement in visibility, the train was moving a little faster. Now, something of the trackside could be seen from Spray's position at its rear. The rattle of wheels passing over points alerted him to the presence of yet another quarry, but with their speed undiminished the train wasn't stopping. Only as the last wagon – with Spray on board – clattered past the quarry entrance did he realise it was Grin No. 2. With Ladmanlow and its marshalling yard little more than a mile away, it was time to start walking again.

Back in his stride alongside the track, he watched the train as it melted away into the mist. He was counting paces now to keep awake: two hundred and fifty, two hundred and fifty one, two hund—boom! The sound of a collision up ahead burst suddenly through the fog.

I believe that there is incontrovertible evidence as to how the theft is undertaken, and that the tallyman at Grin No. 2, and the foreman shunter at Cromford Wharf, are implicated.

By the time he had finished reading Spray's report, Wayland had turned puce.

"Good heavens, man, surely all you have to do is to take a constable with you on Monday and arrest these two scoundrels!"

Spray couldn't stop the outburst and wasn't sure he wanted to. Wayland was making a fool of himself. He didn't want to humiliate his superior, but such displays certainly had the effect of preserving the relationship between the two men. The eruptions kept them on an equal footing, despite the difference in rank that lay between them.

"I really can't see why I have been brought here *on a Saturday* to consider matters that are little more than routine." There was more where that came from, and Wayland looked ready to continue.

Spray managed to interrupt the tirade, "There are two further issues to consider, sir, which do not, at present, appear in the report." He continued, "There are the matters of who benefits from this fraud and by what means. How it is carried out on the ground is clear enough, but who collects the money? Where is it collected from? In other words, who is in control? I cannot believe it of either the tallyman at the quarry, or the shunter at Cromford. Unless we can uncover this man, or men, we cannot be said to have solved the case."

It was on the tip of his tongue to say that arresting them now would hinder further progress, but Spray thought better of it.

Wayland grasped the implication of what he had been told, but was still not happy, "I do not see that I have any reason to be troubled by this today."

"There is the second matter to consider, sir."

Amid his bluster, it had slipped Wayland's mind. As he listened, the sinking feeling returned but slowly, and his indignation subsided.

"Yesterday, there was an accident on the C&HP. There were both fatalities and injuries. I was close by at the time and joined the assembled crowd." Spray handed his superior a second report.

I proceeded to the scene of an accident on the C&HP about a mile and a half south east of Ladmanlow.

The sergeant related the details of the accident. News always leaked out slowly from the White Peak, so Wayland had not heard about the tragic event of the previous day.

"The matter that concerns me is one of the two deceased men I saw lying at the trackside." Spray explained, "Everyone I spoke to assumed he had died in the accident, but I couldn't find the man who had retrieved his body from the train. There were no injuries to suggest he had died in the crash, but he had livid bruising around his neck. It is my opinion he had been murdered by strangulation."

If he could, Spray usually kept any information collected during an investigation well away from Wayland. Experience had taught him that life was easier that way, and in truth it also suited the senior officer. Wayland was a man who liked certainties, and these were to be found at the end of an investigation, not part way through. However, Spray felt he had to divulge what he knew to obtain Wayland's cooperation.

"As I walked back along the track towards Whaley Bridge, sir, thinking that the murderer must have passed that way, I found a hat, somewhat damaged, lying in the cess. At the time I was unsure of its significance. It was some distance from the site of the accident and seemed unlikely to have been associated with it. Equally, it was so unusual as to require an explanation."

Wayland returned to reading Spray's report.

After completing my investigations, I made my way to Whaley Bridge, where I was able to establish the identity of the murdered man.

By the time Spray arrived back in Whaley Bridge it was mid–afternoon. He let himself in with the latch-key Mrs Oldroyd had given him. He'd managed to banish 'Lizzie' from his mind, replacing it with 'Mrs Oldroyd', but the sound of her voice instantly brought her back as Lizzie.

"Is that you, Mr Spray?" she called, stepping out to the hall to greet him.

Noticing his dishevelled, unshaven condition, she insisted on taking his greatcoat to the kitchen. He climbed the stairs to his room and opened his small suitcase to prepare a change of clothes. Answering a soft knock on the door, he discovered that Lizzie had left a jug of steaming hot water on a small table right outside. He smiled at her kindness.

She was on her way back downstairs, but turned her head and, looking up at him, said, "You must be perished with cold, Mr Spray. I'll take a pot of tea into the front parlour for you in a quarter hour."

At the appointed time, and in a proper state to take tea with a lady, he entered the welcoming room. The fire was blazing, and he was dazzled by its warmth, its comfort, its civilisation. In the two days he'd been out there, living rough, such things were so far from the reality of his life that he'd hardly dare think of them.

"I'll be through in a moment," Lizzie called from the kitchen. By the time she came in, with a tray laden with the necessities of afternoon tea, he was in a dream-like state: not quite a trance, not quite asleep, but feeling as if he was floating.

"There we are, Mr Spray. My, oh my, you really do look all in."

"Mrs Oldroyd, this is really most kind. You'll join me, I hope?" Only as his landlady sat down did he notice the little stack of two cups and saucers.

They talked about nothing very much, but he enjoyed the conversation. It was only when Lizzie returned to the kitchen for more hot water that he realised there had been no enquiry as to his unkempt state, despite her initial exclamation. As he stood up to stretch his legs, he was grateful for her discretion.

Standing in front of the fire, a photograph caught his eye. Lizzie on her wedding day was her usual composed self, with a rather wooden version of her infectious smile bestowed on a slim, but un-athletic looking man, about ten years her senior. To Spray's casual glance, he seemed oddly familiar. Flanking the newlyweds were two people. A man in his fifties; possibly her father? Yes, the family resemblance was there all right. Presumably, the fourth person was the best man. Although more robust, with broader shoulders and standing taller, he bore a family resemblance to the bridegroom. Spray recognised the face. He had seen it earlier in the day: bluish, cold and stiff, above a livid bruise of strangulation.

"Another cup, Mr Spray?" Lizzie had returned to the parlour bent on resuming their agreeable conversation.

Spray was relieved to see she had resumed her seat. "Mrs Oldroyd, there's something we need to discuss," with his change of tone, Lizzie's animation evaporated and she sat, gravely, waiting for him to continue.

Not quite knowing where to begin, there was a deal of throat clearing, rearranging of hands and more than one false start: "It's… it's about your wedding photograph."

"Yes, Mr Spray, what about it?" Her tone was quizzical.

Having second thoughts about starting with Lizzie's nuptials, he promptly changed tack, "There was an accident on the Cromford line earlier today."

Lizzie had heard nothing of it, so he gave a brief account of what he'd seen: "I was close by at the time. There were, er, fatalities." He was reassured by her calm acceptance. "I'm sorry to say that one of the deceased is in that photograph on your mantelshelf," he began. Before he could specify which, Lizzie cried out, with a hand to her mouth and eyes filling with tears.

"Oh no, you mean father, don't you? You're saying he's dead?" Even in her extreme distress, Spray noted, she was facing the prospect of tragedy squarely in the face.

"No, no; the other gentleman. I am guessing that he was a groomsman." The relief spreading over her face was matched only by Spray's more subdued feelings.

"Oh, that's Arthur – my late husband's brother. You're quite correct in thinking he was a groomsman; our best man, in fact. You are saying he is dead? Oh my, that is terrible news. Poor Arthur."

"Did he live here in Whaley Bridge?" The professional was having a tussle with the personal in Spray's mind. If Lizzie noticed, she gave no sign.

"No, over in Cromford, but he often had business here and he always stayed in this house. In fact, he has a room on a permanent basis."

Before proceeding further, I prepared this report and made arrangements to lay it before my superior officer.

Superintendent Wayland finished reading the report and his sergeant, taking the opportunity of the ensuing silence, said: "I informed Mrs Oldroyd that her brother-in-law's body had been found at the site of the accident at Ladmanlow, and left it at that, not wishing to publicise my suspicions before discussing them with you." Wayland accepted this without comment. He had other things on his mind by then.

"This will be a matter for the local constabulary, of course."

Spray had not finished. "It is quite possible, sir, that unless we take some action, the murder will be overlooked. When I left the scene, it was generally believed that the man had died as a result of the accident."

"So you think the murderer will escape retribution?" Wayland tended to be sanctimonious when faced with manifest wrongdoing.

"Yes I do. Unless we take urgent action to prevent it," Spray advised.

There was a pause, and the superintendent looked pensive. It would not go down well with *his* superior, up at Euston, if he were to be found disturbing a hornet's nest that could perfectly well have been left alone. Whilst ignoring a specific request to investigate the loss of revenue, to boot.

"I established that the deceased, Arthur Oldroyd, acted as agent to what remains of the original board of directors of the old C&HP. He would have had unrestricted access to railway premises, and, therefore, was ideally placed to be involved in the fraud that is currently under investigation." At this from Spray, Wayland's reservations seemed less pressing.

"Have you any evidence to support this suggestion?" Wayland asked.

"It's a connection that I feel requires further examination." It was the best Spray could do.

"You cannot see any other way forward?" They were back on the detective's territory now.

"No sir, in my opinion, this is the only line of enquiry I can think of." Spray hoped his clenched jaw wouldn't betray his anxiety. There was a pause. Wayland trusted Spray and finally came to a decision.

With the decision made Wayland was a changed man: eager

and alert. "Very well, how should we proceed? You mentioned earlier that I could be of assistance, how may that be?"

"Well, sir, if you were to travel to Buxton and speak to the coroner, you may be able to establish whether a murder has been reported to him. If it has not, you might remedy that omission, and then suggest the railway constabulary undertake the investigation ourselves."

It said a lot about the relationship between the two men that, once the decision to pursue the case had been taken, Spray had no doubt that his superior would back him to the hilt. Wayland would do whatever was necessary to convince the coroner, and afterwards, his own superior, on the wisdom of the course he was about to undertake.

"Right, sergeant, when is the next train? There is no time to be lost!"

Part 2

Chapter 5

Buxton, Saturday, 18th December, 1875

The Cheshire countryside swept by, but neither man paid it much attention. The physical comfort they both enjoyed in a first class compartment was illusory.

"One first class single to Buxton." A perplexed Spray stood near enough to the ticket office window to hear his superior officer's request. They could both travel free whilst on Company business.

"Here, sergeant, take this." The ticket passed to Spray hurriedly, and Wayland looked away as he spoke, "Get a shift on, man, or we'll miss it!"

Despite his limp, Wayland made good progress through the crowd, and such was the press of travellers that Spray found himself trailing behind. He fingered his official, third class pass, redundant for this journey, as he contemplated the luxury he was about to experience. Arriving just in time, they stood together on the platform as a locomotive clanked past them, followed by its carriages. The business of finding a first class compartment kept the daunting prospect of the journey at bay for a time. Even then, the presence of another passenger as far as Goostrey was sufficient to justify their silence. When the traveller alighted, the two detectives were without excuse. Superintendent Wayland knew his duty as architect of the encounter: he harrumphed.

"You come from the county of Derbyshire, I believe," Wayland felt better for making a start.

"Yes sir, I was raised in Chesterfield."

"But not born there?"

"I cannot say where I was born, sir; I was brought up in an orphanage." There was a pause. "It was run by Quaker folk, and that is all I know."

Searching his mind, all Wayland could come up with concerning Quakers was chocolate, banking and a refusal to fight. He couldn't comment, so struck was he by the unlikely alignment of his sergeant's upbringing and his subsequent career.

Spray carried on, "They taught me many things in the orphanage, but above all else, to accept no man as superior based on worldly wealth or position."

As an officer and a gentleman, Wayland was steady under fire, but this revelation threatened him. He'd always felt secure in his position, and yet here it was being declared worthless.

"I learnt that all men should be judged on their merits. It has stood me in good stead throughout my life, sir," Spray's affirmation was unsettling.

To Wayland's relief, another passenger entered at Wilmslow. He'd heard enough; his impulsive ticket purchase for the sergeant had been a mistake. They travelled on, further conversation impeded firstly by the presence of a third person, and later by the need to change trains hurriedly at Stockport. By the time Wayland had regained his equilibrium, their locomotive was straining noisily uphill into the Goyt Valley.

"Come along, sergeant, do keep up." Trying to get a look at the engine, Spray had dropped back. The scattering of people on the platform at Buxton offered no excuse. "You're the one who set this investigation in motion. The least you can do is to make an effort now." The scent of battle was lifting the old soldier's spirits.

A telegram had been sent before they left, so they were expected:

IMPORTANT WE MEET TODAY STOP ARRIVING BUXTON TWO THIRTY STOP WAYLAND STOP SUPERINTENDENT OF RAILWAY POLICE.

They were still made to wait. Wayland was fuming by the time the two of them were ushered into the presence of the coroner, who ignored Spray.

"Ah, Superintendent Wayland," the coroner, a Mr Walters, managed a perfunctory handshake. "Perhaps you would be so good as to tell me what this is all about?" The man's eyes were bleary, probably from an after-dinner nap, thought Wayland. "You realise this is all most irregular. I normally keep office hours, y'know?"

"It is most kind of you to see us, Mr Walters," said Wayland. He received no invitation to be seated, and so the two men faced each other like prize fighters. "We're here in connection with the railway accident near Ladmanlow yesterday."

"That can wait until Monday," Walters replied, dismissively.

"But there were fatalities, have you not heard?"

"So I believe. Two men were killed in the accident and their bodies lie at Dickens's premises in the town. They'll handle the matter. It's pretty clear what happened to them. I don't think they'll trouble me much."

"My sergeant has reason to believe that one of the deceased may be the victim of murder."

Caught off guard, the coroner could only bluster, "That is ridiculous, superintendent, they were both found at the accident!" He glanced across at Spray, "Surely you can't be relying on *this* man's word?"

"Sergeant Spray arrived at the scene shortly after the collision," Wayland replied, nodding in his direction. "Present your report to Mr Walters, if you please, sergeant."

The coroner's attitude might have worried a lesser man, but Spray, quite untroubled by his disdain, stepped forward and gave his report verbally.

"I arrived at the scene within about half an hour of the accident. There was, as you may imagine, a lot of confusion. An unfortunate fireman had fallen in such a manner as to be caught up by the wheels of his engine, and had been extricated, only with some difficulty. I assume he died instantly; at any rate, he was clearly dead by the time I saw him. His driver was alive but seriously injured. In my judgement, he had a broken thigh and will be lucky not to lose his leg."

"I should have thought that only a medical man could draw such an inference."

Wayland, indignant, tried to interject, but Spray cut across him.

"Well, sir, I had the honour to serve in the Crimea alongside the superintendent, when he was a colonel. We became familiar with death and its causes, having attended injured and dying soldiers on numerous occasions."

The two old soldiers had Walters beat. He remained silent until Spray completed his testimony by explaining that he could find no one who had extricated the second body. He repeated what he had told his superior earlier in the day. His recount made it plain that he believed the cause of death was strangulation. The state of the corpse suggested that death occurred at least one, or possibly two days previously.

By the time Spray had finished the coroner was subdued. He agreed, albeit reluctantly, with Wayland's suggestion that they proceed forthwith to inspect the body.

By way of expediting matters, a footman was sent on ahead. "Why don't I accompany you?" said Spray, falling into step beside him. They headed for the premises of Dickens &

Nephew, undertakers. The footman drew the bell-pull three times before it was finally opened.

"Yes? What d'ye want?"

"Good afternoon, we've come from the coroner," said the footman. "He needs to view the bodies brought in yesterday from the railway. And he's bringing two policemen: this sergeant and a superintendent."

The undertaker recognised Mr Walters' servant. He plucked at his shirt and put a hand to his absent necktie, embarrassed by his crumpled appearance.

"The coroner? Coming here? On a *Saturday*?"

Spray stepped into the unpromising exchange, and proffering a hand, announced in a respectful but friendly tone, "Good day to you, sir; I am Sergeant Spray of the railway police. I take it you must be Mr Dickens."

His pleasant manner mollified the undertaker, who corrected Spray as they shook hands: he was, in fact, the nephew mentioned above the door. "Robert Akers. Always happy to oblige the agents of law and order."

"My superior officer and the coroner will be here presently," Spray informed.

Spray took Akers confidentially by the elbow, and leaving the footman in the outer parlour, stepped into a back room. A disagreeable smell of putrefaction hung heavily in the air. Two corpses lay in rough-hewn boxes serving as makeshift coffins. They were supported by trestles and covered by coarse canvas sheets.

"See here, Mr Akers, I'd be grateful if you would arrange things in a certain way. The bodies are very different, are they not?"

A look of surprise crossed Akers's face.

"When the others arrive, I would be obliged if you would

show them this one first, and make a bit of a show of it." Spray folded back the canvas, showing the mangled and bloody corpse of the unfortunate fireman.

He then drew back the cover of the second cadaver. *No harm in another look.* There, on the side of Arthur Oldroyd's head, was a scraped area, a bit flattened and missing some hair. The paucity of blood revealed that it must have been an injury sustained after death. Spray had missed it the previous day, but it was clear enough now: Arthur Oldroyd had been dragged along by his feet after he was killed.

A knock at the outer door drew Robert Akers away to greet the senior members of the party. Spray dipped swiftly into Oldroyd's pockets. Time was short, although a confusion of etiquette arising between the undertaker and the footman, as to who should open the door to the coroner, gave him just enough to pocket the cadaver's wallet. As the new arrivals were ushered in, Walters sent his footman home and then pressed a handkerchief to his nose, as the odour of death wafted through the door.

"Well, Superintendent Wayland, here we are. What is there to see?" the coroner asked.

As requested, the fireman's body was exposed first. The stench intensified as Akers swept off the canvas, and Walters, his grip tightening on the square of fine silk at his face, stepped back at the sudden exposure of the mangled corpse.

"No, no, Mr Akers, not that one, if you please, the other cadaver is the one we're interested in," Spray winked at the confused Akers, who removed the other canvas.

The apparently undamaged body was exposed.

Spray began, "If I may show you, sirs, this is the critical issue."

As the coroner stepped forwards, he froze. Spray saw fear in the man's eyes as a look of recognition crossed his face.

"You will see that death must have been caused by strangulation. To produce this injury, a garrotte would have been used. In my opinion, it has to be murder."

Shaken by what he had seen, the coroner could only agree.

The inspection had taken about three minutes. There was silence as they returned to the front parlour. Walters made one last effort to deflect the investigation, but in his agitation, the words died on his lips. All that emerged was an incomprehensible mumble.

As the two senior men stepped outside, Wayland began to speak, "I assume I have your agreement to an autopsy? My department is pursuing the case, and I would be obliged if you would instruct the local constabulary to cooperate."

Walters could only agree.

Inside the parlour, Spray addressed the undertaker: "Thank you, Mr Akers, we're most grateful for your kind assistance, especially as it is a Saturday afternoon. Can I help you restore order in there?" he nodded towards the back room. "I need to have a few words with my superintendent, but afterwards perhaps you could introduce me to your local hostelry."

It seemed that Akers thought the cadavers could very well look after themselves, but the offer of a jug of ale was eagerly accepted.

By now, Wayland and the coroner were parting. Spray caught up with them.

"I shall be in a position on Tuesday or Wednesday to bring someone to identify the body, sir. I take it that will be in order?"

Walters assented, shook hands with the superintendent and left.

"A satisfactory outcome, don't you think, sergeant? All you have to do now is find the culprit." Wayland felt his remark merited a chuckle. Spray managed only a wan smile in response.

"What do you make of the coroner, sir?"

"A bit of a young upstart. Not much weight to him, couldn't stomach the blood and gore: got him on the run."

"You didn't notice anything else?" Spray realised he was being a bit unfair to his superior, who had been standing a little behind the coroner when the body of the murdered man was exposed.

"You couldn't have seen, sir, but as Mr Walters was about inspect the garrotte marks, I feel sure that he recognised the dead man. It is also significant that he made no enquiry as to whether we knew the man's identity. He recognised him, and in my opinion, didn't want to be drawn into conversation on the subject."

"That is most interesting, sergeant," Wayland replied, raising an eyebrow. "What do you propose to do next?"

It would be so much easier to just get on with the job and tell Wayland afterwards, but Spray couldn't avoid it. He needed the superintendent's consent to obtain the services of a constable.

"My first priority is to get more information about the victim. We know who he is, and that he lived in Cromford, but that's all."

He hoped he'd got it right about Cromford. His conversation with Lizzie Oldroyd had been clouded by his feelings for her. Cromford had definitely been mentioned, he was sure of it.

Wayland, nodding, seemed satisfied, "Yes, I see, and then?"

"From such information it might to possible to establish a motive. The murder probably occurred nearer to Whaley Bridge. I would be much assisted in my investigations if I could be assigned a constable to make some enquiries there."

Wayland was in a quandary. If things went badly... a vision of the resulting interview with his chief, in London, floated into his head. And then there'd be a quill-pusher from finance, too. But, of course, a *successful* outcome – now *that* was an entirely different matter.

"You're sure you can sort this out, sergeant, not forgetting the original problem of the missing limestone? That was the original case, and I'm quite certain our superiors will be much more impressed with a solution to that mystery than any number of murders."

"Yes, sir, I'm certain," Spray was adamant.

It was enough for Wayland, "Right, I suppose you would like Constable Archer to assist?"

Spray was suitably grateful for the offer, "Thank you, sir. Perhaps you could give him this note?" Some furious scribbling ensued. "And would you also be so kind as to ask him to go to Whaley Bridge on Monday. It would be convenient if he could take lodgings with Mrs Oldroyd. Failing that, have him leave a message there saying where he can be found on Tuesday evening."

That was it. Spray had obtained exactly what he had wanted: agreement that the case was his and an assistant to help towards its investigation. Wayland had more information from his taciturn sergeant than he could usually count on at this point in an investigation. Both satisfied, they went their separate ways. One back to Crewe, and the supervision of a now-depleted establishment, the other to a tryst with an undertaker.

Chapter 6

Cromford, Saturday, 18th December, 1875

Spray only just made it in time for the 5:15, Saturdays only Midland Railway service from Buxton to Miller's Dale. The handsome station façade had all but disappeared into the gloom by the time he walked through to the booking hall.

"Your ticket, please, sir?" The stern collector was unimpressed by a LNWR pass. Embarrassed, Spray turned back to the booking office.

"A third to Cromford, if you please."

"Best look sharp, sir, it's off any time now."

This time, the man at the barrier waved him through. Spray hurried onto a platform that was suddenly enveloped in steam, as an ancient tank engine blew off its safety valve.

"Hurry along there!" The door was slammed shut behind him. Guard and engine were both eager to get underway. As Spray sank into the unaccustomed comfort of MR third class travel, the train set off with a jerk, exchanging the gloomy, gas-lit station for the blackness of a winter's evening.

Spray was finding it difficult to concentrate on the investigation. An image of the station façade demanded attention and preoccupied him all the way to Miller's Dale. But why? The business of changing trains at the junction came as a relief. Traversing the wild and windy overbridge drove out the persistent image.

He wondered at the surprising extent of Miller's Dale Station. Down below, in the valley, a few chinks of light, distant and faint, suggested the modest size of the village it served. After bursting from Cromford Tunnel, his train drew to a halt. Coughing on the fumes that had seeped into the carriage, Spray stepped onto the platform. No gaslight here. Only an oil lamp spluttering where passengers crossed the track to exit the station from the down side. Perched high up on the edge of the Derwent Valley, the route to the village was all downhill. Spray had cleared his lungs by the time he entered the Bell Inn.

"G'd evening, sir," the inn was warm and inviting.

"Good evening, landlord." A few moments elapsed as Spray removed his hat and coat.

"Nah then, what'll you be havin'?" The man stood aside to better show off his row of barrels on a shelf behind. Spray took advice, and with a full tankard, sat by the fire. He contemplated both the local brew, and what he had learned from Akers earlier that afternoon.

They had repaired to the undertaker's favourite public house, where he talked about Buxton and its various drinking dens.

"There's one for everyone, y'know?" Akers explained. "Railwaymen 'ave their own – two, if truth be told – one for each company, y'see. Then the farmers down by the market and this one, fer the likes of small shopkeepers." Akers took a pull at his ale and raised an unsteady hand in the general direction from which they had entered. "But yer wu'nt want ter sup ale in that un ower the road, there."

Spray looked across, but all he could see was the Coachman Inn, a neat and tidy public house. The windows were perhaps cleaner than most; the customers that could be seen looked highly respectable and orderly.

"Why not?"

His companion began to exasperate Spray. Whilst sober, Akers wasn't the gossip that he hoped for. Now, tipsy, he was becoming increasingly difficult to follow.

"Yer know, they're all…" Akers rummaged for the right word. The best he could manage was '*them* sort'. He paused, hoping that Spray would understand without having to become too specific, but Spray looked at him blankly. Finally Akers mumbled, a hand covering his mouth, "Yer know, *mandrakes*."

Spray did know, although he was surprised to find a molly house in an isolated market town like Buxton. Manchester, London, or the major ports, yes, but *Buxton*? He suspected he may have served with a few such men in the army. The subject of their amorous preferences had crept away to a rarely visited part of his mind.

"Tha', there coroner's man; I see him go in there." At this point the effort of conversing became too much for Akers. He slumped forward onto the table and promptly fell asleep.

It was getting dark and Spray had a train to catch. He shook the sleeping man awake and offered to escort him home, but was told to be off: "There's still ale int' pot."

So little information having been elicited, Akers' words received more of Spray's attention than they might otherwise have merited. Was there a connection between the certainty, at least in Spray's mind, that the dead man had been recognised by Walters, and Walters' subsequent failure to discuss the man's identity? And what about Walters' servant? Did he harbour a guilty secret? It was quite possible that this last titbit was mere idle gossip and of no consequence. Though, if it was true, Akers had certainly tied himself in knots to impart it.

A dish of mutton chops arrived, and, for a while, Spray concentrated on the needs of his stomach rather than those of his mind. As he mopped up the last of the gravy with a hunk of bread, the landlord began clearing away the empties and wiping down the tables.

"Would you have a drink with me, landlord?" It was a spur of the moment invitation on Spray's part and was accepted with apparent pleasure.

Spray began his covert questioning, "Heard about the accident?"

"Aye. No one around these parts can understand why two trains were on the line at the same time."

Spray nodded, but said nothing. His companion wiped his mouth with the back of his hand.

"I get mostly Midland men in here," the landlord continued. "They often laugh about the old relics the Cromford railway is still using."

The ancient locos and parochial employees certainly didn't rate highly in their eyes, thought Spray.

"They're saying a fireman and a passenger died. No one's sure, but some think it were Arthur Oldroyd. He lives here in Cromford, you know?"

"They're right," Spray confirmed, "it was Oldroyd, sure enough. Can you tell me exactly where he lived?"

Seeing the suspicious look come into the landlord's eyes Spray realised he'd have to explain himself. "His body was found on the railway, but it wasn't the accident that killed him."

"So, that's how it is." The landlord was curious, yes, but he seemed strangely unsurprised by the news. "And how come tha knows so much abaht it?"

Spray admitted to being the officer in charge of the case. He was halfway to extracting his warrant card but was told not to bother.

"Tha's all reet, ah see it now. Couldn't place yer fer a start off. Ah can see yer a Jack fine enough. So, how were it done?"

"He appears to have been garrotted, perhaps in the middle of the week, a few days ago, at any rate."

"Any idea who done him in?"

"Bit early for that yet. Where did Mr Oldroyd live?"

The man jerked his thumb at the door. "Up Scarth Lane. He's well known in these parts – lived here for as many years as I can remember. My cousin Ellie does for him; you know, his washing an' housework, like. She don't live in, though; he won't 'ave that. But she calls 'erself his 'ousekeeper all the same. She's fond of 'im, too. Won't 'ave a word said against 'im; says what a gent he is and how clean and tidy he is, never anything out of place. Some days she cooks for 'im, too. Not that regular, though, he's away a lot."

"Any idea where he goes?"

"Well, he's a sister-in-law in Whaley Bridge. Says 'e goes there on business, but no one's sure what business it is. 'E's s'posed to be looking out for the people with money in the old C&HP – as their 'agent', whatever that means. Any case, there can't be many left by now. That solicitor Jones, and Mr Fitzroy Tarp, are the only ones, far as ah know."

"Anywhere else?"

"Ah've seen 'im boarding a Manchester train before now, but ah 'aven't been following 'im around. Oh yes, 'e goes to old Tarp's place often enough." This last observation was accompanied by a knowing look that Spray couldn't interpret.

"That would be on account of his connection with the old railway company, would it?"

The landlord explained that when Oldroyd had been a very young man, Tarp had taken him in and made sure he had an education. In due course, Tarp had found him a position as agent to the original investors in the company. Quite why, no one knew.

"They say Tarp was sweet on Oldroyd's mother."

At this point the knowing look flitted across the publican's face again, but he wouldn't be drawn further.

Spray thanked the landlord for the splendid mutton dinner and congenial company, and enquired about accommodation for the night. After placing his small suitcase in the room, he went out into the cold dampness of a misty December evening. Now fortified, he set off to familiarise himself with the village, get his bearings, and find Oldroyd's house. As he walked towards it, up Scarth Lane, two men erupted onto the street. From the detective's position it wasn't quite clear where they'd come from, but it must have been from a house close to Oldroyd's. The taller of the two pushed at a shorter, rotund individual whose silk hat was already awry.

It would be an exaggeration to call it a fight. Fists were raised but the smaller man's punches failed to land. They were more like bantam cocks showing off than combatants with serious intent. The taller man, cloth cap still in place, did little more than hold the other at arm's length. Spray heard shouting: "Why the hell are you here?" and "You've no right..."

From what Spray could make out, about twenty yards away, the two men had found themselves at the same place. Each had not expected to be discovered by the other. After a minute or so, they parted, startled by Spray's approach, and set off in opposite directions. Collar up and hat pulled down, Spray loitered for sufficient time to see the younger, taller man cross the road and disappear into the Boat Inn a few doors along. He paid no attention to the detective. In the doorway of the inn, a shaft of light fell on him briefly, and Spray recognised the man as the head shunter of the railway yard at High Peak Junction. But who was the other combatant? Spray looked around and saw the portly figure waddling away, heading downhill.

As Spray watched from a discreet distance, the man turned off the Derby Road. Fumbling for a key in his waistcoat pocket, he let himself into a door opening directly off the street. Spray waited a minute or two then strolled past the premises. Next to the door, an imposing brass plate glinted in the faint moonlight.

Barford & Smythe
Solicitors
Nathaniel Jones

He returned the way he had come, pondering the possible connection between a dishonest railwayman, a lawyer and a violent death. By the time he reached the Bell Inn, the bar was almost empty. He bade goodnight to the landlord and took himself off to bed. Tomorrow he'd have to rummage through his ragbag of information, and see if he could make sense of what he'd collected so far, but, for the present, sleep called.

Chapter 7

Cromford, Sunday Morning, 19th December, 1875

Sunday arrived much as Saturday had departed. After his breakfast, Spray found himself walking through a grey, misty gloom in the company of his landlord. The fried bacon and black pudding had come with a suggestion.

"Ah told you about our Ellie, who looks after Mr Oldroyd's, she might 'ave more to tell than ah 'ave. I'll take you to meet 'er if it'll 'elp."

Mrs Ellen Bagshaw's habit was to brave all winds and all weathers to attend the eleven o'clock service at chapel. She was heading there when the two men intercepted her. Spray found himself shaking hands with a reticent woman of slight build. She had a long, narrow face, her hair shot with grey and tied neatly into a bun. She looked every inch a domestic servant, dressed respectably for weekly worship.

"I'll have to get back t'the Bell, Ellie, but Sergeant Spray has some news for thee." The landlord hurried off, and Spray found himself walking briskly in the direction of Mount Tabor Chapel.

"You'll have to tell me as we walk, sergeant. And hurry along, I mustn't be late." There was a firmness about Mrs Bagshaw that he'd missed on their introduction. "Now, what is it?" she asked.

"You've heard about Friday's railway accident?"

"Of course, and what's more, I've heard that Mr Oldroyd was killed." Ellie's step remained firm. "I mean, it's only rumour, but I'd have expected him back by now. Is that what you came to tell me?"

"The rumour's true, I'm afraid."

Ellie walked steadfastly on.

"But there's more, Mrs Bagshaw. I have reason to believe that he'd been murdered some time earlier."

She halted abruptly.

"Oh dear, oh dearie me." After a short silence, Ellie continued, "You're sure, I suppose? Yes, of course you are. You wouldn't be here talking to me, else." She resumed walking, less purposefully now. "So, it's come to that, has it?"

"I'm investigating the case and I need to look round his house. I was hoping you might let me have the key."

"Well now, I'm not so sure about that. How do I know… ?"

Spray reached into his pocket for his warrant card.

"Oh yes, I see… I suppose it's all right then." She handed the key over. "It's for the back door. You have to go down the jitty and it's second along." She stopped and turned. "It's just back there."

Spray realised with some surprise that they'd followed his route of the previous evening. The two parted, Ellie Bagshaw on her way to commune with her God, and the detective to attempt the same with the spirit of Arthur Oldroyd.

One small mystery was resolved immediately. The two men from last night must have started their argument in the jitty and emerged in full flow, hence their sudden eruption onto the street.

Spray entered the narrow opening, and ducking to avoid the odd bramble, wound his way to the back yard of Oldroyd's house. It was dainty and fastidious to the point of being fussy. Dominating the scene was a large, fluted and crenulated bowl above a slender stem, set on a tapered plinth. The climbing plants behaved impeccably as they crept up the walls. The usual contents of such a place, the coal store and rubbish bin, were decorously obscured. Spray was at a loss. With no aesthetic sense – his Quaker upbringing had put paid to that – it failed to impress him.

It came as a relief to find the back door ajar; he could swiftly return to the world he did understand. Noticing a key in the lock as he entered, he wondered if there was anyone already inside. He walked quietly past the scullery door and through to the kitchen. Still, there was silence. Bolder now, he went into another world. The kitchen, workaday with its flagged floor and black-leaded range, gave way via a passage into an entrance hall. To the left, an imposing staircase rose to a half landing and turned through a right angle to reach its destination. The front door, to his right, was flanked by two narrow windows, and hanging from the ceiling was an elaborate chandelier, cut glass gleaming in the winter light. He stepped back a few paces and opened the door off the passage.

The scene was at such variance with any dining room Spray had ever seen that he stood mesmerised. Quite apart from the scale, its style was unlike that of the heavy, dark sideboards, lumpy square tables, and solid chairs characteristic of the gentry. Even his rather blunted aesthetic sense realised he was looking at rare elegance.

Across the entrance hall a door opened into the parlour. A large room, it was comfortable rather than refined. There were heavy, leather chairs, a large fireplace with an ornate brass fender, glass-fronted bookcases, and prints and pictures on the walls. Spray suppressed the urge to head straight for the roll-top desk. He made his way into the room, just standing and looking, inch by inch, instead. He didn't expect a blinding flash to reveal all, but the essence of a place, and of its owner, was important.

Finally, he approached the desk. He expected the roll top to be locked against curious intruders. To his surprise, it slid upwards smoothly and revealed not very much. There was blotting paper, a bottle of ink, pens on a cut-glass rest, and blank sheets of headed writing paper inscribed: *11 Scarth Lane, Cromford, Derbyshire*. Either side of the kneehole were drawers, mostly unlocked. Their contents comprised mainly small items, the possessions of any man of business.

Two drawers caught his attention because both appeared to have been forced open. There were scratches around the locks and damage to the polished woodwork of the drawer fronts. One was empty, but a reserve supply of paper lay in the larger one. Spray considered why there should be so much of it. As he idly ruffled the sheets, the reason emerged. Although the top few sheets bore Oldroyd's home address, beneath them were others with an entirely different heading.

Time was passing, and it seemed unlikely to inspire Ellie Bagshaw's trust if she returned from chapel to find Spray rummaging through the open desk. He slipped one of the sheets into his pocket, did his best to return things as he had found them, closed the drawers, and drew down the roll top. All looked as it had done before his inspection.

He thought he was ready for anything as he reached the top of the stairs, but the master bedroom was a shock. It was dominated by a four-poster bed, swathed in drapes. The bed was echoed by a dressing table hung around with swagged fabric.

Spray felt distinctly uncomfortable. Prints of classical statuary adorned the walls, depicting naked young men of remarkably fine physique. They forced him to confront a truth he had been avoiding: this was the house of a man who loved men. His distaste for such matters had kept him in total ignorance about them, but duty now demanded he open his mind.

Ellie would be back from chapel soon, and Spray set out to meet her. She would be more co-operative, he reasoned, if she didn't have a picture of him making free with her master's property.

"Mrs Bagshaw," he held out a hand, which was shaken firmly.

"Sergeant."

Greetings completed, they proceeded to the back entrance, where much surprise was expressed about the open door.

"Well really, what will Mr Oldroyd say?" For Ellie, her late employer remained in the present. "Did you leave it like this?" She looked accusingly at Spray.

"I'm afraid not. The door was open, with a key in it, when I arrived. Here is the one you gave me." He returned it to her.

She looked exasperated, "It must be the one from under the urn. I kept asking him not to leave it there, but he would still do it. I only found it by accident one day, and he seemed quite flustered when I mentioned it. He just told me not to tell anyone."

"Did anyone else know about it?"

Ellie didn't know. It seemed that there were very few visitors to the house whilst she was there, although there were duties of one sort or another most days of the week. On the odd occasion when she cooked tea, she departed by half past five, leaving the meal warming on the range.

"Very particular, he was, never wanted me to stay later." After a few moments of thoughtful silence, she added, "I suppose he must have had visitors in the evenings after I left. Sometimes there would be dirt on the floor at the back entrance and in the kitchen. I remember a pair of gloves, in the entrance hall, that certainly weren't Mr Oldroyd's. I thought I recognised them, though. As soon as he saw them he picked them up and I never saw them again. That was some years ago."

"Whose did you think they were?"

"Mr Jones, the solicitor. You see I used to work for him, too, up till about two years ago. It was all very strange. Mr Oldroyd seemed very upset for a while, but I put that down to the death of his brother, who died young and left a widow in Whaley Bridge, you know?"

Spray nodded.

"All of a sudden, he said he didn't think I could work for him and Mr Jones at the same time, and said I had to choose. I don't think he wanted me to go because he said I could have extra hours working for him. So I gave in my notice to Mr Jones. He seemed much happier after that."

Her manner took on a conspiratorial air, "I didn't tell Mr Oldroyd, but I put in a word for my sister and Mr Jones took her on. In fact I sometimes help her out with his washing, she brings it home, you see, and we help each other out."

Spray steered the conversation back to Oldroyd's visitors.

"There have been times when he was very insistent that I shouldn't go upstairs. Very inconvenient, it was. I like to keep a routine with the cleaning, never know where I am else. There may have been a hat and scarf that I didn't recognise in the entrance hall occasionally, but I can't remember when. The dirt on the kitchen floor, that's quite another matter. Quite regular it is; well it's worse when it's wet, of course, but there's usually some to do on a Monday morning. You'd think he'd had his feet in the ashpan, clogs and all."

"So, you clean upstairs, and in the, er, rooms, too?" Spray tried to introduce the subject of Oldroyd's flamboyant bedroom as cautiously as possible.

"Ooh yes, quite a sight isn't it? Mr Oldroyd always said how artistic the pictures were, and historical, too."

"Were Mr Oldroyd's, er, *tastes,* gossiped about in the village?"

"I never talked about it, well, except to my sister, but we don't gossip around."

They wandered through the house, Ellie mentioning items she thought might interest the detective. He listened attentively but heard nothing to add to what he had already learned. Apart from the dining room and bedroom, there wasn't anything exceptional to his eyes. As they headed back toward the kitchen, Ellie was apologetic.

"You must be famished with cold, but I can't offer you anything to warm you up; the fire's not lit, and…" She paused, then added, as an afterthought, "It's not mine to offer, anyway."

Spray wondered to whom 'it' might now belong.

Before he could frame the question, she continued, "If you have any more to ask, we can go to my cottage. I've a fire going, and I could make us a pot of tea."

The offer was an inviting prospect and he agreed. He told himself that there were still questions to be asked, and that the possibility of refreshment, warmth and congenial company had nothing to do with his acceptance.

Ellie's cottage was clean, cluttered and, above all, warm. A kettle hung to one side of the stove and was half way to boiling. She swung it closer to the flame and set about tea-making. Finally, they were settled around the tea-table, and Spray addressed the question that had come to mind just before they set out. He approached it obliquely.

"I wonder, do you know anything of Oldroyd's family?"

"There's not a lot to know. He had a brother who died about two years ago, but I told you that, didn't I? Then there's the brother's wife. That's it really. Oh, I think there's an aunt as well."

After the briefest of pauses she remembered, "Oh, there's old Mr Fitzroy Tarp, I suppose. I've heard it said that he's Mr Oldroyd's natural father. If that were true, then young Mr Jarvis Tarp would be his half-brother."

"The young Mr Tarp?"

"Old Mr Tarp was married and without children for many years. Later his wife bore him a child they called Jarvis, but she died having it. Father and son live in some style out toward Crich."

"How old would you say Mr Jarvis Tarp is?"

"In his twenties or thirties, I suppose."

"Did Mr Oldroyd ever say anything about his will?" Spray's question finally made it to the surface.

"I don't think so." There was a thoughtful pause. "Well, not what was in it…"

Spray looked at Ellie quizzically.

She answered his tacit question: "After his brother died, and just before the to-do about who I was to work for, I remember him returning one day with a big envelope. He was flustered and muttering to himself, and I thought I heard the word 'will', but I'm not really sure."

"You never saw the envelope again?"

If it had been a will, she had no idea whose it might be. In no uncertain terms, Ellie told Spray her knowledge was exhausted on the subject. It was time to go and he did so as diplomatically as he could.

"Mrs Bagshaw, it's all been very interesting, and you've been so helpful, telling me what I needed to know. I'm sure I can find the truth about your late employer's death now." He rose to go. "Just one more thing, could you explain how to find Mr Tarp's house?"

Of course she could. It was called Cromford High House

and turned out to be above the Lea Bridge Road, with views across the Derwent Valley. To get to it, he had to go in the direction of the station and then head up Willersley Lane toward Starkholmes.

They shook hands and parted, she feeling she might have said more than was wise. Spray, whilst admiring her discretion, wondered if he had gained anything from the conversation.

Chapter 8

Cromford, Sunday Afternoon, 19th December, 1875

Spray was becoming breathless as he climbed upward, away from the river, and in between gulps for air he tried to plan the interview. An elderly man of business seemed as unlikely to be stealing limestone as he would be committing murder. No, what he wanted was some sense of the extent of Oldroyd's connection with the old C&HP, and a clearer idea of what the remnants of the old company amounted to.

He stood, slowly regaining his breath, propped against a dressed-stone gatepost with Cromford High House carved into it. With its twin, it helped support a pair of wrought iron gates that were functional rather than showy. By the time he'd walked down a driveway that cut through a well-tended garden running wild at its edges, his breathing was back to normal. Clinging, as it did, to the steep side of the valley, he thought it must be a nightmare to keep the unruly from encroaching into the ornamental.

Spray tugged on a wrought iron bell pull and was rewarded with a distant tinkling sound somewhere inside the house. Almost immediately, the door opened and a maidservant asked his business.

"If you would be so good as inform Mr Fitzroy Tarp that I would like a word with him, I should be much obliged."

"Er, well sir, I'll…"

"I'm Sergeant Spray of the London and North Western Railway constabulary." At least that got him through the door and into the entrance hall.

Whilst the maid was away consulting her master, a tall, fair and self-possessed man walked through the hall.

"And what dealings can the constabulary possibly have with my father?" He looked haughtily at a point somewhere above the policeman's head.

Spray fixed him with a steady gaze, demanding attention.

"Unfortunately, sir, that will, so far as I'm concerned, have to remain between Mr Fitzroy Tarp and myself."

A door closed and the maid started across the hall.

"I take it you are Mr Jarvis Tarp?" Spray asked.

"Damn your impudence," the younger man spun on his heel and stalked off.

The maid, all but falling as the young Tarp brushed past, regained her balance.

"Mr Fitzroy Tarp will be pleased to see you now, sir."

Enveloped in the faint tang of expensive tobacco, Spray found himself surrounded by shelves of books. Wherever the shelves ended, oak panelling started, and at the far end was a huge bay window giving a magnificent view across the Derwent Valley.

"Sergeant Spade?" A hand was proffered and accepted.

"It's Spray, sir, how do you do."

"Yes indeed, my apologies, I'm a little hard of hearing these days."

The detective found himself shaking hands with an elderly man, slim almost to the point of gaunt. He had once been tall and straight, but was now rather bent, though the aura of an erect posture remained. Bald on top and grey where he still had hair, he had a long, narrow, lined face with blue eyes that were alert and intelligent, despite his age.

"How may I help you? I can only suppose it's in connection with Friday's accident. The maid brought news of it this morning. She didn't know much, just that it was a head-on collision and that someone was killed. Please be seated and tell me all about it."

Spray was ushered from the polished floor, across a Turkish rug, to one of the comfortable leather armchairs flanking the fireplace. He noted that it was positioned in such a way as to give Tarp a better view of him than vice versa. Had Spray been about to interrogate a suspect, he would have done the same. But, then again, perhaps it was an arrangement bred only of failing eyesight.

Spray had imparted some of the details when the maid reappeared with tea and a well-loaded cake-stand. Such was the promptness of her return that Spray mused whether all was pre-prepared to detain any chance visitor – with a view to enlivening a dull Sunday afternoon, perhaps. Turning to leave, she caught her foot at the edge of the rug, and in not quite falling, dropped the empty tray with a clatter.

Without giving any thought to whether such a thing was proper between servant and guest, Spray rose from his chair, picked up the tray and opened the door for the embarrassed girl. As he did so, he was aware of movement, and thought he glimpsed Jarvis Tarp retreating from the doorway.

"You'll take tea with me?" the invitation sounded like an order. The prospect of hearing about a railway accident seemed to have animated the old man.

"You say the trains were travelling towards each other on the same stretch of track. Who had the token, that's what I'd like to know? It's disgraceful." The old man was fuming. His railway experience was plainly still fresh in his mind. "We'd never have tolerated that sort of operational sloppiness in my day!"

Both men knew that only the driver with the token had the right to proceed onto a single line.

"How many casualties, sergeant?"

"Well, sir, the business is not entirely straightforward."

"How d'ye mean?"

"One of the deceased was a fireman. He was on the foot-plate at the time of the accident, and was killed as the other locomotive reared over the tender and came into his cab. The other man was found by the track."

"Clearly a passenger thrown from the train at the moment of impact." The old man was having difficulty seeing beyond the accident.

"No, sir, the signs are that he may have been murdered, and that he had been there for some hours, if not days." There was a pause.

"Who was he? D'ye know?"

"Mr Arthur Oldroyd," Spray held his eyes steady.

The news sent the old man into a shocked silence. Not for long, though.

"Sergeant Spray, would you pour the tea? I'm a bit unsteady with the pot these days."

Teacups were filled and cakes placed on bone-china plates. Tarp regained his composure and was ready to rejoin the fray.

"What can I do to further your enquiries, sergeant?"

"There are two areas in which I would value your knowl-edge and experience." Spray was back on more familiar ground, setting the agenda and asking the questions. "I want to get some background on the C&HP. The body was found on its land, the victim had connections with the railway, and I can't help wondering if the crime has its roots there."

The old man's eyes lit up and he launched forth.

"Back in the twenties, railways, as we know them, were in their infancy. They were mostly horse-drawn and carried minerals to ports or canals. The odd steam locomotive was a novelty, and in many cases, a liability. The Peak was a prolific producer of limestone, but the problem was, how to get out large quantities? In the last century a canal was proposed to connect with waterways on both sides of the Pennines, but the plan fell through. There's no water up in the Peak."

Spray looked puzzled. Up on the high ground it seemed to rain most of the time. Tarp explained that it all seeped away through the limestone, and could not be collected in a reservoir at the head of the canal.

Tarp explained thoughtfully, "A group of local business-men, my father among them, thought that a railway was just the thing: if they could do it in the coalfields of Durham, why not here? They raised some capital, got hold of the canal plans and set about it. It was the mid-twenties when they got the Parliament Act through, and by 1831 it was operational. Sadly, my father didn't live to see it; he passed away in twenty-seven. I inherited his estate, including his interest in the railway, and a limestone quarry. I was young and energetic and made myself useful to the other investors. They were mostly my father's generation, and being good businessmen, saw the advantage in it, but didn't understand the thing itself. I was just the reverse. What intrigued me were the locomotives. Just think, in twenty-nine they ran the Rainhill Trials. I was enthralled by the whole thing. I even got the others to fund me to attend!"

Tarp paused for breath. Spray wondered if the old man's constitution was up to relating the heady excitements of the old days. He also wondered what Tarp supposed this ancient history was contributing to his current investigation.

"I was hoping we might explore Arthur Oldroyd's connec-tion with the company."

"Yes, yes, I'm coming to that." Tarp was testy at being interrupted.

"The old C&HP wasn't in the same league as the Liverpool & Manchester. Apart from anything else, we had no steam locomotives. It was all winding engines and horses to begin with. By God, that irked me. A few years later I had my way, and we acquired locomotives for some sections of the line. I only got away with it because most of the investors were either dead or so infirm as not to care. You've got to understand, we never made much out of it. The people who profited were the quarry owners, of which by then, I was one."

When Tarp paused for breath, Spray took his chance, "Which quarry would that be?"

"Grin No. 2. Why do you ask, are you familiar with the quarries in the Peak?"

"I have a passing acquaintance with them."

The old man might have to take a breather now and then, but was sharp as a knife nonetheless. He continued.

"By this time, the early forties you understand, I was pretty well the only active director. We had a general manager for the operational side, but I was busy with my own work. It was here that Arthur Oldroyd came into it. He was only in his teens, but I'd kept an eye on him growing up. He was a bright lad, so I took him on as an apprentice really, but he learnt fast and within a few years I couldn't manage without him."

A question hovered on Spray's lips, but discretion won out over curiosity, and it remained unasked.

"Finally we got steam onto every section of the line. The problem was we didn't have enough capital. It was a very hand-to-mouth affair. There'd been a huge increase in traffic, and I thought that the addition of steam locomotives would help us cope. We even tried building a couple ourselves. They were all right, I suppose, but all the extra traffic played havoc with the old rails we had laid, and we still didn't make enough money. By 1860 we were in serious financial difficulties, but the London and North Western came to our rescue. Up till then, our only rail connection to the outside world was at the Cromford end of the line onto the Midland. At the Whaley Bridge end, a connection was proposed that would give us access to the L&NW. If they could get control of our line they could, how shall we say, encourage traffic onto their metals."

"It must be a cut-throat business, running a railway company." Spray was accustomed to the physical cutting of throats, but never ceased to be surprised by the bear pit that was the world of commerce.

"We managed to keep our perilous financial position from the L&NW and negotiated a quite advantageous deal, considering we were staring bankruptcy in the face. By then, the shares of the original investors had passed to their heirs. As they hadn't paid a dividend in years, everybody had lost interest and in some cases, I suspect, actually discarded the certificates. Barford & Smythe dealt with all that, they were the company's legal advisors in the beginning. Both have since passed on, and Nathaniel Jones has the firm." A look of distaste flitted across Tarp's face.

After a brief pause, he continued, "It happened at about the time we negotiated the lease. Very inconvenient it was; Barford was pretty well out of things by then, but Smythe was involved, and he passed away suddenly in the middle of it. I'll say this for Jones: he picked it all up very quickly, and I suppose I have to admit he turned it in our favour, better than Smythe could have done."

Spray wondered if Tarp would ever get back to discussing Oldroyd.

"How did Mr Oldroyd fare in all this?"

"Yes, all right, I suppose you're eager to get to him. I see

I've been unduly prolix. By the time we were in trouble, he was more or less in charge of the business side of things. I depended on him and he knew it. I let him know that, if he did what he could to facilitate the lease, he would be taken care of. In the end we negotiated a lump sum and an annual payment related to the level of business. The cash went to pay off our creditors. I was so relieved to have avoided bankruptcy that I made over the annual payment to Mr Oldroyd, to keep an eye on the L&NW, and act on our behalf whenever necessary."

"That was fourteen years ago! Has the arrangement lasted all this time?" Spray found it difficult to keep incredulity out of his voice. "Aren't there any other interested parties to query this arrangement?"

The question flustered the old man. "Well…" he paused for a moment, "No one has mentioned the matter."

"Not even this legal chap, Jones?"

"No."

"What do you expect will happen to the annual payment now Mr Oldroyd is dead?"

"It will probably become redundant. The L&NW is offering to buy out the C&HP completely. Really, Mr Spray, you intrude too far into sensitive business matters of no concern to a policeman."

Spray was pleased to hear Tarp becoming rattled: it suggested he was getting somewhere.

"Mr Tarp, I think you should consider this. An associate of yours has died in suspicious circumstances. Both you and he are linked with the railway company on whose property he was found and most likely killed. You have both been involved in a business arrangement that at best can be described as irregular. I would be in dereliction of my duty if I did not make enquiries along these lines. I take it you are as anxious as I to uncover the truth about Mr Oldroyd's death?"

Tarp didn't quite run to an apology; a policeman couldn't expect such a thing from a gentleman. Though it was a subdued man who explained that the L&NW had approached him with an offer to buy out the shareholders of the C&HP. In Tarp's view, traffic must have increased to the point where they wanted a free hand to expand, and the annual payment irked them. He had convened a meeting with Jones and Oldroyd and any shareholders Jones could contact. Jones arrived alone, and said he had been empowered to act on behalf of the other shareholders. He had no written confirmation of this arrangement, but Tarp accepted his word. Oldroyd, however, had been reluctant to follow suit.

It sounded to Spray as if there'd been a blazing row between the solicitor and the company agent, much to Tarp's discomfort. He asked Tarp how an employee might be able to prevent a transfer of ownership of the company.

"As Mr Oldroyd took increasing responsibility for the running of things, I felt that we couldn't manage without him. By then, there were no other investors paying any attention to how things were run. I considered he would be more committed to the company if he owned some shares, so I made some of my holding over to him. As a result, he had some say in the matter of the L&NW approach."

"Could he block the sale with his shareholding?"

"Not with what I had made over to him. It was strange: in the end, although Jones was very angry, he didn't press the matter, and went away with his tail between his legs. I was just relieved when they departed. I'm not up to that sort of thing anymore. Afterwards, though, I was puzzled by the outcome."

It seemed that Spray was right about a row.

"What was your view of the offer?" he questioned.

"It was the best thing that could happen, but quite honestly, I was past caring about it." A weariness descended on Tarp.

Spray was unsure whether it was provoked by the rigours of the interview, or the wider malaise of a man tired of this world and its doings.

"I hadn't the stomach for an argument so I just let them get on with it," Tarp offered resignedly.

Spray began to feel sympathy for the old fellow. He had provided a lot of information, some with a possible bearing on the case.

"You have been most helpful, sir. I thank you for your hospitality, and will take my leave." Spray had risen from his chair and Tarp was rising, too.

"Just one last thing." Spray may have felt for the older man's weariness, but he couldn't avoid the question.

"I understand that you had a…" there was a slight pause, "… a connection with Mr Oldroyd's mother in the distant past?"

"Really!" Tarp had risen to his full height; a hand was extended, propelling Spray to the hallway.

Before Spray knew it, the front door separated the two men – one to return to his fireside, the other sent on a long walk in the winter gloom. Spray had to admire the adroit manner by which it was done. Tarp may have become weary of the world, but he still retained the skills required to survive there.

Chapter 9

At 7am, Constable William Archer wound his way through the crowds milling about on Crewe Station. It would get worse later but, even so, he already had to use his elbows to be sure of arriving at work on time.

"If that's you, Archer, come in here now!" Superintendent Wayland was in early today. He usually arrived an hour later than his staff.

Archer knocked and entered.

"Now, see here, constable, I've a particular job, and it requires you to take yourself off to Whaley Bridge and nose about a bit." Wayland could never quite grasp what his men got up to when engaged on detective work; 'nosing about a bit' was the closest his imagination got to it. "I've Spray out there already, he'll tell you what to do. I've some instructions from him here, so you can make a start." He handed over Spray's note.

"Am I to know what the case consists of, sir?"

Wayland searched for insolence in this rather pointed question. He could find none, but wasn't entirely convinced. The constable habitually wore such an amiable, self-effacing air that Wayland often wondered what he was doing in a police force at all. His confusion was all the greater because he had to admit that, whenever there was anything difficult or dangerous to be done, Archer would volunteer and succeed. All the while, he'd still wear the same expression, and, apparently, without discommoding himself one jot.

"Well, I suppose you'll have to know." Wayland instantly regretted his surly tone, "Yes, of course, the matter stands like this…" He related the events of the previous Saturday and even went so far as to show him Spray's report on the fraud investigation.

"Are we proceeding on the assumption that these two cases are connected, sir?"

The superintendent was in a quandary. He couldn't, for the life of him, see how. On the other hand, Spray had left him with the distinct impression that they were. He couldn't quite recall it being said overtly, but Spray was clearly proceeding as if the cases were two sides of the same coin. Head office was the decisive consideration. He had been instructed to investigate the fraud, but had acted on his own initiative, or at least he had acted – the initiative was his sergeant's – in the matter of the murder. It would ease relations with his superior if there were a connection.

"Yes, constable. At present we are. We must all be guided by Sergeant Spray."

Wayland instantly regretted his final sentence, even as he uttered it. It subverted the chain of command in front of a mere constable. It was, however, the truth, and he let the remark stand unqualified.

"You have your travel pass and the department will pay a reasonable sum for your accommodation. But you pay for your food, and particularly, your drink. Remember, this is work, not a holiday." With these remarks the senior officer persuaded himself that he had reasserted his authority.

"Oh! The sergeant was most insistent that you take this hat with you. Better wrap it up, not sure what it signifies, but he thinks it's important," Wayland concluded.

"Will that be all, sir? There's a train for Stockport in a few minutes."

Twenty minutes after making his escape, Archer was sitting in a third class compartment, on a wooden seat, with the hat in brown wrapping paper beside him. He perused his sergeant's note.

Go to Whaley Bridge. Seek lodgings at 37 Old Mill End. If none available ask advice about alternative. Meet me there Monday eve. Ask about town to establish most recent sighting of Mr Arthur Oldroyd, his regular habits and associates. He lodged at the above address. I will make enquiries there when I arrive. Also, show hat about, see if anyone recognises it, or knows its owner. Sgt Spray

At Stockport, Archer had time for a cake and a cup of tea in the refreshment rooms. He took good care of his stomach when he had the opportunity and could never understand his sergeant's casualness about meals. Spray could go a whole day without eating, and, sometimes, when the two were working together, his constable had to follow suit. Today, on his own, he could do as he pleased, so he sat contentedly, gnawing on a rock bun.

Notwithstanding Sergeant Spray's eccentric dietary habits, their first murder investigation was an intriguing prospect. They'd worked together before, but nothing as exciting as this. He mused on his senior officer as the train was dragged, alternately panting and wheezing, up the more or less continuous climb to Disley. Though generally honest and straightforward, Spray was not above a little deceit whilst in pursuit of a larger truth. What most intrigued Archer was Spray's ability to separate head from heart. It was not that he was heartless. Quite the contrary; Archer himself had been in receipt of many acts of kindness from his hand, as had many others. Though Spray remained unmoved in the face of experiences sufficient to touch the hearts, or turn the stomachs, of apparently much more hardened officers.

The train entered the Goyt Valley, and rattled along at an easier pace to New Mills and Furness Vale before stopping at Whaley Bridge. As he left the station, a grim and untidy town met the policeman's eye. Terraces of soot-stained cottages lining the valley bottom and creeping precariously up its sides, were punctuated by mills with belching chimneys. It was all set against a backdrop of spoil tips, and in the distance, the White Peak dominating everything. Along with the shops and public houses in the foreground, it did nothing to commend itself to a son of the Cheshire plain. It was quite unlike Crewe, where Archer had been born. There, the neat rows of brick-built railway houses and modern civic buildings, surrounded by lush countryside, were his ideas of a proper town.

By mid-morning, a thin, watery sun was failing to improve Archer's first impressions as he enquired after Old Mill End. At least, as he approached No. 37, he was beginning to leave the industrial wasteland behind. He was heading toward the edge of town and the hills beyond.

By the time he arrived, the terraced houses had given way to detached properties; still modest, but a step up from mean. His knock on the door was answered by a demure woman some years his senior, with a steady, no-nonsense air about her.

"Good morning, ma'am. I understand you might have lodgings?"

After a moment or two, the corner of her mouth showed a twitch of recognition. Yes, there was a vacant room. It was very modest. One of her other rooms was reserved for a gentleman whom she thought to be returning this evening, and the other, her best, well, she really couldn't let it at present.

"Perhaps I'd better show it to you, Mr... ?"

"Archer, ma'am, that is, Mrs... ?"

"Oldroyd, Mrs Oldroyd."

The widely-spaced hazel eyes, even features and a trim figure were a pleasure to behold. He knew his limitations, though: quite apart from the black armband and jet pendant at her throat, she was beyond him.

Modest it was, but the room was cleaner and tidier than his quarters back home in Crewe, and the terms most reasonable, with breakfast included. Archer was not sure how to square that with the superintendent's warnings about paying for his own food, but time enough for that later. He left his meagre belongings and descended the stairs, still clutching the parcel containing the hat that Spray thought so important. He made to go out, but Mrs Oldroyd offered him a dish of tea as repast after his long journey.

"Have you travelled far, Mr Archer?"

"I came on the five-and-twenty past eleven from Stockport." Quite true, of course, but he knew it was not quite an answer to the question. "I hope you don't mind, I've taken a liberty. I have to meet someone later, we have some business together, and I have asked him to come here."

"That will be quite in order, Mr Archer; what time will you return?"

"A little after six o'clock." Such was Archer's unease that he failed to notice the difficulty his landlady was having in keeping a straight face during the exchange.

It was a relieved young man who made his excuses and left. He didn't know he'd been rumbled, but he knew he was out of his depth.

He tried unwrapping the hat as he walked back to the town, but the knots in the string defeated him. He'd intended doing it before leaving his lodgings, but had forgotten in his hurry to depart. Finally, he gave up the struggle and sat on a low wall to concentrate fully on tackling the knots.

"Wot yer doin', mister?" an urchin – perhaps nine or ten years old – with something green dribbling down his upper lip, stood in front of him. Scruffy? Yes, but not destitute. His boots had soles, and his head was topped with a cap set at a jaunty angle.

"Coo, er, I seen an 'at like that afore."

Archer came from a big family; conversing with the young was second nature to him. If you wanted information, just biding your time usually worked.

"Really? What you doing here, young man?"

"It's me dinner break."

"Shouldn't you be having your dinner?"

"No one at home. If we ain't got no one home we'm supposed to stay in school. I 'opped it."

"What about your dinner?"

A look of exasperation came into the urchin's eyes, "I don't get no dinner."

"Ah, we'll have to see about that; what did you say about the hat?"

"Oh that," it was clearly a matter of little importance compared with talk of dinner. "I see a body wearin' a hat like it a bit ago."

"Can you remember when?"

There was much umm-ing and err-ing. It turned out that ma was in the habit of roasting a joint for Sunday tea, with cold meat and pickles on Monday, and, if it stretched, Tuesday. What was left next day went into shepherd's pie or hot-pot. The urchin may not get his dinner on a regular basis, but it seemed his tea made up the gaps in his diet. Archer could not bear to think of a day with no dinner.

After some uncertainty as to whether or not the joint had

stretched last week, it was established that the body with the hat—'like wot yer got there'—was seen the evening they had ''ot pot', so it must have been Tuesday.

"Eer mister, you got a tanner, cos I give yer wot yer want didn't I?" He had indeed.

It turned out the urchin had a name: Jimmy Allcroft.

"See here, Jimmy, you come with me and we'll see about that tanner." As they walked into town Archer enquired after the time and place that the 'body wearin' that hat' had been seen. It turned out that Jimmy could be surprisingly accurate on the point.

"I were on an errand fer me mam. It were about a quarter after seven."

"How can you be so sure?"

"Ah, well, ye see now…" there was a certain reticence, but the urchin pressed on. "It were band night. Me mam told me t'follow me pa and tell her where he went."

Archer suppressed an almost irresistible urge to ask where Mr Allcroft ended up.

"Band's at half past; me Dad has a cornet, ye see."

"What sort of body was wearing the hat?"

"Well, that's tricky," Jimmy became serious. "There's two sorts of people: them, wot's like us, and then the other lot, wot's like them."

Archer held his breath.

"Trouble is, he weren't like us, and he weren't like them, neither. Yer see, he didn't have clothes like me, dad and everyone round here. They were sort of smart, but not like a toff. Really, the only proper smart thing were that."

He pointed at the hat Archer was carrying. It seemed that in Jimmy's mind, at least, the 'hat' had definitely become the property to the 'body' under discussion.

"And where did you see him?" Archer had withdrawn a coin from his pocket with his free hand and let it be seen by Jimmy. No harm in a bit of encouragement, and they were nearly there, both conversationally and geographically. The urchin looked pityingly at his companion.

"Where you were sittin', of course. Well he were sittin' when I set out, but he were just walkin' off when I got back."

"How long did your errand take?"

"Well me dad went straight to band, but there were no one there! Could tell that cos door were locked, so he went t' the Jodrell." Archer was unfamiliar with Whaley Bridge and asked for clarification. The pitying look returned. "The pub, yer know, the Jodrell Arms."

"So that would be ten minutes?"

"Suppose. Saw him agin, though, at least I think it were him."

"When would that be?" They had stopped outside a pie shop with a delicious aroma wafting from the door. Jimmy seemed unmoved, after all he usually 'didn't get no dinner'. Archer, on the other hand, couldn't dismiss the mouth-watering display in the window and was distracted by it.

"Well, I told me mam where me dad were," Jimmy explained, rolling his eyes dramatically. "She didn't half go on, so I hopped it. Came back when she'd calmed down, and she told me ter go and get him home. So I went back to the Jodrell and told dad what she said an he looked a bit down, but he come home. He don't get difficult, me dad, when he's had a few, just a bit soppy. Said he'd get me some cornet lessons if I were good. Mind you, he's said that afore when he's had a few an I ain't seen none yet." Jimmy's manner became wistful. "I do want ter play the cornet like me dad, I really do."

Archer was ashamed of his own hunger in the face of the

boy's longing, but the feeling disappeared as soon as it had arrived.

"Anyway, I got him home, and he started swearing somethin' awful. He'd left his cornet at the Jodrell. So I said I'd get it for him an' I hopped it again. Well, there were goin' ter be a racket when he got in, weren't there? So I went back to the pub, an' just afore I got there, I saw this body again." By this time Jimmy's doubt had dissolved. "He were goin' down there."

There was just one more question, "Where does it lead to, down there?"

"To the wharf, everybody knows that, and the railway yard." Jimmy's voice didn't hide his exasperation.

The pie shop had become irresistible. Despite a disapproving look, from across the counter, in Jimmy's direction, they had a pie each. Archer also bought an oatcake wrapped round some cheese, in greaseproof paper, for emergencies. As they came out, a tanner changed hands and another was promised if Jimmy could remember anything else later.

"If you do, come to Mrs Oldroyd's at No. 37 on your street, tomorrow, before school."

Jimmy considered this for a while.

"She's one of the other lot, ain't she? But she's all right, gave me a penny t'other day. See yer there." And the young boy was gone.

<hr />

Spray was on his way early the next morning. With breakfast inside him and his bill paid, he stepped out from the Bell to join a surprising number of people – mostly men, but one or two women – on their way to work. He turned for the station and barely noticed the girl across the road. Having consulted his *Bradshaw,* he was aiming for a train departing Cromford at 7:15am, and he needed to hurry to the Midland Station, high up the side of the valley. He made good progress to start with, but was breathless by the time he presented himself at the window to ask for a ticket to Buxton.

He stepped onto the platform to the distant sound of an approaching train. Through the railings, he could see someone toiling up the station approach. *She'll be lucky to make it in time,* he thought. A smart Kirtley 2–4–0 came to a halt with a sigh. He was just getting into a carriage when he thought he heard his name.

"Hurry along there, sir!" A porter ushered him on board.

Hearing his name spoken as the door was closing, he turned, and to the disapproval of those already comfortably seated, he opened the window. By now the girl was level with his compartment.

"Sergeant Spray," she gasped, "I have something to tell you… it may help your enquiries."

The tightly-timed train was already moving.

"Go to the Bell Inn and tell the landlord your name and address. I shall be back." By now the train was leaving her behind. "What's your name?" Spray shouted.

Her reply all but disappeared as cylinders full of steam discharged their exhaust noisily up the chimney and the engine whistled. He thought he may have heard the word 'Tilly'.

Spray was condemned to travel with those he had disturbed. The Midland Railway had abolished second class travel earlier in the year. In the process, it had given all its passengers upholstered seats. Unfortunately, the early morning Derby, all-stations-to-Manchester 'stopper' didn't run to corridor stock. He did his best, shutting the window and trying to slip, unobtrusively, into a less-than-adequate space on the bench seat. There were no welcoming nods. It was a relief to change trains at Miller's Dale.

Buxton, it seemed, wasn't popular this morning, so he had the waiting room to himself. He set about a task that required privacy and should really have been undertaken earlier. He'd glanced only momentarily at the headed paper he had removed from Oldroyd's desk.

Flegg & Co.,
Supplier of Minerals,
Coachman's Passage,
Buxton.

Initially, he had thought it writing paper, but now, on closer examination, he saw it was laid out as a *pro forma* invoice, with space for items, costings and total due. Next, he produced the wallet dipped from the inside coat pocket of the murdered man. He wanted to lay out the contents to view them as a whole, but his privacy was at the mercy of any traveller wishing to shelter from the cold. He contented himself with exploring the compartments one at a time. It was nearly his undoing. The wallet was heavy, heavy enough to suggest coins, and indeed there were some. What he nearly missed were the keys in a smaller pouch, sharing the same compartment as the cash. It opened in the reverse direction, so he had to get to the deepest recess of the first to find the opening to the second.

There was much clanking of worn bearings and hissing of steam escaping from leaky joints as the Buxton shuttle drew in. Spray stepped out onto the platform and watched with the curiosity of a true enthusiast. Not a smart engine this time, but one of such decrepitude that Spray wondered at its ability to move at all. All the same, he was fascinated. Despite his misgivings, the train completed the short journey to Buxton Midland, and Spray left the train in search of Coachman's Passage.

Retracing his walk of Saturday afternoon, he found himself outside the pub where he and the undertaker, Akers, had shared a drink. He rather hoped that Coachman's Passage and the Coachman Inn were connected. Although there was the pub, clean and respectable as before, no Coachman's Passage was to be seen.

Setting off along the street to his right, the sergeant looked across the other side for a likely alleyway. The row of shops was broken by a turning onto a side street with no name. He crossed over and walked alongside the gable end of the corner property. Perhaps five yards down, Spray turned into a trackway running behind the shops, giving them rear access. He walked past four gates before his progress was blocked by a more-substantial pair of doors set in a stone wall. The sour smell of stale beer hung in the air.

It was a long shot, he knew, but it was the best lead he had. Taking the larger of the two keys he'd extracted from Oldroyd's wallet, he tried it in the lock of a wicket gate set in one of the doors. The ease with which it opened came as an anticlimax, and as he slipped through, it all seemed too easy. The place had seen busier days. Before the railways finished it off, the yard must have teemed with men and horses engaged in the coaching business. Now, with empty stables put to more mundane uses, it was deserted – well, almost. Two of the stables were still occupied, and an open-sided shed housed a trap, so there must still be some local trade.

Other doorways revealed an assortment of old barrels, broken furniture and discarded junk, disused items that had accumulated to fill the available space. Next to the open bay, Spray came across something very different. What had once been the entrance to more stabling was now framed, and filled, with a solid-oak door adorned with an escutcheon.

A rumbling sound took him by surprise. It was still barely light, and he hadn't seen the cellar man until unexpected footsteps and muttered oaths alerted him. Spray made himself scarce behind the trap. For a panicky moment, he regretted his clandestine approach, but as the man went, untroubled, about his business, and disappeared back from where he'd emerged, the detective regained his composure. With the yard quiet again, he returned to the locked door and, fumbling, tried the second key.

Suddenly, there were more footsteps as a second empty barrel followed the first. In a panic, he tried to turn and withdraw the key at the same time. It jammed. He slipped behind the trap again. This time, he had the key to worry about, but the second barrel came to rest and nothing seemed amiss. Expecting the man to head back inside, Spray was startled by the clatter of buckets. The cellar man was reborn as a stableman. Creaking, clattering and splashing suggested a yard pump: the horses were being given fresh water.

Vulnerable as he was, Spray mused, with wry satisfaction, on the irony of providing dumb creatures with bucketfuls of a commodity high-priced in the Buxton Spa. The behaviour of the moneyed classes fascinated him. They could be persuaded to spend large amounts on any useless fad or fancy, if packaged in the right way. The Nonconformist in him deplored such exhibitions of wealth. As his mind wandered, his position became ever more precarious.

The open bay housed not only the trap, but also a stack of hay. The horses also needed to be fed, so the stableman passed within a few feet of him, pitchfork in hand, to spear a bundle of fodder. Spray feared that he would be discovered, but the man turned away and headed for the nearest stable and then repeated the process for the second horse. The pitchfork was replaced, and the man ambled off, Spray hoped, to find his breakfast.

At his third attempt, Spray managed to free the key. He forced himself to replace it in the lock, this time with a gentler touch. It turned smoothly, and the door opened. As he closed it behind himself, he became disorientated when the light all but disappeared. As he stood inside, at last, pulse settling and eyes gradually accommodating to the gloom, a skylight materialised above his head.

If the railway yard had been the direction taken by the man with the hat, it was the direction for Archer to follow. He wasn't sure what to expect. He hadn't asked for enlightenment from Jimmy – the lad had been sufficiently scornful of his local knowledge as to discourage further enquiry – but it was a railway yard like no other he'd seen. The picture in his mind was of the extensive layout at home, with engine running sheds, hangars for the construction of new engines, a turntable, goods yard and the rest. Not at Whaley Bridge. Here was a modest and eccentric affair. It was an interchange point between railway and canal, and much of the traffic consisted of limestone being shipped out from the quarries of the Peak. Most intriguing to Archer was the use of heavy horses to move the wagons about. Railway access was via an incline so steep, that wagons ascended and descended by being attached to a continuous rope that was wound around a capstan at the top.

The mechanism was driven by a docile horse walking round in a never-ending circle.

There was nothing like this at Crewe, and he was determined to investigate further. His instructions had not extended to this foray, but curiosity got the better of duty, and he walked confidently through the yard gates and started to explore. For a while, he wasn't challenged, but his interest in the sweating, heaving horses finally drew attention. A shunter broke off from urging one of the beasts to move what looked to be an impossibly heavy load.

"Oi, you! what yer up to? You ain't got no right bein' here. This is railway property."

"Good day to you, sir. If you have a look at this, I fancy you will see that I am indeed allowed." Archer displayed his warrant card.

"Wot's that?" asked the shunter, squinting at the small print on the card.

Archer thought: *the man could hardly distribute wagons according to their correct destinations if he couldn't read, but the writing on the dockets attached to each one was written in big, black letters. Probably his sight had deteriorated with age.*

"It's a railway-police warrant-card. I am Constable Archer."

"Is it now? Yer a bobby, are you? My name's Pott, Timothy Pott. He must have telt thee, then. I told him not to bother. It were only kids, tha knows. You'll never get 'em, and if yer do, all the little beggars need is a clip round th'ear."

Archer's mystification showed all too clearly.

"You know, the yard foreman. I had to tell 'im cos Star weren't so good when I got here." The man squinted at Archer, "You don't know what I'm about, do you?"

"Er, no. It's another matter entirely." Archer was interrupted before he could explore the 'other matter'.

"She were in a right mess, tha knows. She'd been out in the yard all night. Must have rushed about a bit and worked up a real sweat, all caked on, it were; and her standin' there shiverin' by time I got 'ere. Yer see, osses get a thick coat in the winter, and them as works hard like Star sweat up and get too hot, so we clip them. Problem is, when they've been workin', we have to rub them down ter dry 'em off, an' then put sacks on 'em to keep 'em warm. No one had done that for poor owd Star in the middle of the night. Got a right chill, she did; she's better now, tho."

The man's voice rose with indignation, "D'ye know, they'd closed the door to the stalls so she couldn't have got back in if she'd wanted to."

As a youngster, Archer had helped in the family-bakery business by grooming the cob, tacking her up and backing her into the shafts. On occasions, he'd even been allowed to take the van out on the road by himself. The shunter's story did make sense. His love for horses shone through, especially for one that had been ill treated.

"Is Star on her own in a box? Could I have a look at her?" asked Archer.

"You int'rested in osses?"

As they walked across the yard, Archer related anecdotes about the family cob. He ingratiated himself by implying that he had a greater involvement with caring for the horse than was strictly the case. Inside the box stood an enormous, heavy horse, on pristine straw, coat shining, water bucket topped up, with a hayrack stuffed full. Star was clearly the recipient of much loving attention.

"We'll 'ave 'er back in work afore Christmas."

Archer felt he had indulged the man's passion for horses sufficiently to move on.

"I'm here on quite another matter, Mr Pott. I know how important Star is, but I didn't know about this incident till I met you. I'm trying to get a fix on a cove who wore this hat. He's not a gent but probably tries to look like one." This was the best interpretation of young Jimmy's description he could manage.

Pott looked at him pensively, "No, I s'pose yer wouldn't come all this way for the oss. But, anyways, I ain't seen your cove, not never."

"What about Mr Arthur Oldroyd? Do you know him?"

"Oh, 'im. Well I know who he is – was. I 'eard he died in the accident on Friday. That's why yer eer, in't it?" Pott's disappointment was palpable. He clearly felt that the death of Arthur Oldroyd was an insignificant matter as compared with the abuse of his horse.

"I'm just making a few enquiries. Did anybody else here know him better?"

"Well, Fred don't, that's fer sure." Pott lowered his voice to produce a faintly conspiratorial tone. "He's a furriner, tha knows."

Archer's curiosity got the better of him, "Where from?"

"Across t'watter, o'course. Eats some funny vittels, keeps goin' on about summat called spaghetti. A relative of his brings some from over there. Looked all white an wrigglin' when 'is missus cooked it. Offered me some. Told 'im it'd be like eatin' worms. He's all right, tho'. Him and his missus 'ave a lot o' gran-kids, they're good littl'uns, but I lost count how many."

The subject of foreigners seemed to be exhausted. "Yer'd best speak ter Riggott. 'E's foreman, I'll show yer where 'e is."

They approached an old wagon body in the corner of the yard where a man – a rather truculent man – stood in the doorway blocking any further progress.

"Mr Riggott, this eer's a bobby."

Riggott grunted uncooperatively.

"Bin askin' after Arthur Oldroyd. Told him you an' 'im was thick, cos I see you wiv 'im a lot. You 'eard e's dead, din't yer?"

Riggott exploded, "What the 'ell d'ye say that fer, yagret-puddingead? Ah'll cloth yer one, get back to work and stop bloody moonin' ower that Star!"

With increased venom he added, "She's not yower oss, tha knows; belongs t'company, and they can tek her away any time if she won't work!"

Pott walked back to the patient horse he'd been working earlier. Archer was sure he detected a swagger in his step. The baiting of Riggott had gone well.

"Nah, Mr Bobby, we got rid of him," Riggott glared at the back of the departing shunter. "Let's be seeing yer warrant card." Riggott peered at it with more success than Pott and read out Archer's name and rank slowly, accompanied by a faint sneer. "What can I do for you, Constable Archer? It ain't no good asking about Oldroyd, I 'ardly knew the man. See him about a time or two, tha's all."

"Mr Pott seemed to think you saw quite a lot of him."

"Oh, 'im. Yer don't wanna tek any notice of 'im. 'E ain't reliable, tha knows, tells lies an' that. 'Im and that furriner Maida are in't pocket of management."

"So, what it boils down to is that all the staff here are rogues, except you, and you have no connection with the dead man," Archer deadpanned.

"That's 'bout it," Riggott said, with an air of satisfaction, as if the matter was settled.

Archer did not hide his scepticism, but the conversation moved on.

"Have you seen anyone about wearing this hat?" the constable asked.

Riggott seemed happier with this line of questioning and became more cooperative. "We... ll, not much to go on, is it? S'pose I might have, not 'ere tho', in the town, last week p'raps. Can't be sure."

Where the truth lay was anyone's guess. Archer felt he would get nothing of any further use. Bidding Riggott good day, he contrived to pass close enough to Pott to suggest they meet for a drink – 'my treat, of course' – that evening.

"Bring your foreign friend Fred along, if he'll come."

From Pott's reply, it seemed that the offer of a free drink would be sufficient enticement. With that, Archer walked out of the yard to hawk the damned hat round Whaley Bridge.

<hr />

Meanwhile, in Oldroyd's office in Coachman's Passage, Spray waited, silent and immobile. Mostly, he wanted to be sure there was no hue and cry provoked by his entry. His eyes adjusted slowly to the gloom. Whilst he waited, he wondered at his good fortune. With only the faintest hope of success, he had found his way into the centre of Oldroyd's business affairs.

He was in a clean and tidy room, with whitewashed walls, boarded floor and gas lamps. How long ago had gas arrived in Buxton, and at what cost had it been installed here? A box of safety matches lay, temptingly, on the desk. Could he risk the glow from a gas mantle giving him away? After several minutes he still couldn't see well enough to examine the myriad ledgers and papers. In amongst them must be proof of Oldroyd's fraudulent business dealings and, through them, perhaps some clue as to who murdered him. Spray took the plunge and struck a match, turned on the gas and started searching.

It wasn't that difficult. Oldroyd had been a methodical man and he'd organised his papers as if he were in a perfectly legitimate line of business. There was a stack of ledgers itemising consignments of mineral, mostly limestone, with a delivery date, customer's name, address, value and payment date. There were statements from a bank in Manchester, which held an account in the name of Flegg & Co, where monthly deposits had been made. All transactions were in cash, and when Spray added up a month's earnings he could match the sum with a corresponding bank deposit.

There were surprisingly few withdrawals over the years; Oldroyd must have had other sources of income. There was, of course, the stipend from the rump of the C&HP; Tarp hadn't revealed what that might amount to, but it was doubtful if it could support Oldroyd in the style that the Cromford house represented. Then there were the inevitable expenses of the business: men to pay, travelling and suchlike. Spray was mulling this over, idly thumbing through the ledger, when he realised he'd underrated the scope of Flegg & Co.

All his investigations during the previous week had been centred on one quarry: Cross & Blackwood at Grin No. 2. The consignments he had tracked ended up at High Peak Junction, at the Cromford end of the line. Without giving it too much thought, he had assumed that this covered the whole enterprise. But within the ledger were addresses to the west, in Cheshire, and that had to mean that consignments were being passed through Whaley Bridge as well. The operation was far bigger than he had imagined.

Spray finished with the business accounts and, having jotted down a few details, turned to other matters. There was a bundle of letters from a solicitor in Buxton, the first one, dated May 1871, agreeing to undertake some business 'as previously discussed'. Others confirmed that the business was progressing, and then one dated October 1873 read: 'Matters have been arranged as per your instruction. All documents are in safekeeping at the above premises. Should I be incapacitated at such time as further action is required I have left instructions for my successor as to how to proceed. As our business is now completed I enclose my account'. It was signed *Ezra Brook, Attorney-at-Law.*

Another batch of correspondence was from *Nathaniel Jones, Attorney, Cromford,* but no letter was dated later than January 1873.

With the paperwork exhausted, Spray turned to the rest of the office. There wasn't much to see apart from the desk, an office chair, a tier of shelves, a comfortable armchair and – lurking in the shadows and flush with the wall – the door of a safe. Noises from outside broke his concentration: a horse clattered on the cobbles and wagon wheels rumbled. After some shouting, full barrels thudded dully onto the ground and, in exchange, the hollow ring of empty ones being loaded suggested that perhaps this was an opportune moment to make his exit.

Opening the door a crack, Spray could see a dray drawn up parallel to the back of the public house. All the bustle was between the two, with nobody on the yard side. Once he'd turned off the gas lamp it only took a moment to slip out, lock the door and stroll towards the hubbub. "Excuse me, sir, where would I find the proprietor?"

A big, muscular man looked up from rolling an empty barrel towards the dray. He scowled, or perhaps he always had a malevolent look on his face.

"'Nah then, wot yer doin' here? How'd ye gerrin?"

"I walked in through the gate. It's open, you know."

"Oh yeah, s'pose it is. I had ter let the dray in." The scowl faded. "Yer want ma? She's the gaffer. In there." He pointed to a door.

"I need to talk to her about Mr Oldroyd," said Spray, but the name did not prompt even a flicker of interest. Either he'd not heard about the man's death, or he didn't care.

A lobby, barely wide enough to accommodate a flight of stairs with a passageway alongside, took Spray to a doorway opening into the serving area behind a bar. A backside of ample proportions came onto view. Its owner, bent double, was loading glasses onto low shelves.

"That you, Perce?" The backside acquired a top hamper as its owner straightened up. "'Ave yer finished? Oh! Who the hell are you? And what yer doin' behind my bar?"

Vera Pidcock was well endowed with rosy – perhaps ruddy – cheeks, but the habitual twinkle in her eyes was diminished by the sudden appearance of a stranger. There was no sign of fear, only indignation. "You got no right bein' here. We ain't open, an even if we was, that's where you should be." She gestured with a short, heavy staff that had somehow appeared in her hand. On a dark night, held by one with evil intent, Spray would have described it as a cosh.

Looking suitably chastened, and happy to get out of range of the weapon, he stepped smartly round the end of the bar and into the saloon. "Good day to you, ma'am. I apologise for startling you. I'm Sergeant Spray, here to speak to you about Arthur Oldroyd."

The indignation began to subside. She was now more wary than assertive, but still every inch Mrs Pidcock, landlady and licensee.

"What about 'im? He's usually about here this time of a Monday mornin', but I ain't seen 'im yet." Clearly the news of Oldroyd's demise hadn't made it to the Coachman Inn.

"You've heard about the railway accident up by Ladmanlow last Friday?"

It had been mentioned in the bar, she replied, but she hadn't taken much notice. "Too busy, yer see; but they did say some was hurt." It began to dawn on her that there was a connection between this intruder, the accident and Arthur. "Yer don't mean 'e were one of 'em, do yer?"

"Well, yes and no."

"What sort of answer is that?" she asked, her mockery tinged with apprehension. "Either he were or he weren't."

"All will be explained. Do you know him well?"

"Course I do: he owns the place and I'm 'is tenant." Both of them were finding the conversation confusing. "Wot's more, he's my nephew, so get on wi' it and tell me what's happened!" She frowned with concern.

"There were two men found dead at the site of the accident. One of them was a fireman, who had, clearly, been thrown from his engine. But the other hadn't died in the accident; he was found beside the line. We believe this man was your nephew, Mrs Pidcock, and I am sorry to have to tell you that we suspect he may have been killed before the crash and left in the scrub beside the line."

Mrs Pidcock's indignation and wariness evaporated. She was visibly shocked. "My poor Arthur, who could have done for 'im?" There was a pause. "I loved that boy." Another pause. "Are you here to find out who dunnit?"

The atmosphere had changed. Grief now prevailed, but Spray felt that far from being the intruder he was now a welcome visitor. The cosh had been put aside and the landlady was pouring herself a brandy and offering one to Spray.

"On the 'ouse, of course," she said, sadly.

He declined.

"Why, why would anyone do such a thing? 'E were a good man: well, 'e were good to us, anyways."

"I am sure he was, Mrs Pidcock. Perhaps, if you could tell me about Mr Oldroyd, you know, who he knew, how he lived, and what sort of business dealings he had, it might help us find whoever did this terrible deed."

She was flattered at being drawn into the heart of the investigation and responded accordingly, and at some length.

Vera was Arthur's mother's younger sister. She was ten when Arthur was born and looked after him as a baby and a toddler. His father was absent much of the time. 'He went fer a sojer, ye'see. Wern't never home.' As a former soldier, Spray couldn't resist exploring the byways of her story.

Spray asked, "Do you know which military campaigns he fought in?"

"Good Lord above, why would I know that? There's allus wars goin' on, but they don't trouble me, an' I don't trouble they. Well, not unless a man don't come home in the end. But then, who's ter say if he's dead, or just gone off? That's what 'appened ter Arthur's ma: her man just didn't come home. Mind you, Arthur done all right: that Mr Tarp took 'im in."

She suddenly looked rather pensive. "I've often wondered 'bout that."

It emerged that Vera's husband had 'just gone off' as well, leaving her with a son, Percy, the man Spray had met in the yard. As young Arthur had made his way in life, under Mr

Tarp's benevolent eye, he'd been able to help Vera and Percy get by. Eventually, he obtained for Vera the tenancy of the Coachman.

"Been the makin' of me and Perce, this place has, ever so kind of Arthur; but we've done him proud."

Spray looked around the clean and tidy public house. Indeed they had, though there was no doubt it was the landlady who was behind its success.

Mrs Pidcock wiped away a tear. "He 'ad one room upstairs," she explained, gesturing towards the lobby where Spray had entered, "and another in the yard. Very pertickler 'bout that office in the yard, never let anyone near, and told me and Perce to make sure no one got near, neither."

It struck Spray that Percy wasn't too mindful of his duty in that respect.

"Can you remember any times that Mr Oldroyd had visitors, either in the office or upstairs?"

Vera looked wary, "Difficult ter say. He could let people in t'yard office and I wouldn't know."

"And the upstairs room?"

Vera had tried to avoid the question but its reiteration forced her into the open.

After a pause she answered reluctantly. "He did have visitors up there. I almost never saw them, but I heard them goin' up."

"Lady friends?" He asked, gently, acutely aware of the scandalous nature of his line of questioning.

"Gentlemen friends. That were more to his likin', yer see, an' there was plenty as liked 'im, too."

Spray was astonished at how nonchalant she was about her nephew's activities. *Perhaps she didn't understand* he thought.

"I met one of 'em once. Very nice 'e was. Passed the time o'day, said how nice the pub were, an asked me how I was and that. Sort o'man yer could talk ter, nice-like. Never brought them through the bar; he'd allus let them in through the yard. That's why I 'ardly ever saw 'em, 'cept that once."

"Can you describe him?"

"Yer don't think 'e dunnit, do yer?"

"At present, Mrs Pidcock, I've no idea who was responsible, so you see, anything you can tell me might turn out to be very important," Spray explained.

"I only saw 'im in dim light. He were tall, taller than you, and clean shaven, smart clouts and is coat were a belter."

"And his hat?"

"Nah, didn't see no 'at. But he looked a proper gent."

"Can you tell me anything about the mail Mr Oldroyd received? Did he get the same sort of correspondence at regular intervals, for example, or were there any oddities? Can you remember any postmarks, or return addresses?"

"Well I got my letters, but I ain't so good when they get joined inter words. I can do me name an me sums well enough," she added, helpfully. "Some o'they wot come reg'lar had different colour writin' on the outside, well I 'spose it were printin' really, and some had a funny smell, like flowers and that."

Spray thanked her for her assistance and asked if he could see the bedroom. As he followed her up the narrow staircase, her slim ankles and tiny feet came into his line of sight. In her youth she might almost have been petite.

A bed, square in the middle of the large floor area, gave an aura of spaciousness, but when he entered Spray found he had to duck beneath the eaves. He could stand upright in the dormer, though, and it was the light from this which enabled him to inspect the contents of a closet beyond. The clothes inside would have created a very different persona from the man who occupied the office in the yard.

In the attic room there had been no space for pictures, but on his way back down he found himself face to face with a lithograph of the Crystal Palace on the staircase wall. If it had been there since the Great Exhibition, it was in remarkably fine condition. Idly, he ran his finger along the top of the frame. No dust. Somebody took good care of it.

"That's a fine picture, Mrs Pidcock."

"Ooh yes, Arthur took pertickler trouble over it. Dusted it heself, he did, wouldn't let me touch it."

They descended to the bar, more brandy was poured, and this time, Spray found himself with a glass in his hand. They sat together in companionable silence for a while.

"I just r'membered summat as might help. Few weeks back, this gent came in askin' after Arthur. 'E weren't here but I knowed 'e'd be back dreckly, so I bid the gent sit down and wait. 'E were calm but 'e didn't look too happy, and when Arthur came in 'e weren't happy neither. They sat ower there," she pointed to a secluded corner, "'an had words. I couldn't hear, o'course, but yer could see it weren't friendly, very het up with each other they were, but quiet with it."

"Can you remember what the gent looked like?"

"Oh yeah, I had a good look at him. Tall 'e were, an' smart, an' fair, an' young. Well, younger'un Arthur. 'Spose 'e might be same age as Perce, somethin' short o'thirty, anyway. I wondered if 'e was one of Arthur's, er, friends, but I weren't sure. Seemed a bit too sure of 'isself."

She fell silent. The detective could see tears running, silently, down her cheeks.

Then she looked up to heaven and continued, "Oh, Arthur,

I wouldn't a-talked like this if yer'd been here, y'know. I'd have seen him off; that I would. But yer not here, are yer, and yer's not coming back, are yer? And this bobby-man sez 'e can find out who dunnit, an' if 'e can do that, I got ter help 'im, ain't I, fer you and yer ma's sake."

Spray patted her hand in an avuncular fashion and she broke from her reverie, unsure whether it had all been in her head or she had spoken out loud, or a mixture of both. The tears subsided and the comforting hand was withdrawn.

"With your leave, Mrs Pidcock, I must go now, but I'll be back. If you remember anything else, you know, about the tall, fair gent, or anything, you can tell me then."

Chapter 10

On a Monday afternoon, the population of Whaley Bridge seemed to consist principally of women, small children, elderly men and the odd layabout. Constable Archer, a high-crowned bowler with a vulgarly ostentatious hatband in one hand, tried them all. The women were too harassed to give him more than the time of day, however politely he approached them. Talking to the elderly was a struggle too: they were either too deaf or too garrulous – in most cases, both.

He approached the odd idler but none would talk without a drink inside him. In desperation, he even resorted to bribery in the form of a jug of ale, but not one admitted to seeing anything useful. Publicans, almost to a man, held out on him. Bobbies were not good news either, to them or their customers, and they made no distinction between the railway constabulary and the generality of Peelers.

The man at the Jodrell Hotel was more helpful, but his information was of dubious value. Yes, he thought he may have seen the hat last week – 'Not the sort of thing yer see round here, more like at the seaside' – but could remember nothing of the wearer. 'Must 'ave been later, when we're busy.'

That was it. Archer dawdled until the town-hall clock crawled round to six and then made his way to the Railway Hotel to meet up with Pott and his 'furriner' mate. He didn't have long to wait and was soon paying for a couple of jugs of ale for the railwaymen.

Frederico Maida was small, dark, stocky, but agile and alert. On being presented to Archer with the words 'here, this is the bobby wi' all the questions', a hand shot out and gripped Archer's, shaking it with a vigour that the policeman found slightly embarrassing.

"I Fred, please to meet."

"Bill." The little man's genial manner was infectious, drawing the constable into a greater familiarity than he was used to in the line of duty

"Tim, 'e say you very good man." Both Archer and Pott looked a bit startled at this assertion.

"I didn't quite say that, Fred."

"You say 'e don't like Riggott, an anyone not like Riggott is good man."

"What's between you and Riggott, Mr Pott?" asked Archer. "I couldn't help noticing you riled him and then looked rather pleased with yourself. I'm damned if I can see how you get away with it as he's the senior man."

With the cares of the day rapidly dissolving in alcohol, Pott allowed himself a smile and a little more familiarity.

"Yer can call me Tim. Well, yer see, Bill, this is the way of it…" The 'way of it' turned out to be a combination of incompetence, uncontrolled temper and animal cruelty.

Riggott was working a horse in the yard and the animal slipped on the setts, falling onto its knees. The wagon was on a slope, and as the horse fell, it started to roll back slightly.

"Riggott should have braked the wagon and unhitched the horse," Pott observed.

Instead, he'd lashed out with a stick to try and get it to rise. The poor animal made an effort to comply, but the unbraked wagon pulled it over again. At this point Tim saw what was happening, rushed over, applied the brake and went to rescue the horse. Riggott lost his temper, aimed a blow at Tim and caught him in the face. Unbalanced by his swing, Riggott was in no position to avoid Tim's well-aimed kick to the groin. As a fight, there wasn't much to it, but the result was Riggott lying on the setts, writhing in agony.

"It were almost worth it, just fer that," remarked Pott, with a satisfied grin.

Pott had unhitched the much abused animal, taken it back to the loose box and set about treating its wounds. Fred had arrived late on the mishap, but had seen enough to corroborate Pott's report to the head shunter at Shallcross yard.

"He shoulda got ridda 'im."

Fred, indignant, saw the failure to sack Riggott as a slur on his testimony. Tim was, however, given sole responsibility for the horses in the wharf yard and was now senior to Riggott in that respect.

Tim supped the dregs of his ale, and as he wiped a hand across his mouth, Archer paid for refills, wondering the while if the outlay would pay a dividend. His companions were agreeable enough and talkative with it, possibly too much so, as they drank their way through a second pint, but was he going to learn anything new?

"Tell me about Riggott and Oldroyd. How do reckon they were connected?"

"Oldroyd would come down t'yard reg'lar of a Monday, round knocking-off time and say 'how d'ye do' ter anyone as was about. Then he'd walk past the cabin, stick 'is head through the door, an' then bobby off."

"You mean the box van in the yard where you got at Riggott?"

"S'right. 'E has a cubby inside and keeps records an' stuff there. That's not all of it, though. Them nights when 'e'd been round, Fred an' me would see Oldroyd an' him goin' in the Jodrell; not with each other, like, an' then they'd get their heads tergether in the snug, an' then go out, separate like. We didn't allus see all of it, but enough bits an' enough times ter know them's thick."

"What about the other man?" asked Fred.

"Bobby ain't intrested in 'im."

The bobby certainly was, "What other man, Fred?"

"'E come week or two ago. Ask 'bout Oldroyd. 'E ask anyone see him in bar. You remember, I was a bit…" Fred made wavy movements with his hands, "… so you carry drink for me – I still pay, though – and tell 'im Oldroyd not here, but his friend Riggott in corner."

"Can you describe him, Fred?" Archer asked hopefully.

Fred looked dubious and repeated the wavy movements.

"Not so good to remember, but 'e tall."

Coming from a man of Fred's height, that could mean anything.

Tim added helpfully, "I didn't see him close, like Fred, but I 'old my ale better than 'im. He were quite tall, and dressed like a gent with smarmy hair, fair like."

That was that. The second jugs were nearly empty, and Archer was reluctant to pay for more. He inwardly justified this parsimony on grounds of social responsibility. Mrs Maida would hardly thank him for sending her man home drunk.

"Bill, Bill, you come to my 'ome one day, see bambinos, have tea, meet wife. Maybe I remember more."

Outside it was dark, cold and damp. Constable Archer made his way through the grim streets of Whaley Bridge to 37 Old Mill End.

Sergeant Spray squared his shoulders as he was ushered out of the front door of the Coachman and set off in search of the offices of two solicitors. He had been unwilling to tell Mrs Pidcock any more of his business than was absolutely necessary, so he had not asked for directions, preferring to nose about on his own. There were a few people about on the chilly, damp streets, but he kept his own counsel, telling himself he needed to learn how to find his own way around.

He stumbled across Ezra Brooke first, thanks to a nameplate fixed alongside a heavy oak door, brass fittings gleaming, front step swept and scrubbed. In response to a couple of 'rattats' with the door-knocker, he was admitted by a maid, who presented him to a small, rather stooped man with a beaky nose and intelligent eyes.

"Good day to you, sir, how can I be of assistance?"

Solicitor and detective introduced themselves, and in one seamless move, Spray found himself ushered across a hallway, into an office and seated. The room was businesslike and comfortable at the same time. A mahogany, glass-fronted bookcase faced a black-leaded fireplace, across an expanse of heavily patterned carpet. Spray, Brooke and a desk occupied the space in between. The window was behind Brooke. Spray looked across the desk at the man's intelligent eyes. They exuded an air of honesty – no, not honesty, professional rectitude, a rather different trait.

"Now, sir, what is it you want of me?"

Spray revealed his connection to the railway constabulary. Brooke had heard of the accident at Ladmanlow and of the deaths that had occurred.

"I suppose you have an interest in the causes and consequences of such an affair?"

"The railway inspectorate will take care of that, Mr Brooke;

it's quite another matter that brings me here. Of the two bodies found at Ladmanlow, only one died as a result of the accident. The other man appears to have been killed beforehand. Possibly murdered."

Brooke was visibly shocked. "You're sure of this?"

"I inspected the body myself on Friday and brought the matter to the coroner's attention on Saturday."

Brooke looked impressed. "How did you manage that? I've never seen him lift a finger at the weekend."

"I took along some heavy artillery in the form of my superintendent, he was quite sufficient for the undertaking."

Brooke looked quizzically at the sergeant, "This is all very interesting; indeed, I'm grateful for the intelligence, but I'm at a loss to see how I can help."

"The deceased was, I believe, a client of yours. A Mr Arthur Oldroyd."

Brooke looked both startled and impressed. "This is terrible news. May I ask how you have come to make a connection between the late Mr Oldroyd and myself?"

Spray parried the question with another, "I wondered if his death may be connected in some way to his last will and testament. Furthermore, it occurred to me that you might be in possession of such a document and may possibly be his executor."

There was a silence – quite a long silence – it seemed to Spray. The solicitor considered his position.

"I can confirm that I drew up a will for the deceased between three and four years ago. I am named as sole executor. Provided no more-recent will is found revoking it, I am confident that it cannot be challenged."

"And the beneficiaries?"

Brooke admired his audacity but would not be drawn.

"Come, come, sergeant, you don't really expect me to answer that question before the will has been read and a grant of probate made." The man adopted a more confidential tone, "However, I can tell you one thing without breaching any confidences: I would wager my entire worldly wealth against the name of the perpetrator of your suspicious death being found on the document in question."

Both men had gained something from the conversation, and as they commenced their leave-taking, Spray felt honours were even. Brooke's professional integrity was intact and nothing had been revealed of his own sources.

"I intend returning to Buxton tomorrow to have the body of your late client formally identified. I initially considered his aunt, Mrs Vera Pidcock, for the task, but his sister-in-law, Mrs Elizabeth Oldroyd, seems more suitable."

"Is that so? Um, I see."

Sensing the solicitor's uncertainty, Spray felt they were no longer even, but could not discern why.

The coroner's office was only a couple of minutes' walk away, and Spray found it easily. The advantage gained by his parting remark to Brooke had emboldened him to ask directions. They brought him to a modest establishment: an entrance door with tired paint, not quite peeling, and a brass knocker in need of polish. A plate read *J. W. Walters. Her Majesty's Coroner*. The door opened to his knock and a pair of protuberant eyes with a sloping forehead above, and weak mouth below, peered out at him.

"Can I help you, sir?" The man didn't quite cower, but Spray felt it would have been unwise to raise his arm.

"Good morning. I am Sergeant Spray of the railway constabulary."

"Good morning, sergeant. Ezekiel Nightingale, chief clerk

114

to the coroner," said the man, inviting Spray into the inner hallway.

"I have come about the affair at Ladmanlow on Friday."

"Really, sir, what affair might that be?" Clearly, Walters hadn't bothered to inform his staff of the collision.

"A fatal railway accident. I assumed the coroner would have instructed you to put matters in hand."

"Oh, no sir, I doubt he has even been informed yet. I've never known him to undertake official business over a weekend."

"He did this weekend, Mr Nightingale: I accompanied him myself to the premises of Dickens & Nephew, where we inspected the two cadavers."

The man's eyes bulged even more than usual and his weak mouth hung open, flecks of spittle on his lips.

Spray continued, "I rather expected this office would be arranging an autopsy by now and preparing to open an inquest."

"I never see Mr Walters here on a Monday, sergeant. If he wants anything he sends his man round. I haven't seen him since last week. He always goes to Lea Bridge…" At this point the clerk realised he was saying more than was wise, "… or somewhere, anyway."

"Perhaps you would be good enough to inform Dickens & Nephew that I intend to return tomorrow with someone able to identify one of the bodies."

"Oh, I, er, I'm not sure…" Apprehensive of doing anything not expressly ordered by the coroner, the man was about to refuse.

"There is a suspicious death involved, so I need to see Mr Walters urgently. What is his home address?"

The clerk immediately became evasive. Mr Walters was not at home, he could not say when he would be either at home or at his office. He could not promise to convey a message to him the next day.

Eventually, Spray's face grew dark with frustration, prompting the clerk to offer him just enough to avert an angry outburst: "Perhaps, if you wrote him a memorandum, sergeant, I might get it to him tonight."

He gestured towards an ornate chair placed close to a mahogany console table, upon which were sheets of laid paper, a blotting pad, a quill pen and a bottle of ink.

Having completed the note, Spray turned his attention to questioning the clerk.

"You frequent the Coachman Inn, do you not, Mr Nightingale? It has quite a reputation, I understand. You find what you want there, do you?"

"What are you implying, sergeant?" the man's colour was rising and Spray noticed his fists were clenched.

"You go there regularly, so I assumed..."

"Assumed what? That I'm one of *them*? Is that what Akers told you? I saw you go off with him on Saturday."

"Not at all. The matter came up whilst I was at the Coachman; they seemed to know you there." Spray could lie convincingly if he had to. He did not wish to implicate Akers.

"I assure you, sergeant, that I am a perfectly normal man, not one of those... of those..." he tailed off, leaving the word unsaid. "The reason I visit that place is because Mr Walters sends me there once a month with a package for the landlady."

"I see. What sort of package?"

"Don't rightly know, never took much note of it."

Spray shaped up his hands to suggest an envelope that might contain a thickish wad of banknotes. "About this size?"

"Suppose so, could be."

"Do the packages have anything written on them, such as the recipient's name?"

"I don't know any more than I've told you."

"Then I shall bid you good day, Mr Nightingale. And, if you please, do not forget to give the note to Mr Walters as soon as he returns." He paused briefly, "And thank you for all the information."

An effective detective needs a lively imagination, but to survive in institutional life it's a positive hindrance. Spray had managed by treating his creativity rather like a working dog, chained in its kennel until whistled up for duty. It was as if the railway constabulary, from time to time, gave him permission to let it off the leash.

As he walked toward the station, a picture came into his mind of a rill, polluted at its head and depositing poison at intervals as it flowed downhill. It was conjured up whilst he contemplated the Buxton office of the coroner. At its head, a pompous, self-serving bully that probably mistreated his clerk, who in turn grew to resemble, but not to like, his employer. Alongside this fanciful idea, inside Spray's head, there was an annoying buzz, as if two bluebottles were trapped in a jam jar.

There were connections he couldn't quite make, one to do with the picture of the Crystal Palace hanging outside Oldroyd's room at the Coachman. The other about the brass plate outside the office of the coroner.

As he approached the ornate, paired façades of Buxton Station, the buzzing stopped. Both the Crystal Palace and Buxton Station were designed by the same man. Joseph something or other. Paxman? Plaxton? Before he quite hit on the surname the other pairing surfaced. The name on the brass plate appeared on a list he had scribbled down in the office at the Coachman. With time to spare before his train departed, he settled down in the refreshment room, a cup of strong tea, and a ham sandwich of uncertain age, in front of him, alongside his scribbled list of Flegg & Co's customers. There it was: *Walters & Co., Suppliers of Processed Lime Products*, above an address near Lea Bridge.

The train was due, and Spray hurried to his platform. As his attention was devoted to this simple activity, a name, *Paxton*, slipped into his mind. That was it. The bluebottles had escaped!

Chapter 11

Old Mill End was steep. Previously Spray had walked up it with ease, hardly breaking his stride from the bottom to No. 37. Not this afternoon; his legs were lead weights, his breathing laboured and progress slow. Finally, he reached the door and was greeted with a warmth that only made matters worse.

He'd been dreading this moment for most of the journey from Buxton. Progress had been made during the morning. As he boarded the Stockport train and settled in his seat he was rather pleased, but by Dove Holes the euphoria had evaporated. When they stopped at Chapel, he'd have got out and returned to Buxton for two pins. All he had to do was tell Mrs Oldroyd that he was a policeman investigating her brother-in-law's suspicious death, ask a few questions and invite her to identify the body tomorrow. But for two weeks now he'd hidden his true identity. Two days ago, he had extracted information about her personal life whilst being aware that a member of her family had been killed. His list of perceived wrongs went on, and by the time the door of No. 37 opened it was nigh-on unbearable.

"Mr Spray, come in, how good it is to see you again. Take off your coat – here, let me take it. I'll prepare refreshments," Mrs Oldroyd fussed.

Whilst the sergeant sat in front of the fire, the singing of the kettle, the clinking of cups and the clatter of teaspoons wafted through the open door. The familiar sounds made him feel even more wretched. But why? He was here in the line of duty, wasn't he? And duty was what he was about, wasn't it? It had never felt like this before.

Mrs Oldroyd entered from the kitchen, preceded by a tray containing all the paraphernalia needed for the ritual of afternoon tea. When all had been properly arranged the dreaded moment arrived.

At first all he could manage was a rather croaky, "This is very kind of you, Mrs Oldroyd," but suddenly the floodgates opened and he was in confessional mode.

"I have some difficult things to say to you, Mrs Oldroyd. I hope you won't mind if I say them now."

She composed herself and murmured consent.

"I regret to say I have been less than honest with you concerning the reason for my presence here." Damn it – he knew he sounded like an official report, but he didn't know how to stop.

Mrs Oldroyd put her hand to her mouth and averted her usually steady hazel eyes.

"The matter in hand was confidential, so it seemed necessary to obscure its true nature." It was getting worse, and he knew it.

Meanwhile a rather unladylike snort escaped Mrs Oldroyd and her eyes began to crinkle. Such was Spray's preoccupation with himself, he failed to notice her demeanour.

"I have to tell you that I am a police detective in plain…" at this point, a giggle escaped and was obvious even to Spray. "… clothes," he concluded.

After the giggle had passed into a full-blown laugh, and finally subsided, and a crestfallen Spray had more or less regained his dignity, matters were clarified.

"I realised you were a policeman within the first few days. You had to be that, or on some criminal enterprise. I wouldn't last long as a landlady if I couldn't tell the difference. You were obviously an honest man, so policeman it had to be. I do apologise for my unseemly behaviour, but," she hesitated whilst the right words were found, "you were so solemn, and I already knew, and you looked so mortified and..." another giggle escaped.

It was at this point that Spray realised he wasn't being laughed at; it was just a funny situation. Suddenly the leaden legs and knotted stomach evaporated, and he laughed along with his landlady. With a lightness of heart, most inappropriate, given the rest of the conversation, Spray started again.

"I can't really tell you why I've been ferreting about for the last few weeks." He now came across less like an official and more like a chatty friend. "However, as a result, I was at the site of Friday's accident, where I found your brother-in-law's body. I didn't know who he was at the time, although he looked familiar. It wasn't until I came back here and saw your wedding picture that I realised why."

Spray felt an apology was due, but it was waved away.

"I imagine that detectives don't have a choice as to where their investigations take them," she said.

He could have kissed her! What? What was he thinking? Was this the reason for his earlier reluctance? He could feel matters slipping out of control. Had she noticed his turmoil? She didn't change; the steady, hazel eyes showed nothing but genuine interest in what he was saying. With a superhuman effort he returned to the purpose of his visit.

"I am extremely sorry to have to tell you this, Mrs Oldroyd, but your brother-in-law did not die in the railway accident. He was deliberately killed and his body left by the track." He watched Lizzie's (oh no: he'd started thinking of her as Lizzie! Stop it!) composure finally crack. She was visibly upset.

"But how? Why? Who would do such a thing? Are you sure?" Lizzie was not given to floods of tears and tortured sobs, but something glistened in each eye, only to be brushed away brusquely. Order was restored.

He addressed her questions, avoiding how the man had died. But she pressed him, and with great reluctance, and as much tact as he could muster, he explained the victim had been strangled with a garrotte.

"Oh! That's all right then," she replied.

Spray was startled at her matter-of-fact attitude.

"A few weeks ago, one of my kitchen knives went missing, and I wondered if he'd been stabbed. Silly of me, I apologise."

They talked at length. Spray asked the questions and was impressed by the clarity and coherence of her replies, not to mention her occasional frankness. It emerged that Lizzie's late husband, Albert, was known to her father from their railway employment. At the time, she hadn't realised how close he was to his brother, Arthur, but after the wedding, she was obliged to welcome the older man as her kin.

"I was surprised at how generous Al was with the house-keeping money. Things were always tight at home, and after ma died, I knew exactly what pa earned. Al always gave me three times as much as my ma had got and said there was more if I needed it."

"May I ask, of what did your late husband die?"

"I always understood it was consumption. He certainly had a terrible cough towards the end."

"Did anything unusual happen after he passed on?" Spray knew it sounded a silly and perhaps heartless question, unless something unusual had happened, and it certainly had.

"The first thing was the house. I understood Al owned it and had left it to me in his will. He always seemed so straightforward and honest about such things. In the event, he left me everything he owned, but this property was only half his. The other half belonged to his brother, and still does – well, *did,* I suppose. Oh dear, someone else will own his share now. You don't think they could somehow take away my home and livelihood, do you Mr Spray?"

Spray thought it quite possible, but no purpose would be served by saying so. He mumbled something resembling a reassuring platitude and Lizzie continued.

"The next thing to deal with was a letter from a solicitor in Cromford. He said Al had owned some shares in the Cromford mineral railway, and if I would sign the form he sent me, he would take care of the transfer. I really don't understand such things, so I showed the papers to Arthur. He flew into such a temper about it! I'd never seen anything like it. Both he and Al were most even-tempered; well, I suppose I'd never given them cause to be otherwise. It was terrible. Arthur said a few choice words about the solicitor. 'Jones', I think he was called. I wouldn't like to repeat them in your presence."

Spray got the distinct impression that it was his blushes that were being spared, not hers.

In the event, Arthur had taken his anger off to Cromford, along with the paperwork, and Lizzie heard no more about the matter for quite a while. Later, she learnt that signing the paper would have transferred the shares to Jones. Although they were worthless then, Arthur said they would be valuable one day.

"Arthur was very good to me about the house; he said I was to treat it as my own. It was his suggestion that I let rooms, and he started my business off by reserving one, permanently, and paying in advance. At the beginning, it seemed he had done it just to help me over Al's death." There was a moment's pause, after which, she added, "I wasn't so sure about that later on. It seemed highly convenient for him, too."

It occurred to Spray that it was a very good way for Oldroyd to keep his sister-in-law dependent, and, therefore, compliant.

"There's one more thing I must ask you. I need a formal, positive identification of Mr Oldroyd by someone who was close to him. I was hoping you would accompany me to Buxton tomorrow for this purpose."

He rather expected the tears to reappear, but Lizzie agreed readily, and so it was arranged.

———

There was a certain amount of bustle outside the front door of No. 37: voices, a ripple of laughter and a rather deep chuckle. Finally, there was a knock. In the parlour, the conversation had moved on. Afterwards, Spray couldn't remember what the talk had been about, but that didn't diminish the glow of pleasure that remained long after it was over.

Miss Maisie Hartle and Constable William Archer had trudged up the hill simultaneously. Realising, as they neared No. 37, that they were bound for the same destination, they struck up a conversation and walked alongside.

Lizzie answered the door. "I can see there's no need to introduce you two to each other," she remarked with a smile.

Maisie giggled and Archer gave her a conspiratorial wink.

"But you must come and meet Sergeant Spray, although I rather think that he and Mr Archer are already acquainted." Lizzie was enjoying herself with a little harmless fun at the two policemen's expense.

It wasn't until they were inside the house that Maisie noticed the hat that Archer had been touting around all day.

"Mr Archer, I wonder where you acquired that hat? You

see, the last time I saw it, it was being worn by a gentleman who was staying here. Did he lose it?" She turned to Lizzie, "Last week, wasn't it?"

"Yes, you mean Mr Markham? He stayed two nights. He was quite nosey, always asking questions. First, it was how to get the Fly to Cromford, then later he was looking at my wedding picture and asking who was who. And then he wormed out of me that Arthur had a permanent room here; then he wanted to know which nights he stayed." Indignation appeared in Lizzie's voice, "I told him to mind his own business, but I think I may have let on earlier in the conversation, though. Oh dear, do you think it mattered?" she asked Spray.

It was with relief that he found himself back on familiar territory, where he could regain control of his feelings and start to use his brain. He managed to settle Mrs Oldroyd's anxieties without admitting that she had been dangerously indiscreet. He wrote down the inquisitive guest's name. Mention of it had generated the biggest prize of all.

"Lizzie, you recall that day trip to Blackpool, with Emma and the others?" asked Maisie.

Lizzie remembered it very well.

"And the ball we went to? I danced with a young man called Eddie. And afterwards, when we were getting ready to go home…"

"Yes?"

"And you dropped your bag?"

"Yes?" The story was taking some time to unfold.

"Well, that Eddie fellow helped pick up your things, and then we had to rush off for the train."

Lizzie had a vague recollection of the event but certainly not of the man. Maisie was adamant. By this time, she had picked up the hat and was idly fiddling with it. Had either

Spray or Archer examined the hat more carefully, their blushes might have been spared. Maisie's fingers found their way into the hatband and emerged with a small, pale-blue card printed in black: *Comfortable lodgings by the night or the week. Mrs Elizabeth Oldroyd, 37 Old Mill End, Whaley Bridge.*

"Look, Lizzie, he must have picked it up when you dropped your bag," Maisie concluded.

Despite the embarrassing little matter of being shown up as sloppy detectives by an eighteen-year-old girl, the two detectives were jubilant. The two women between them had put the man's name together. To Lizzie, he had been Mr Markham; to Maisie, Eddie. There it was: a Mr Edward Markham, of Blackpool, had been asking about the movements of Arthur Oldroyd shortly before his death, and had probably disappeared on the same night as him.

Spray and Archer eventually repaired to the White Hart at the bottom of the hill and sat in a secluded corner, tankards in hand. They began to discuss Archer's information, gleaned from the young urchin, Jimmy. More specifically, the lad's sighting of Markham in the town, and on his way to the railway yard, on the night of the dead man's disappearance. There were unwritten rules to be followed first. During detached assignments together, the usual formalities of rank slipped, but the manner of that slippage was itself formalised. As the senior, Spray had to make the first move.

"So, Bill, what do you make of this?"

"Well, sarge…" At this point, a small gesture was made by the sergeant and the ritual was complete. "Well, Sam, we're making some progress."

After a while, what seemed a very persuasive case started to look a bit threadbare. For a start, how had Arthur Oldroyd's body been transported to Ladmanlow? Alternatively, how had he been induced to go there under his own steam? Was the matter of the horse, loose all night in the yard, relevant? Archer had established that it was a shire of at least seventeen hands. To lift a dead body onto its back single-handed would be well-nigh impossible. From what was known so far about Edward Markham, it seemed unlikely he would be up to it. It would also require a certain amount of horsemanship to manage the animal. And why take the body all that way?

"Ladmanlow is as close as the C&HP gets to Buxton," said Spray. "Before the other two railways got to the town, Ladmanlow offered the only access to the railway for people from there. What if the killer went to Buxton to get away from the scene of the crime? That rather suggests he came from there or wanted to use its railway connections. It all implies local knowledge. From what Mrs Oldroyd and Miss Hartle said, Markham is not a Derbyshire man. And why was he heading off to Whaley Bridge railway yard when young Jimmy saw him?"

Come next morning, a gleam of light fell on this last conundrum.

Chapter 12

Bacon was sizzling nicely in the heavy, cast-iron pan when the sound of guests filtered down the passage from the parlour and through the kitchen door. It was open a crack for that very purpose, and upon hearing them, Lizzie poured boiling water into the teapot before taking a tray containing the first instalment of breakfast through to the men.

"Good morning sergeant, constable. It'll take a minute to brew." With that she returned to the frying pan.

"Good smells coming from down there, Sam." The younger man nodded toward the kitchen.

"S'right William, looks as if Li…" – he corrected himself – "Mrs Oldroyd does a good breakfast, not that I've had much of a chance to try one yet. Ah! Here it comes."

Lizzie returned carrying a large tray containing two plates laden with rashers of bacon, black pudding, two eggs apiece, and bubble and squeak. William immediately got to his feet.

"My, that looks heavy, Mrs Oldroyd, let me help." He took the tray from her and was rewarded with a pleasant smile.

"Thank you, Mrs Oldroyd, that looks grand. I was just telling Constable Archer that, for all the time I've stayed here, I only know your breakfasts by reputation." He turned to William, "I was always out so early, y'see."

Lizzie, trying to suppress a giggle, turned back towards the kitchen, "I'll be back presently." *Those men are so funny*, she thought, *why do they have to be so much on their dignity, even at breakfast?* She hugged the memory of yesterday's conversation to herself.

"Now, see here, young William, I want you to walk the track from Whaley to just beyond Ladmanlow. I know I've been along it before, but it needs a fresh eye, and anyway, we've got more to go on now. Just search for anything that looks out of place or suspicious." With Lizzie in the scullery, attending to the pots, and two half-cups of tea on the table between them, the two had reverted to informality.

"I'll take Mrs Oldroyd to Buxton to identify the body and then put her on the train back here while I go on to Cromford and see what I can make of this fellow, Jones." He'd gained Lizzie's agreement to the plan, and she had suggested catching the 9:14am.

"I'll be back here by dinner time," she had said, then, rather more uncertainly, "It won't take long, will it? I do hope not."

Lizzie had replied quite sharply to the suggestion that she might need escorting home: "Thank you, sergeant, I can manage a train journey quite well on my own."

"After you have walked to Ladmanlow, William, I want you to visit as many of these firms as you can manage." The list from Oldroyd's office at the Coachman was handed over.

"They're all businesses that have been invoiced by Flegg & Co. Ask them about their dealings with the company, how it all started, and who paid for the canal transport. Try and get an idea of whether they were trading in good faith, or realised there was something fishy going on."

Lizzie, still in the kitchen, answered a knock on the back door.

"Jimmy Allcroft, what are you doing here? Shouldn't you be at school?"

"Yes, missus," Jimmy's tone was contrite, "But Mr Archer

telt me ter come 'ere this mornin' if I thought of owt else 'bout the cove with the fancy hat." There didn't seem a need to pursue the matter of school any further.

"Gentlemen, you have a visitor," announced Lizzie, ushering Jimmy into the parlour. If the boy was perplexed by the sergeant's presence, he didn't show it. He addressed himself solely to Archer.

"Yer r'member I telt ye 'bout cove with the fancy hat goin' to the railway yard? Well, afore I saw him, another feller went down there. Bit funny really, not many folks g'down there of a night time in the winter. See a few lads and lasses in summer, tho'." From his slightly coy tone, it seemed he had an inkling as to the purpose of such visits. But he certainly had no idea why a couple of men might make the same excursion.

"It were that chap as lives 'ere, missus, well some o't' time, any road."

If Lizzie was shocked, she managed to hide it from Jimmy and the others.

"'Ere, that's worth a tanner in't it?" Jimmy set off for school with the satisfied air of someone who'd made a good bargain. Sam gave William a conspiratorial wink as Lizzie showed the lad to the door. Sixpence must be well worth a wigging for arriving late. When she returned, he had a question for her.

"Was Tuesday the last time you saw your brother-in-law?" It turned out that it was, and what's more, he and Markham had been at the guesthouse, together, for a short while. She had even introduced them.

"Arthur kept very irregular hours; I never enquired where he went or who he saw, and he never said."

Constable Archer strode confidently into the wharf yard, although he hardly relished the long walk ahead.

"Morning Meester Archer." Fred was already at work.

"Morning Fred." Somehow the sight of little Italian raised his spirits, and dodging the horse, Archer watched him manoeuvre a heavily laden truck into the transhipment shed.

In the canal arm, waiting to enter, was a line of empty narrow-boats, high in the water. They looked very different from the one just then emerging, with only a few inches of freeboard showing and a hold full of limestone.

Archer turned and set off for the foot of the Whaley Incline on the other side of the River Goyt. An elegant cast-iron bridge was shared by pedestrians and rail traffic. Managing to avoid being run down, he walked on, past the points where the track divided, and started to climb. Half way up, he was flagging, but even so, was moving faster than an empty truck which was being hauled silently uphill on a continuous rope. For a moment, ascending and descending trucks were in a line with Archer across the tracks, then each went their own way. At the top, the twin tracks rejoined and passed beneath the main line. It was the bridge that prevented steam working in the wharf yard: it was so low that only horses could pass beneath it. Now, free of the need to avoid horse droppings, he strode more freely, making good progress past Shallcross yard. He wasn't entirely sure what he was after. Sam had told him to look out for anything out of the ordinary; but what was 'out of the ordinary' on this extraordinary railway?

He crossed, with a locomotive clanking along at leisurely pace hauling a handful of re-railed wagons from the accident. A cheery wave from the driver was his only human contact for an hour or so, until he got to Ladmanlow sidings. The going had been tough: three further inclines in a chill December wind were taking its toll. A wide panorama of bleak moorland hardly compensated for the effort, neither did distant views of Buxton.

"Oi, what you doin' up 'ere? This is railway property and you ain't allowed." Ladmanlow wasn't much of a station – even if you could join the Fly there – but it boasted a station master and he was a worried man.

"Perhaps you would be good enough to look at this." The sight of Archer's warrant card pacified, but hardly reassured, him.

"I see, a rozzer, eh? 'Spose you're here 'bout the accident. Well I can tell you right now it weren't my –"

Archer Interrupted, "No, no, not that, it's about another matter entirely. I'm Constable Archer, and I'm here about the suspicious death. You know, Arthur Oldroyd? His body was found just along where the crash happened."

The man's relief was almost indecent at the news it was Oldroyd's death that interested the constable. His lack of useful information was exposed over a pot of tea in his office. But rested and warmed, Archer was a new man as he struck out on the last stretch of his walk to the site of the accident and the place where Oldroyd's body had been discovered.

A number of men were trying to tidy up the mess and clear the line. Progress had been slow, hampered by the difficulty of getting heavy lifting equipment up on the Peak. The inconvenience of a single track, covered in debris from the accident, prevented a crane from getting close to the cold, life-less engines, one reared over the other, unmoved since Friday morning. A sorry sight, indeed. He sought out the foreman and presented his warrant card.

"Fine by me mate, g'where yer want. Just be careful we don't drop owt on yer."

William wondered if this last comment was a threat. Policemen are habitually suspicious, but they were also skilled at reading body language and facial expressions, and he could discern only friendly concern in the man's face. He walked over to where Oldroyd's body had been found. Spray said it was adjacent to a rail-side hut. He found a hut and some dried blood on the ground nearby. *Must be from the fireman*, he thought. Closer to the low doorway, and lying partly through it, was a piece of jute sacking.

"Ouch!" Something sharp dug into Archer's palm as he grasped the rough fabric.

Closer examination revealed a buckle, the spike of which had jabbed into him. All at once, the item took shape: it was a horse blanket. He felt sure he'd come across something similar recently. This one had seen better days. The tongue was still inserted into the buckle, but the other end of the strap was hanging loose where it had torn free from its stitching. The significance of the rug was far from clear to Archer, and he cursed it heartily. He knew he had to carry it the five miles back to Whaley Bridge and so took his first step in that direction.

"Damn and blast!" One foot had sunk into the soft mess of a pile of horse droppings.

As he walked on, the rug appeared to become heavier. The track was to his right, as it had been on the outward journey, so he was on the other side of the rails on the way home. Seen from a different angle, something shiny caught just enough light to attract his attention. Poking out from between two chairs, and mostly hidden by the rail above, was a horseshoe. A gleaming horseshoe that couldn't possibly have spent more than a few days of a Derbyshire winter out in the open and still look like that. Dropping the rug over it, he hurried – half walking and half running – back to Ladmanlow. The station master tried to offer him tea, but the constable politely declined: he had only one thing on his mind.

"Could you tell me if they have been using horses up at the accident site?"

"Nah, work up there's a sight too 'eavy for them; never see 'osses hereabouts. Down int'canal yard, yes but not up here."

Archer returned to collect the rug and the horseshoe and set off for Whaley Bridge. Strangely, his burden seemed lighter now.

The journey to Buxton was a sombre affair. Gone was the relaxed conviviality of yesterday afternoon. The man and woman were seated side-by-side. Although closer physically, it was less demanding socially and seemed to be more comfortable than sitting facing one another.

Sergeant Spray, when on official business, was a very different companion from the man with whom she had spent a congenial hour or so previously. Lizzie, for her part, was in a serious mood; it was no light matter to identify the corpse of one's brother-in-law at the behest of the constabulary. She had no qualms about the sight of a dead body. In the past, her deceased mother had lain in the front parlour for two days. Lizzie had been quite able to separate the sense of loss, which she felt acutely, from the inert form, which troubled her not at all. Today was different. There was no sense of loss. She had merely tolerated Arthur, and in fact had resented how close his relationship was with his brother, her husband. But the notion that Arthur may have been murdered troubled her deeply. Nevertheless, she was determined to cope, her self-respect demanded it. Eventually, the pair presented themselves at the premises of Dickens & Nephew and were attended by Robert Akers, sober both in dress and manner. His excess of Saturday afternoon was not habitual.

"Sergeant Spray, a pleasure to meet you again." He couldn't shake off the unctuous tones of his profession.

They shook hands and Mrs Oldroyd was introduced.

The process of identification was almost an anticlimax. Akers had placed the corpse in a respectable casket and worked his artistry on a tasteful arrangement of drapes so that only the face was visible. He had almost managed to get rid of the stench that had previously prevailed. The air was one of tranquillity, and Lizzie, raising her eyes momentarily, glanced at Spray, grateful for his presence.

"Yes, that is the late Arthur Oldroyd." Such was her self control she managed to get 'late' in the right place.

Lizzie emerged onto the street with a great weight lifted from her shoulders. Spray lingered long enough to ask when the post mortem would take place.

"I understand there isn't to be one. I had a message from the coroner to go ahead and arrange the funeral. I suppose I should be talking to Mrs Oldroyd about it, unless you know of a closer relative."

Spray kept his temper, just. He escorted Lizzie to the station and together they waited for her train over tea and rather unappetising rock cakes.

As her train drew slowly out of the station, Spray's suppressed anger emerged. He stormed off the platform, muttering oaths to himself that he would never normally voice out loud. He went red in the face and even kicked a kerbstone. To the casual observer, he was no more than a slightly agitated man. To himself, he seemed wildly out of control. This wouldn't do.

As he walked to the coroner's house, he tried to restore calm. However, on hearing that the coroner was 'not at home to anyone', Spray's dam finally burst, and he marched in, pushing the footman aside rather more vigorously than intended. Jonah Walters was seated in the front parlour, nonchalantly reading *The Times*, every inch a scion of the establishment at ease. He looked up as Spray burst through his door and then and stood up, four square, in front of him.

"How dare you intrude in this manner! Leave at once. Where is my servant?"

The footman, having recovered himself, appeared behind Spray, who forced himself to adopt a respectful tone.

"Do please forgive me the impolite manner of my entrance, Mr Walters, but I had no choice. I need to speak to you most urgently, in your capacity as coroner."

Walters, pacified by Spray's obsequious attitude, gestured to the servant to leave.

"Well, man, what is it?" the coroner asked, curtly.

"I understand there is to be no post-mortem on the suspicious death at Ladmanlow."

"If there is to be any discussion on this matter, I shall speak with your superior officer," Said Walters, coldly, but he was feeling a little less sure of himself. He recalled being bested by this upstart on Saturday, and his bluster weakened.

"I think, Mr Coroner, that you had better listen to what I have to say." There was a slight tone of menace in Spray's voice. "A man has died under suspicious circumstances and his body found within your jurisdiction. It is your obligation to arrange a post mortem. Before you refuse, I should bring the following matters to your attention."

Spray recounted several relevant details from his investigation so far: that minerals had been stolen in large quantities;

that they had been marketed by Flegg & Co; that – amongst others – a company named Walters & Co was one of its customers; that there was documentary proof of these transactions. He mentioned that receiving stolen property was a crime, and that the prices being charged by Flegg & Co were sufficiently below the market rate as to strongly suggest criminal wrongdoing.

There were, of course, some weaknesses in Spray's rendition. Certainly, Walters & Co had appeared in Oldroyd's ledger, but Spray would have great difficulty in producing the ledger on demand. He had no real idea of the price of limestone, or its relationship to Flegg & Co's prices. And he had no evidence that Walters, the coroner had any connection with the firm of Walters & Co of Lea Bridge. It had been one big bluff, but the sudden and dramatic alteration in Walters's demeanour, from bluster to apprehension, was all the confirmation he needed.

Spray omitted to tell Walters that, as yet, he had been too busy to establish the ownership of Walters & Co, but he had no doubt it could be done if necessary. Walters was cowed, and Spray wanted him to contemplate his defeat.

"Now, Mr Coroner, if you would be so kind as to write a note authorising the post-mortem, I can arrange for the body to be conveyed to the mortuary."

Both men stood in silence for a few seconds, then Walters, in an atmosphere of grudging defeat, began to write out the requested order.

"Oh, and you can add the name of the deceased, now that it has been formally established. He was a Mr Arthur Oldroyd; but of course, you knew that, didn't you?"

Chapter 13

Back in the wharf yard, Fred was still at work with his horse.

"Tim? He's in there, time for 'is dinner jus' now. Always 'as it in there."

Inside the tack room, Tim Pott, seated on a wooden chest, was tucking into bread and cheese. He looked up as Archer entered.

"'Ere, where d'ye find that? I 'aven't seen it since Star went missin' last week."

He'd caught sight of the bundle, carried so laboriously back from Ladmanlow.

"And that looks like her shoe an all."

"Can you be sure about that, Tim?"

"We'll soon see; give 'em 'ere." He examined the horse blanket and pronounced himself satisfied.

"See 'ere, Star allus rubs 'erself ont'right quarter. I've had ter repair this un twice so far. Here, yer can see where it were done. Nah then, let's 'ave a look at the shoe."

They went to the box where Star was still in residence, and Tim, leaning against her flank, bent down and lifted her hind leg.

"Lucky yer came when yer did – I'm havin' the farrier to 'er later. She's back at work t'morrow. See, it's hers all right, fits a treat. Almost good enough ter put back on as tis."

They left the box and headed back to Tim's dinner.

"So c'mon, Mr Clever Clogs Bobby, where'd yer get 'em?

Archer explained where he'd been that morning.

Tim looked taken aback. "That's one hell of a long way for 'er to roam. I can see 'er 'eading back on her own, but she must'ave been led out there."

———•••••———

Having delivered written instructions concerning the post-mortem to the coroner's office (drawing admiration from its hapless occupant at his achievement) Spray went back to Buxton Station and travelled, via Miller's Dale, to Cromford. Assuming he knew the way to Nathaniel Jones's, he set off, but the dark had been confusing, and whilst retracing his steps, he heard a girl's voice.

"Sergeant – Sergeant Spray."

Why on earth was a girl calling his name? He stopped. Damn, he'd forgotten the young woman at the station who'd tried to speak to him as the train was leaving yesterday morning. What was it? Yes, Tilly.

"Oh sergeant, thank you for coming back. I didn't know if you'd want to talk to me." Tilly's gratitude embarrassed him. He'd forgotten all about her.

"Come on, miss, let's go and sit by the mill pond and we can chat."

She was reluctant: "Could we walk on, please, I don't want to be seen with you, and I'm meant to be on an errand. I'm in service at High House, to Mr Fitzroy Tarp and his son, Mr Jarvis Tarp – you do remember me, don't you?"

Finally, he recognised her. "Yes I recall now: you wouldn't admit me on Sunday afternoon."

His half grin and the twinkling eye must have allayed her fears.

"That's Mr Fitzroy's orders, sir, very particular he is,

everything has to be just so. But he's not bad really, if you mind your ps and qs."

They started along Spray's route of two days previously, but instead of turning left, followed the course of the Derwent. The valley sides were steep, and by Spray's reckoning, they were below Fitzroy Tarp's house, which was perched high up on the rim of the gorge.

"You see, sir – I heard you asking about Mr Oldroyd – and I don't think Mr Fitzroy knows – and I only saw him twice – but it could have been more often – and I don't think Mr Jarvis would like me telling you, but I thought it right to speak up – what with Mr Oldroyd being dead." She ran out of breath, much to Spray's relief.

There was a narrow break in the scrub and stunted trees that spread down the valley side to the road. Steps rose upward to a steep path, and Spray realised they had stopped at a short cut to High House.

"Do you think we could start at the beginning, Miss Tilly? I've got a bit lost. What is it that Mr Fitzroy doesn't know?"

She appeared crestfallen, but started afresh: "You see, he came at night – and I only saw him on my way home – and Mr Fitzroy was always in bed by then cos I never leave before he goes to bed – and he must get in by the back cos everywhere else is locked. Mr Jarvis is always in the billiard room, and there's French windows onto the lawn, and you can undo the bolts," she ran out of breath again and made to start up the steps.

The only thing Spray could do was to interpret what she had said and play it back to see if he was right. 'Is this what you're saying?' This time he could see her exasperation. She must think him very stupid, and anyway, she needed to get on. With her foot set on the first step there was nothing else Spray could do but follow her.

"Mr Oldroyd visited at night – late enough for no one else to know, and you saw him some times. And it would have been possible for Mr Jarvis to let him in to the billiard room." The route levelled out for a short stretch and she slowed momentarily.

"I must get on sergeant – they'll be expecting me back."

"Please, Miss Tilly, just two more things." She nodded, and Spray continued, "Was there anything special about the nights you saw him?"

She blushed and reluctantly mentioned meeting someone to walk home with. He'd been late on both occasions.

"So, Mr Oldroyd could have visited quite often without you seeing him?"

Tilly, itching to go, agreed.

"On Sunday, when we first met, was Mr Jarvis listening at the door?"

With that, Spray realised he'd overstepped the mark. Tilly blushed again and was off.

Nathaniel Jones, solicitor-at-law, opened his front door to find Sergeant Spray of the railway constabulary on his step. Each made himself known to the other with a perfunctory handshake before they adjourned to Jones's office. There was no jockeying for position; the office was laid out with a clear indication as to who should sit where. Spray found himself facing Jones, whose back was to the window. He was used to the arrangement, practised by all the professionals and gentry he had met in this case so far. *Had they all got something to hide?*

"Well sergeant, what is it you want of me?"

Spray was familiar with the tone, suggesting, as it did, a busy man with little time for trivialities.

"You've no doubt heard about the accident on Friday morning?"

Jones's reply that he had was accompanied by the expelling of air through pursed lips. It endowed his acknowledgement with a sense that the question was an irrelevance to those engaged in more important matters.

"There were fatalities at the site of the accident." Spray chose his words carefully. Jones continued to look unperturbed. "One of the dead found there was Arthur Oldroyd." Still no reaction. "He was murdered some time before and his body found by chance."

This provoked a response. From a man of affairs deigning to give a little time to an inferior, a momentary look of apprehension crossed his face. He struggled to compose himself and finally succeeded, but he had been smoked out.

"That is most unfortunate, but I don't see that I can contribute to your investigation, sergeant."

"If you would be so kind as to indulge me for just a few moments, sir, there are one or two points I thought you might be able to help me with. Am I right that both you and the deceased had an interest in the old C&HP?"

"Yes, that is so, but the company has been more or less defunct for a number of years, and we have had very little to do in that connection recently. We meet but occasionally."

"Do you remember a meeting in Cromford recently with Mr Fitzroy Tarp and Mr Oldroyd?"

Jones was taken aback; was he frightened or just indignant? Spray couldn't tell for sure.

"I suppose I do."

"I understand it was an acrimonious affair. That you and Mr Oldroyd took a different view of an offer to buy out the rump of the old company, and that his view prevailed. I'm interested

DAVID J. BOULTON

as to how that was so, given that you said you had control of a majority of the shares."

There was a pause in which an angry Jones looked like a man about to beat an impertinent underling and kick him off the premises. During the pause, discretion prevailed.

"I am not prepared to discuss the matter further."

"Mr Jones, what I conclude from this is that either you do not have the shares, or written authority to control them, or both. An alternative conclusion might be that the shares are in your possession and have somehow been registered in your name."

"That is enough, you must go." Jones was shrill rather than authoritative.

Spray stayed where he was.

"Let us move onto another matter…"

Jones was stuttering, attempting, but failing, to say something.

Spray paid no attention, "Can you explain why you were in Mr Oldroyd's house, at night, and only a few hours after his body had been found?"

Spray's guess provoked a surprising response. He hadn't seen Jones in Oldroyd's house, only on Scarth Lane outside it, but the solicitor was quite prepared to admit where he'd been.

"Of course I can. I was there out of loyalty to an old friend. There was no one but me to look after his property."

And Ellie Bagshaw thought Spray.

"Just as well I went there. I was putting things to rights when that working man came in. Gave him a piece of my mind, I can tell you."

"Had you considered the possibility that he had a legitimate reason to be there, and that you were the intruder?" Spray retorted.

"Don't be preposterous, man," Jones had retrieved his bluster. "What would my old friend Oldroyd be doing with such a person, late at night?"

143

"How did you get in?"

"The back door was open, not only unlocked, but ajar."

For the first time since the beginning of the interview, Spray had the impression Jones was telling the truth.

"And you definitely arrived before the other man?"

"Of course, that's what I said."

Spray had created a moment's calm by asking the same question twice. Jones was more confident now.

The sergeant continued his questioning, "What were you putting to rights when the man came in?"

"My friend's desk was in disarray, and I was just tidying things up."

"I put it to you that you were looking through his paperwork for anything that might prove damaging to yourself," a thinly-veiled accusation from Spray.

"How dare you!" Guilt and indignation vied for primacy on Jones' face. Indignation won, hands down: "You barge in here and call me a liar to my face!"

Spray had him on the run.

"There is one other matter to discuss. What can you tell me about an Edward Markham? I understand he visited you here recently."

"I can say absolutely nothing about him; client confidentiality is absolute. Like the confessional."

"So, if I were to return in a few days and put it to you that this man was implicated in a murder shortly after visiting you, you would still be unable to assist my enquiries?"

Jones looked petrified. Spray rose, bid Jones 'good day', and left feeling triumphant. By refusing to speak, Jones had unwittingly confirmed what Spray had wanted to know.

Chapter 14

Blackpool, Wednesday Morning, 22nd December, 1875

The whole thing was a mystery to Spray. He sat in his seat as the Manchester train ran easily down the Goyt Valley and onto the Cheshire plain. He tried to explain to himself how it had happened.

On Monday evening, a rather embarrassed William Archer had been unmasked as a policeman, and by Wednesday breakfast, he, and the source of Spray's discomfort, were on familiar terms.

"Lizzie, let me help you with…"

"William could you just…"

Even Spray had been drawn into the family atmosphere, in spirit if not in name.

"Sergeant, could you pass these over to William? Thank you, that's very helpful."

Back in Crewe, he'd been to the Archer home on the odd occasion. An orphan with no experience of family life, he'd felt slightly uncomfortable. Here was that same feeling again, engendered by William and Lizzie acting brother and sister. Confused he may be, but Spray was beguiled.

With his ultimate destination still some way off, he alighted into the smoke and grime at the terminus and sought assistance. At least this time he wouldn't be the only one asking. The route between two of Manchester's main stations could have been recited by a parrot, so often did the ticket collector repeat it to enquiring travellers.

"Down the station approach, up London Road, through Piccadilly and str…"

Spray took it all in and set off. He kept a weather eye open for the old man. It'd caused a fair old rumpus last night when he'd tried to rouse the postmaster, after hours, to send a telegram, but in the end, his warrant card had done the trick.

> HAVE IDENTIFIED SUSPECT STOP REQUIRE ASSISTANCE AT HIGHEST LEVEL STOP MEET MANCHESTER VICTORIA ELEVEN THIRTY STOP DESTINATION BLACKPOOL STOP

Brevity and economy went hand in hand when it came to telegrams. He hoped Superintendent Wayland would take that into account when contemplating its peremptory tone: it was his department's money, after all.

Spray was relieved not to have bumped into him already. Wayland's route from Crewe would take him through London Road Station, as had Spray's, but the old man would take a cab. Spray, on the other hand, wanted to get his bearings and think about the case whilst walking alone.

The previous evening, William and Sam had taken their pints to a quiet corner in the White Hart and compared notes. They reviewed progress to that point.

1. *It was certain that an Edward Markham of Blackpool had been enquiring about the victim shortly before his death.*
2. *Markham had spoken to the victim on the day he disappeared and had later been seen to follow the victim down toward the wharf yard.*
3. *An item of clothing belonging to Markham had been found by the track, between the last sighting of the victim and the place where his body was found.*

4. It seemed probable the victim's body had been transported on the back of a stolen horse, from the site of the murder, to where it was found.

When the two policemen considered this list, it seemed a bit thin. If it was all that could be presented in court – assuming they were permitted to get the case to court – 'not guilty' would be the possible outcome. What persuaded Spray was Jones's reaction to questioning about Markham. The man had been almost paralysed with fear. The only way to progress the case was to question Markham, and that meant finding him. To do this, the cooperation of the police in Blackpool was required, and to get that the superintendent was needed.

What about motive? The two of them put their heads together. There were loose ends aplenty. The front runner had to be the blocking by Oldroyd of the business deal put together by Jones and Tarp. Try as he may, Spray couldn't see Tarp arranging Oldroyd's untimely end. He was much too sophisticated a man to resort to anything so crude. If he wanted to neutralise Oldroyd, he would have found a more subtle way of doing it. In addition, he didn't seem to have the drive for such a project. No: if the sale of shares was at the bottom of it, Jones was the man.

What if Oldroyd threatened to expose, or even blackmail, Jones over the shares he had been accumulating in his own name? This possibility created a loose end of its own, since there was no proof, as yet, that he had succeeded in such deception. The only case he knew anything about was Lizzie's, and Oldroyd had prevented the transfer.

Archer had wondered if the motive might be found elsewhere in Oldroyd's life.

"Perhaps he was blackmailing one of his sodomite friends

and got done in for his pains?"

Spray was more comfortable with the next possibility.

"What if someone from Oldroyd's life as Flegg & Co thought he could be taken over, and he resisted?"

Neither man could see anyone they had come across, so far, making such a move. Certainly Riggott was capable of the act, but having met him, Archer said he couldn't see him managing the business side of things and certainly not planning anything. Anyway, it was still conjecture that he was the inside man at Whaley Bridge.

Finally, they got to the will. Who would benefit was unknown, Ezra Brook had seen to that. But the will would be read in a few days, so they would have to wait.

•◦•◦•

The two policemen arrived at Victoria Station at more or less the same time. Wayland was climbing down from a cab as Spray approached.

"Ah, there you are, Spray, we'd better get our tickets, and then you can tell me why I'm here."

"Very good, sir."

Memories of their last journey together were forgotten as Wayland bought two first class tickets.

As they settled themselves into the comfort of the Lancashire & Yorkshire Railway's most expensive seats, the superintendent gave one of his penetrating looks.

"Now, what's this all about?"

Spray gave a tidied-up version of the previous night's discussion.

"So you see, sir, we have to find Markham and question him. He's certainly implicated in the murder. If you could persuade the Blackpool constabulary to mount a search for him, we ought to be able to close the case."

"And what if he isn't in Blackpool?"

"He has to be, sir: he comes from there and we have evidence that he intended to return."

Wayland didn't pursue the matter further. He was enjoying himself, and if Spray had no other plan of action, he was quite happy with this one for the moment.

"Very well, I'll see what can be done there." He was tickled pink to be at the heart of an ongoing investigation, although he would never admit it. "And you, what are you about? I'll need you when I see the superintendent." He was confident of managing the man but perhaps not the details.

"I thought I'd visit the premises that Markham uses as a postal address, sir. Mrs Oldroyd kept a record of it," Spray replied.

It crossed Wayland's mind that Mrs Oldroyd had become more involved in the investigation than might be expected of a respectable widow of unblemished character.

"I propose staying the night. If they find Markham, it'd look bad if there was no one on the spot to question him."

"Quite so, Spray, quite so; I don't suppose you have anything else for me to do," his voice trailed off wistfully. "I see you don't. Very well, I shall return to Crewe when all is arranged here."

After a long silence, there was a minor eruption, reminiscent of a whale surfacing for air.

"See here, Spray, you haven't said anything about the fraud case you're meant to be pursuing." The superintendent was back in charge. "It's all very well you chasing off after a murderer, but you're being paid to stop Company revenue being leeched out into someone else's pocket. So what about it?"

"Ah, yes sir, my mistake, of course," proper deference had been re-established. "I have evidence that the dead man, Oldroyd, was at the heart of a criminal conspiracy to steal and transport minerals, and then sell them on through a company called Flegg & Co. He was the sole proprietor of this company as far as I can tell. I have clear evidence that it operated to the south of Cromford, through High Peak Junction, and I know who else was involved there. I'm pretty certain that it operated through the wharf yard at Whaley Bridge, but I have no firm evidence of his accomplices at that end of the line."

"So that's it then, chief suspect dead, no more losses, mention in despatches for Sergeant Spray and home for tea." The superintendent was prone to a little jocularity at such moments. His sergeant was disappointingly downbeat.

"There is a problem with that analysis, sir."

Wayland had never understood irony and the moment passed without comment.

"The matter of motive needs a little clarification. One possibility is that someone murdered Oldroyd, or had him murdered, to take over his operation."

"Any others?"

"The sale of the Cromford railway's residual interest and the issue of who controls the shares have to be considered.' Spray described his interview with Jones, Tarp's comments and the rupture of relations between Jones and the dead man over Mrs Oldroyd's shares.

"Might I suggest, sir, that we wait a little before informing Euston that the matter is closed?"

Ordinarily Wayland would have been summoned by now to give a report on the case's progress. His senior officer must have been distracted by the proximity of Christmas.

"Very well, if you think it best, but I must have a report no later than the second of January."

The train slowed and then, clanking and bumping, came to a halt. Wayland stepped out into a rather depressing Talbot Street Station. It was gloomy and empty; Blackpool in winter was not a popular destination. Limping toward the exit, he was lucky to find a hansom cab. Spray followed him onto the platform and dawdled past the locomotive. The driver was at his cab window and the two nodded, about to strike up a conversation. The engine was waiting to be released from temporary captivity by the station pilot. Even then, it was being attached to the train's rear; the fireman was down in the four foot, uncoupling the leading coach.

"Move along smartly, Spray, this is your skirmish, show a bit of enthusiasm." Wayland was recalling past campaigns in preparation for the coming encounter. He climbed stiffly into the cab, the damp air off the Irish Sea was not doing much for his rheumatics.

Spray followed obediently.

"Central police station, cabbie, prompt now."

They arrived at a newly opened building housing the recently constituted Blackpool police force. A sergeant guarded the entrance hall, and Wayland addressed himself to the man.

"I wish to speak to your most senior officer." Wayland was rather unsure of the rank assigned to an officer in charge of such a force. They were a very new innovation.

"That would be the superintendent, sir." The man recognised from Wayland's uniform insignia that he was of a similar, lofty rank. "May I ask your name, sir?"

"Superintendent Wayland of the London & North Western Railway Constabulary."

"Please wait here, superintendent, and I will see if he is free to receive you."

The sergeant returned shortly and ushered Wayland and Spray into a spacious, but unostentatious, office. A small, wiry man, purposeful and alert but with nothing of the parade ground about him, stood up and shook hands, first with Wayland and then with Spray. He was a modern man, one whose authority owed nothing to background and breeding, his rank had been hard-earned. Wayland sensed this immediately and mused for a second on what an intolerable place today's world was when a man of equal rank to himself wasn't a gentleman.

When all three were seated, the situation was explained by Sergeant Spray.

"So, you want me to arrange a search for this man Markham, who you think comes from Blackpool and is possibly involved in a murder on your territory? Hmm." He looked doubtful, "Rather a needle in a haystack. Could be worse – the haystack's considerably larger in summer."

He turned slightly in order to reach and pull a bell-lever on the wall by the fireplace. In seconds, a sergeant appeared. Upon enquiry he did not know an Edward Markham.

"If Sergeant Spray would be so kind as to repeat the man's description?"

Spray did his best: bit of a ladies' man; tries to look smart but doesn't quite make it; probably gambles. He wasn't quite sure why he said the latter, but it provoked a response from the sergeant.

"Lotta gamblers in Blackpool. This time o'year they're at a loose end – no trippers to fleece, so they squabbles amongst their selves. Got one in the cells from last night. Could do worse 'an talk to 'im. He might respond to a little inducement."

Leaving their chiefs, the pair went down to the cells: two seasoned officers, essentially honest, both struggling with disillusion at the imperfect mass of humanity around them.

"I reckon, if this cove sees a way out o' eer without charge, he'll tell us anything he knows 'bout Markham. Trouble is he'll tell us what he don't know as well."

A dejected, scruffy individual with a grazed cheek and ripening black eye sat in the cell as the sergeants entered. He was still suffering from the previous night's excesses, but roused himself sufficiently to complain about his situation.

"You can't keep me eer like this. I got me rights y'know, an' anyways, I ain't done nowt."

"'Cept causing an affray, behaving drunk and disorderly in a public place, threatening someone with a broken bottle and, finally, taking a swing at a nice, kind bobby who was trying to stop you killing him."

"He weren't so kind – it were 'im what gev me this," he said, pointing to his eye.

"And bloody lucky you were he stopped you from killing the other man, cos if you had, you'd be on a charge of murder and we wouldn't be havin' this conversation."

"Ow d'yer mean?"

"If, and only if, you answer some questions that me an' this officer puts to you..."

"Ee's a rozzer as well, is 'e? Where's 'is uniform?" The prisoner giggled. There was obviously some time to go before he sobered up.

"And you don't tell no lies," the sergeant continued, "and if you don't vomit on the floor agin, I might – just might – see my way to letting you go without charge. But not until you're sober, mind."

The offer was given due consideration, as if the decision was finely balanced.

"What d'ye wanna know?"

"Markham – Edward Markham. Where do we find him?"

There was another giggle.

"I'd like ter find him, too. 'E owes me money. 'Eard he 'ad a big win last weekend and he's disappeared. Allus does when he's chink in is pocket."

"Do you know where he lives?"

"'E don't live nowhere," the man guffawed.

"See here. If you can't do better than this, I'll have you up in court tomorrow; and it won't just be drunk and disorderly. How about attempted murder? That broken bottle would tell against you."

A douche of cold water couldn't have worked better.

"Nay, what I mean is, he kips down in other people's drums; he's allus got girls, and when no one'll have 'im, he'll find a deadlurk. Yer know, empty-like."

"Know any specific places?"

Several possibilities dotted around the borough were mentioned and duly recorded in a notebook.

Chapter 15

Having escorted the Whale onto his train back to Manchester, Spray found his way to Talbot Road in search of Markham's postal address. A bow-fronted shop with window panes bulging provocatively outward had initially seemed an unlikely candidate. He'd walked past, and back again, before realising that the purveyor of 'Health Foods, Patent Medicines and Surgical Appliances' was indeed the place he sought. The nature of the business and the name of its proprietor were picked out in gold lettering above the window. He gazed through the glass at an array of rubber pipes and mysterious metal devices with a squeamish fascination. Behind them, cardboard posters advertised all manner of items purporting to be essential to good health: Carter's Little Liver Pills dominated, with Goody's Headache powder and Lydia E. Pinkham's Vegetable Compound also in attendance. Suddenly, a pale face topped with greying hair receding at the temples was peering at him above the advertisements. Spray went inside.

"Good afternoon, sir, how can I help you?"

After a few moments of uncertainty, Spray identified the shopkeeper's accent. It must have waned over the years, but the Welsh lilt was detectable still. Before the detective could identify himself, he was enveloped in the delicious aroma of baking.

"Ah, that's Mrs Griffiths doing her good works in the kitchen," the proprietor nodded toward the rear of the premises. "My dear wife bakes bread with special, health-giving properties. I would be pleased to wrap some for you, sir, while it's still warm."

"It is indeed a tempting offer, Mr Griffiths, but I am here on police business. My name is Spray. Here are my credentials." He proffered his warrant card. "I understand, sir, that you hold mail on behalf of other people."

"Yes, that is so, Sergeant Spray. We started the service some years ago. Blackpool wasn't like it is now, you know; many new buildings were being constructed, and the itinerant workmen needed somewhere to collect their mail."

"And someone to read it aloud to them, I shouldn't wonder?"

The shopkeeper nodded, "Indeed, most of the fellows could not read. I was happy to provide that extra service for a very reasonable fee. I had recently opened the shop and had to turn a penny where I could. We had many more customers back then," he continued, pointing to a small box with marker cards. "In those days, a box of this size would have been quite insufficient. Now the workmen have gone, but we still help a few customers by handling their mail."

"I am interested in one customer in particular, sir, a Mr Markham. I wish to question him in relation to a suspicious death," said Spray.

Both men were distracted by the sudden, loud jangling of the bell above the front door, and a youth entered the shop.

"Ah, Ernest, you're back. Ernest does odd jobs around the place for us, sergeant. Now, look lively, lad, go and see if Mrs Griffiths has any errands for you."

The youth nodded silently in reply and walked towards the smell of baking bread.

"Markham, you say? I have nothing for him at present. He doesn't get many letters. The most recent must have been, ooh, let me see, about five or six weeks ago. A rather official-looking letter arrived for him." He paused and added: "Oh dear, I can't remember what happened to it."

"Do you think you can help me to find Mr Markham?"

"I don't see how I can be of assistance. I don't know where he comes from or where he goes to. He only appears in the shop occasionally, and I've never seen him with anyone else."

A young voice piped up from the kitchen, "I seen 'im wiv another cove, Mr Griffith, outside the shop, an' I knows…"

"Be quiet, Ernest!" Griffiths cut in. "The sergeant is not interested in your tittle-tattle. He's got proper work to do."

Ernest's head peeped round the door and Spray winked at him conspiratorially. The lad understood, nodded and retreated.

"Thank you for your time, Mr Griffiths, you've been most helpful. I shall be in Blackpool until tomorrow. I will call in again before I go to see if you've remembered anything else."

Griffiths, evidently still keen to turn a penny, asked if Spray had anywhere to stay.

"This town is full of lodgings, sergeant, but most are closed in the winter. My wife takes in guests on occasion, only of the best quality of course. She would be most honoured to attend you."

Spray found the smell of baking bread irresistible, and matters were swiftly settled.

"You'll take supper, of course, for a small consideration?" Griffith's entrepreneurial spirit was admirable.

Spray announced his departure loud enough for the alert young Ernest to hear, and the lad caught him up only a few paces along Talbot Street.

"You really a Jack?" asked Ernest, wanting to establish that he was dealing with the genuine article.

Spray confirmed his status with the LNWR, but this was not well-received.

"We got Lancashire and Yorkshire Railway 'ere; I reckon they're the best. Go all the way from Liverpool to Hull an' back. Imagine that!"

Spray looked benevolently on this partisan view of the railways: living in Chesterfield when he was Ernest's age, he had held a similar view of the Midland. Once they had turned a corner and were out of Griffith's line of sight, he got down to business.

"What was it, Ernest, that Mr Griffiths told you not to bother me with?"

"Old Griffiths don't think I know nothin'. He's all right, though, he helped me wiv my reading – well, it's so's I can read what's on the boxes and orders an' such like." There was a pause. "Oh yes, Markham; I don't like 'im. He gimme a clip round the ear few weeks back, said I was a cheeky little sod."

"And were you?"

"There was a letter waiting for him, in his box. I only said it were a bit posh for t'likes of 'im, an' he clipped me one!"

Spray struggled unsuccessfully to suppress a grin, "What was posh about the letter?"

"It were big an' stiff, an' it had printing on the back."

"Did you see Mr Markham with someone else outside the shop?"

It seemed that after the contretemps, Ernest had watched Markham leave and whilst pulling faces at him through the window, had seen him meet a man. This other man had raised his fist at young Ernest.

"But 'e didn't mean nothin', cos 'e grinned at me. I knew who the cove was. Mr Griffiths had sent me on an errand to his 'ouse last summer."

———•◦•———

Enid Brash stood in her freshly cleaned parlour preening herself. She felt queen of all she surveyed. She'd married for love and they had a place of their own. Come spring, she'd be taking in holidaymakers, and she and Harold would be set up for life. Her mother, who had always claimed to be a widow, died, and after the requisite year of mourning, Enid had married Harold. Her mother would not have approved. She called him 'unreliable' and made it plain that the house would go to cousin Hetty if Enid married him.

Harold had a bit of a past, it was true. Some unsavoury friends from his youth had been a problem, but Enid knew that she could change him. Well she had, hadn't she? He'd got that job at the council offices at her instigation. It was in the department that dealt with rubbish and drains and the like, but with her support, he would soon work his way up to something more highly regarded. Enid suppressed a small voice in the back of her mind which wondered if he really had given up the old life. It sounded too much like her mother. Safe in her complacency, she answered a knock at the front door. Her sense of well-being survived the sight of a respectable man standing a polite two steps back from the threshold and asking to speak with her husband. She thought it must be something connected with his job; after all, he said he'd be out of the office today.

"He's not here just now. Can I tell him whose asking?"

"Sergeant Spray of the LNWR Railway Constabulary." Unknowingly, he had lit a fuse, and he continued, "I only want to ask him some questions about his friend, Edward Markham."

The spark reached the explosive, and suddenly Mrs Brash was shouting and screaming. Expressions such as 'blackguard', 'never again' and 'over my dead body' could be distinguished. 'Respectable people', and 'changed man' gave way to something about mother being 'right all along', when the sobbing eventually subsided.

Feeling embarrassed, Spray saw that the woman was overwhelmed by despair. Finally, the storm passed. After apologising for the distress he had inflicted, Spray ventured two questions.

"Has Mr Markham been here? Do you think your husband has seen him recently?"

Mrs Brash returned an emphatic 'no' to both questions. Asked when her husband might return, she asserted tearfully that she 'didn't know anything anymore' and closed the front door.

Spray turned, and as he walked up the garden path, a man was just entering the gate. The two introduced themselves, and Spray manoeuvred himself and Harold Brash tactfully out of earshot and sight of the house.

"When did you last see your friend Edward Markham?"

"A few weeks ago, sergeant, but not by appointment; I bumped into him unexpectedly in town. I don't see much of him these days; the wife doesn't approve."

He was convincing, Spray had to hand him that. Perhaps it was just as he said, a chance meeting and nothing more.

"Mrs Brash was greatly distressed when I mentioned Mr Markham. To begin with she didn't think you had seen him, but then she wasn't sure."

This reconstruction of the interview, whilst correct in its way, was not an exact reflection of what had occurred, but the fear in the man's eyes suggested he'd seen through the deception. He was well able to bluff the likes of policemen, but couldn't lie convincingly to his wife. He had something to hide.

What a place, thought Markham, *no better than a paddingken. Cold and draughty with a leaking roof in one corner turning the floor to mud.* The only dry place was a kife made of planks, raised from the floor on battens, where he spent his nights, shivering, under a thin blanket. He'd put his two bottles of gin, piece of cheese and a tuppenny loaf on an upturned box. They were just visible now he'd lit the candle.

That damned Craker woman hadn't done anything on the allotment since her husband died – if he did indeed die, and if he were her husband. Still you can say one thing for her: she kept a bloody close eye on her daughter. Why the hell did the old girl have to go and croak? That upset everything.

Edward Markham was not happy. He never really was. If things were going well, they ought to go better; if things were bad, it was someone else's fault. Occasionally, it was a bit of each. So, the money he'd won at the weekend was good, but not good enough. At least it was still in his pocket, though. Trying to keep it from his many creditors was hard; that's why he was hiding out in a garden shed.

The clanks, squeals and puffs from the goods yard on the other side of the fence had long since faded into the background, and he hardly heard them. Useful though: he'd acquired the contents of the shed from there. Mind you, he'd had to hack a way through the brambles to get to it. After that, it'd been a cokum; over the fence and through the nearest open door to see what he could find. He'd had to jump around a bit – there were people all over the place – but he could look after himself. He really came alive on such capers.

What was that? There was a faint scraping sound outside. He'd snuffed out the candle before a familiar voice called his name.

"Eddie, are you there? It's Harry." *Phew!*

Eddie's view of himself didn't include the dishonesty and egoism so obvious to others. Deceit was at his core, with one small and inexplicable exception. Eddie had extricated them both from some youthful escapade with a particularly fine stroke, and the pair had become good mates. Until, that is, Harry fell for Enid. Even then, Mrs Craker kept a lid on things, but the old bat had to go and die. When Enid married Harry, she dragged him back to respectability. Even then the connection between the men was not completely broken. Wearing thin, perhaps, but still with sufficient strength for Harry to offer a safe haven to his old mate: in the late Mrs Craker's allotment shed.

"There's trouble, Eddie: a Jack was at the house asking after you. I told him I hadn't seen you in weeks. He mentioned you to Enid and she got upset." The connecting thread between them was stretched to breaking point. "You've got to get out of here. When I go home she'll give me hell, and I can only cope if I don't know where you are."

The bloody weakling can't stand up to his missus, thought Eddie.

"What have you done? There's rozzers all over. They must be after you," Harry spoke worriedly.

Eddie had seen them, and from habit he'd kept out of their way, but he hadn't given them a second thought. Now, fear started to spread through him. He was not a man to make plans; he just reacted to whatever life threw up. Getting out of Blackpool was the only thing he could think of, and the means lay just over the fence at the bottom of the allotment. He grabbed the gin and was heading for the door.

"Hadn't you better take the scran and the blanket if you're riding the wagons? You've no idea how long you'll be or where you'll end up."

There wasn't enough light for the relief on Harry's face to show as Eddie headed for the door.

"Better I don't know where you're off to. Just in case," Harry suggested.

There was no friendly farewell. Eddie disappeared down the allotment and Harry went home to face Enid's wrath.

Once he was over the fence, Eddie's problems started. Scouting around for whatever came to hand was one thing; finding a comfortable billet on a train was something else. He could see railwaymen moving about across the other side of the yard. Nearer, a line of wagons was silhouetted against the gaslight, its end disappearing into the gloom. The train looked as if it was complete: he could hear, rather than see, an engine at one end puffing gently, the familiar clanking noises as it buffered up to the train confirmed his thoughts.

Eddie slipped into the shadows close to the trucks. They were open-topped. A box-van would be no good anyway: previous, illicit forays into railway yards had taught him that. The doors could be opened only from the outside. If he hid in one, someone would shut him in, and he'd be trapped. Once, a mate had locked him inside for a lark. It had been Harry who had released him. *That was in the days before Enid, damn her!*

At the head of the train, the guard and driver were exchanging information about its weight and details of the journey. Formalities completed, signed logbook safely in his satchel, and using a distant gas lamp to see his way, the guard set off along the six-foot towards his van. Eddie held his breath as the crunch of the man's boots on the ballast got louder, echoing across the track beneath the train. As a precaution, Eddie headed in the other direction.

Even the petulant Eddie had to acknowledge what happened next as pure good fortune. Stumbling, he put out a hand to steady himself, and once recovered, found he was holding the bottom rung of a short iron ladder. Looking up, he realised he'd been mistaken about the train's composition: this was a box-van. The ladder led to a passenger door, and swinging it open, he was delighted to see a handle on the inside.

He heard a couple of crows from the engine and realised that the guard must have reached his van and given a green light to the driver. The driver responded by tooting the engine's whistle. A ripple of movement ran down the line of wagons as the engine drew slowly forward.

Damn and blast! thought Eddie, realising he had left his victuals on the trackside. As the clatter of tightening couplings drew nearer, he jumped down and swiftly snatched up his supplies. The ladder started to move away, and in desperation, he chucked the bundle through the open door. He hauled himself up on the handrails and threw himself in after it. Pulling the door shut behind himself, he heard the satisfying clunk of the catch. Self-congratulation seemed in order. *Eddie Markham does it again,* he chuckled, but his feeling of triumph was short-lived.

Another ripple of movement traversed the train from end to end. The train, so briefly in motion, came to a halt. *Bugger it: the bastards must have seen me!* He opened the door slightly and peered out, prepared to jump and make a run for it. There was no one to be seen, but the shunting signal was in the 'on' position, explaining why the train had come to a standstill. A couple of engine whistles, longer this time, alerted the signalman. He set the road, pulled a lever that changed the ground signal from 'on' to 'off', and the train was in motion again. Creaking slowly over the points onto the main line, the vehicle began its unhurried journey across the Fylde and beyond.

Chapter 16

Two Journeys, Thursday, 23rd December, 1875

Supper with Mr and Mrs Richard Griffiths was, in Spray's opinion, devoid of proper food. The vegetarian meal he was served was more suited to an animal: nuts, seeds and greens. A working man needed meat, and he left the table hungry. The next morning he descended for breakfast without enthusiasm. Over an unappetising repast of porridge and arrowroot, Griffiths gave Spray a lecture on the adulteration of food. The issue was, he told his guest, the subject of a recent Act of Parliament. The man's dreary eating regime didn't seem to dull his intellect, although Spray wondered if it had had a limiting effect on his range of interests.

"Will you be staying long?" they had asked. "I hope you got what you came for … sorry we couldn't be more help." It seemed the couple had discussed his business, and why not, he thought, *I need all the help I can get.* He settled his account, having explained that he would be on his way that day, but as he was leaving Griffiths rushed after him, as near to animated as Spray had seen him.

"Sergeant, I've remembered something. That letter for Markham. I still don't know what happened to it, but the post-mark was somewhere in Derbyshire and it was embossed with the name of a firm of solicitors. I believe it was Barford and Company. Does that help?"

Spray thanked him.

Later, having drawn another blank at the police station, Spray boarded a train for Manchester. It was just beginning to snow, and as he travelled across the Fylde, the weather became steadily worse. Big flakes flashed past his window. From time to time, he saw a goods train loom out of the whiteness. It would wait patiently in a siding, its locomotive quietly simmering, to allow the Manchester Express to pass.

By the time Spray's train reached the vast, dingy cavern of Victoria Station, the worst of the snowstorm had passed. Plenty had settled, though. As he set out along Hunt's Bank, he was stepping on solid, but slippery, snow, packed down by the hundreds of be-clogged feet belonging to the hard-working folk of Manchester. For some it proved too treacherous: Spray hauled an old crone upright to find her rather less than grateful.

"Forty years past you'd have had to pay fer 'andlin' me like that, young man." She gave a cackling laugh. "But thanks t'ye, all t'same."

As he walked, Spray was reminded of his stroll the previous day, when he'd seen something out of the corner of his eye. He was in Market Street, when a sign for Sickle Street attracted his attention. He had no idea why he thought it significant, and certainly couldn't remember now, but he had turned into it, hoping for enlightenment. There it was: Arbuthnot & Stein. The same words he'd seen on the bank statements in Oldroyd's office. It was here that Oldroyd squirrelled away his money.

Before he realised what he was doing, he was through the door and asking the floor-walker if he might see the manager. The man invited him to traverse the expensive marble floor to an elegant, French-polished mahogany counter. A wing-collared clerk looked disapprovingly at his warrant card.

"I'll see what I can do, Sergeant Spray. Please wait here a moment." He disappeared behind a handsome screen of etched glass, leaving Spray to contemplate his surroundings.

He hated this sort of place: it stank of power used to intimidate – the poor on the outside and the rich tucked up comfortably within. Spray understood small money, the kind of money too insignificant to come to the attention of Arbuthnot and Stein. The kind of money that bought a train ticket or a night's lodging. The kind of money that a tooler might lift from a toff's pit without him realising.

Big money offended him. The kind that a bank such as this would deal in: hundreds and thousands rather than pennies and shillings. He didn't trust the people who owned it or those who handled it for others. Above all, he didn't believe that it could be multiplied without dishonesty.

"If you would kindly follow me, sir?"

The clerk ushered Spray along a passage lined with opulent rosewood panelling, and cowered slightly as they passed a gentleman walking in the opposite direction. The other man was tall, fair and bore an air of disdain . He wore a frock coat and carried a silk top hat.

Spray was left in an antechamber protecting the manager's office. He wandered around the room, idly examining the pictures hanging on the walls. Not that he was an art lover, it was something to kill the time.

He was intrigued to come across something he recognised: a lithograph of the Crystal Palace. At the bottom right-hand corner was the artist's name and what looked like a fraction: 1/4.

"Ah, Sergeant Spray, I see you are interested in our little collection," said a voice that startled Spray.

Thanks to the sumptuous Persian rug, a tall, authoritative man had entered the room noiselessly. "That's a particularly fine lithograph, and very valuable, as you will no doubt have realised. It's one of a very limited print run."

Spray had no idea what he was talking about, but shook the proffered hand.

"My name is Ferrison, I am the assistant manager of the bank. Are you wishing to open an account?" The words were gracious, but Ferrison's manner delivered a contrary message: it was highly unlikely that a policeman's small nest-egg of savings would be welcome here.

"Oh no, Mr Ferrison, nothing of that kind. I am here on official business. It concerns Mr Arthur Oldroyd. He is – pardon me sir, I should say *was*, as the gentleman has lately passed over to the Other Side – proprietor of Flegg & Co in Buxton, which holds an account at this establishment."

Ferrison flinched slightly when Spray referred to Oldroyd's demise, but remained silent.

Spray added: "I have reason to believe that he was murdered, and am investigating the matter." His words produced a reaction.

"Oh dear! How shocking! Poor Mr Oldroyd. Was it a robbery or some such?"

"We are looking into it, sir. My presence here is in regard to an issue connected to the enquiry; it may, in fact, be central to it. I have established that Flegg & Co has been trading illegally, and that the proceeds of that activity have been deposited here."

Ferrison became vehemently defensive. "The bank has no knowledge of, or complicity in, any illegal activity. Furthermore, it can neither confirm nor deny that the firm you named has an account here."

"I do not seek confirmation of the bank's connection with Flegg & Co. We have documents to prove that. I need to know if anyone other than Oldroyd has access to the Flegg Account."

"The bank respects the confidentiality of its clientele, sergeant. I have nothing more to say on the matter." He operated a richly ornate brass bell-pull set neatly into a wall panel. Within seconds a liveried commissionaire appeared. "Good day to you, sergeant," said Ferrison.

His manner made it clear that the interview was over. As the commissionaire accompanied him through to the antechamber, Spray noticed a plaque on the outside of the door. It bore the words *J Tarp Esq, Managing Partner*.

After the pantomime with Enid Brash, and the interview with her husband, Spray had braved the December weather and wandered about Blackpool in an attempt to get his bearings. By the time he'd reached Blackpool Police Station, he was grateful to get out of the biting wind, straight off the Irish Sea, and hear Sergeant Parker's progress report.

Parker had offered no news of Markham: 'The drunk must have been right', he'd remarked, 'when Markham has money he disappears', but had suggested they meet at the end of his twelve-hour shift. By 6pm Spray had been seated in a quiet corner of a public house, tucking into a much appreciated plate of stewed mutton and enjoying Parker's congenial companionship.

"One of my constables remembered old Mrs Markham when she first came to Blackpool," Parker told him. "Her boy Eddie was a young scamp then, and she was always going on about how they had come from what she called 'the cradle of the cotton industry'. Myself, I always thought it was Lancashire, but she was adamant that it was Derbyshire. I've forgotten the name of the town... Let me think... Hmm, it definitely began with a C. Does that mean anything to you, Sam?"

The goods train headed slowly westward, its jerky, random movements making sleep impossible. Even sitting was uncomfortable. Eddie was tormented by the cold and the incessant rattling – *Damnation! Would it never stop?*

There wasn't much to the compartment. He explored it in the darkness. It ran from door to door, giving access from both sides of the track. He came across three holes in the partition, at shoulder height, between him and the rest of the wagon. This explained two things. Firstly, that the wagon was for horses, and secondly, the cause of the pungent stench. Years of urine were soaked into the wooden floor, and residual fragments of droppings suffused the stalls with an aroma that wafted into the groom's compartment. The wagon's motion had caused a stack of buckets to work their way out slowly from under a wooden bench. Tripping over them, Eddie finally realised the source of the annoying rattling.

It began to dawn on him: this was as much a prison as an escape. He ate half the loaf and some cheese and then started on the gin. Time passed in a blur as the level in the first bottle dropped. He was still able to stand when he needed to answer a call of nature and was just sober enough to reach for one of the buckets – they had their uses, after all. His aim wasn't too good, but so what, it wasn't his floor. Finally, after wrapping himself in his blanket, he dozed off. The train rattled slowly on.

The stops and starts that inevitably accompany a journey on a slow freight train were unknown to its illicit passenger. He had drunk more gin during the night and had stopped caring where he was, or even why. The train halted at a freight yard, where the engine was detached and replaced with a fresh one. The guard had returned the log to the driver and fireman. Nothing amiss had been noted. After being relieved by another crew, the three went to find the train they were rostered to take back to Blackpool. The procedures of the previous evening were repeated by the new crew, the train having had a few box vans added before it resumed its journey.

Eddie slept on until daylight brought him a fresh revelation about his compartment: there was a small window in each door. In fact, it was the grey light of a winter morning creeping through them that had wakened him. He felt freezing cold, nature's two calls were desperately urgent, and his whole body craved water. He was sober enough to appreciate the limitation of a bucket in his present predicament. The newly discovered windows slid open, but the gap was too narrow to accommodate the widest part of the bucket. He had no faith in his ability to project the contents through the opening with any accuracy.

He had just decided to share his quarters with his slops when the train slowed and then stopped. He looked out of the window and could see a small ditch alongside the track, and behind that, an embankment. Neither end of the train was in sight; he was on the outside of a curve. This was his chance: he would jump down onto the bank, do what was necessary and be back in a trice.

He even had the forethought to take a clean bucket with him to get water from the ditch. Just as he reached the point of no return, a couple of crows rang out from the engine and the train was on the move again. *This is the end: it has to be.* He was in the middle of nowhere with his trousers round his ankles and snow was beginning to fall. To cap it all, he had even managed to contaminate the water he was hoping to drink. His luck had run out. All his other problems were subsumed into this calamity. He was going to die of hypothermia, in a snowstorm, on a railway embankment.

It was all their bloody fault, of course it was. He'd never had a decent break. That Mrs Craker, her damned daughter, the bloody rozzers, the Jack from god-knows-where… He was so busy compiling his hate-list that he did not heed the two more engine whistles in the distance.

The rear of the train halted almost level with him before he realised what was happening. It stopped almost exactly where it had started, but on the parallel line, so there were now two sets of tracks to cross to get back on board.

Eddie climbed back into his horse-box and tried to take stock of his position. It's the business with Jones. It has to be. Thoughts of the consequences were more than he could bear. He reached again for the gin bottle in the hope that it would stop the pain. Two more crows on the whistle and the train lurched forward again only to jerk to a stop, then backwards, then… Eddie lost count of the movements. Finally everything went quiet.

The train was stationary for a long time. It was snowing hard now and settling. Before he became too drunk, it dawned on him that the snow might solve his thirst problem. The drink had made him just reckless enough to climb down to the track again and scoop some into a bucket. As he climbed back into the waiting freight train, a Manchester bound express roared past.

Chapter 17

Buxton & Journey's End, Friday, 24th December, 1875

It was breakfast time at 37 Old Mill End, and the mouth-watering smell of frying wafted through the house. The two detectives had spent the previous evening in a different sort of fug. The White Horse at the bottom of the road had been quiet enough to talk and noisy enough to avoid being overheard. Pints in hand, they had sat together comparing notes.

"So, what did you find in Blackpool, Sam?"

"Not Markham, that's for sure. He's known there all right, amongst the gambling classes. He bumps into the police occasionally, but nothing serious. Usually has no money, and when he gets his hands on some he goes into hiding." Spray continued, describing his experiences with Richard Griffiths, Purveyor of Health Foods, Patent Medicines and Surgical Appliances.

"You've no idea the things he had in his window – come to think of it neither have I, and I had a good look at them. But I did obtain an address for an associate of Markham's."

Spray solemnly described Enid Brash's reaction to Markham's name. His straight face only made the story funnier and in the end Archer burst out laughing.

"It's all right for you, you weren't there." Spray looked rueful, but even he laughed in the end. "Clearly, she does not approve of the friendship."

"What kind of a man is Harry Brash?" asked Archer.

"He was certainly a smooth talker, but he looked guilty when I told him about my conversation with his wife. I couldn't tell if he was just scared of her or hiding something from me."

The conversation moved on to Arbuthnot & Stein.

"The place reeked of money and hypocrisy." This sort of comment was usually followed by a diatribe about the evils of excess, but Spray changed tack.

"I didn't learn much there, but the man was rattled when I told him about Oldroyd's murder. And he protested loudly when I suggested the bank was holding money he'd earned illegally – too loudly, if I'm any judge."

"Is that all?"

"Well, the managing partner is a man called Tarp. I am wondering if this is Jarvis Tarp. How about you? Anything useful?"

Archer's tour of Flegg & Co's customers was of little help. They each claimed to have been trading with the company legally. Also, the prices were keen but no more than that, and one had complained that this week's delivery hadn't arrived.

By the next morning, their dull mood had vanished as Lizzie served breakfast. Then – unusually in such circumstances – she sat and ate with them as though they were a family.

"Have you any plans for tomorrow?" she asked.

Confused, Spray and Archer looked mystified.

"Don't be difficult: you must know it's Christmas Day! I have a proposition to put to you: my father and I always have a meal together here; then he goes to sleep by the fire and I visit Maisie's family."

Lizzie continued her offer: "If you two would be so kind as to go into the town and order a bird, I'll arrange with the baker to roast it tomorrow. Then I'll feed you both the best Christmas dinner in Whaley Bridge."

There was no dissent. Archer still had memories of family Christmases and couldn't think of anything finer. Spray was more equivocal. There'd never been a Christmas celebration at the orphanage, and as an adult he'd generally taken his festive meal in a pub.

Spray watched a busy Whaley Bridge going about its business in the snow. He and Archer had stood in a queue outside the butchers with what appeared to be all the women and children of the town. They'd finally made it into the shop, but Spray was driven out by sharp elbows and bulky wicker shopping baskets. A bar full of drinkers getting the next round in was a vicar's tea party by comparison.

Archer, amused, watched Spray's retreat. *The man doesn't live in the real world*, he thought. So tough and determined at work, and intelligent too, but all at sea in this place. Getting an earful for tripping over a customer's toddler or bruised ribs from a determined housewife's basket had all been Archer's life before he became a policeman.

"What yer doin' 'ere, mister? Thought yer were off chasin' criminals." Jimmy Allcroft had popped up next to Archer and went on in a more confidential tone: "My mam sent me fer't giblets; the butcher ad took 'em out."

It was quite a performance: Archer watched as Jimmy confronted the errant shopkeeper and shamed him into handing over the missing innards. The lad grinned at Archer as he pushed his way to the door, a gleam of triumph in his eye.

"You up our road wi' missus Oldroyd termorra? Spect yer'll be at Mr Maida's after, cos she allus goes there." The whole town seemed to know one another's business.

Polite as usual, Archer's progress was slower than the lad's, but finally he emerged carrying a fat, white goose with its giblets intact. Jimmy always had something useful to say, it seemed, if only about shopping. He'd spoken to Spray as he passed. "Oh yes, I know who he is." Archer had looked quizzically at his sergeant. "He must have seen us together. He came and asked me if I were 'one o' they Jacks, like Mr Archer'. And had I 'caught any legs wi'out 'ats'."

With the matter of tomorrow's meal arranged, the two detectives left Lizzie plucking the goose and set out for the station. Spray was going to Buxton to see about the post-mortem. Archer went south to the Cromford canal, to interview some more of Flegg & Co's customers.

The previous day had passed quickly for Eddie. He was unconscious or asleep, or a bit of both, most of the time. As soon as reality intruded, he drowned it out with more gin. On one occasion, when the noise and jerking of a shunting operation had shaken him into life, he'd looked through one of his little windows to see hundreds of coal wagons. A voice, so close it made him jump back, called out.

"This un's not for Wigan, leave it wi' t'other wagons."

There was an answering shout followed shortly by another jerk. A couple of swigs from the bottle, and Eddie Markham was able to retreat once more into alcoholic oblivion.

Much later, he awoke to more bumping and shouting. He ventured another look. In the back of his mind he knew he had to get off the train, but the gin always seemed a better option – he was well into the second bottle by now. This time, the guard was walking back to his van. A couple of blasts of the whistle and they were off again. The cold wasn't worrying him so much now, even in his more-sober moments; he was just stiff and sluggish. He swigged more gin and slept until daylight.

—•••—

The doctor's house was everything a professional man's premises should be. A polished knocker adorned an oak-panelled door. The brass plate to one side announced his credentials, and the man himself lived up to them. The three-piece suit was immaculate and the tie subdued.

"Sergeant, do come in. The coroner's man said you would want to see me. I completed the autopsy only yesterday."

The thought of this gentleman in his finery poking about in a dead body intrigued Spray.

"Most, how shall we say… perplexing. Not at all what I'd been led to expect. Something about a rail accident, that fool Walters said. Never get any sense out of him, don't y'know?"

Littering the consulting room were tools of the doctor's trade. The two men sat across a desk.

The doctor explained, "He was murdered, of course, but you knew that. There were conclusive signs of strangulation with a garrotte. The hyoid was ruptured, and there were characteristic marks on the neck. There was, however… how shall I put it… a diversion. He was in a state of, er, tumescence when he died. No stains, though. I considered the effect of the garrotte; the hangman's noose can do it, you know? I saw a case in the dissecting room when I was a student, in the old days. Difficult to say if a piano wire would have the same effect. Anyway, someone else must have been involved; the murder weapon wasn't found with him, was it?"

Spray's head was spinning: a garrotte was one thing, but he found the rest difficult to contemplate. He wasn't sure he understood it.

The medical man carried on with his report, "There was also post-mortem damage to the side of the scalp. It looks like he'd been dragged along by his feet, over some rough ground, after he'd been killed. Let me see, he was found last Friday... well, I can't say how long he's been dead, but it was certainly longer than a week. Oh yes, and there were a lot of brown hairs on his clothing. Can't be absolutely sure, but I'd say it was horse."

He looked solicitously toward the detective. "Understood all that?"

No. Spray had not understood it all and wasn't sure he wanted to either, but he certainly needed to.

"I'd be happy to show you the body and explain my findings in the flesh, as it were."

Spray declined, but gritting his teeth, asked for the bits he didn't understand to be rendered in layman's language.

They were at the door shaking hands when the doctor dropped his voice conspiratorially. "I nearly forgot to say, sergeant: I found this in a secret pouch in his coat. Might be of help, so you'd better have it."

Breakfast on the footplate was a triumph of improvisation. Standing in the sidings of Stockport yard with twenty minutes to the off, the crew reckoned there was just enough time.

"Get that shovel clean!"

The fireman swilled it down.

"Right, hold it steady!" The driver unwrapped the bacon and black pudding and laid them on it carefully.

"Ouch, you've got the damn thing bloody hot already!" He

nursed a burnt knuckle.

The crew watched through the fire hole as the bacon started to sizzle. The aroma was swept into the boiler tubes by a gentle forward draught.

"Don't leave it in too long, I like mine juicy!" The shovel was withdrawn and the smell of fried bacon filled the cab.

"Here y'are," the driver held out two tin plates, and the bacon and black pudding slipped off neatly, their places on the shovel taken by four eggs.

"Don't get 'em overdone, yolks just runny, mind."

After two days in a horsebox, this was a kind of torture for Eddie. The aroma had crept through the gaps in the planking and enveloped him as he woke. It was just daylight now, and he could hear voices from the crew of an engine standing alongside. The snow he had collected had melted, and he'd drunk the pitifully small quantity of liquid it produced. He'd been without water for several hours and his food supply had given out well before that. He reached for the gin bottle.

The signal came off, and with a couple of crows on the whistle, the engine eased its train forward, out of the yard and onto the main line.

———

Tilly was blacking the kitchen range when she heard the front door bell. With lampblack all over her hands, it was as well she'd rolled up her sleeves. She made haste, but by the time she'd opened the door the florid, portly man on the step was not at all pleased. He muttered something about a 'Damn long wait' and then, more clearly, stated: "I have an important meeting with Mr Tarp senior."

Through the open door, Tilly could see a horse and trap,

reins thrown carelessly over a garden seat. That wasn't right, she knew, but the unpleasant visitor was barging through the door without waiting to be announced. Unexpectedly, Jarvis Tarp came to her rescue.

"Mr Jones, that your nag out there? I'd say you've had it drag you all the way up here from Cromford, by the way it's sweating. If something isn't done it'll get a chill." He turned to Tilly. "You be about your chores, I'll deal with this."

"I didn't expect to see you today." Jones found himself speaking to Tarp's back as the younger man stepped out to call for the gardener to take care of the horse. "This is supposed to be C&HP business. I can't see how you can be involved."

Much of what he said was drowned out by a shouted conversation about stabling. As he returned to the entrance hall, Jarvis Tarp chose to ignore it.

"We'll go and talk with father, please follow me," Tarp said.

They entered the room where Spray had consumed tea five days earlier.

"Ah, Mr Jones, do sit down." Fitzroy Tarp's courtesy was cut short.

"This is really too much, Mr Tarp. I didn't expect young Jarvis here to be involved. This isn't his business, you know."

"Since Arthur is no longer with us, I feel the need of an assistant. I'm not as young as I was, and he looks out for me. You're not going to be difficult, are you?"

Jones, sulky at being outmanoeuvred, had to concede.

"Right then, now we can begin," said Jarvis.

It was Fitzroy's turn to be disconcerted by his son. "I think I'd better hear what Mr Jones has to say first, Jarvis, then he and I will decide what is to be done. You are here to take notes and advise."

Jones pointed out that Oldroyd's death had put a different complexion on things. If he and Fitzroy Tarp so decided, they could reverse the decision taken at the previous meeting and pursue the LNWR offer.

"The bank will take care of the financial side of things, of course…" began Jarvis.

Fitzroy broke in: "Just because your late mother was an Arbuthnot, Jarvis, and you're the director of a bank, I cannot see that you have any part to play in this arrangement. I am perfectly able to deal with the matter on my own." Then, to Jones: "Arthur may have been obdurate at our last meeting, unreasonably so, you might say, but he made a point that is, as yet, unresolved. We have still not seen any evidence that you have authority to act on behalf of the legatees of the original shareholders."

Jarvis nodded in agreement, "The bank would have to be reassured on the issue. Documentary proof is required."

Jones was cornered. He knew it. Desperate to deflect attention from his duplicity, he launched an attack. It was the only way he could see to avoid exposing the wrong-doing Arthur Oldroyd had come across following the death of his brother.

"Your protégé, Oldroyd, wasn't what he seemed." Jones's eyes began bulging and his face turned puce. "I called at his house the other evening," he began, assuming an air of self-righteousness, "and there was a working-man there."

"What prompted your visit, Mr Jones?" Jarvis broke in.

Jones began to bluster. "I'd heard he'd died. Just wanted to make sure everything was all right."

"Apart from a meeting here, I'd heard you hadn't spoken to Oldroyd for over four years." Jarvis spoke calmly, but managed to make his words sound like an accusation.

Jones ignored the interjection and ploughed on.

"He was a railwayman from High Peak Junction, and he looked it, I can tell you. Now you tell me, what was Oldroyd doing, meeting a fellow like that, in the middle of the night?" He shot a glance at Jarvis. "Well, you'd know, wouldn't you?" He left the imputation hanging.

There was silence. Fitzroy Tarp had observed Oldroyd's unmarried status, but had not cared to dwell upon it. Now, he looked mortified at having to consider the issue. Jarvis smouldered with suppressed anger. All three, each in his different way, was so disconcerted by the foregoing, that they failed to consider any other reason for clandestine meetings between Oldroyd and an employee of the railway.

———•◆•———

Having set off from Blackpool two days previously, the 5:10 pm train completed the final leg of its journey. It had trundled across the Fylde and through the cotton and mining towns of Lancashire, slipped into north-east Cheshire and had come to rest in Derbyshire. Along the way it had lost and gained wagons, but had remained essentially the same entity until it arrived at Shallcross yard. Here it was, separated into what remained of its constituent parts. They would be used to form other trains on other days.

In his horse box, Eddie was, for the most part, oblivious of the changes that had occurred around him. Apart from having heard someone shout 'Wigan!' some hours previously, he had little idea where he was when the tantalising aroma of breakfast had crept into his van.

"This'll be the last afore Christmas, then."

"Right, we'll leave the mineral wagons in this road, an' put oss box-van ower there. It'll not be needed till the new year.

Some gent's been goin' out with t'Cheshire hounds. He'll be takin' his hunters 'ome come January, I reckon." There was a series of soft puffs and a clank as the van was coupled to the engine.

Eddie heard this exchange, but did not appreciate its meaning. He'd had the last of the gin and its effects were wearing off, but the cold was really getting to him. He lay on the bench and clutched his threadbare blanket. The sky was clearing as darkness fell. The stars appeared and the temperature dropped further.

—•••—

"Now, William, I want you to take this goose along to the bakery in town. They'll be expecting you. Well, not you, perhaps, but the bird. And you'll benefit from stretching your legs, too, Sam. I'll have breakfast ready in one hour, so mind you are back in time."

The pair strolled companionably down Old Mill End to the baker's. Not many homes in Whaley Bridge had ovens big enough for a Christmas roast, and he was happy enough to help out, for a fee.

"Oh ah, Mrs Oldroyd's goose, is it?" The baker studied the creature, calculating its weight. "My lad will deliver it about midday." He opened up a huge oven, slipped the bird in to join the earlier arrivals, and scribbled a note of whose it was.

As the detectives left they were enveloped in the unfamiliar aroma, for a bakery, of roasting meat.

Back at No. 37, Lizzie had, with some difficulty, produced breakfast as usual. Hitherto, when the meal was over, the men had been the first to rise from the table, bent on a day's constabulary duty, whilst their landlady lingered over a second cup of tea. Today, on Christmas day, the roles were reversed, and the harassed cook bustled off back to her kitchen whilst the two men wondered how to spend the morning.

"William," Lizzie called from over her shoulder, "do you think you could give me a hand in here?" It could have been his mother's voice. Then, rather more uncertainly, she added, "Sam, would you be good enough to go round to father's and keep him company for an hour?"

He could hardly refuse and set off down the hill for the second time that morning. He had to admit that it had been deftly done: Lizzie had marshalled her troops to best advantage and made it palatable to them at the same time.

Sam Spray and Isaac Bennett spent a congenial hour together, then ambled slowly to No. 37. As they entered, they spotted Archer wearing Lizzie's apron. Both men laughed heartily as Archer immediately untied it and cast it aside. His cheeks were red.

Lizzie giggled as Archer came forward to greet Isaac. "Merry Christmas, father," she said, kissing him. "Have you been well looked after?" She turned to Spray and enchanted him with her smile and her gracious appreciation. "You've no idea what a help you've been in looking after father."

"The pleasure was all mine. Mr Bennett has been kind enough to share with me his extensive knowledge of racing pigeons."

"And in exchange, I have learned much about the railways in the Crimea! And I've brought along a little something to contribute to the meal." Isaac gestured to a wicker basket that Spray had carried for him.

Removing a cloth that covered its contents revealed an assortment of bottles, one containing a fine sherry and the remainder, ale. The four settled themselves around the large table that William had set out in the parlour. He then carried in the roasted goose whilst Lizzie followed with the vegetables. Spray was invited to carve the bird.

Spray had never experienced this sort of family Christmas before, and it disturbed him. He could feel the tight lacing that held his emotions in their proper place loosening, and he was frightened at what they'd expose when the knots finally came undone. Lizzie made sure everyone had large helpings, the gravy boat went from hand to hand, and beer tankards were filled and refilled. Their easy intimacy flourished and amusing conversation flowed. By the time a flaming plum pudding arrived, Spray was enjoying himself without reservation.

Afterwards, over-stuffed with food, drink and good humour, the three men sat in wing chairs by the crackling parlour fire. They passed the sherry bottle back and forth whilst Lizzie clattered around in the kitchen. Sam's head spun; he had no idea what was happening to him, but just at present he didn't care.

The sun was working its magic in Shallcross yard. On the southern edge of Whaley Bridge, the horse van, with its matt-black roof, had been warming up all day. Inside, it was like an oven. The groom's door opened and a dishevelled figure peered out. He made an attempt to climb down the rungs of the ladder to the trackside. The yard was deserted; there would be no traffic on Christmas Day. There was no one to see him miss his footing and fall before he reached the ground.

Eddie was so stiff and weak it took him some time to get to his feet. Having almost frozen to death overnight, the sun had brought him back from the brink. In his hypothermic state, he'd stopped feeling anything. Now his aches and pains, ravenous hunger and desperate thirst had returned, seemingly multiplied tenfold. Worse still, the reality of his situation returned. Sober now, he couldn't dodge the need to leave the train and make his way in the real world again.

The sharp, clean air smelled strange after being cooped up with his own slops for two days. He stank of unwashed body and soiled clothing; he was unshaven and his hair jutted out at crazy angles. As he walked, he caught sight of a tramp inside a shop, only to be shocked by the realisation that it was his own reflection in the window glass.

"A Merry Christmas to you, sir!" chirped a passer-by. He hurried on, no doubt grateful to leave the stench behind.

So, it's Christmas Day, thought Eddie, getting his bearings at last. He noticed a pain in his thigh. Slipping a hand in his pocket to investigate, he found a knife he'd forgotten he had. He must have stabbed himself with it as he fell. Even now he shied away from contemplating its original purpose. He used his remaining energy to stagger and stumble downhill towards the town.

Reaching Market Street, he drank eagerly from a drinking fountain erected by the charitable citizens. Assuaging his hunger was his next priority. Despite his tramp-like appearance, he would have to eat, and the only place open was a public house. He dragged his fingers roughly through his tousled hair and tried to make some adjustments to his clothing in a futile attempt at making himself presentable. Then he walked towards a door from which emanated the sounds of laughter, noisy conversation, calls for more beer and all the hubbub created by a busy, convivial tavern. The urge to join in was irresistible; well, almost. As he admired the impressive frontage, his attention was drawn to the sign above the windows: the Jodrell Arms.

Eddie reeled in shock. The Jodrell meant this was Whaley Bridge, and Whaley Bridge meant he was back where he started. But he soon realised that, if this place was a problem, perhaps it was also an opportunity.

They must be at the right house. The door was open and the decorated knocker unusable, even if it could have been heard, which seemed doubtful. Sounds of laughter, jolly piano music and a background hum of conversation spilled onto the street. Above the hubbub, the higher register of children's voices left no one in any doubt: a family party was underway. The late-comers walked in unannounced. Almost immediately, Lizzie was whisked off by a friend and became part of the family. The strains of Barbara Allen poured out of the parlour. The piano was all but drowned out by the lusty singing of a group of women, the elder ones sitting, comfortably ensconced in armchairs, the younger and noisier ones standing around the instrument. Amongst them, Archer caught sight of Maisie, the charming young lady he'd met when they were both walking to Lizzie's.

"Meester Archer! You come! I so pleased! This your friend?" Fred Maida presented Spray and Archer to his wife.

"You must have something to eat!" she insisted.

Neither detective had the heart to refuse, despite the goose and all that had gone with it.

"I make ver good Italiano dish, it called la-sagn-e. Made with pasta, all in layers, and baked. It cold now, so it fredo. I Freddo, ha-ha, but I not cold!"

The food was better than the joke, but no one minded in the infectious party atmosphere.

"I go hot it for you," concluded Fred Maida, and hurried off to the kitchen.

The pianist took a break, and so the singers took a rest, giving Archer a chance to chat with Maisie. Spray used the hush to chat with Fred over a plate of lasagne. Both men had served in the Crimea and soon they were reminiscing about old times, with much being made of Italian bravery at Chernaya and the contribution of railways to the campaign. When the music restarted, and the singing recommenced, Fred went off to attend to his other guests.

Spray stood and wandered through the house. He spotted Lizzie standing in a doorway that led out to the back garden. As he joined her, the backs of their hands touched gently. Showing any sign of what had happened was unthinkable, but each took the brief contact away to treasure later.

Jimmy Allcroft was sure of himself. He was quite definite about what he'd seen. What's more, he knew who to tell about it and where to find him.

"Mister Bobby! I seen 'im! Just now, in't town, yer know, the man yer were lookin' fer on Monday. Come on, yer got ter get 'im!"

Archer was very reluctant to leave Maisie.

"Are you absolutely sure, Jimmy?"

"Course I am, I knows what I saw an' if yer don't 'urry he'll 'ave disappeared agin!"

The two made their way through the crush to find Spray. Jimmy told his story again and the threesome set off for the town. The hunt was on.

The party continued unabated: as Fred was playing a sentimental Italian tune on his accordion, Lizzie started to worry about her father. Waving her goodbyes, she set off for home. Walking briskly up the hill, she was so preoccupied that she paid little attention to an unsteady, decrepit figure across the road. On arriving home, she looked in on the somnolent figure of her father asleep by the fire. The old man hadn't been himself lately, but he seemed peaceful enough now. She quietly closed the door.

Archer had done his best, helping her to clear up earlier, but her kitchen was still a mess. As she set about putting things to rights, a noise in the hallway surprised her.

"William, is that you? You really didn't need to come back, I can…"

An unfamiliar voice croaked her name weakly, "Mrs Oldroyd?"

Hoping to avoid waking her father, she went into the hallway to find herself face to face with Eddie Markham. Such was his dishevelled state that she didn't immediately recognise him, but she knew desperation when she saw it. Lizzie stepped back, and he followed her into the kitchen. In the better light she realised who it was and saw his plight even more clearly.

"Mr Markham, this is a surprise. Do come and sit down." Despite his weakness, Eddie remained standing.

"I need bed for the night and some victuals."

Spray, Archer and young Jimmy were in search of Markham. He'd been outside the Jodrell Arms when Jimmy had seen him, facing along Market Street toward the canal crossing. Archer ran toward the bridge, stumbling in the dark; the moon had yet to rise.

The propriety of taking an eleven-year-old boy on a man-hunt would have to wait till later. Spray and Jimmy crossed the road into Canal Street and down to the wharf yard. Just now, he was the only one who'd seen Markham before, and he knew his way round the town. By the time he'd tripped over the rails twice, all but impaling himself on a points lever the second time, trying to keep up with the lad, Spray came to his senses. Where was the one place a desperate man would go to in an unfamiliar town? Instructing Jimmy to go after Archer and tell him to follow, he set off for Old Mill End.

Out of breath, Spray stood for a few moments listening in the hallway. The voices were indistinct, but he was sure he could distinguish Lizzie's and one other coming from the kitchen. At least they were calm; that was something. Closer now, stepping as lightly as he could, Lizzie came into his view through the doorway, speaking to an apparently empty room. The other person must be out of sight, standing to one side of the entrance. Spray's movement in the shadow caught Lizzie's attention momentarily.

"Who's that?" The voice was weak and filled with fear.

Spray stepped forward.

"It's one of the other guests, Mr Markham, I did say we were full, you know."

He could see Markham now; the man had moved to stand beside Lizzie.

"He's been staying here for some time with another gentleman," Lizzie explained.

Mistakes are made with the best of intentions, and Spray had admired Lizzie's handling of things until she went a step too far.

"Let me introduce you." Spray winced as she said it: "Mr Markham, this is Sergeant Spray."

Weak and frightened he may have been, but adrenaline shot through Markham's body at the word sergeant. Galvanised, he stepped behind Lizzie, pinioning her, and pulling a knife from his pocket, he held it to her throat. To Spray the tableau seemed frozen for an eternity.

Jimmy caught up with Constable Archer in Market Street, on his way back from the canal crossing, and delivered his message. It was busier here, and there was more light. The policeman set off running and despite having to dodge the Christmas revellers, outran the more nimble Jimmy. Like Spray, he was gasping by the time he climbed up to No. 37 and had to stand a moment or two to let his breathing quieten down. There was something wrong; he could sense it. The front door, standing ajar, was part of it, and so was the way the muffled voices from the kitchen stopped so abruptly. Quietly, he edged his way through the hall toward the open door into the kitchen.

Mostly, what he could see was Spray's back, almost filling the doorway. Light glowed through a small window to the side of Spray's head, framed by his shoulder, the door jamb and lintel above. Smack in the middle, like a living portrait, were Lizzie's head and shoulders with a knife to her throat, held by an alien hand.

By the time Archer had made it round the house to the back entrance into the scullery, Lizzie, calm and controlled, was speaking.

"Oh, Mr Markham you've found my knife! Wherever was it? I missed it over a week ago."

The restraining arm round her chest relaxed perceptibly, and the knife sagged slightly. Seeing this, Spray stood immobile, hardly daring to breath. As Archer appeared in the doorway behind the hostage and her assailant, he willed the constable to stand still, too. It was no good; Markham saw the flicker of recognition in his eyes.

"Stay just there, whoever you are." The adrenaline had strengthened Markham's voice and he sounded menacing. He glanced over his shoulder as he forced Lizzie to turn with him, so she stood between him and the newcomer.

Markham realised he could not keep watch on Spray and Archer simultaneously, and that either could jump him at any moment.

"You!" he shouted at Spray. "Get over there with your mate!"

Spray intended to make a lunge for Markham's arm as he passed, but thought better of it. He could not bear Lizzie to be hurt. They'd just have to wait it out. After all, the man could not hold that pose forever. He was both astounded and impressed with Lizzie, who had managed to remain as cool as a cucumber so far and continued in that vein.

"You look all done in, Mr Markham, you really do." She sounded sympathetic. "And on Christmas Day, of all days. And you must be so hungry and thirsty. Why don't all of you gentlemen make yourselves comfortable, and I will brew a pot of tea. Or would some ale suit you better, Mr Markham? My father brought some excellent bottles this morning, and I'll wager you would really enjoy a glass along with a big hunk of bread and some cold roast goose. I've some tasty pickles, too. Now, you sit yourself down and I'll prepare it right away."

It might have been the thought of a draught of ale that did it, or maybe it was the thought of food. It offered the prospect of an end to two days of extreme privation, and Markham gave up. It was as if the adrenaline, which had propelled him into action, could find nothing left to stimulate in a man whose energies were spent. Weak with hunger, parched and physically, mentally and emotionally exhausted, his grip relaxed, the knife clattered harmlessly to the floor, and he sank heavily into a chair like a marionette with its strings cut.

The crisis was over.

Part 3

Chapter 18

Cromford High House, Monday, 27th December, 1875

Stan was a worried man. He'd had no word for over a fortnight. It hadn't been a problem until now. The boss gave him
the order every Sunday evening for the next week, with a
provisional order for the week after. It had rolled on pretty
well for several years. To begin with, it was only one wagon
load a week, but now there'd be at least four – forty tons –
each time. He hadn't heard the news by the time he'd turned
up for his instructions last Sunday week. But he'd realised
something was up, what with the door being open and that
fat sod nosing about. He didn't know why, but the boss had
dropped a word a couple of years ago to steer clear of him.
Not that their paths had crossed until that evening: why the
hell had the door been open?

Next day, of course, it was all over the yard, and he realised
where the poor bugger was. He didn't see the problem at first.
The stuff had rolled in, he sent it on its way, according to the
provisional order from the week before, and everyone was
happy. He hadn't been paid of course, but someone else would
be along with instructions and money, wouldn't they? By the
end of last week it finally dawned: there wasn't anyone else.

To start with, there'd only been the one from Whaley
Bridge, but soon enough his brother started to run things at the
Cromford end, and it had settled into a comfortable routine.
He'd heard the brother had died, but it didn't seem to have
affected things much. Without thinking about it, Stan had
assumed there was a replacement at the other end of the line.

Usually, he didn't see much past his next grind, preferably followed by drink and then sleep. Now he had to start thinking. Just being good at his job in the yard wasn't enough.

He'd expected alcohol to help matters along. It always had on previous occasions when there was a problem. Drink, shouting and, if necessary, fists had done the trick. Not this time though; well, not until Cadd had turned up. In his hazy mind it had seemed so simple: arrange for those two Irishmen to load his boat the next day; no more problem. That was Sunday.

By Monday he realised it hadn't helped: not when he'd seen Cadd and his tribe arrive in the village. With the *Jane* loaded, he was going to want to know where to take his cargo; Stan bloody well didn't know so he made himself scarce. In the process, he caught sight of Tilly Mutton; nice little lass, though he'd never managed so much as lay a hand on her kettledrums. Sex wasn't what preoccupied him this time though: she worked for the Tarps and that gave him an idea.

———

Standing in the well-appointed billiard room of Cromford High House, they looked an ill-assorted pair. Jarvis Tarp, son of money and influence, free of the contamination of a caring mother who might have laced his self-indulgent persona with a modicum of empathy toward his fellow man. Tarp faced Stan Bardell: failed father and husband, drinker, womaniser and artisan. They shared more than met the eye at first glance.

Both were totally without scruple, both would take money wherever it could be found, and each allowed their lust a free reign. Their proclivities, however, were not identical, and their failure to understand that difference was to have consequences for both men.

"This is a considerable intrusion, if I may say so – who the hell are you?" Tarp thought there was no harm in starting with a question, the answer to which was already known.

"Stanley Bardell – sir." He was sobering up fast and the 'sir' seemed like a good idea. "I've come to offer my condolences for Mr Oldroyd's death." It was the best he could think of. "You knew him well I believe?"

There was a pause in which Tarp grunted assent.

"Mr Oldroyd and I had an arrangement, affairs in common you might say, and I wondered if you would be in a position…"

If Bardell had been a more perceptive observer of his fellow man he might have been warned by the glint in Tarp's eye at the word 'affairs'. As it was, he just thought that an afternoon's drinking was having its effect on the other man.

Tarp broke in, speaking with an icy tone, completely missed by Bardell: "We'd better not speak of this here. I'll get my coat and we can step outside."

Chapter 19

Crewe, Tuesday Morning, 28th December, 1875

It was mid-morning in Superintendent Charles Wayland's office, where he and Sergeant Sam Spray sat either side of the desk. It was warm, or rather, warmish. The fire was burning brightly but had to compete with the bitter cold outside. A telegram had arrived late on the previous afternoon warning Wayland of Spray's arrival. The meeting was anticipated with relish on Wayland's part: the arrest of a suspect amounted to 'case closed' in his book.

"The problem is sir – I don't believe he could have done it – not on his own, anyway, and probably not at all."

"Oh?"

"He threatened Mrs Oldroyd – but didn't put up a fight in the end." This would have been enough to serve as an official record but Spray couldn't let it rest there. "Mrs Oldroyd behaved with a cool courage such as I have rarely seen in a man, never mind a woman." He warmed to his subject and had he not been so taken up with it, might have seen a twinkle in Wayland's eye. "Whilst Markham had a knife to her throat, she talked to him calmly and in the end persuaded him to give himself up."

"So you could say, sergeant, that she effected the arrest herself."

Spray looked sharply at his superior; was he having his leg pulled? Before he could reach a conclusion as to this unfamiliar eventuality, the conversation moved on.

"So what did he have to say for himself when you questioned

him?" Wayland prompted.

"He confirmed pretty well all we knew of his movements. He admitted to returning to Mrs Oldroyd's house, asking after Arthur Oldroyd and later speaking to him in the early evening of December 14th."

He ran through Markham's words in his mind: 'I could see 'e weren't straight, so I did a bit of the camp stuff, and gev 'im the old c'mon, an' 'e said 'ed meet me a bit later. Said 'e'd be at the Jodrell, an' I was to wait outside an' watch where 'e went an' foller 'im after a few minutes. I ain't no mandrake, but I can act it up if I need to.'

"We don't have any more sightings to go on."

Wayland was eager to get on with the story. "Well go on man, what did he claim happened next."

"Markham said that whilst he was waiting, a 'wild lookin' cove' came out of the pub, so he stayed put to let him get out of the way. When he got to where Oldroyd had said they should meet, he realised the 'wild lookin' cove' had got there first. 'Standin' over 'im wi' a piano wire in 'is 'and 'e was.' That was his description."

"Do you believe such taradiddle?" Wayland clearly didn't, but there was, none the less, a touch of curiosity in his voice.

"I do, sir. Markham's story – and his behaviour – was convincing. He said the other man was weeping, but as soon as he saw Markham he pulled a gun on him. It seemed to Markham that either running or tackling the man was going to get him shot, so he stayed and did what he was told."

Wayland had to agree with this last point. "I suppose he's right there; if you believe his story."

Spray nodded again. "Markham said the man ordered him to get the body on the back of one of the horses, but he needed a hand so the other man gave a shove. Markham was instructed to cover the body with a blanket and strap it on with a roller. The doctor certainly found horsehairs on the cadaver at the autopsy, sir, confirming the story about the horse."

It may not have been believable, Wayland mused, but it was certainly possible.

Spray continued, "Markham claimed he was forced to lead the horse and its load up the two inclines out of Whaley Bridge and for five miles or so further on. Why that spot he didn't know, but I believe it would be because it's the closest the line gets to Buxton. The murderer must have a good idea of the local geography. In daylight, you can see down into the town from there. I saw just that panorama when I was at the site of the accident."

Wayland steepled his fingers. Encouraged, Spray went on.

"According to Markham, he, the man and the horse with its burden stopped by a line-side hut. Markham was told to undo the roller, take off the blanket, pull the dead man off the horse's back onto the blanket, and drag the body toward the hut."

Spray smiled grimly as he recounted the next bit of Markham's testimony.

"He said, 'it were a ghost, Mr Spray, a gret-big white ghost come out of the shed.' It scared him, and it scared the horse, which reared up, knocked the other man over and bolted. Markham followed. He wanted to take the gun but didn't see where it fell and left it."

The 'ghost', they both agreed, could well have been a barn owl.

"They can certainly look ghostly coming on one at night." Wayland was beginning to waver. "The evidence from the line side and the stables supports the story pretty well, I suppose." He desperately wanted a nice, clear conclusion, but the counter argument was beginning to tell.

"Then there's the autopsy evidence, sir." Spray's initial report had not quite done the findings justice. He realised he would have to bite the bullet if he was to convince the Superintendent. "You see, sir; the doctor said he was in a state of tumescence when he died."

The point was not taken. Wayland looked mystified.

Spray explained, "He had a stand on, you know, a stiffy, a boner; he'd got an erection." Once the barrier was down, Spray didn't know when to stop.

Wayland held up his hand. "Yes – alright, Spray – I understand – you can stop that. But I still don't quite see how it bears on the case." The subject was easier to discuss now.

"He must have been in a state of sexual excitement when he was killed. Now, I can accept that Markham could act it up a bit – he's a conman – but what I heard about him in Blackpool suggested he's a ladies' man through and through. I can't see him getting that far with Oldroyd. He'd have killed him first."

Wayland was getting the idea. "So you're suggesting that the assailant came from that other part of his life."

There was the sound of a high-pitched voice from the outer office: "Telegram for Superintendent Wayland." The call was repeated until the boy was shown into the inner room. "Is there a reply, sir?" The lad was cheeky, or perhaps in a tearing hurry.

"Hold on there. I've not looked at it yet." The message was unfolded and spread out flat.

CORPSE FOUND AT HIGH PEAK JUNCTION STOP PLEASE ADVISE FURTHER ACTION STOP. It was pushed over to Spray.

"I think I'm persuaded; you'd better go and look into it." Wayland wrote out a reply, and the lad went on his way.

Two days earlier, Sergeant Spray had interrogated Markham. The previous night, he and Archer had had to decide what to do with him. After he'd dropped the knife and sunk onto one of Lizzie's kitchen chairs it became clear that he was in a bad way. With little water and even less food for three days, quite apart from a substantial hangover, he needed some restorative care before much could be expected of him. Lizzie took control of the situation, not that she or the others would have put it that way.

"You can take him upstairs and put him in Arthur's room. As long as you keep an eye on him I really don't mind. He can stay there until morning."

At various points during the long night, all three of them were struck by the irony of a murderer being detained in the bed of his victim.

"He's very cold you know." Lizzie knew that better than the other two, having been embraced, albeit forcibly, by him. "He needs warming up, slowly mind, and giving water. When he's back to normal he can have some food." She spoke with authority, but not authoritatively. The two policemen followed her instructions without demur; Markham did what the policemen told him.

He was taken upstairs, and precautionary cuffs attached him to the bed head. A fire was lit and Lizzie's most decrepit blankets draped over him. In these civilised circumstances he looked, and above all, smelt, even worse than he had when he left Shallcross yard. Whilst Markham dozed in unaccustomed comfort, Archer took the first spell watching over him: slumped in a chair, he was having difficulty keeping awake himself. Not that it mattered; the prisoner wouldn't cause trouble for several hours.

Downstairs, Lizzie was attending to the details of chicken broth; well, goose in this case, but her pragmatic approach seemed to be paying off. The remains of the bird had been stripped of any bones it could spare, and they were being boiled on the range. The aroma was enticing, and the broth would serve as breakfast for the arrested man upstairs. Lizzie had great difficulty seeing the bedraggled specimen who had threatened her as a murderer. Certainly, she had allowed herself a slight weakness at the knees in the aftermath of her ordeal, but concern for her father had soon put paid to that.

Isaac Bennett, however, had continued to sleep off his lunch until the disturbance in the kitchen was all over. His concerned daughter had given him a censored version of proceedings, and he had taken himself off home without a care in the world, having had a very happy Christmas day.

Spray relieved Archer half way through the night and giving the fire a good poke, took up guard duty. Arthur Oldroyd had left the room for the last time some ten days before, and Spray looked around with mild curiosity in the flickering firelight. There were few signs of its previous occupant to be seen. Oldroyd had been sufficiently mindful of his sister-in-law's sensibilities to leave the room as he had found it. There was, however, one small embellishment: a picture hanging at the edge of Spray's vision. He got up from his chair and lifted it from the wall to have a closer look.

It was a lithograph of the Crystal Palace. *Why had that irritating bluebottle started buzzing in his brain again*? He sat down with the picture on his lap and tried to think of other things, but the buzzing persisted. The fire was burning low, but as is sometimes the case, it gave a last flare before settling down to a comfortable glow. He turned the picture to the light: in the bottom right-hand corner was what looked like a fraction, 2/4, and the artist's name.

By morning, Markham was more his usual self, both physically and mentally. After wolfing down the broth, he then demanded something more substantial. Lizzie, who had made sure he was looked after properly when he was so weak the night before, wasn't to be pushed around; after all she had a business to run.

"You'll be paying for the night and breakfast then," Lizzie asserted.

Whatever he'd expected from being arrested, he certainly hadn't supposed he would have to pay for the privilege.

"Whad'ye mean? I'm under arrest, quite wrongly, I might say – it's their call." He gestured as best he could, given the cuffs on his wrists, in the direction of the two detectives.

At this point the anger, fear and resentment at her treatment last evening welled up in Lizzie. During the tirade, words such as 'vermin', 'vicious' and 'ungrateful' could be distinguished, along with 'dirty', 'smelly' and 'deceitful'. By the time she'd finished, she felt a lot better. Markham, on the other hand, was subdued. The women he usually dealt with would shut up when he gave them a good slap. This one had spirit.

"I've got money, how much do you want?" The cost was settled and breakfast provided.

Spray and Archer had listened to this performance, fascinated. Not only had a side of Lizzie Oldroyd been revealed that neither had suspected, she also displayed an ability to subdue a criminal by force of personality, without the use of violence, as was the usual way. This impressed them enormously.

———

A room was commandeered at Whaley Bridge Station, and the interrogation commenced.

"Let's start with Jones. We know about your connection with him: what have you got to say about it?"

Markham tried to bluff it out, "I don't know what you're on about. I never met any Jones."

Spray was at his most intimidating. "Stop messing about, Markham. We know you received a letter from him, which you collected from Griffiths' shop. We know you travelled to Cromford from Blackpool, stopping the night at Whaley Bridge. We know you visited Jones; he told us all about it."

This last was untrue, Jones had just about confirmed the visit, but that was all. Markham, however, faced with a detailed rendition of his movements, caved in.

"Alright; I got a letter from Jones sayin' I was to go an' see him – yer know, something to my advantage – with a bit from a newspaper. Well I din't understand it all, but I went anyway. I knew Jones 'cos 'e worked fer my aunt. When the old crone died she left all 'er money to a companion, as long as she looked after the bloody cats. All I got was some useless shares in a railway wot din't pay an' a free travel pass I couldn't use. I din't even get the shares till the cat woman died."

"So when you got to Cromford what did Jones have for you?"

It emerged that Jones had precious little to offer, at least up front. He talked about the LNWR taking over the C&HPR and the profit that would accrue to shareholders if that happened. He also said it wouldn't happen unless something was done about a man who was holding things up. 'Thing is, Markham, we need to do something about him, and I reckon you're just the man.'

"He wanted you to kill Oldroyd?"

"Yes."

"Would you say that in court?"

"Yes." There was a pause, "Will that get me off?"

"No, of course it won't, but if you're believed it might make a difference."

"But I didn't kill him, honest I didn't"

"Alright, if you didn't do it, tell me what happened?"

The story poured out, and wherever he had evidence, Spray had to admit, to himself at least, that it bore out what was being said.

"I were just going ter frighten him, that were all."

"With the knife you threatened to kill Mrs Oldroyd with? I don't believe you. A man like Oldroyd would find some way of protecting himself once you let him go. You only had one chance and that was it. There are just two last questions: why did you run if you're innocent?"

"There was rozzers all over the place. Didn't take too much notice till I heard there'd been jack askin' after me 'at 'arry's place. Then I put two an' two tergether an' scarpered. I knew if you caught up wi' me, you'd reckon I did it even tho' I hadn't."

"Alright, second question: why did you choose to come back to Whaley Bridge?"

"I didn't choose, I got brought. Never thought 'bout getting off when I got on that train. Goods trains ain't like ordinary ones where yer can see where y'are when it stops. Anyway, I was asleep most of the time."

Drunk more like. "So you arrived here by chance?"

"That's about it. I realised it'd stopped fer good, so when I felt better I climbed out. Didn't know where I was ter start with, but there aren't many places wi' a pub called Jodrell; I recognised it then."

"Must have been a shock?"

"S'pose so: but then I knew where ter find a soft touch fer a bed an' some scran."

Spray, who had kept a cool head until now, was overtaken by anger at this casual reference to Lizzie. He was half out of his chair, with fists clenched, before he got control of himself.

Markham cowered, unaware of why he had provoked such a reaction.

"I'm going to take you before a Magistrate, and you're going to be remanded in custody, accused of murder."

Having disposed of Markham in the town gaol – no mean feat on Boxing Day, requiring, as it did, the signature of a Magistrate – the two detectives had caught a train for Buxton. Spray was about to introduce Archer to the delights of The Coachman Inn. He didn't say why or where they were going, but he wanted to check out an idea provoked by the irritating bluebottle from the night before.

As they entered, Spray said, "I want to introduce you to Vera Pidcock. She's Oldroyd's aunt; I told you about her, didn't I? You be nice to her, whilst I slip upstairs and look at a picture."

They found their way to the bar and were bid a happy New Year for their efforts.

"Vera this is a colleague of mine; find him a pint and have something yourself. He'll tell you how things stand." Spray put some money on the bar. "Do you mind if I have one more look at Arthur's room?"

No, she didn't mind, Perce would cope with the customers. So, having poured a pint for Archer and a brandy for herself, she was all ears.

Spray, meanwhile, went round the back of the bar and up the stairs. He didn't need to go further than the landing; what he was after hung on the wall just outside the bedroom door. Yes, there it was: a lithograph of the Crystal Palace. He took it down and stood under the skylight in the bedroom. In the bottom right-hand corner, by the artist's name, was what he was after: 3/4.

When he regained the bar a pint of ale was waiting for him, and Vera insisted on hearing the story again from Spray. No doubt it would be round the district by morning, but that suited him perfectly well. Finally, the bar filled up, and the staff needed two pairs of hands to satisfy the customers. Spray and Archer were able to retire to a quiet corner.

"So tell me, William, what do you think of Markham; did he do it?"

They had not talked on the journey to Buxton, there had been too many passengers for privacy, but here in the corner of a noisy pub no one would overhear.

"He told a good tale in the end." The constable had sat in on the interview. "Trouble is he's an inveterate liar; it's difficult to know what to believe." William obviously had doubts and seemed keen to voice them.

Sam put forward the contrary view. "Well, for the moment, let's just assume he's telling the truth. Let's work on the assumption there was someone else involved. I suppose it's possible he was an associate of Markham. But what if there was a coincidence, and he and the murderer were completely separate? We know Oldroyd was a mandrake; what if the murderer came from that part of his life? There's evidence from the pathologist to support the idea that sex was involved."

William had been told about the pathologist's findings.

"What if Oldroyd and the murderer knew each other and were…" Sam had some difficulty with the notion, "… lovers? It would explain how the assailant could get close enough to put the garrotte round his neck."

William was sceptical and allowed it to show.

"There's something I haven't told you. I only just worked it out," he gestured upwards, "when I went upstairs."

Sam explained that he had come across three lithographs: a limited edition of four, probably quite valuable, three of them in the possession of the victim or people connected to him.

"There's Arthur Oldroyd's here, and one in a room at 37 Old Mill End." He couldn't quite bear to describe it as Lizzie's house; not in this context anyway, "which probably belonged to Albert Oldroyd." He went on to describe, in detail, his visit to Arbuthnot & Stein.

"Should have taken it more seriously at the time, but I just didn't see it. There has to be a connection between the lithograph numbered 1/4, which I saw there, and these other two, numbered 2/4 and 3/4. We know that Oldroyd banked there, and some big wig in the bank is called Tarp. And then there's the other Tarp/Oldroyd connection in Cromford."

Archer wondered where the fourth lithograph was, but held his tongue.

Spray banged on Jones' door until he got an answer. He'd left Archer in Buxton asking discrete questions about Jarvis Tarp, whilst he took himself off to Cromford to try and squeeze more out of the attorney. With Markham in custody, he calculated that Jones would tell him anything that might save his neck. Jones' indignation soon wilted as his situation became clear.

"Markham is claiming that you put him up to murdering Oldroyd. He says Oldroyd was holding up a business deal, and you wanted him out of the way. If this were to come out in court, I can't see how you would avoid being implicated in the murder."

Jones was rattled and began to bluster. The words 'liar' and 'scoundrel' were thrown around, not to mention 'bastard'. Spray let it be known he thought the language most unbecoming of a professional man, particularly if he were innocent. Then he changed tack.

"What can you tell me about Fitzroy Tarp and his son?" Jones was only too happy to talk on this subject; it seemed much safer ground than Markham.

"The old man has been a long time in business, and in the past, very successfully. He seems to be under the influence of his son too much lately."

Spray asked what he meant by that. Jones wished he'd been less forthcoming and made some anodyne observation about the young wanting to run before they could walk.

"I understand Jarvis Tarp is connected with a bank."

Jones felt he was safe with this subject. "Yes, he's a partner. His mother was an Arbuthnot, the Bank bears her family name; it's in Manchester, you know."

Spray was non-committal. "Did young Tarp do anything with himself before he went into the bank?"

Jones said he'd been in the Yeomanry for a while and couldn't resist gossiping.

"He left in a hurry. No one knows why for sure." He dropped his voice confidentially, "I did hear he was found with another man in, how shall we say, unfortunate circumstances."

"You're saying he's a mandrake?"

Jones was happy to confirm the fact, "It's quite widely known," he sniggered.

"Did you know about Oldroyd?" Jones confirmed that he did know about him and his late brother.

"The Oldroyd brothers and Jarvis Tarp knew each other?"

Jones confirmed this was the case. "There's been a rumour

about for many years that Fitzroy Tarp was Arthur Oldroyd's father. It's never been confirmed but…"

"If Jarvis was in the Yeomanry, he must be a horseman; they're a cavalry regiment." Spray was musing rather than asking a question.

"Oh, I don't know about that, I don't think he has much experience with them." It still rankled with Jones that Jarvis had been so high handed about his horse two days ago. He wasn't going to admit this humiliation to himself or Spray. "Jarvis puts on airs, but he doesn't amount to much." This was said with a self-satisfied tone; Jarvis Tarp had been put in his place.

"It would, sir, be of great assistance to the enquiry, if I could prevail on you to go to the barracks of the Derbyshire Yeomanry Cavalry and make some enquiries about a Jarvis Tarp." Spray had tried to explain to his superior the importance of the connection he had uncovered between the two Oldroyd brothers and Tarp. It had been an uphill struggle.

Whilst Spray had a certain diffidence in discussing homo-sexuality, he was in no doubt about its power to induce an emotional attachment. The sharing of tokens, like the numbered lithographs, could be a part of such a relationship.

Wayland would have none of it. In his eyes, the whole thing consisted of a bunch of perverts behaving obscenely and was best ignored. He considered himself to have a dangerously liberal viewpoint. Most of his circle would go for the horse-whip, imprisonment or hanging.

He was, however, finding Spray's carrot irresistible. It was the third time in this investigation he had been asked to participate, and he was getting a taste for it.

"So what do you want to know about Tarp?" He had taken the carrot.

"Well, sir, he seems to have left the Regiment in a hurry, and with his tail between his legs. It must have been quite a disgrace for him, but above all, for the Regiment. I would like to know what he had done, and in particular, if violence and relationships were involved."

It was quite understood between them that Spray, as an ex-sergeant, would cut no ice with the CO of a regiment of cavalry. This was the real reason for Wayland's involvement.

"May I suggest you take Archer with you to Derby, and then send him on to Cromford with whatever information you acquire? It will save time; you can return direct to Crewe and Archer can come straight on to rejoin the investigation."

There was more to this suggestion than one of simple convenience. Archer's enquiring mind might well light on something the older man had missed.

"Very good, Sergeant, if you think it best."

Chapter 20

There was no confusion about the travel arrangements to Derby. Superintendent Wayland travelled first class and Constable Archer third. Quite apart from the distinction in rank, real money was involved. The journey to Derby would be on North Staffordshire metals, first to Stoke, and then to their destination. Their L&NWR passes would not serve, and tickets had to be paid for. They arrived at Derby Midland to discover that Normanton Barracks were some two miles away. A cab was secured, and at this point reason prevailed. The two policemen travelled together at Wayland's expense.

On arrival at the Barracks, they announced who they were, and an enquiry was made for the commanding officer. The corporal on duty at the gate looked as unimpressed as his lowly status permitted. The messenger he'd sent for orders returned, and reluctantly the pair was escorted to the appropriate door.

"Leave this to me, Archer. No doubt he'll talk more freely to a fellow officer."

Not quite what Spray had in mind, but Archer was powerless. The situation did, however, create a problem for Corporal Brabbins who had orders to deliver the party to his CO in person and not let them out of his sight. The two waited outside the CO's door, which through inadvertence, or possibly design, stood ajar.

A cavalry regiment is essentially an offensive outfit: its officers and men are imbued with this single minded approach to the enemy. The engineers have a more measured view of things. Much of their work is defensive; though some considerable time since Wayland's military service, this was essentially his stance. The two men eyed each other with suspicion.

"Now, superintendent, what is it you want?" The tone was even more abrupt than the words.

Wayland's reply was neutral, giving no ground, but offering an honourable truce. "We are engaged in a murder enquiry. It is possible that you may be able to provide some information that would be of assistance in the matter."

There was a harrumph that suggested that this was a most unlikely eventuality.

"I would be grateful for anything you could tell me about a man called Jarvis Tarp, lately an officer of this reg…" Wayland got no further.

"How dare you, sir! You come here interfering in matters that don't concern you. Matters that are properly internal to the regiment, that you have no right know about." There was more in this vein, delivered with increasing choler.

Wayland held his ground, just.

It would be charitable to put the intemperance of this outburst down to matters outside the issue in question. The CO was an acting Lt Colonel, with substantive rank of major. Recent reforms had removed the right to advance through the purchase of commissions. True, the War Office had compensated officers holding such commissions, but only at the standard rate. Of the unofficial premium required to join a cavalry regiment, there had been no mention. So here the man was, out of pocket, dependent on his own limited abilities for further advancement, and faced with the exposure of a regimental scandal whilst he was in temporary command. Wayland was shown the door and an order barked.

"Corporal; these two civilians," the description spoken with particular venom, "are to be seen off the premises in short order. They are to speak to no one whilst in the barracks."

"Sir."

Colourful though some engagements may be – The Charge of the Light Brigade might well be cited as one such – battles are usually won elsewhere, in less glamorous actions. Whilst Wayland and the CO were one side of the slightly open door, Archer and Cpl Brabbins were on the other.

Not all of the extreme language passed through the crack in intelligible form, but the name Tarp was heard clearly. It had an immediate effect on Brabbins. First he spat in a most un-soldierly way, given that he was on guard outside his CO's quarters, then he looked at Archer, knowingly tapped the side of his nose and winked.

The pair of them had stepped smartly away from the door as the two combatants emerged, and as ordered, they set off for the gatehouse. Wayland felt dejected, not that he allowed it to show, quite unaware that he had obtained valuable information. To Archer, the CO's outburst confirmed that Tarp had been an officer at Normanton and had been ejected in circumstances that discredited both him and probably the regiment.

"Sir, with your permission, I'd prefer to walk back to the station. We are in any case going separate ways from there. Would you like me to tell Sergeant Spray of the uproar we have caused here and leave him to make his deductions accordingly?"

Archer was being as tactful as he could, and Wayland felt rather better about himself. If Spray could deduce something from what had happened, perhaps he hadn't failed completely.

"Very good, Archer, as you wish. Good day to you." With that he climbed stiffly into the waiting cab and was gone.

Brabbins and Archer were left standing at the guardhouse with a private.

"Here you, cut along for a piss or a smoke or something, and come back in five minutes." The private who'd been left to guard the barracks in his corporal's absence made himself scarce, grateful for a brief respite. To Archer: "Now see here, constable, I'll tell yer what this Tarp business is all about."

It was a sorry tale and had made the lower ranks very angry. Tarp was a junior officer and generally disliked by the men. He had his favourites amongst them, and it was widely understood he chose them for their sexual preferences. That would have been overlooked if both parties had been willing and discrete. Initially they were, but Tarp got a reputation for sadistic violence, and he had to resort to ordering the men to satisfy his needs. He made the mistake of approaching a trooper who didn't share his tastes. Indeed, this man had quite a reputation with the girls of which he was very proud.

"I din't see this y'understand, but there were a lot o'noise in t'officers' quarters, shoutin' an' swearin' an' that, an' another officer went in. 'E found Tarp wi' 'is britches down an' a stand on, wi' a black eye, an' t'other feller bout ter 'it 'im again."

Archer asked how Brabbins knew the detail if he hadn't been at the scene.

"I'm commin' ter that, don't rush me. Tarp 'ad disappeared by the time I got there. A couple of us were told ter arrest the trooper, put 'im into a cell an' no one were ter speak ter 'im. Well that weren't goin' ter work, were it? 'E told me all about it."

"So you never saw Tarp again? What happened to the trooper?"

This was the part of the story that caused all of the resentment and was leading Brabbins to break ranks and talk to an outsider.

"Well 'e were punished an' given a dishonourable discharge. 'E'd 'ave been flogged, probably to 'is death, which would 'ave been convenient for them," he jerked his thumb in the general direction of the barracks. "But it were 'bolished a few years back so they 'ad 'im in solitary, then got rid. Might 'av 'ad 'is mouth stuffed wi' gold cos' no one's seen 'im since."

So that was it. Jarvis Tarp was a sadistic and predatory sodomite. Jones' story was true. The other sentry returned, and Archer set off for the station.

Spray sat alone in the second class compartment to which his pass entitled him and watched the rugged scenery of the Goyt Valley as it rushed by his window. He was getting to know this journey well: first the Cheshire plain, then Stockport and a change of both train and terrain, then the long haul to Buxton. The engine was working hard, he could hear it chuffing away loudly. The regular beat was occasionally broken with a run of rapid puffs as the wheels slipped, and the driver quickly brought things under control.

Setting out from Crewe, he could have travelled to Stoke and Derby on the Knotty, along with Wayland and Archer, and then north on the MR mainline to Cromford. The journey might have been a bit faster and with only two changes, more convenient. The overriding consideration was money. At least two thirds of his present journey was on the L&NWR, and no expense would accrue to the department. Wayland would not have countenanced any extra cost for budgetary reasons, and Spray had no quarrel with that.

Money was a problem to him, or at least, large quantities of it were. The ethics of money were addressed during his time in the orphanage. It could hardly be otherwise; the place was controlled by people who took the high moral ground on pretty well everything. But it was funded by wealthy bankers and industrialists. Spray had found the accommodation between money and morality as unconvincing as the likelihood of its receiving divine approval. He was happy to take the cheaper route to Cromford.

With the change of station and train at Buxton, he was on the distinctly down-at-heel shuttle to Millers Dale. Not for long though; it was only just over five miles before another change for a much more comfortable ride to Cromford. The MR certainly had the edge. He had watched admiringly as the smart Kirtley 2-4-0 sighed quietly as it drew in. Spray's interest in locomotives was undiminished, despite working cheek by jowl with them.

Finally, Cromford; all this daydreaming was put aside as he turned left out of the station approach and left again into Lea Road. On the way, he made a mental note of the steep access to Cromford High House before reaching the canal crossing into High Peak Junction. He'd been here before, of course, but clandestinely at night. It seemed rather smaller in the daylight. To his surprise, things looked to be proceeding as normal. A little shunting engine was fussing over a line of loaded trucks that looked as if they were destined for the main line running alongside the yard. On another siding, a train of empties was waiting to be hauled, three at a time, up Sheep Pasture Incline and back to the limestone plateau that was the White Peak.

He made his way to the hut where he had secretly examined transhipment records twelve days previously. The door was ajar, and he entered.

"Sergeant Spray, Railway Constabulary." The man inside was sitting at a desk surrounded by piles of paper. To Spray, it looked like utter chaos, but the man had an untroubled air and was welcoming enough to the detective.

"Good day to you. Henry Dobbin, I'm the yard foreman."

"So you must have sent the telegram?"

It was indeed, although Dobbin was a little apprehensive on the subject. "Hope I did the right thing. It's not quite straight-forward. He wasn't exactly in the yard when he was found."

Spray was curious, "I see; where then?"

It turned out that the body was found in one of the narrow boats moored at the wharf. It had been loaded, but for some reason Dobbin didn't know, it was still in the basin. Usually, the craft moved as soon as it had a cargo.

"Come and have a look."

As the two of them picked their way across the yard, a shout from a shunter warned them of a silently coasting wagon, and disaster was averted. At the canal side, there was a more-fevered atmosphere. Boatmen and their families stood around, curious, but also concerned that the investigation might interfere with their livelihoods. One boat, the *Jane*, was at the centre of all the interest. She was fully loaded, with a tarpaulin covering her cargo of limestone. One corner, at the bow, was hanging loose, and Dobbin lifted it to show Spray the reason for his telegram.

"So this is it." Spray clambered aboard and ducked under the canvas.

There wasn't much space between the top of the limestone and the longitudinal ridge that supported the tent-like covering. Grateful to be hidden from the crowd on the wharf, he felt for evidence that the man had died in the same state as Oldroyd. Fumbling around inside the britches of a dead man tested his professional duty to its limit. Having established the man's flaccid state he called out.

"Could we roll the canvas back? I'll need to move about a bit in here."

He was already getting white powder all over his boots. With daylight on the scene he could see the victim more clearly. He didn't recognise him at first, but the cause of death was clear enough. The livid line round his neck was an exact replica of that seen on Oldroyd's corpse.

"Just before we move him, I want a look round."

As he straightened to get off the boat he realised who the man was. It was the head shunter from the yard. He turned to Dobbin. "You realise who it is don't you?" It seemed that a combination of reluctance to get too close, and the gloom under the canvas meant that no one had investigated closely. "It's your head shunter. I don't know his name, but I'm sure that's him and he's been murdered."

There was a mixture of emotions on the faces crowding round. At least it explained why the man had been absent from work since Christmas, but there was also shock that someone they all knew had met a violent end. It had been generally assumed that the dead man had crawled in drunk and frozen to death. No one had thought of murder.

Spray's announcement gave him much greater authority in the matter, and he was able to clear the small crowd away from the canal edge. It seemed to him inconceivable that the man had met his end in the cramped environment of the loaded boat. He must have been dragged into the hold from the bank after he was dead. Spray would have liked to find evidence of this in the muddy surface of the wharf, but when he looked he realised there was scant chance of it now. So many feet had trampled the ground that it was hopeless.

"Whose boat is this?"

A man stepped forward. "I'm Thomas Cadd, skipper and

owner of the *Jane*." The weather beaten, gnarled man in his forties, rather bow legged, but sure on his feet and confident was almost defiant. "She's my boat, so what of it?"

Spray was at his most polite, "Well, Mr Cadd, it would help me unravel this mystery if you could answer a few questions. Do you think we might step aboard, somewhere a bit quieter?"

As he spoke he cast a knowing glance round the group of sightseers. Cadd took the point and shooed the residual members of his family out of the tiny stern cabin. The two men stepped into a waft of warm air. A small stove to the left-hand side was burning well, with a kettle on top singing away tunelessly.

It seemed to Spray that the two of them filled the small space to bursting point. Yet Cadd and his wife – recently ejected into the cold outside with a babe in arms – and goodness knows how many other children lived in these cramped conditions. Everything was spotless: brasswork gleamed, varnished wood-work shone, and elaborate paintwork dazzled. He marvelled at the colourful mugs and plates tidily arranged in a cupboard whose bottom, hinged door was let down to form a table.

Spray wondered if he had made a mistake coming into this space in which he felt such an interloper. Cadd was so much at home that Spray was acutely aware of being at a disadvantage. Too late now; he was invited to sit on the bunk opposite the stove and offered a brew. It was poured from a brightly decorated teapot in which the dark liquid had spent a long time.

"Well, Mr Policeman, what do yer want to know?" Cadd was not a man to be intimidated.

"Could you tell me how long the *Jane* has been at the wharf?"

"We arrived three days ago."

"That would be the twenty-fifth; no day of rest, even on

Christmas Day?" Spray was surprised.

"See here, Mr Policeman, if the *Jane* ain't moving, I'm losing money, and I can't afford that." Cadd started to look worried for the first time. "We shouldn't be here now, by rights, we should be on our way south."

"Where too?

"That's the bloody problem. I don't know." He jerked a thumb in the direction of the bow. "He should be telling us, 'cept he's dead. We get paid at the other end."

The system was for the *Jane* to arrive empty and the Head Shunter, Bardell, to arrange for a load and tell Cadd the destination.

Spray asked how this arrangement had come about as it seemed a bit casual. Cadd told him he'd been at the wharf hoping for a cargo about two years ago. A 'gent' came up to the *Jane* and suggested they met in Cromford at his house.

"Offered me regular cargoes at a pretty good rate. Bardell would arrange loading and the destination. I was to get paid on delivery. That was the only bit that worried me, usually I get paid up front: but I hadn't got much to lose, so I chanced it and it paid off; haven't looked back since."

"Ever been to Walters & Co?" asked Spray.

"Along towards Whatstandwell? Oh aye, I go there regular like."

"Did you ever wonder about this singular arrangement?"

For the first time since they'd met, Cadd looked uneasy. "Well, I thought it must be above board. Bardell was in charge of the yard movements, and the gent was free and easy there as well."

Spray asked if he knew the 'gent's' name. At this, Cadd had to admit he didn't, but he knew Bardell, so it had to be alright. Spray left the subject; Cadd was guilty of carelessness, certainly, but with both Oldroyd and Bardell dead it was unlikely he could be charged with anything.

"When did you last see Bardell?"

"We got here pretty late on Saturday, and the yard was empty, so I didn't go looking for him till the next day. I got a dusty reception at his home, I can tell you. His woman started shouting and carrying on as soon as I mentioned his name. Seems he hadn't been home that night. In between the shouting, crying and swearing it seemed he was either drunk or with a trollop or both and it wasn't the first time either."

"What happened then?" Cadd said he knew the pubs where Bardell drank so he went round asking for him and finally tracked him down.

"He were the worse for wear, that's fer sure: I don't think he were looking forward to going home so he agreed to round up a couple of men who'd load us up and I came back here. We were loaded by the end of Monday, but I didn't see Bardell again and he hadn't told me who the load was for."

Cadd had gone off with his family to Cromford at the end of Monday to find Bardell. Mrs Cadd insisted she needed a few hours away from the boat over Christmas so they all walked along the towpath to the village in the fading light. A comfortable seat in the corner of a warm bar was found for mother and baby whilst the older kids ran about the village with a bottle of ginger beer each. Meanwhile Cadd searched for Bardell. He wasn't to be found in any of his usual haunts so Cadd braved Bardell's home again. This time his reception was more subdued.

"He never stays out this long, I ain't seen him since you were here yesterday," the woman had told him.

Cadd was able to reassure her to the extent that he had seen him on his way home on Sunday evening. He had, though, delayed him with the request for labourers to load the boat.

"I didn't get many thanks for that, I can tell you, Mr Policeman. She seemed to think I'd done away with him."

"Well, did you?" The question was more a matter of form on Spray's part rather than an accusation. Cadd had a convincing answer.

"Don't be a bloody fool, I needed Bardell ter tell me where ter take my cargo. If I'd murdered him, it'd be after he'd told me, and I wouldn't be here now wasting time when I could be earning."

Spray had to agree and the matter was dropped. He moved on, "Do you know who the two labourers were or where I could find them?"

Cadd said they were Irish and did casual labouring when the yard was busy. 'Not regulars like', but they were often employed to load the boats because the skippers were always in a hurry to get off.

"They're called Paddy and Michael," Cadd explained, "don't know their surnames, but you'll find them drinking in the village in any pub that'll have them. They cause plenty of trouble when they've had a skinful."

Spray asked if Cadd thought them capable of murdering Bardell. The answer was yes, but only by accident, when they'd had too much drink. And it would have been a smashed head with blood everywhere and the body left where it had fallen.

"Nice enough lads really, wouldn't hurt a fly when they're sober: the kids love 'em."

Henry Dobbin felt he'd been abandoned by the detective and had gone back to his office, if not in a huff then in a quandary about what to do with the body. He'd sent for help to settle the matter, and when it arrived it had disappeared into the bowels of the *Jane*. The crowd of gawpers had wandered off when he and Spray had replaced the tarpaulin, and things were slowly returning to normal. Loaded wagons were descending Sheep Pasture Incline as empty ones ascended, and it dawned on him that he was in dire need of a head shunter to control movements in the yard.

How on earth did that detective know what the dead man's job was? Even more mysterious: if he knew what he was, why didn't he know Bardell's name? These thoughts began to trouble Dobbin. In particular, he realised how much latitude he'd given Bardell. He'd have to be more careful with his replacement, keep a closer eye on him and that sort of thing. More work! He was getting too old for all this.

What if Bardell had been up to something, and that was why he was killed? If that was the case, Dobbin couldn't decide whether it was better to know or not. Being next in line for the garrotte, or not knowing and having this nosey detective show how inept he'd been seemed like a no-win situation.

Spray knocked politely and re-entered the office. He'd established roughly when the Cadd family had returned to the *Jane* on Monday. It wasn't until Tuesday morning, after a windy night, that Cadd noticed the flapping tarpaulin at the bow of the boat. When he investigated, he'd seen that it had been badly lashed and initially blamed one of the Irishmen. As he went to redo the lashing, the wind, still unabated, tore the canvas from his grasp, and as it flew up, he'd seen the corpse.

"Sorry about that; thought I'd better strike whilst the iron's hot with the skipper. There was no knowing when he'd be off." Spray apologised with an explanation.

Dobbin was somewhat reassured by the sergeant's reasonable tone. "So, what do we do about the corpse?" He was anxious to see the back of such a disagreeable item.

"The coroner in Matlock should be informed; he'll tell

you where the body should be taken. They usually use a local undertaker. Then he'll arrange an autopsy, and after that, an inquest." Spray was reminded at this point that he'd heard nothing about the inquest into Oldroyd's death. He'd have to chase up the matter in Buxton as soon as he could.

"You mean, I've got to do this?"

Spray explained that, strictly speaking, Cadd should go as he had found the body, but he didn't see him being keen, and it would be best if Dobbin reported the death.

"Before you do that, perhaps we could talk? I need to know something about the dead man." Spray wasn't quite finished.

Bardell, it seems, had worked in the High Peak Junction yard, man and boy; longer, in fact, than Dobbin who had arrived as a promotion in mid-career. At this time, Bardell was junior shunter, but Dobbin promoted him as the result of a retirement. He was competent and reliable at work, and Dobbin admitted to depending on him for the smooth running of the yard.

"I hardly ever have to go out there – he's usually got everything under control." Dobbin said.

"What about paperwork?"

This was a joint effort. Bardell kept a day book, and Dobbin, with a clerk, used it to make a permanent record of freight passing through and then raised bills to customers.

"So, you were entirely dependent on Bardell's record for knowledge of what passed through the yard?"

Dobbin looked uncomfortable at this. He claimed that he made regular inspections.

Spray pressed, "I thought you said that you hardly ever go out into the yard."

At this, he admitted that he had left the shunter to his own devices for several years.

"You see, Mr Dobbin, I started investigating a fraud some

time before either Oldroyd's or Bardell's deaths. It turns out that both dead men were involved in passing freight out of the quarries and through the yard without a record being made of the movement."

Dobbin looked pale and shocked. "You don't think I'm involved?" For the moment he was referring to the fraud. It took him a moment or two to see that such an accusation, if made about the fraud, would be equally valid in respect of the murders.

"At the moment, Mr Dobbin, I have an open mind on the matter."

All this observation did was to leave a black cloud over Dobbin. Spray realised that news of Markham's arrest had not reached Cromford and could see no reason to enlighten the man. He was unlikely to have been involved in either crime, but at the very least, he had been lazy and careless and caused his employers a considerable loss of revenue.

"When did you last see Bardell?"

"He didn't come in to work on Monday, most unlike him, but he must have set the two Irishmen on. It would be at the end of the twenty-fourth. The whole line closed over Christmas and Boxing Day. I can't remember the exact time, but he worked the day and went home with the rest of the men about six o'clock."

"Ah yes, home. What do you know of his home life?"

Dobbin, relieved that the questioning had moved on, told Spray that when he first knew him, Bardell was married and had children, but he couldn't remember how many. Later, Bardell was on his own, and without the children, so he'd assumed that his wife had found a more congenial partner.

"He always had a reputation for drinking and womanising, and a he was free with his fists; but he always turned up to

227

work on time and got the job done. Looked a bit the worse for wear sometimes."

"Tell me about the two labourers who loaded the *Jane*?"

Dobbin would have talked all day on the subject. If he could enhance their reputation as layabouts and drunkards, he felt that suspicion might move in their direction.

"A couple of shirksters and lushes, handy with their fists, live in a tent in the woodland along the river. No one goes there; they're not keen on visitors. No knowing what they get up to." Having done his best to blacken them, he finally produced their names: Paddy Regan and Michael Byrne. "Don't know why Bardell used them so much."

Spray couldn't resist a dig at Dobbin's inefficiency. "You were the gaffer: if you didn't like it, you could have got out there and stopped it."

Dobbin fell silent. The real reason for their employment had been their hard work, availability and low rates.

With nothing more to learn in the yard, Spray bid Dobbin good day, leaving him to contact the coroner and sort out the mounting chaos in the yard.

William Archer arrived at Cromford Station by late afternoon. Following Sam's instructions, he had no problem in finding the Bell Inn or Al Croker behind the bar.

"No, I ain't seen the sergeant, but I'm expecting to. Heard there's a body along at the junction: been done in by all accounts."

William explained that he was to meet his sergeant at the Bell and had just ordered a pint when Spray walked in. He looked, with some asperity, on the ale, and more particularly its recipient, but settled finally for one of his own. They had to compare notes after all. After passing as little information across the bar as possible, commensurate with civility, the two settled in a quiet corner and took stock.

When William had nearly finished, he found himself addressing the matter of how the Superintendent had fared. "You could say he conducted a very effective diversionary engagement, allowing a successful conclusion elsewhere on the field of battle."

Sam saw immediately where he was coming from. He had no wish to see Wayland humiliated. "Don't you fret, by the time this is finished he'll be happy enough. You managed alright though."

This was high praise from someone usually so reticent.

Sam concluded, "So, you've established that Jarvis Tarp is a homosexual who was discharged ignominiously from the army with a record of violent sexual assault. He could well have retained a firearm and be confident with horses. It was a cavalry outfit after all."

Sam recounted his discoveries. In particular, he established that the time of death, or more precisely, the time of embarkation of the corpse onto the *Jane*, to be Monday evening, after loading was complete, and before the Cadd family returned later on.

"Of course, he could have been killed earlier and hidden until the coast was clear. That's the next thing to sort out. We'd better find the two Irishmen and ask around for a last sighting."

In their search for Paddy and Michael, the two detectives should have started with the most disreputable drinking dens in the village. As it was, they made enquiries of Croker and started at the most respectable. They drew a blank at the Greyhound, the Boat and several others from which the two Irishmen had been banned. Finally, they ended up at an unnamed establishment; no more than the one time parlour of a terraced house.

They were both unhappy men and surprisingly sober. The drinking den gave no credit and they had little money.

"That bugger Bardell – disappeared he has – owing us for a day's work. And after we took him in when he was in drink." They glowered across the table, feeding each other's indignation.

"How about if we buy you each a drink. Perhaps we could have a little chat?" Spray had introduced himself and Archer, only to evince the sort of universal suspicion that lay between hard drinking Irishmen and officers of the law. This offer threw up a conflict of interest for Paddy and Michael. It was soon resolved.

"That's mighty kind of you sor. Wid a bit of something to whet the whistle we'd have some craic wid anyone."

The first pints disappeared in an instant, and there was a certain disagreement as to whether the conversation would start before or after the pots were replenished. The matter was decided in the end by those with the money – a fill up was promised after the chat.

"We're looking to find out where Stan Bardell got to yesterday?"

"Ah well, sor, that's something we'd like to know too. He owes us money, y'see."

"But you loaded the *Jane* on his instruction, didn't you?"

Paddy agreed that they had done just that, but the arrangement had been made the evening before. They had then got down to some serious drinking with Stan.

"He didn't want to go home, y'see. His woman was going to play up cos he hadn't been home the night before. They get in the way of serious drinking do women – that they do. You're better off wid out them. I told him – but I think he'd got past hearing me."

After that they had taken pity on him and half carried him back to their hideout in the woods to sleep it off.

"He don't carry his ale too good, y'know, so we left him sleeping in the morning. Michael and I went off to load the *Jane*."

The men had returned in the late afternoon expecting to find Bardell and get their wages for the day's labour, but he'd gone. They went looking for him, but all they found was Cadd on the same quest.

"So the last time you saw him was Monday morning?"

Paddy agreed that it was.

"You see, my problem is, Stanley Bardell was found dead aboard the *Jane* this morning – lying on a pile of limestone that you have just admitted to loading yesterday. The two of you could have just popped him under the tarpaulin when you'd finished and lashed the cover down. Next stop – who knows where?"

The two Irishmen were flabbergasted. They were quite sure the last time they had seen Bardell was early Monday morning sleeping off a hangover. They had been away from Cromford early in the day, looking at a labouring job in Wirksworth and knew nothing of the goings on at High Peak Junction. The issue of who was to pay them for Monday's work soon surfaced.

"We wouldn't have wanted him dead – not before he'd paid us anyway. Might have knocked him about a bit till he did, I suppose." This time it was Michael who spoke. "We wouldn't have killed him – he keeps us in work through the winter."

Despite his suggestion to the contrary, Spray was convinced of their innocence, at least so far as Bardell's death was concerned. He had to agree with Cadd's assessment. They wouldn't have had the guile.

With the promised second pints paid for, 'thank you very much, sor, you're a real gent, sor, anything else we can help wid, sor,' Spray and Archer found their way back to the more salubrious end of Cromford and as they walked they talked.

The pair of Irishmen were discounted out of hand, as were Cadd and Dobbin. They had to talk to Jarvis Tarp. The numbered lithographs, his violence and his sexual preferences put him in the frame. This last issue had its problems. Whilst it seemed pretty clear that Tarp and Oldroyd were well matched, Bardell had emerged as a womaniser with no hint of any other proclivity. Could it just be that business, not pleasure, was what bound the three together? Either way, Tarp had to be found, so the detectives set off for Cromford High House.

Chapter 21

Cromford High House and Cromford Station, Tuesday Evening, 28th December, 1875

The search for Jarvis Tarp did not turn out as hoped. Before Spray and Archer had got to their destination, they knew their quest was doomed. They walked along Mill Road and turned into Lea Road; Spray was aiming for the steep path down the valley side from the house. As they passed the end of Willersley Lane, a figure appeared out of the gloom. It was hurrying towards the village. At the sight of the two men, it crossed the road and was clearly hoping to pass unnoticed. In this endeavour, she was unsuccessful.

"Tilly; Tilly Mutton, it's Sergeant Spray. You remember me; we talked a week ago about Mr Oldroyd."

Tilly did remember and surprisingly, given their previous abrupt parting, sounded relieved to see him.

"Oh sergeant, I'm so pleased to see you. When I heard this afternoon I felt so embarrassed. You must have thought me very rude last Tuesday, but I really didn't know what to say. I mean, when you're in service you're not supposed to gossip and I don't…"

Spray cut in with a kindly intervention. "Tilly, my dear, you behaved quite properly, and I admired your reticence. Why don't we start again, and I'll introduce my colleague, Constable Archer."

Up to that point, Tilly's attention had been on Spray. Once it was drawn to Archer she instantly liked what she saw. The little curtsy would have been more appropriate when aimed at a guest at the big house, but it served its purpose in stimulating William's interest, and their eyes met.

Spray cut in, curtly, "Now, Tilly, first things first, what have you heard?"

Whilst his sergeant was sensible of Archer's glance having restored Tilly's equanimity, it had gone quite far enough.

"About the murder at the yard – and how the body was found in a canal boat – and how…" At this point the headlong rush faltered, "… It had come about." Tilly wasn't quite up to discussing strangulation with a garrotte.

"So, what do you want to tell us?" Spray was at his most benevolent.

"It's the man – the man who was murdered – Mr Bardell – I saw him. He was at the house with Mr Tarp."

"Would that be Mr Fitzroy or Mr Jarvis?"

"Not Mr Fitzroy – he'd gone up to his room by then. He gets very tired and has to go to bed early; he's nearly eighty, you know – I take his cocoa up to him and…"

Spray cut in: benevolence was all very well, but he needed to keep Tilly on track. "Did Mr Jarvis bring Mr Bardell to the house or…?"

"Oh no – I saw him when I was going home for my tea – like now. He asked if the 'young Mr Tarp' was at home. I said he was, and he asked me to go back to the house and show him in ''cos I got'…" Tilly wavered ,trying to summon up the wording, "'a bit o' business he might be interested in'. That was it, that's how he put it." Tilly was sure on the point.

Spray asked her to go through it again, and the same wording was repeated.

"So you showed Bardell in – into where exactly?"

The nearest way in was the garden doors through to the billiard room. Tilly had last seen Tarp in there and she had taken Bardell in that way.

"So when you left, the two of them were in the billiard room, and no one else in the house had seen Bardell enter?"

Tilly agreed and explained that the only other people in the house were, "Mr Fitzroy, upstairs in his room; old Addie, who had a room over the kitchens; and the outside man, who lives over the stables."

"Did you go back that evening?"

"Oh yes, sir. I'm not supposed to, but Addie's usually a bit unsteady by then, and I wouldn't like to see her in trouble, so I go back and do round a bit."

Spray admired her tact. He presumed Addie would have been drunk, but Tilly wasn't letting on.

"What about locking up?"

"Mr Jarvis does it if he's at home – if he's away, the outside man does it. He goes round and then lets himself out through the back door and locks it with his own key."

Spray enquired after last night.

"Oh, Mr Jarvis didn't do it. I saw him leaving when I came back. In a tearing hurry, he was, with a Gladstone in his hand." Tilly told how she was just at the point where the path met the garden and saw Jarvis Tarp emerge from the billiard room. "I could see he was very agitated when he got a bit nearer – he frightened me really, so I kept in the shadows, and he didn't see me."

Just as well. "Can you say what time this was, Tilly?"

She explained that she only reckoned to spend half an hour saving Addie's bacon. She always got the time from the grand-father clock in the hall before she started.

"It was half past nine when I arrived. There was a right mess in the billiard room, I can tell you."

Both detectives imagined they were to hear about the debris

to be found after a struggle: broken glasses and furniture, blood stains on the carpet and such like. Not a bit of it.

"It was the floor, covered in muck, well, white stuff mostly, mixed with mud. Footprints through the house to the bottom of the stairs. Well, up the stairs as well, but I don't go up there at that time in the evening. It was still there in the morning when I took Mr Fitzroy his breakfast."

Spray asked whether everything had been locked up after she finally left, and about the unlocking of doors in the morning.

"I don't know for sure. Addie always has the scullery door open by the time I arrive, so I don't have anything to do with it. She did say the outside man hadn't done his job last night – I think she meant that the locking up hadn't been done right."

Archer had become increasingly curious about Tilly's way of talking of the 'outside man'.

"This outside man, has he a name?"

Tilly became a bit flustered, "Sid – Cedric really – Sid Mutton." This last was muttered as Tilly turned her head away; clearly an uncomfortable subject. She gathered herself up and turned back to her questioner. "He's my Pa's cousin, and he's no gentleman." Archer regretted asking: the answer added nothing to their investigation and he wouldn't be getting any more curtsies.

Spray rescued him with another question, "Has the mess been cleaned up?"

Addie and Tilly had swept it up and dumped it in a bin outside the scullery door earlier in the day.

"I could show you if you like, come on."

It seemed that Archer's intrusion was forgiven, and Tilly was doing her best to help.

The little party climbed the steep path to High House garden and then round the back to the scullery door. There was an almost full moon. Archer was detailed to investigate the bin and resurfaced with a handful of muddy mess. On closer examination, it turned out to be mostly soil, laced with white granules and powder, which had to be limestone.

"Do you think Addie would be…" Spray was just about to say 'sober', but in deference to the proprieties by which Tilly lived, it came out as, "steady enough to talk to me just now?"

Tilly was sure it would be alright 'as long as she's sitting down'.

"Right then – this is what we're going to do. You're going to take me to Addie, and then Constable Archer is going to accompany you to your home. You are not to come to work until I say it's alright…"

Tilly cut in, "But sir, I've got to…"

"No buts, Tilly. You stay at home and only go out with your pa or big brothers, if you've got any."

She was slowly coming to the realisation that Spray was in earnest.

"You mean," it took a moment to frame her reply, "you mean you think he did it, and I saw him, and…" she came to a stop, unable to voice the unthinkable.

"Now come along, if you do as I say there's no danger." This was said with rather more confidence than was felt. "Show me to Addie and then off home. William, when you've done that, I want you to go to the station and get the departure times and destinations for any trains leaving Cromford after half past nine of a Monday. And ask the ticket clerk, or whoever was around last night, if they saw Jarvis Tarp and which train he caught."

Addie admitted Spray to her little sitting room. He and Tilly had climbed the narrow stairs, and she had persuaded the old woman to let this strange man in. She told Addie he was a detective investigating Mr Bardell's death and promised her he was 'safe'. Spray was guarded to begin with. It was obvious to him that the beady eyes opposite would ferret out any insincerity. She was seventy if she was a day, but spry and sharp. Her lined face and sunken cheeks belied the lively mind and alert manner.

"Now see here, young man, what is it you be wantin'? I ain't no gossip y'know, I wouldn't 'ave lasted long here if I was."

Spray tried to tread carefully, but it wasn't easy when telling an old retainer that the son of the family, known to her, man and boy, was suspected of murder.

He needn't have worried, Addie's response was surprisingly matter of fact: "So it's come to that at last, has it? Something of the sort was bound to happen: surprising it's took so long, really."

Spray asked what she meant.

"He was always a wayward child. Killed his mother at his birth, he did. Well, to be fair, I don't suppose he could help that. But it was downhill from there on. He got his teeth early and gnawed the tit something awful. I should know; I wet nursed him. As a child, he liked nothing better than destroying things, particularly if they were living. He never loved anything 'cept himself. Mind you, he could be charming if there was owt in it for him. Get anyone to do anything he wanted if he set his mind to it. But he never understood the pain he caused: or perhaps he did and enjoyed doing it anyway." Addie paused for breath. A lifetime of discretion had suddenly burst open; the relief of justifiable revelation was palpable.

Spray took advantage of the pause. "Can you remember any times when he was violent – perhaps injured someone – even killed and got away with it?"

Addie told him that he'd been at 'some school for toffs the other side of Derby'. She couldn't remember its name, but thought it might have begun with R.

"Got sent home from there and never went back. Not sure what for, but I don't think he killed anybody. Then there was the army. Mr Fitzroy thought that would be the making of him – heard him say so; but it weren't no good. He were home inside two year, under a cloud. He didn't seem one whit abashed though – just carried on as normal. Even brought a gun back – keeps it in his bedroom, he does. Then he went to the bank. I ain't heard anything since then."

Spray asked about his relationship with Arthur Oldroyd: were they friends? If so, for how long? That sort of thing…

"Now that's the funny thing. Those two always got on – Mr Oldroyd was a deal older, but he was the only friend that lasted any time. Mind you, they had arguments. Very possessive was Mr Jarvis – if he thought something was his, you didn't go near. Like that about Mr Oldroyd, he was. Not sure about the younger Mr Oldroyd. They certainly knew each other, saw them together a time or two – not like Mr Arthur though. The younger one died you know." Addie was beginning to dry up: whether through tiredness or lack of anything to say, it wasn't quite clear.

Suddenly, she was alert and leaning forward again. "Here, you don't think he did for Mr Arthur as well, do you?"

Spray had to admit that it was a possibility. Again, Addie's reaction took him by surprise.

"That makes sense. I can't quite see him killing Stan Bardell; not his sort at all. But Mr Arthur – yes – I can see that. Mr Arthur was his, you see – and if he looked like he was going off somewhere else… Yes, I can see that." Addie sank back in her chair and she suddenly looked spent. The interview was nearly over.

"One last question. This morning, when you went round to open up, were the doors locked as usual?"

No, they hadn't been, and initially Addie had blamed the outside man. But when she realised Mr Jarvis had left last evening, she thought he'd forgotten to tell him. So it must have been Mr Jarvis' fault.

By now Addie's eyes were drooping, and she was nearly asleep. Spray thought perhaps he had done her an injustice over the evening drinking. She was just old and tired. He bade her good evening and left.

———

Constable William Archer was a happy man. He'd just been offered twenty minutes' dalliance with an eligible young woman, on the Company's time, and with the approval of his senior officer. As Tilly came downstairs he constructed his opening gambit.

"I'm sorry if I upset you about the 'outside man'. I didn't mean to make you uncomfortable."

Tilly, finding herself alone in the company of a nice young man, wasn't going to waste an opportunity by holding a grudge.

"Oh, that's alright. It's just embarrassing that he's so rough and dirty and a member of my family; with us working at the same house, you see."

Archer wasn't sure he'd had the whole story, but let it rest. They were heading across the lawn for the point where the path from Lea Road emerged from its long climb up the valley side.

"Where were you when Mr Jarvis left last night?"

Tilly explained she was a few paces from the top of the path when she saw Tarp. It was a moonlit night but windy with clouds scudding across the sky, so that the light would suddenly disappear without warning.

"I just stepped off the path into the wood when I saw him and waited. It was lucky, really, the light disappeared just as I stepped aside, so I wouldn't have been seen anyway."

Archer was struck by the way she phrased her last observation. "What happened then?"

Nothing happened, and it had puzzled Tilly. She had expected to hear him on the path, hoping he'd pass without noticing her, but she heard nothing.

"I stood there for a few seconds, waiting, but when the cloud moved away from the moon, and I could see again, there was no one there."

Archer went over the story again with her, but she was quite certain: she had seen Tarp, he was hurrying toward the path carrying a Gladstone bag, and he looked wild and flustered. Tilly had hidden for a short while to the side of the path, at the same time as it had gone suddenly very dark. She expected him to pass by, but he'd disappeared in the space of thirty seconds or so. She was sure she would have heard him if he'd passed her. It was too far for him to have gone back to the house, or even round it to reach the front gate, in the time the moon was obscured. He had just disappeared.

The two descended the steep valley side and emerged onto the road below. Conversation was difficult when they were in single file, and Archer used the silence to consider what he might say when they arrived at Tilly's home. It would be difficult to explain why Tilly needed protection without alarming her family, perhaps provoking a violent response. He comforted himself with the thought that one possible victim of such a reaction was dead, and the other had disappeared.

The two chatted as they walked, side by side, toward the village. What they discussed was of intense interest to them, but of no consequence to anyone else. By the time they reached Tilly's home, Archer was prepared.

"Pa – Pa this is William," they had progressed to first names during the walk, "William Archer – he's a policeman."

Tilly's Pa was a middle-aged man of medium height and amiable countenance who obviously doted on his daughter. He found her arrival in the company of the detective rather disturbing and started fussing over her. She directed him toward Archer with a seriousness that was not lost on the older man.

"Very well, young man, you'd better explain yourself."

First Archer told Mr Mutton who he was, and that he and his sergeant were investigating the murder of Stan Bardell.

"Oh him." This was said in a disapproving tone, leaving no room for doubt as to his opinion of the murdered man. "Yes, I heard about that. It's all over the village, but I don't see what our Tilly can have to do with it."

Archer told him how it was likely that Tilly had been the last person to see Bardell alive, with a man who was possibly implicated in the murder. "You see – Mr Mutton – if our suspicions are correct, it's possible that he sees her as a danger to himself and might wish her harm."

The usually mild-mannered Herbert Mutton took on a belligerent air. "He'd better not try. I'd soon see to him."

Tilly tried to calm him down, with little success: "Don't be like that, Pa, I'm safe enough here. William says I'm to stay at home until it's all over."

"And what are the Tarps going to say to that? I got you that job there – my name'll be mud."

Archer broke in, "There are more important things to worry about than that, sir. I'm afraid the man…" Archer had some difficulty framing the next bit, "we, er, want to question is Mr Jarvis Tarp."

"You mean he did it?" Pa Mutton's face was a battleground of conflicting emotions.

Herbie Mutton was a builder, like his father before him, and the two generations of accumulated skill had rendered him a genuine all-round craftsman. His cousin Sid was no more than a handyman, and whenever anything was beyond him, he called in Herbie. As a consequence, Herbie was held in high esteem at the High House. Between him and Mr Fitzroy, there had grown a relationship more akin to friendship than master and artisan. Not that either man would have seen it that way: it was, and always would be, 'Mutton and Mr Fitzroy'. Over the years, there had been one small advance: Mr Tarp had transformed into Mr Fitzroy. Even this small change, though, was more to do with the need to distinguish between father and son.

Jarvis Tarp had never been part of this relationship, but Herbie Mutton had always afforded him sufficient deference to keep the peace between them. Now the whole thing was blowing up in his face, and he wavered between anger at any threat to Tilly, and his long-standing allegiance to the Tarp family. Of course, Tilly won out, and there was an explosion of anger at Jarvis Tarp and the rest of his family. During the tirade, two reassuringly large young men came in. Archer was relieved to see that Tilly would not lack protection if required. By the time he was able to break in, the two brothers were in no doubt as to where their duty lay.

"At this time, Jarvis Tarp is only being sought for questioning. It is possible that he has a firearm and a garrotte though."

Archer felt he had just stayed on the right side of impartiality whilst leaving no doubt about Tilly's position.

———•••••———

It was more or less an afterthought that took Spray round the back of the house to the stable yard and Sid Mutton's little cottage. Curiosity about the odd way he was described by the two women clinched the matter. The door was opened, reluctantly, by an unkempt and truculent individual in a collarless shirt, once white but now grey, a greasy waistcoat of indeterminate colour and kecks to match.

"Yes? Whad'ye want? Can't a body get some kip? It's bloody late y'know?"

Spray explained who he was and what he was about. "Would you mind if I came in? I think you might be able to help me."

"S'pose so. You ain't told me anything I don't know yet. I heard Stan were dead. Hadn't seen him in a long while though. We used to go drinking till he started up wi' all them women. Don't 'old wi' women. Can't see what they're for. Nothin but trouble, if y'ask me."

Spray began to see how 'the outside man' had got his name.

"I gather there was a misunderstanding about locking up last night?"

"Weren't no misunderstandin'. I do it when I'm told; an' I weren't told, so it were 'is fault."

"His?"

"Bloody Mr Jarvis. He usually does it. I gather he's buggered off – so they women were saying anyway."

"I think Bardell was here at the High House just before he was murdered and that Jarvis Tarp's departure is connected."

"Oh, you do – d'ye. You think he did it then? Well, I'm

244

not surprised. Something like this was going to happen one day. Can't see Stan Bardell as the victim though. I mean, what would Mr Jarvis want wi' him?"

Spray was struck by the similarity between this observation and Addie's.

"That Jarvis always was a bad'un. Right from a kid he were trouble. He'd get up in the hayloft and sit quiet for a bit, then use a catapult to upset the 'osses. One thrashed about so much it broke a leg an' had to be put down. Very pleased wi' himself about that 'e were. Never got punished neither."

Sid thought for a bit, then continued, "Later on, he used to go down to the railway and throw stones at the trains. He never got punished for that neither – not even when he nearly killed a man on the footplate. Little bugger got up the bank over th' entrance to the tunnel and dropped half a brick into the cab of an engine travelling tender first. Knocked the fireman unconscious, he did. Then he came off the bank onto the up platform and into the woods behind. Knew the woods better 'an me. Back here before the train had stopped, I reckon."

Spray asked when Sid had last seen Jarvis Tarp, but it had been earlier than Tilly's sighting and didn't move things on one bit. It was time to go.

"Bid you goodnight, sir. My apologies for disturbing you."

Sam got a grunt in reply, and the door closed noisily on his heels.

Cromford Station nestles into a niche carved from the valley side. Its connection to the village is via a steeply rising access road, and then through the booking hall to the down platform. The up platform is reached by a footway across the tracks at the north end, used by passengers travelling south. Virtually all station business is conducted from the buildings on the down side. It was here that Archer started his enquiries.

There were only two men on duty at nine o'clock of a winter's Tuesday evening. In the absence of anything better to do, they were huddling over a fire in the booking office. Archer put his head through the ticket window.

"Anyone at home?"

There was a scraping of chair legs to be heard followed shortly by the appearance of a surprised-looking clerk. There were only two more stopping trains expected that night, and they weren't due for over half an hour.

"Can I help, sir?"

Archer explained who he was and stated his business.

"You'd better come through – you'll be reet nesh out there."

Although the invitation was motivated by the clerk's wish to get back to the fire, Archer was grateful none the less.

"I'm interested in any passengers who might have caught trains yesterday evening after – say – nine o'clock?" Archer was direct.

"Well, there's only two – two stoppers anyway – the 9:40, all stations to Manchester and the 9:52, Ambergate and Derby."

The other man beside the fire grinned. "We're reet busy 'ere of an evening."

"So, the 9:52 stops on the other platform?"

"Aye, it does that," the porter spoke, "I goes ower before it's due to see t't' carriage doors and collect tickets."

"So you would see anyone getting on the train as well?"

"S'pose so. Don't pay too much attention to them. Hubert here keeps an eye on who's coming onto the platforms. Anyway, last night it were different. The Manchester train arrived late, just as I was going to go over for the 9:52. The locomotive were across the footway – anyway, I couldn't be both sides at once, so I checked the doors this side, and the train drew out. The 9:52 were mankin' abaht. The driver overshot the platform by a couple of coach lengths, so 'e 'ad to set back. It's tricky coming straight out of that tunnel onto a platform – they're allus doin' it. When he'd come to rest, the rear coach were still across the footway, so I waited to see if he'd move again. Anyway, he were off in a trice, and I never got to check the doors. The guard must have done it. He'll put in a complaint a've no doubt…"

Archer cut in: he could just see the hard life of a porter being compared, at length, with the easy one led by a passenger guard. "So you couldn't see who was on the up platform to catch the Derby train?"

Hubert spoke up, "There wouldn't be anyone. No one bought a ticket for either train last night, and I'm damned sure no one came through here for the other platform.

"So you didn't see Mr Jarvis Tarp boarding a train last night? You know who he is I suppose?"

"Oh 'im. We know him alright." The acknowledgement was suffused with disapproval and resentment in equal parts. "Yes, we know 'im alright, don't we Hubert.

Hubert agreed, "Known 'im since 'e were a nipper. 'E weren't any good then, and 'e ain't any good now. 'E comes through the station reg'lar, but I don't see him 'cos 'e's got a special pass 'e gets in Manchester, so he don't need no ticket."

The porter broke in. "S'pose I ought 'a insist on seeing it, but I don't fancy tangling wi' 'im if ah don't 'ave to. Gaffer says it's alright – says 'e checks wi' Manchester time to time, an' they say e's got a pass."

"Gaffer?" Archer enquired after other members of the staff.

"Mr Irwin Pink – calls 'isself Station Master. 'E aint master of much, but you wouldn't think it from the way 'e carries on. Well, I ask you: there's me an' Hubert, a signalman and a shunter at the goods yard, that's the lot, and we don't see much of them two anyway. He puts on airs and graces – just 'cos he lives in that gret house," the porter waved toward the platform outside. "An' walks across the line wi' his thumbs in the armholes of his weskit just as if he owns the place. Always arrives just before the first train of the day. 'E's never-sweat an' I've been here an hour by then."

Hubert chipped in: "Worst thing is 'e don't come from round here, somewhere down south, I reckon." From his tone this seemed a worse crime than hubris or laziness.

Archer wondered how South Cheshire would fare in Hubert's estimation. "So the station master's house is just across the tracks at the north end of the up platform?"

"Tha' catches on quick fer a bobby."

"Is that the only way to get to it?"

"Tha's reet again; 'cept you come through the woods, down the valley side. He'd never go there; get 'is shiny boots dirty." Hubert gave something between a snort and a laugh at the idea.

At this point, there was the sound of someone in the booking hall. Spray arrived and was introduced to the two railwaymen.

"Bad news usually comes in threes. Is there another on his way?" Hubert's lugubrious comment was accepted as a joke by the policemen, though it was not entirely clear that it was intended as such. "By rights you lot shouldn't be in here. We're not supposed to let just anyone in. Particularly if you're from the competition."

The whistle of an approaching train was heard; the porter got to his feet and glanced at the clock. "9:40's on time tonight: I'd best get out there."

Three of them, Spray, Archer and the porter, emerged onto

the platform as the train drew in, each intent on his duties. The porter went to collect tickets and attend to the carriage doors, the detectives compared notes. Archer described the procedures adopted to manage the arrival and departures and what had happened the previous evening.

"They're both adamant that they know Jarvis Tarp, and that he couldn't have boarded either train, Sam."

Spray gave the gist of his encounters with Addie and Sid Mutton. "It's plain that no one has a good word to say for Tarp. The general opinion is that he's a nasty bit of work, and they aren't surprised we're looking for him in connection with murder. The odd thing is, neither Addie nor Mutton could see him being mixed up with Bardell."

Archer's reply was hesitant, but he spoke up none the less. "Sam, you don't think we've got this wrong? What if we've been concentrating on Jarvis and his 'little friends' when all the while it was to do with Oldroyd's business?"

The 9:52 came and went with only a cursory glance from the two men engrossed in conversation. They paid no attention to the cold and had barely noticed the porter crossing the line, with time to spare tonight, to collect tickets and attend to the carriage doors. Curious glances were cast in their direction by the handful of passengers as they hurried past, homeward bound, on a winter's night.

Finally, Hubert approached them. "Ain't you got nowhere to go, then? No more trains tonight y'know. I'm locking up, and then we're off."

The pair walked down the station approach, toward the village. Still exploring the intricacies of the case, they were making slow progress. As they turned into Lea Road they were overtaken by the two station staff.

"Gerronwi' it lads you're wastin' good drinking time." It

was clear where Hubert was heading.

His companion had other ideas: "I'm off home – the missus'll have some snap ready."

They walked on ahead and had disappeared across the Derby Road when a train whistled in the distance. It made good progress up the valley, the pulsing beats getting louder as it passed high above the detectives. When it disappeared into Willersley Tunnel, the silence of the night returned.

A few paces further on, Spray stopped. "Those two said there were no more trains tonight. We've just heard one. They're idiots."

Archer tried to be reasonable. "They said there were no more stopping in Cromford. That one went straight through."

All he got in reply was a grunt. They walked on in silence.

"Come on, we're going round the pubs," Spray was a changed man. Something had happened to him in the last minute or so.

Archer had seen this before. His sergeant had an idea, and there was no stopping him.

"We've got to have another word with Hubert."

The last thing Archer wanted to do was retrace their steps of earlier in the day. What he wanted was his bed, already booked, at the Bell.

In the event, it wasn't such an ordeal. The first pub they came to was The Greyhound at the bottom of Scarth Lane, where it meets the Square. Hubert's thirst had been such that he'd gone into the first pub he'd passed. Sitting in a corner by the fire, glass in hand, he was less than enthusiastic at the sight of the two policemen.

"Wot you two doing follering me abaht. 'Taint good for my reputation being seen wi' you. Yer from the wrong company and yer peelers – neither of which I like. Bobby off."

Spray was at his most affable. "We're sorry to trouble you again, sir. If you could clear up one point we'll be on our way."

He took the grunt, in reply, as an agreement to his proposal.

"Just after you left us, we heard a train pass through the station."

"So what? It don't stop at Cromford."

"No – quite so. Could you tell me where it does stop?"

"It's the early mail. Starts at Derby, stops Ambergate, Matlock, Millers Dale, then I'm not sure. Ends up in Manchester. Now are you goin' to leave me in peace?" Hubert turned away, but the questioning wasn't quite over.

"Does it take passengers?"

"Yes, but they can't board at Cromford 'cos it don't stop. That's it." Hubert rose to his feet and left the fireside to join the throng round the bar.

Chapter 22

Cromford, Ambergate and Buxton, Wednesday Morning, 29th December, 1875

Come next morning, Archer was to be found back at the station. He was on the up platform, having crossed in good time to avoid the 7:40, which was due in the down platform, and would have impeded his progress. In contrast to the night before, the station was busy with early morning passengers. Many of those were waiting for the Manchester train initially, but after its departure, even more people crossed the tracks, joining Archer for the Derby service.

The two detectives had agreed today's schedule last night and fine-tuned it over a hearty breakfast. Not quite up to Lizzie's standard, but Al Croker at the Bell had done them proud.

With his ticket for Ambergate in his pocket, Archer took his seat on the 7:52. It was a simple enough assignment, but he was excited none the less. It was moments like last night that made working with Sam Spray so rewarding. With Hubert's grudging co-operation in The Greyhound, and a brief glance at Bradshaw, all the pieces were there. Both men had them to hand, scattered and disordered as they were, but it was Sam who had assembled them into a useful picture.

"What do you think of this, William? Tarp leaves Bardell for a moment or two cooling his heels, in the billiard room, after Tilly had shown him in. He comes back with his service revolver and persuades or forces Bardell to go down to the wharf. There's no one about, so he can kill Bardell and dump him on the *Jane* without being seen."

So far, William had come to the same conclusions. All pretty straight forward.

"Tarp returns home and decides to disappear. He brings some mud into the house, mixed with limestone from the *Jane*'s cargo, and leaves with a Gladstone bag. Tilly sees him, and then he disappears."

William had got that far on his own, but no further.

"What if he disappeared into the woods down a different path from the one we know about and reached the station from the valley side? He knew the woods from boyhood, and Hubert said there was access from the stationmaster's house to the hillside. So Tarp could have waited until the 9:52 drew in and got aboard unseen. It was convenient, from his point of view, that the porter couldn't get across, but he'd probably have made it unnoticed even so."

Archer was in unexplored territory by now, "So he's on a train going south, and nobody's seen him. What next?"

"Well, he has a problem. Sometime soon he's going to be asked to show a valid ticket, but he doesn't have one. What he does have is a pass to travel between Cromford and Manchester."

Archer grasped the point immediately: "He needs to buy a ticket or get back to the part of the line where his pass is valid!"

They had consulted Bradshaw, and the 9:52 departure from Cromford reached Ambergate before the early mail train arrived there.

"He could catch the mail, and be on the train we heard passing through last night."

Archer was impressed by Spray's reasoning, but did have a reservation, and it was the reason for his present journey. Even if Tarp returned to the part of the line for which his pass was valid, he was on a train that didn't stop at the station where that validity commenced. A sharp-eyed ticket collector might notice this and confront him. The alternative was to spin a tale at the barrier at Ambergate and go to the ticket office and buy one for the remainder of his journey.

Spray countered with an alternative: "He could have made himself scarce at Ambergate, boarded the mail train and left it wherever he saw a lot of other passengers alighting, hoping the discrepancy wasn't noticed."

Archer was on his way to make enquiries at Ambergate. The journey down the Derwent Valley only took a few minutes, with one stop: Whatstandwell. Despite its brevity, it was a striking experience. For much of its length, the line clung precariously to the steep, eastern side of the valley. It afforded a magnificent view across the Derby Road and the river, to water meadows in the valley bottom. Beyond that, rising wooded ground just caught the winter sun as it rose behind the train.

Ambergate Station was like no other. Railways are constructed to be straight or gently curving. The platforms, cuttings and tunnels all conform to this imperative. Arriving at platform one offered Archer a different perspective.

The station lay in the 60° angle created by the junction of two gently curving lines. A third, short, connecting line closed off the open side, creating an equilateral triangle of track. Each side of the triangle sported paired platforms. Inside the enclosure, each met up with the other at its end. The outer platforms connected to the inner ones by footbridges.

It was possible to walk a continuous circuit around the three inner platforms. Archer saw immediately that it was an ideal place for a fugitive to remain unnoticed between trains.

The ticket collector replied to his enquiry: "The 9:52 Cromford train arrived before the late mail, sir." To a further question: "No, sir, no funny stuff Monday night. No excess fares for out of area passes – nothing out of the ordinary at all. I recognised all the passengers who left the station." And finally, "Yes, sir, the late mail is the last train to call here."

So that was it. If Spray's theory was right, Tarp must have departed on the late mail. Archer caught the next northbound train on the Midland mainline and followed in his tracks.

———

Spray was not looking forward to the day ahead. First, he was going to upset an old man, who must secretly have been expecting such a day for much of the last fifteen years. Then he was going to persuade a middle-aged woman to allow him to violate the privacy of her grief. After that? He didn't know what after that, but the gloom hanging over his first two tasks seemed to spread beyond them. There was nothing to lighten his mood.

He forced himself to stride out as he walked along Lea Road. He continued to climb energetically up the steep path to Cromford High house. He could have dawdled on the road and rested at intervals on the path. He could even have taken the much longer route up Willersley Lane, as he had done on his first visit, but Spray was not a procrastinator. If it had to be done, best get it over with.

Addie showed him into the breakfast room. Fitzroy Tarp may have needed early nights in old age, but he was still an early riser. He had finished his breakfast by quarter past eight and was reading, with the aid of a glass, a copy of the *Times*. If he was surprised at Spray's early call he didn't show it.

"Good morning, Sergeant. We meet again; how can I help you? Our last meeting ended rather disagreeably, I recall.

I trust we shall avoid parting with any such discord today."

Spray doubted it, but made a suitably anodyne reply. He was being warned off the subject of Oldroyd's parentage; the old man wasn't quite out of the game yet. He could live with that limitation. There were more immediate concerns to air.

"You may have heard that a man was found murdered at High Peak Junction yesterday morning."

Yes, Tarp had heard, but failed to see how he could help.

"I wonder if you could tell me where I might find Mr Jarvis Tarp?"

"He's away at present – he's on business in Manchester, you know – he has to stay there overnight on occasions. Why do you ask?"

Spray ignored the question. "Could you tell me when he was last here?"

For the first time there was a flicker… of what? Fear, anger perhaps, or was it panic? Composure was regained in a trice, and Tarp answered steadily enough.

"Oh, he was here Monday night; we ate together."

"What time would that be?"

"About six o'clock. After that, I retired to my bedroom. Really, Spray, this is too much. Our domestic arrangements are our own business, and I must insist you leave the subject alone. In fact I must ask you to leave." He was rising; his poise was finally shattered.

Spray remained seated. "You see, Mr Tarp, your son is wanted for questioning in connection with the murder."

A man of the world, urbane, if elderly, had risen from the chair, but a broken and desperate man sat down. He blustered and protested, but his mask of authority was gone. All Spray could see now was a pathetic old man finally confronting his demons. It gave him no pleasure, but it had to be done.

"The man who died was seen here on Monday evening with Mr Jarvis Tarp. Later on, your son was seen leaving with a Gladstone bag, in a hurry. Around your house was found an amount of material, which in all probability came from the place where the body was found."

Tarp had nothing to say and Spray continued. "He has not been seen since, but we have reason to believe he left the station aboard a train travelling south, and then caught another train going northward."

The old man made a despairing effort to contradict this conjecture. In the end, he wished he hadn't. "Don't be absurd, man. If he'd caught a train, the staff at the station would have seen him. You have asked them I suppose?" A note of triumph entered his voice. "They didn't see him, did they?"

Spray mentioned the little matter of childhood misdemeanours involving exploring the woods and throwing stones… He didn't have to press the matter. Fitzroy Tarp put up no more resistance.

He agreed to answer any questions Spray wanted. The first concerned the dead man Stan Bardell: "No – I don't know him. If he worked at High Peak Junction I may have seen him in the past, but I haven't been there for some years." Tarp was heartened by this. At least he could be truthful with a good heart. "No. As far as I can say, Jarvis didn't know him either."

More worryingly, the matter of guns was addressed. The manner of Bardell's death had not been mentioned.

"Is that how Bardell died; in a shooting?" He was reassured by the answer. "Yes, Jarvis has a revolver." Thinking he was justifying its possession, Tarp added, "He was in the Army, you know – a cavalry regiment."

Spray made it plain that enquiries had been undertaken about Jarvis' military service. The old man wilted.

"Do you know where it is, the gun?"

"In his room, he has a case for it."

It was agreed that Addie would show him where it was kept before he left.

"I've instructed Miss Mutton to stay at home until this is over."

Fitzroy Tarp had been wondering where the maid was all morning. He was half way to accepting the explanation, when the implication of Spray's advice struck him.

"You mean, she saw Bardell and Jarvis," there was a pause, "and you think," he could hardly bear to say it, "you think Jarvis might try to murder her?"

Spray nodded, and was quite nonplussed by Fitzroy's next remark: "Bloody servants – why can't they keep their noses out of things? They should damn well know their place. I pay 'em and feed 'em and get damn all in return! All I expect is for them to keep their mouths shut and do what they're told."

By this time, indignation had replaced surprise. Being Spray, it was carefully controlled. "If I understand you correctly," the 'sir' was omitted deliberately, "servants are non-people owing their whole life to their employer – and in particular, have no right cooperating with the constabulary – against his wishes. By the same token, I imagine you consider your own cooperation optional?"

Whatever had happened to Tarp in the past few minutes, it had driven out his common sense. "You have the right of it there, sergeant."

"I think you should understand, Tarp, that your arrogance and stupidity have led to two deaths. By covering up Jarvis' uncontrollable and violent behaviour all his life, you have contributed to the murder of two people, and, I trust, the execution of a third." Noting the question in Fitzroy's eyes he went on: "You see, I believe he murdered Oldroyd as well."

At this, the old man collapsed into tears. The interview ended where it had begun, in the shadow of Arthur Oldroyd's parentage.

———————

Archer was at a loose end. He and Spray were due to meet later in the day, in Buxton, but the trains were so timed that he found himself aboard a down stopper, with a couple of hours in hand. If Sam's theory was correct, Tarp could have left the early mail at any of a number of stations on Monday night. Why not investigate the possibilities?

The train burst out of Lea Wood Tunnel and came to a halt where William had started out an hour or so before. No problem about overshooting the platform on a down train; Cromford Station was over a mile away from the tunnel mouth. As the locomotive pulled away, it disappeared straight into Willersley Tunnel, suddenly full of choking smoke as it strained to get its heavy load moving. William hadn't much time for Sam's enthusiasm for railways. But he certainly felt for the men on the footplate, enveloped in the acrid fumes of an engine hard at work, trapped inside nearly half a mile of tunnel. The passengers could at least shut the windows and keep out the worst of it.

Not much point in opening them at the other end either, although the next station, hard on the exit and only a mile or so from Cromford, was worth a look. To reach Matlock, less than two miles further on, the line passed through three more tunnels under High Tor, after passing Matlock Bath. It was alpine terrain in the heart of Derbyshire. The station buildings enhanced the impression, looking, as they did, for all the world like a Swiss chalet.

The village, with its warm springs, had become a spa, attracting both summer visitors and distinguished residents. Its raffish sophistication was something of an anomaly amongst the dourness of the Peak. However, on a cold day in late December, its charms were well hidden. William stayed in his seat. The early mail had not stopped here, but it had done so further on, in Matlock.

He alighted and started asking questions. Nothing positive emerged, but the ticket collector said that there were very few season-ticket holders using the station, and he would certainly have remembered one from Monday night.

With forty minutes to wait for the next train, William's enquiries at stations down the line were going to take a long time. By the time he arrived in Buxton, he'd stopped at three more and drawn a blank at every one.

———•••———

Sam Spray was oblivious to the charms of the Derwent Valley as his train steamed on its way. He was sunk in thought, wrestling with an ethical problem that had lain corrosively at the back of his mind since Christmas Eve. The item, slipped into his hand when he parted from Dr Astley, was a key. Not a very large key, but big enough to have 'Chubb' imprinted into the bow. It should rightly be in the possession of Oldroyd's executors, and ultimately his beneficiaries, but there it was, in his hand, and he was on his way to use it. He squared this with his conscience on the grounds that his duty was to find Oldroyd's murderer, and after that he could get it back where it belonged; but he was still uneasy.

As soon as he'd examined it, Sam had realised what it was.

It had to be the key to the safe he'd seen on his clandestine entry into Oldroyd's office. This time, he would opt for a more-direct approach and hope for Vera Pidcock's cooperation. He achieved it alright, but not quite on the terms he'd anticipated.

"Go on then, yer know the way don't yer?" Seeing the surprise on Spray's face, she continued, "I realised where yer'd been when I first saw yer – not straight away, mind, but later that mornin' after yer'd gone. I mean ter say – coming in through t'yard like that. Perce wouldn't notice anything," then, more confidentially, "he's none too bright, yer could 'ave got away wi' murder." She clapped her hand over her mouth at the inappropriateness of the comment. "If yer'd just wanted to speak to me yer'd 'ave just come through the front."

Spray was beginning to doubt his suitability for plain clothes work. Vera Pidcock and Lizzie had both rumbled him, or his intentions, in short order. Now he could only think of the victim's sister-in-law as 'Lizzie', since their Christmas together. He knew it to be most unprofessional; what he felt about it was quite different.

By the time he reached the door of the converted stable, he was back in detective mode. No sticking key and dodging behind hay stacks this time: he went straight in, leaving the door open for extra light and lit the gas lamps. Only then, with the draught making them flicker, did he shut himself in and tackle the safe. There was always a chance that Oldroyd had owned more than one, and the blade of the key in his hand wouldn't fit the safe's keyway. It jammed on his first, rather tentative, attempt, but it slid in easily on a second try and turned smoothly.

The safe's interior was rather disappointing. It was less than eighteen inches deep; the size limited, no doubt, by the depth of the wall into which it was set. There were a few documents laid flat, a photograph and a bundle of letters tied up with pink ribbon. It was an untidy affair, with sheets of different sizes, some flat, some folded and others in envelopes. As he took them to the desk, it struck him that the bundle would have fitted nicely into the empty desk drawer at Oldroyd's Cromford house. At the time he had been there, the state of the drawer front, showing as it did every sign of being forced, had suggested to Spray that the contents had been stolen. Perhaps he'd been mistaken, and they had been removed for safe keeping before the break in. If so, the implication had to be that Oldroyd was worried enough about his security to start taking precautions.

The letters proved a daunting task. They were in chronological order, broadly, but there were sufficient exceptions to require careful attention to their dates. In some cases, no date appeared, in others, there was some such note as *Thurs pm*. In yet others, the year was missing. They were written in a variety of different hands, but in the end, Spray realised that the bulk of them had been written by one of three people. Confusingly, they didn't always sign off in the same way. There was a *J* and a *J T,* which correlated well with the abbreviated address of *H H*. There were some from *Al,* and in one case, *A,* but they ceased over two years ago. Mostly, they were from *37* or *W B,* although a couple were from *Alpine Villa* and one from *M B*.

All this desk work was hard for a man of the outdoors, and Spray's head was beginning to spin. He started muttering to himself in an attempt to keep his mind clear.

"Suppose *J* and *J T* have to be Jarvis Tarp," was his first conclusion. "*H H* is probably Cromford High House." This followed, as they always appeared together on the same letter.

He had created a second pile signed *A* or *Al*. "Got to be the brother, Albert, with 37 for an address, and that means *W B* must be Whaley Bridge." In addition there were a few headed *Alpine Villa* and one with *M B* as the address.

The third pile was the most intriguing. These were all signed *G, GA* or *Gerry*. "Must all be the same person. What's this though?" Most of the pile were headed *Alpine Villa* or *A V.* "Those two sound like the same place but what about this one? *S C*; what the dickens does that mean?" Again there was a smattering of *M B* as the originating address.

If the morning's work so far had been taxing, Spray was dreading the next stage. He'd been taught from an early age that other people's correspondence was sacrosanct, and whilst business correspondence didn't trouble his conscience, personal letters did. It was time for a break.

"You alright me duck?" Spray had repaired to the bar of the Coachman and Vera was in a motherly mood. She was no longer in awe of Spray, if she ever had been, and could see a man with a furrowed brow in need of a release from his cares. "This'll set thee up." A pint of ale was set on the bar.

"Vera," she'd invited the familiar address when they first met, "did Arthur Oldroyd ever talk about anyone called Gerry, or even bring someone of that name here?"

"Can't say he did. Not that I knew of anyway. But as I said the first time you was here, he took a lot of people up to his room an' I never met 'em, 'cept that once, an' I never got 'is name."

"Did he ever talk about a villa, possibly Alpine Villa?"

No, he hadn't mentioned such a place. "I seem ter r'member 'im saying 'e was off ter a cottage once; but I never knew where it was, and nothing got said 'bout it again."

It was very clear, had been for some time really, that Oldroyd kept the two sides of his life separate. Business was based at the Coachman and operated from various parts of the

C&HPR. The rest of it revolved round his home in Cromford and Alpine Villa, wherever that was. The room upstairs was an anomaly, but he kept that pretty-well separate with the almost-private entrance through the yard.

Spray's imagination stirred into life. What if the two lives had collided, and his death was the consequence. What if the encounters here and at the Jodrell were the points where the two sides had met? Despite being witnessed by different people, each had produced remarkably similar descriptions, both of the other man and the nature of the encounters. It was all speculation, and Spray wished Archer was around to share it with.

The bottom of the glass was in sight; it was no good; he had to get back to the letters.

"Vera," she had been busy at the other end of the bar during his reverie. "I'm expecting Constable Archer in a while. Tell him where I am and send him over, will you?"

With the letters in four piles he had to decide where to start. The smallest contained a miscellaneous collection with no pattern to them in terms of sender or address. He put them to one side and tackled the ones from *A* and *Al*. They were clearly between brothers, and the contents were largely unexceptional, although one discussed the advantage of marrying, *given our particular circumstances*. Then, one asserted, *I've found just the right young woman, very agreeable, and I feel sure she won't give any trouble*. When Sam realised it was Lizzie, about whom such a cavalier attitude was being taken, indignation overrode his scruples, and he proceeded in better heart. The very next letter agreed: *your intentions are wise and should keep us all out of trouble*.

The pile signed *J* and *J T* was next. The letters were more distasteful to read, but perhaps more illuminating, so far as the case was concerned. Spray, who had never sent or received a love letter in his life, was astounded at the passions, felt so deeply and expressed so freely, to be found on the written page. Despite his naivety, he did recognise elements other than love: there was a possessiveness of dangerous intensity that emerged here and there. Such phrases as, *I cannot allow it* and *do not dare to do such a thing again,* were interspersed with more affectionate writing, suggesting a fraught relationship. There were no letters after mid-October, and the last one, dated the eighteenth, was the most revealing of all. It was clearly written as the affair was breaking up. The pain in earlier paragraphs was replaced at the end with anger and threats. *You cannot do this to me. I will not allow it,* and a bit further on, *life will be lost on the altar of my pain.*

It was simple enough; Tarp and Oldroyd had come to the end of a liaison. In the break up, the rejected lover wanted death. As it turned out, the death of his ex-partner.

Letters from the third pile were different again. It took Spray a while to realise they were addressed to two different people. The smaller portion was all headed *Dear Arthur* and signed *G A* or *Gerry*. They consisted of mundane matters and innocent arrangements, all being sent with *Regards* and *Best Wishes*. The remainder were quite different. Each was to *Dearest A* and was signed *Your Loving G,* with *Ever* inserted on occasions. Despite his reserve, Spray recognised a tenderness and affection quite unsullied by the fierce possessiveness of Tarp for Arthur Oldroyd. Whoever *G* was, he lived at *Alpine Villa* and had been the late Albert Oldroyd's lover – Albert, who married Lizzie despite his attachment to *G*. Arthur must have acquired the letters on his brother's death to keep them from Lizzie. If this was done out of consideration for her, Sam was in no mood to credit it. So far as he could see, it was an entirely self-interested act to save the skins of the others.

Spray was contemplating the conundrum of who the mysterious Gerry was, and where he might live, when there was a knock on the door.

"I've got to the right place then?" Archer stood in the doorway surveying the scene: Sam at the desk amid piles of paper was an unusual sight in itself, but the room was a surprise as well. Outside, he thought himself entering a stable, but inside the gas light illuminated the well-appointed office.

"Shut the door, William." A gust of wind had entered along with the detective and scattered some of the letters onto the floor. Sam bent down to retrieve them and found himself holding an envelope he'd missed earlier.

With the door shut and order restored, the two of them got to comparing notes. William was rueful about his apparently wasted morning, "Couldn't get a sniff of him. If you're right about the journey south, with an about turn at Ambergate, I might well have drawn a blank there. It's an ideal place to pass unnoticed between trains. But he had to get off the north bound one somewhere, and I haven't found where yet."

Sam described his dead end: "*Alpine Villa, M B and S C.* I just can't get any further." He tapped the desk pensively with the edge of the stray envelope. "They're connected with Gerry, and he was connected with the late Albert Oldroyd, whose brother, Arthur, was certainly connected to Tarp. It's all in there somewhere, but where?"

William had a moment of inspiration. "Did you notice anything particular on your journey this morning?"

Sam had to admit to being sunk in thought for pretty well the whole of the time; "Why do you ask?"

"You travelled through Matlock Bath; may even have stopped there. If you'd looked out of the widow, you'd have seen a station looking like a Swiss chalet. The area round there is called Little Switzerland, you know?"

Sam continued tapping the desk. He didn't know, but was grateful that William did. That was why they worked so well together, each valued the other's contribution. The envelope slipped from his fingers and swooped to the floor.

"Perhaps M B is Matlock Bath and…" Sam bent down and picked up the fallen envelope, "and Gerald Arbuthnot lives at Alpine Villa!" There it was staring him in the face: *Albert Oldroyd Esq., c/o Gerald Arbuthnot, Alpine Villa, Matlock Bath, Derbyshire.* He'd had the answer in his hand for the last five minutes, and it'd been in the collection of letters all along.

"I suppose rank gives you the right to trump my ace." William was a whist player and lapsed into the jargon occasionally. "I don't expect you noticed how far Matlock Bath was from Cromford this morning did you?"

No, Sam hadn't been paying attention, but William had: "It took about six minutes, and I'm wondering if Jarvis Tarp might have walked there on Monday night and not caught a train at all?"

Suddenly, the fog of uncertainty, which had surrounded Spray in the search for their suspect, vanished: "That's it, that's where he went and may even still be there. We'd better move."

William forbore to mention who had held the ace of trumps; no point in overplaying his hand.

Chapter 23

Matlock Bath, Wednesday Afternoon, 29th December, 1875

With a squealing of brakes and a sigh of escaping steam, the train drew into Matlock Bath. William was right, the station looked as if it had been lifted out of an alpine scene he'd come across in an advertisement for one of Thomas Cook's tours. Sam was rather shamefaced at not noticing it on his earlier journey.

The two of them had left the Coachman having replaced the letters in the safe, minus those involving Albert, G, and the two mentioning Lizzie. Whoever inherited Arthur's estate, Lizzie's humiliation wasn't going to feature in it if Sam could do anything about it. He'd also taken the photograph: a tall, fair man in military uniform, looking straight ahead, lacking emotion as such portraits do. On the back: '*you are my all. Jarvis*'.

On the way to the station, they had called at the office of Ezra Brooke, Oldroyd's lawyer, to leave the keys that had troubled Sam's conscience. Most of what was to be found at the Coachman concerned the misdeeds of a man beyond the reach of earthly retribution. He felt that keeping them was not going to further the investigation. A certain evasion was required from Sam, and a delicacy on the part of Brooke, to effect their transfer without exposing how they had come into his possession. It was in neither man's interest to pursue the matter.

"I understand you made an arrest in connection with Oldroyd's murder over Christmas, Sergeant. And now there's this other affair in Cromford?" News of Bardell's murder must have reached Buxton. "It would be inconvenient to find they had been committed by the same hand."

The canny lawyer, having put his finger on the major flaw in the case against Markham, was trawling for gossip, although he might have described it as seeking information.

"The case is not complete yet, and investigations are proceeding." Sam could prevaricate if he had to. "Good day to you."

With that, the two detectives took their leave and headed for their train. The two stations, MR and LNWR, stood side by side, with a gap of thirty yards or so separating their identical facades. As they arrived at the MR entrance, they found themselves engulfed in passengers pouring out from the LNWR exit next door. A familiar voice called from the crowd.

"Sergeant, how nice to see you, and Constable Archer too." Here, in the public world of a station forecourt, the intimate ways into which they had all fallen recently seemed out of place to Lizzie. "How pleasant to see you and convenient too. I have been wondering how much longer you would need the rooms."

After expressing pleasure at the happy coincidence, Spray explained they were furthering their enquiries at Matlock Bath, and had every intention of returning to Whaley Bridge shortly. He would be most obliged if the rooms could remain available for a few more days.

"And what brings you to Buxton, Mrs Oldroyd?" It was an innocuous question, asked more out of politeness than curiosity. The answer, as it was given, seemed equally innocent.

"Oh, I've an appointment with a lawyer: something to do with Arthur's death. He wrote, asking me to go and see him."

Spray felt he couldn't probe, and as the matter was being treated as of no importance, he learnt no more. In due course, the issue would make its reappearance.

As the two men alighted onto the platform, it became apparent that the bulk of Matlock Bath lay on the western bank of the Derwent. It left the opposite side to the railway and precious little else, before a steep, wooded slope formed the valley side. The ticket collector proved most helpful and set them on their way to Alpine Villa. This turned out to occupy the same bank as the railway but much higher up. They were out of breath by the time they arrived at a pair of semi-detached houses nestled in a niche in the hillside. The surrounding trees looked like a cushion against which the two-story, wooden-clad building, with its low pitched, overhanging roof, reclined. The large gable end spanned both houses and faced out across the valley, with a first floor balcony giving a magnificent view across the Derwent to the Heights of Abraham. The first house was indeed well-named: Alpine Villa.

A path led to the front door. Spray knocked, and knocked again but to no avail. There was no answer. The two of them came away from Alpine Villa and approached its mirror image next door. At this point, one of their remaining questions was solved. A discrete nameplate proclaimed Swiss Cottage to be next door to Alpine Villa. SC and AV were virtually the same place.

This time, the door was opened cautiously by a wiry little woman, rather bent, with a deeply lined, weather-beaten face.

"What do you want?". There were few teeth to be seen when she opened he mouth. "I don't have nothin' from hawkers, and I don't hold wi' tramps."

"Very wise, I'm sure, in a remote place like this." Spray was at his most emollient. "Fortunately, we are neither. I am Sergeant Spray, and this is Constable Archer, of the Railway Constabulary."

The old crone was not to be outdone. "So what yer doin' up 'ere? Railway's down there." She waved a hand toward the river. "I don't need no rozzers."

"We'd like a word with Mr Arbuthnot. We understood he lives next door. Is he about? We've tried knocking."

"That won't do no good. Ain't no one in." An air of satisfaction accompanied this last pronouncement. The woman plainly felt she was one up on the two detectives. "Good day to you." The door was closing. Archer stuck his foot in it. "'Ere you can't do that." The time for emollience had passed.

"I think we'd better come in, Mrs?" by this time, the door had been firmly pushed open, and Spray, followed by Archer, was inside. "You're Mrs?"

"Miss; Miss Hannah Mutch, if yer must know. But yer've still got no right ter be in 'ere."

By this time they were in a comfortable parlour, the front window of which looked out below the balcony and took in the same magnificent view.

"We're investigating a crime committed in Cromford two days ago…"

Hannah cut in. "I ain't been near Cromford in months." Then after a moment thought, "Years, and I ain't committed no crime, neither."

"I'm sure you haven't, Miss Mutch. It's just that I think Mr Arbuthnot may be able to help us with our enquiries. Since he's not next door, could you tell me who owns Swiss Cottage?"

A gleam of devilment showed in the dark, deep set eyes. "Don't rightly know."

Exasperation showed on Spray's face. "Miss Mutch, we are engaged in a murder enquiry, and your failure to cooperate could be seen as obstruction."

The devilment turned to triumph. "You lot'd know better'n

me. I know who used to own it, but he don't no more."

Archer chipped in. He should have known better than to cross swords with Hannah, "So, why did he dispose of it?"

"He didn't. It was him what got disposed of."

Understanding dawned on the two policemen.

"You mean it belonged to Arthur Oldroyd?"

"He-he; took yer time getting there di'n't yer?" The old woman cackled away to herself.

"Have you ever seen this man here or next door?"

Hannah glanced at the photograph of Jarvis Tarp, but looked away immediately. To Spray's eye it was too hurried, as if she didn't want to look long enough for her memory to be triggered.

"Can't say I have or I haven't. 'E looks too swell fer me in that uniform."

"The man in the picture is a suspect in our enquiry. He is a Mr Jarvis Tarp." As he was talking, something clicked in Spray's mind. "He owns a bank in Manchester; it goes under the name of Arbuthnot and Stein. Would that be the same Arbuthnot family as Mr Arbuthnot, who isn't at home next door?"

Hannah was getting flustered. "I don't know anything about no Bank; you're confusing me. I ain't used ter this sort of thing. I'm a spinster, and I don't get out much. Why can't you leave me alone?"

Archer found himself rather discomfited by her distress and escaped back to the hallway. It was an entirely professional move, he told himself, to have a look round, make sure they hadn't overlooked vital evidence; that sort of thing. As he turned away from the front door to explore the darker recesses of the house, he found himself face to face with a familiar image.

"Sergeant, I think you should look at this."

Hanging on the wall was a lithograph of the Crystal Palace. Spray lifted it from the picture rail and the two men returned to the parlour window. There it was, bottom right hand corner, under the artist's signature: 4/4.

For a moment Hannah gathered herself up, indignant at the violation of her home. "Here, leave that picture alone, it's valuable and it means a lot to Mr G…" The name died on her lips as she realised her mistake.

She was saved by the bookcase. Covered in confusion, she watched as a door opened that was decorated with the false spines of books, and a man, medium height, slight of build, fair and in his thirties, stepped into the room. He, totally ignoring the intruders, spoke to Hannah.

"That's quite alright, Nana; you don't need to worry about me anymore. Why don't you go up to your room and have a sleep. You look all in. I'll take care of things now. I'm sure these gentlemen don't mean us any harm."

Archer watched her face and tried to untangle the mixture of emotions to be found there: worship, as that of a mother for her favourite, certainly, also relief at the shedding of responsibility. There was also affection as she tenderly touched a bruise developing around his right eye. The mischievous, spiky old spinster was no more, and a gentle, motherly soul took herself upstairs.

"I take it you're Mr Gerald Arbuthnot, sir."

"I am, and you are?"

As this brief exchange developed, the assured man, who had confidently soothed the agitation of an old lady, sank into a chair and began to wilt. The bruise around the eye wasn't the only sign of injury. A split lip was swelling, and scraped knuckles were seeping a smear of blood.

Spray introduced himself and Archer. "You appear to have been in a fight?"

"My cousin would always beat me, right from childhood, this way and any other you care to mention. The only people who could stop it were Albert and Arthur, and now they're both dead. That's why I hid; I thought he was coming back."

The man was a picture of abject misery. Whether it was out of grief for the death of friends or for himself, now exposed to the renewed onslaught of his bullying cousin, wasn't clear.

The door of book spines stood open. Behind it was a surprisingly commodious space made up of the interior of the book cases and the dividing wall between the two properties.

Archer looked inside what amounted to a modern priest hole. "I thought these things belonged to the past."

There was a silence. Arbuthnot tried to frame a reply. Policemen were policemen, wherever they were from. "People don't understand us," was the best he could manage, "it seemed a prudent arrangement."

Spray immediately saw the man's dilemma. "I think you should understand we're here in the pursuit of a violent criminal, and we think you may be able to help us. Nothing more." His obvious sincerity was reassuring.

"Very well, sergeant. What can I do for you?" The thinly veiled allusions to a suspect, a cousin and a crime were all stripped of any ambiguity, and the three men shared their information. Jarvis Tarp and Gerald Arbuthnot were indeed relations. Tarp was suspected of the murder of Oldroyd and Bardell. Tarp had left Cromford on Tuesday night and walked up the Derwent Valley to Matlock Bath and had demanded Arbuthnot take him in.

"I didn't know what he'd done, but I realised it must be serious. He looked really wild when he arrived."

Tarp had then demanded that Arbuthnot go to the station in the morning, buy a ticket for Chapel en le Frith and find out the time of the next train. He was to bring the ticket back for Tarp.

"He knows how to get onto the platform without passing the ticket collector. He was always doing it when he was a child, at lots of stations. I don't suppose he's forgotten."

"How did you get beaten about like this?" Spray felt real concern for the battered Arbuthnot.

"He threatened Hannah and said he'd hurt her if I didn't do as he asked. I couldn't have that, so I stood up to him." His voice trailed off to a whisper. "It didn't do any good though – I did what he wanted in the end." He brightened a little. "But he didn't hurt Nana."

Spray found himself intrigued by the relationship between the two. With no experience of an intimate family himself, he found he was at a loss to explain what lay between them.

"She was my nanny when I was young. She's the only person who cared about me as a child, and I've loved her ever since. My mother wasn't…" Whatever his natural mother was or wasn't, Arbuthnot found it beyond him to go any further.

Spray broke the silence; both as a kindness to the tongue-tied man, but also out of curiosity. "So what's her position here?"

"She's a sort of housekeeper." Arbuthnot went on to explain that the two properties were originally owned by the Oldroyd brothers. "When my, er, particular friend, Al, died, I inherited Alpine Villa. I'd been living here for some time by then, and Al would come when he could."

Spray seethed at this oblique reference to Lizzie's passion-less marriage, but kept his indignation to himself.

"Arthur never really lived here in Swiss Cottage; he just used it occasionally. In the summer, he let it out to visitors to the Spa. Hannah and I took care of everything for him."

The lithographs of Crystal Palace had run like thread, insubstantial but never broken, through the investigation. Spray asked about them.

"It was several years ago now, Jarvis bought the set of four and gave one to each of us. He said it would bind us all together forever." Arbuthnot shuddered. "He was just wanting to control things. He was always like that."

"One last thing – did Tarp have a gun when he came here?"

Arbuthnot couldn't say; "But he could have had anything in that Gladstone bag of his, and I wouldn't have known." Indignation welled up. "How can he do it? That bag still has Lt. J. Tarp, Derbyshire Yeomanry Cavalry on it. He was thrown out in disgrace." Then, in more a measured tone, "I suppose you know that anyway. You seem to know pretty well everything else."

Chapter 24

Chapel en le Frith, Thursday Morning,
30th December, 1875

It had been a cold night, and the waiting room benches were hard and unforgiving. Spray and Archer had arrived the evening before and investigated the matter of the first and last trains out of Chapel en le Frith. It was not quite as simple as it sounded. Two stations served this modest settlement. The M R, whose Central Station, on the main line from London to Manchester, had the best position near the middle of the town, was their point of arrival. It was where Tarp would have arrived too, assuming Chapel was his destination.

As they had trudged the mile to South Station, Spray began to have doubts about his employers. The L&NWR had arrived in the town first and had the quicker route to the city. Yet, with a more-central station, and more-comfortable travel for those of modest means, the Midland had the edge. Deep in these disloyal comparisons, the significance of Chapel came to him. It was the next station from Matlock Bath, down the M R mainline, where the two networks came together. Tarp could move onto the L&NWR, Stockport to Buxton line, by just changing stations at this insignificant little town.

The two of them had mulled over the possibilities in a pub, after the last train. Tarp could have alighted at any station between Matlock Bath and Chapel or carried on to Manchester on his season ticket. Either way, he would have attracted more attention than by turning up his collar, pulling down the brim of his hat and discreetly presenting a third class single at Chapel.

They both assumed that the business of getting Arbuthnot to purchase his ticket in advance was a ploy to avoid attention.

Question: was it just natural caution that led Tarp to cover his tracks, or did he think he was the subject of a manhunt? No answer.

"We're Railway Constabulary Officers, and we need the use of the waiting room overnight."

The Chapel South Stationmaster was not impressed and attempted to refuse. Spray adopted his most forceful persona. "We are investigating two murders, and your failure to cooperate might be viewed in a poor light when the case comes to court."

The man gave way reluctantly, "Don't you go using all that coal. It'll be needed tomorrow, and we don't get no more till Monday."

With nowhere to stay, and an early start on Friday morning, they had decided that the waiting room was their only option. It had to be South Station. They were L&NWR officers, and no amount of pulling rank would have got anywhere on the Midland.

They awoke to the sound of a door opening and the rattle of coal in a scuttle. A porter, whose job it was to light the waiting room fire, was surprised to find glowing embers. He looked round as Spray and Archer, stiff from their uncomfortable night, staggered to their feet.

"'Ere, what have you two been doing? This ain't a doss house tha knows. I'll 'ave ter tell…"

"He already knows. We spoke to the stationmaster last night."

The porter was mollified by the sight of two warrant cards. With the workman's 'parliamentary' due shortly, it was time for the two policemen to get to work.

The idea was for Spray to stay at South Station and Archer to go to Central. They would then keep watch for Tarp attempting to leave Chapel and arrest him. As a plan, it was full of holes, but neither man could think of anything better. They made their way to the station exit, past a queue forming up for tickets. A motley bunch of men in rough clothes and clogs were heading for a day's work. Spray glanced in their direction. Tarp was unlikely to pass himself off as a labourer. Apart from his arrogance, there was the matter of suitable clothing. There was something odd about the crowd though. Spray looked more carefully. That was it. A man in a frock coat and silk hat, looking very awkward in such company, was about to buy his ticket. He left the ticket window and turned to face Spray.

"William, just follow that man and see where he goes, before you go to Central." There was no time to elaborate; the man was heading back toward Chapel. Apart from the familiarity of his face and the incongruity of his dress in such company, Spray was struck by the pre purchase of a ticket.

With the arrival of the parliamentary train, the ticket hall emptied. He went to the window and made himself known. Unlike the porter, the ticket clerk had been informed of Spray's presence and was as curious as the policeman about the man in the silk hat. "No, never seen 'im before. There's a fast train from Central to Manchester at about half past eight. Them in business usually get that." Then under his breath, "It's more comfortable on the Midland." More loudly: "Silk Hat bought a ticket for Whaley Bridge."

No more travellers arrived. The next train wasn't for some time, and Spray was alone left with his thoughts. A picture of the Crystal Palace sidled, unbidden into his mind. Why? Before this case, he'd never given it much thought. The Great

Exhibition had been twenty-odd years ago, and he paid precious little attention to it even then. He understood the building had been given over to all sorts of frivolity since it was moved out of Hyde Park. Not his sort of thing at all. He got to thinking about Tarp's conceit in trying to bind people in unwilling, at least on Arbuthnot's part, association with valuable gifts.

Who had told him they were valuable? Ferraby, no, *Ferrison*, that was it. At the bank in Manchester, Ferrison. *FERRISON*, that was him, in the silk hat. He bought the ticket for Whaley Bridge. He did it for Tarp.

With this realisation came the problem of what to do next. Spray was in a quandary. Archer would soon know where Ferrison had gone, but didn't know his significance. He must be taking the ticket to Tarp who might just spot an unwary Archer on Ferrison's tail. Having established where Ferrison went, most likely his home, Archer would go as arranged to Central Station.

At this point, Tarp would be free to leave unobserved and go where? The simple answer was South Station for a train to Whaley Bridge. He'd got a ticket after all.

Spray started talking to himself. "That would be too easy." He never liked 'easy'. If he'd seen Archer he'd know the hunt was on. "Better assume he knows – but what the dickens next. Come on, think. What's he done so far? Walk up the valley to Swiss Cottage then catch a train to Chapel. How far's Whaley Bridge?" Spray didn't know for sure, but thought five miles or so. "He'd do that in less than a couple of hours – be a lot longer if he keeps off the road. He's going to walk it."

"I'm not goin' ter stop 'im tha knows. If e's killed someone already he won't stop there." The ticket collector looked apprehensive.

"No of course not, Ernie." Spray was having to coax the

man. "If you could just watch to see if he comes through the station, and if he does, where he's heading?" It was the best he could do at South Station and Spray set off at a jog trot in search of Archer.

It was soon obvious he was getting too old for this sort of thing, and he settled for a brisk walk. Once he'd got his breath back and settled into the rhythm of it, he made pretty good progress. In under half an hour he was at Central Station.

"He went into a house and came out again pretty quickly. I took a look through the door when he opened it – didn't see much. Someone on the inside slammed it shut. It could have been a man, but I'm not sure. Then I came here." Archer thought he could have been seen from in the house; he was at the gate when the front door opened. "Sorry, I should have been more careful."

Spray reassured him, "You weren't to know. I didn't know for a few minutes after you'd set off. Then it just dawned who he was."

Ferrison had arrived at Central shortly after Archer and caught the Manchester train. If he was aware of the policeman, he'd given no sign of it.

"He looked a bit worried though. Stood there with his gamp – twisting it round and round in his hand – I thought it was going to fall to pieces."

"You'd be worried if you'd left your house and family at the mercy of Jarvis Tarp. You didn't see any signs of a Mrs Ferrison, did you?"

No, Archer hadn't seen anyone else, but he thought it looked like the kind place where a married man, with a job in a bank and a family, might well have settled down. By now, the two of them were walking toward Ferrison's house. Spray hadn't made it clear what he intended to do when they got there, mostly because he hadn't much idea himself. All he knew was that Tarp must either be there or have left recently.

In the event, they walked up to the front door and knocked.

———

"Yes, gentlemen, can I help you?" It all seemed normal enough.

"Is Mrs Ferrison at home?" Spray took a gamble on there being a conventional family attached to the bank official.

"I'll go and see. Who shall I say wants her?"

She looked dismayed when it was explained who they were. Reassurance was in order and Archer was the man for the job.

"Don't be alarmed Miss… er?" He smiled.

"Mary, I'm Mary."

"We only want to ask a few questions about your visitor."

Mary would have liked to be reassured by Archer, but mention of Tarp unsettled her further. She scuttled off to find the mistress.

Mrs Ferrison, when she appeared, was a small, rather dumpy woman, with the kind of face that would have had a babyish charm when she was young. By now, the bloom of youth had faded. She wore a dress of flowered fabric, full but gathered in at the waist, with a high neck. It seemed to Spray, despite his almost total ignorance of ladies fashion, that she was rather elaborately clothed for mid-morning at home.

"Oh, Mr… er?"

"Spray, Ma'am." She hadn't taken in her maid's announcement.

"Yes, of course, Spray. Did he change his mind and send you back for his bag?" She fluttered both verbally and physically. Whilst speaking, she darted around the room adjusting ornaments, flicking imaginary specks of dust off vases and the like. "Mr Tarp asked if he could leave his bag here. He stayed the night, you know; such a nice gentleman. He's Mr Ferrison's employer – quite an honour. He arrived last night and asked if he could stay."

Spray wanted to interrupt and get a bit of order into the flow of information, but couldn't find an opening. Better to pick out what he wanted as it flew by. Mary, meanwhile, had retired to the hallway with Archer. The door into the drawing room, where the other two talked, remained open. At a second assertion by her mistress about the gentlemanly manner shown by Mr Tarp, she sniffed dismissively. The gesture was not lost on her companion.

Mrs Ferrison continued, "He said he had some business in the neighbourhood – it would be a great boon if he could stay. So polite and kind he was – owns the Bank where Mr Ferrison works. Such a gentleman. Then, this morning, my husband had to go out early for something." At this point she sounded uncertain for the first time. "I really don't know why, but as soon as he came back, he was off again to catch his usual train. Then Mr Tarp had to leave. Rather sudden, really; he was a bit abrupt – asked if I minded him leaving his bag, and he was gone." Then rather wistfully: "I thought we might have a little conversation before he left, but no." The stream dried to a trickle, "I'm sorry, Mr Spade, did you want to ask me something?"

Meanwhile, Archer had enquired after the dismissive sniff.

"He's no gentleman; heard him shouting at the master early, before the mistress was up. Don't know what about, but I think they may have been fighting. Leastways, the side of Mr Ferrison's face looked a bit sore, and he were rubbing it."

"Mary, do you think I could just have a look at Mr Tarp's bag?"

Her reluctance related only to getting caught by Mrs Ferrison. With a promise from Archer to act as crow, she agreed to get the bag from a cupboard under the stairs. There was the regimental crest and Tarp's name and rank that had so incensed Arbuthnot.

"'Ere, you didn't say you was going to search it."

Archer had the bag open and was rummaging inside. No sign of piano wire or revolver, just clothes and the necessities for a gentleman's overnight stay.

"You'll get me sent away wi'out a character."

He hurriedly closed it up; "Sorry Mary, no harm done." The cupboard door was shut by now, "But it's really most important – I wouldn't mention this to anyone."

The subject of 'what it would be wise to conceal from who' was in Spray's mind too. If they failed to apprehend Tarp quickly, then he might return for his bag, and Mrs Ferrison may well put herself in danger if he revealed her contact with the police. Suggesting she kept their visit secret was hopeless. She would give herself away in the first sentence. All he could do was try to make her think nothing of importance had happened. So far, he hadn't asked a single question, and it would be best to leave things that way.

"No, thank you, Mrs Ferrison, I think we've made a silly mistake. I don't think you can help us after all. I'm sorry to have troubled you for nothing. Please accept our apologies." He was heading for the door: "Come along constable, I don't think we should waste any more of this good lady's time. Good day to you, ma'am."

By this time the two policemen were on the path outside and heading for the gate.

"So, we think he's going to leg-it out of Chapel?" The two detectives were on their way back to South Station. Archer had voiced the conclusion they had both arrived at. Having pooled their information, they both thought that Tarp wanted to get to Whaley Bridge. Warned of their presence, he would keep off the rail network.

"Smart work there with Gladstone, William. Looks as if he's set off armed. What do you think? Protection from us, or has he something else in mind?" Spray had the beginnings of an idea, but wondered what whether Archer was on the same track.

"He'd have every reason to keep us at bay. We've got enough to hang him, if only we can catch him."

Spray was non-committal.

"I suppose you're right, but..." It seemed to Archer that Tarp was going toward Whaley Bridge for a purpose, not away from Chapel to escape. He just couldn't put his finger on why.

At South Station, Ernie was adamant. "He ain't come through 'ere since tha were 'ere. Wat's more, I sent a porter ower t'other platform before Stockport train came in ter mek sure we didn't have no fare dodgers. Nothing." The ticket collector may have been reluctant at the start, but he'd certainly taken the job seriously.

At Spray's insistence, they were returning to Whaley Bridge on the next train. He was sure, without quite knowing why, that it was to be the scene of Tarp's next transgression. Archer couldn't quite see it, but hadn't anything else to suggest. In any case, it was Sergeant Spray and Constable Archer – in the end – that would always settle such matters.

They had crossed to the up platform at track level: a dangerous arrangement that allowed both trains and passengers to share the same space. Despite warnings in big letters to

'Look both ways before crossing', there was a steady loss of life all over the network at such intersections. The pair had made the other side without incident and were now seated in the very modest waiting room on the far platform. With an armed criminal on the loose, greater risks lay ahead.

"What about this lot?" Archer had pointed to an area of waste ground and scrub behind the platform. "If he knew his way around Chapel, he could hide up there and get on a train without being seen, if he was careful."

"And go where?"

"Anywhere between here and Manchester, I suppose." Archer was still unconvinced, but said no more.

"Well, I'm sorry, William, you'll just have to live with it." Their train was approaching. "We're going to Whaley Bridge. I don't care whether Tarp is on the road, in the scrub," he gestured over his shoulder, "or managed to catch a train earlier; he's heading there. I just know it."

Chapter 25

Whaley Bridge, Thursday Afternoon, 30th December, 1875

By the time Spray and Archer reached Whaley Bridge, it was still light, but only just. The sky had cleared, and as the winter sun was disappearing over the edge of the Goyt Valley there was, for a short moment, a striking sunset. During the surprisingly long journey from Chapel, impeded by a goods train failing to clear the mainline in time at Shallcross Sidings, Spray had been silent. As the train drew to a halt with a faint hiss of steam and creaking of brakes he'd made up his mind.

"He's coming here to kill someone; I'm sure of it. He's killed Oldroyd and his associate Bardell in Cromford. The two people in this town who are connected to him are Lizzie and that man Riggott."

Archer had to agree. "Pott and Maida had said as much about Riggott, and they had told a tall, fair gent that the two were close." True it required some faith to turn the 'tall, fair gent' into Tarp, but nothing was for sure in this world.

"You see if you can find Riggott at the wharf yard, and I'll go and warn Lizzie. We'll meet back here in an hour."

They were on Market Street, outside the Jodrell Hotel. Archer had only to step across the road and on to Canal Street; Spray had at least half a mile along to Old Mill End, and then the climb to No 37. By the time he arrived he was breathless, but relieved to find Lizzie was at home.

"Sam, you're back. How good to see you again." They shook hands, a chaste kiss of greeting, though briefly contemplated by both parties, was avoided. "And William, is he with you; will you both be staying the night?"

She was rather put out, as they went into the parlour, by his manner.

"Lizzie, you have to find somewhere safe. Somewhere you can spend the next few hours with people who can protect you."

She protested: "But why? You haven't let Markham go, have you?"

Whilst reassuring her on this point Spray was insistent. "Go and get some things together, and I'll go with you to Maisie's house. She's got some big, strong brothers, hasn't she? I met them at Christmas."

"But Sam, I've got some news I must tell you. It's about that…"

He cut in, "Go and get ready, and you can tell me on the way."

They took a rather circuitous route, Lizzie insisting that if she was in danger so was her father. Spray doubted it, but they went to collect him all the same.

Whilst they walked, Lizzie spoke of her news, "You remember when we met yesterday? I was going to see a Mr Brook. Well what do you think he told me?"

If he hadn't been so preoccupied with her safety, Spray might have taken more notice of Lizzie's excitement.

As it was, the bombshell struck without warning: "It's Arthur – he's left me almost everything in his will."

Spray was dumbfounded. It took him a while to work out why this news, so happy for one, caused such a sinking in the heart of another.

"Oh, I see, that explains why he asked to see you." It was the best he could do whilst his thoughts and feelings were in such turmoil.

At its core lay a conflict between strict adherence to honesty and truth inculcated at the Quaker orphanage, and the pragmatism suffusing the world he now inhabited. They walked on in silence.

The first and easiest strand to tease out from the tangle in his mind was the source of the wealth. As far as he could see, most, if not all that Lizzie had inherited, had been dishonestly acquired by her benefactor. This presented him with the incongruity of the goodness of Lizzie and the badness of the money.

More difficult to resolve was what he felt about her. He knew something was happening, but what? His upbringing had no place for close emotional ties. He had no experience to call on. Even serial lovers don't really know what overtakes them at the moment of falling: a kind of madness perhaps? Sam was at a loss as to what had been happening to him; all he knew was that it mattered. And now, this.

He could not countenance wealth. Wherever he saw them, riches created corruption, dishonesty and unhappiness. He would have none of it.

"You're very quiet, Sam?" Lizzie said.

All he could do was grunt; with his mind in such disarray he had nothing to say.

Anyway, if Lizzie had money, how could he be seen to be pursuing her? Everyone would think he was after her inheritance. The shame of such a thing would be intolerable. Pursuing her? Was that what he'd been doing? Had the pursuit achieved anything? Was there anything between the two of them to disengage from? How did you end an affair that didn't exist? Despite his attempt to rationalise a way out of the mess, nothing was resolved. All he was left with was a dead weight, somewhere inside, that it seemed he was condemned to carry forever.

Archer walked down Canal Street and into the wharf yard. With the light failing, the day's work was coming to an end. An empty wagon in the distance, at the top of the incline, was being secured for the night. Horses were being led downhill, four in hand, back to the stables. He presumed two had been on the capstan, and the other two, hauling wagons toward Shallcross and back. It all seemed so leisurely, at ease with itself, contrasting with the urgency driving the hunt for Tarp.

"Meester Archer, it so good to see you again. I busy just now, but I come back in minute." Fred Maida was leading the four cart horses back to the stable. He declined a helping hand from the policeman for which Archer was grateful. His experience at home with his father's cob hardly fitted him to cope with one of the giant shires that Fred managed with such nonchalance.

"It's you again, is it?" Inside the stable, Tim Pott was bedding down, feeding and watering his charges. Archer had wandered in after Fred and his quartet. It was marvellous to see the ordered way the animals walked into their stalls unguided and in a trice were head down, munching away at their feeds.

"Whad'ye want? I'm busy just now." Tim was rubbing down each horse and then covering its back with a hessian blanket.

All the while the powerful animals stood passively as he and Fred pushed alongside them into the stalls. They fixed the blankets with rollers round the girth to hold everything in place for the night.

"I'm looking for Mr Riggott," said Archer, "Do you know where I could find him?"

Both Tim and Fred had disappeared momentarily amongst the great animals. A rather muffled voice said, "Tell yer what, Mr Policeman, you go and fill up them buckets whilst we finish off here, and then you can buy us each a pint at The Railway."

Archer stood at the bar ordering ale. He wasn't sure this was what Sam had in mind for him when they parted, but he comforted himself that it was all in the line of duty. The other two had found a corner in the snug and took appreciative pulls at the ale when it arrived.

"Now then, Mr Policeman, whad'ye want wi' Riggott. He ain't much use fer owt, that 'un." Tim was enjoying himself.

"We think he may be in some danger." Archer wasn't sure quite how far to go on the strength of Sam's hunch.

"What? Yer think someone wants ter do 'im in? I don't think we need ter get too upset about that, then." Tim laughed and took another pull at his ale.

"Meester Archer, I tell you about Riggott." Fred was trying to be helpful. After all it wasn't him who'd had the fight with unpleasant foreman. "We not see 'im this afternoon. He go to Shallcross yard. When 'e finish work 'e feeds 'is pigeons."

"Down here, in the wharf yard, are they?"

Fred gave a knowing look and tapped the side of his nose. "They are, an' they aren't."

Riggott, it seemed, kept them in two places, one bunch here at the wharf, and the other a mile or so to the south at Shallcross. Depending on where the pigeons were racing from, he would choose to fly birds from the nearest of the two lofts. To the fair-minded Archer, it all seemed rather irregular.

"Doesn't anyone complain?"

"It secret. He-he." The little Italian giggled. "Tim an' I know, but we no tell. 'E never win anyway, so it not matter." There was a pause, "The day he win..." Both railway men laughed conspiratorially at the thought.

Archer drew the conversation back to the matter in hand: "So you'd expect him back at the wharf any minute now?"

It wasn't as simple as that.

"Sometime 'e go home first or goes for a drink."

It appeared he could be anywhere.

Tim joined in, "I think 'e's got a woman somewhere. I'm workin' on it. Ain't got nowhere yet, but he just disappears sometimes."

Riggott's home was out on the Buxton Road along the Goyt Valley. With that and Shallcross being a mile out of town in opposite directions, the net would have to be spread widely. Fred returned from a call of nature out at the back.

"Bill, Bill," Alcohol brought on greater familiarity. "That man who come looking for Riggott, we tell you 'bout him last time. I think I see him, out the back – but he disappear now."

The Railway was a maze of small rooms with several ways out. At least one gave access to the railway embankment that so dominated the town. By now it was dark, and an attempt to follow would be useless with no lead to go on. It was time to be off.

"I come and help find Riggott." Fred's enthusiasm was infectious – along with the effects of the ale, the evening didn't seem such a bad prospect after all. "Know my way round Whaley better'n you."

It was true his local knowledge might turn out to be invaluable.

The two detectives, Archer with Fred in tow, met as arranged. With Lizzie and her father in a safe place, Spray was free to concentrate on Riggott. The matter of ale wasn't mentioned. He was too preoccupied to notice the alcohol fumes on the breath of the other two. He listened intently to what they had to say about Riggott's movements and the possible sighting of Tarp.

"This is what we'll do. Our man is bound to come back to his pigeon loft at the wharf, in the end. If we split up, and one of us goes out to Shallcross yard and another to his home, then Fred can cover the centre of town and the wharf." It was agreed. "Then we'll meet back at the yard."

Spray took the Shallcross detail. As he walked through the town, the prospect of imminent action went some way to relieve his inner despair. There would be a temporary respite, lasting only as long as the rush of adrenalin; it was why he chose the longest limb of the search. It would stave off the gloom for that bit longer.

Shallcross yard, when he got there, was deserted. Fred had explained where to find Riggott's pigeon loft, and there it was. To his untutored eye, it was full of contented birds pecking away happily at an abundance of grain. They must have been fed when Riggott left work.

Sam chose to return along the track connecting the mainline yard with the wharf. The Buxton Extension, as it was known, was a comparative newcomer compared with the C&HPR. It had elbowed its way out of Whaley Bridge to the south, with scant regard to the convenience of the senior line. It crossed the latter on such a low bridge that locomotives couldn't reach the Whaley Bridge Incline or the wharf below. Horsepower was all that was available. As a result, he had to be careful to avoid the droppings. With a brilliant moon, this wasn't so much of a problem until he came to the low bridge. For a moment or two, all was dark, and his footsteps echoed eerily – then, squelch. He'd carry the smell round with him all evening.

A wagon came into view as well as the capstan for controlling its descent. Some way away, it crept nearer and clearer as he rounded a gentle curve and approached it. From a distance, the line, double tracked by now, seemed to disappear over a precipice. Only as he got closer could he see over the brow and down into the yard.

He started to run.

Archer made his way along Market Street, toward Buxton. After a quarter of a mile, the road forked; to the right a bridge crossed the canal. Fred's instructions were to go on until the houses petered out, keep left, and then go under the railway bridge to the next cottage. In the bright moonlight, there was no difficulty in finding Riggott's home, but to no avail. It was closed up and dark with nothing coming from the chimney. Archer concluded that Riggott must live on his own. After banging fruitlessly on the door, he made his way back toward the town.

The canal provided an alternative route. At the bridge, he dropped down onto the towpath. It occurred to Archer that Riggott would use this way as a short cut from the yard to his home, instead of climbing up to the town along the road. A long line of narrow boats were moored up for the night. They were mostly sitting high in the water, waiting for a load the next day. Wisps of smoke curled up from smokestacks, and enticing smells of cooking reached him as tea was prepared. The cramped quarters housed surprisingly large families. In the past, he'd been put in mind of a conjurer's trick, at the sight of a hoard of children emerging from the tiny cabin. As it was this evening, they'd all been packed away in their magic floating boxes, and he had the towpath to himself.

The yard, too, was deserted. His reconnaissance must have taken less time than the others. He set off for a stroll around the perimeter, driven by no more than idle curiosity. Across the far side, away from the town and over the river, he noticed a row of houses, more substantial than railwayman's cottages, leading off toward a wooded area. The night, though clear, was bitterly cold, and he was warmer on the move than standing about. The walk toward the woodland was uneventful, but as he turned, Archer heard shouting. It seemed to come from the first house in the row, and running back, he was sure a woman screamed. Two men had burst from the door and appeared to be fighting. Watching as he ran, Archer realised one of the men was trying to get away from the other.

The escaping man managed to cross the bridge into the yard. With the gap between the two widening, he was some way to the other side, toward the town. Two parallel rail tracks ran at right angles across his escape route, and in his panic, the prey stumbled on the first rail. Unable to recover in time, he fell heavily as his foot caught the second. He lay, helpless, between the two tracks, and the hunter was on him.

Archer shouted as he ran, but wasn't heeded until he was almost up with the two men. One was motionless in the six foot; the other, satisfied with his handiwork, stood up and turned as Archer arrived. He was face to face with Jarvis Tarp.

———

With the imperative of getting into the fight as soon as possible, Spray had no opportunity, as his temperament would have usually dictated, to devise a considered plan. He just followed his instinct.

The empty wagon, standing on the brink of the incline, had been secured for the night with an old sleeper laid across the rails. It was heavy, and the wagon must have rolled onto it, making it impossible to push the timber off the rails by hand. Spray hunted about for something to help the process along. Laid alongside the track was a long steel lever. No doubt his dilemma was faced daily by the shunters, and it was kept to hand for the very purpose. He pushed it into the triangular space between wheel and scotch and levered the timber free, dragging it to one side, parallel to the track.

A further impediment to his progress seemed easier to sort out. The wagon's brakes had been pinned down. The brake blocks were activated by the rotation of a cross shaft under the mid-point of the chassis. This movement was controlled by a long lever running half the length of the truck. It moved up and down within a slot outside the wheelbase, at the end of the chassis. Holes along the length of the slot allowed for pins to keep the lever in place. Spray, cold fingers fumbling, extracted the pin and lifted the lever into the notch that kept the brakes off when running free. Good operating practice would have had him replace the pin to retain the lever in the notch. There was no time for such refinements.

But why wasn't the damn thing moving. It was at the top of a steep incline, free of restraint and refusing to budge despite his pushing. He grabbed the lever again and managed to get sufficient purchase to edge the wagon forward. The first couple of inches made no difference; the great inert lump went nowhere under its own steam. Another heave and the lever slipped as the wagon started to roll, so slowly at first that Spray stood momentarily to assure himself that something was happening. Then he panicked at the prospect of being left behind. He took a couple of paces, reaching up and failing, to get a hold on the top of the wagon side. He fell heavily, tripping on the old sleeper he'd laid beside the track. By the time he'd picked himself up, the rear of the wagon was almost level with the far end of the sleeper. Jumping up onto it, he ran its full length and launched himself at the rear of the truck. Dangling from its corner, he scrambled to find a foothold. Then, finally, his hands aching, he clambered up to stand on the buffer.

Why was the bloody thing moving so slowly? Having willed it to wait for him a moment ago, he was now urging it on. At this rate, it was going to take an age to get to the yard below. He'd have done better to run.

Fred searched all Riggott's haunts, mostly public houses. He could only look in for sufficient time to catch their enticing, beer-laden warmth for a brief moment, before heading for the next. Over the years, the man's aggressive behaviour had got him temporarily barred from most of the drinking dens in Whaley Bridge. But a drinker of his prodigious habits was too much of a publican's goldmine to be excluded permanently. Between them, the publicans and Riggott had come to an unspoken agreement: they served him as long as he didn't stay too long in one place.

The result was that Fred had to visit every pub in the town before returning to the wharf. As he came round the end of the transhipment shed, he could see a fight in progress across the yard. Two men were still on their feet, slugging it out, when he first saw them. As he ran, one was clearly having the worst of it. Fred recognised William Archer as the constable fell.

To reach the combatants, he would have to cross two sets of tracks. No experienced railwayman would do such a thing without checking for oncoming traffic, and Fred glanced toward the incline. The scene took only a moment to register. A wagon, out of control, was careering down the slope with a man standing on a rear buffer. It was obvious to him that the man was Spray, intent on joining the fight at the earliest opportunity.

The paired tracks on the incline joined, via a set of points, to form a single line at the bottom. The line then crossed a cast-iron bridge over the River Goyt, where it entered the yard. Even if the points weren't set correctly, the wheels of the truck would force the points over, to let it pass without derailment. That is, as long as its speed wasn't enough to throw it off the track whilst traversing the sharp S-bend, where the two lines converged.

This part of the journey was beyond Fred's control. Once inside the yard, assuming the truck was still on the rails, it was a different matter. Here were two sets of points controlled by a two-lever ground-frame. One lever controlled entry via a short spur to the transhipment shed, where track and canal met under cover. If the truck ran in that direction, at any speed, it would come off the track and probably overturn, so steep were the reverse curves. More importantly, it would carry Spray away from the fight.

If the wagon carried straight on at the first set, a second set of points allowed the single track to split into a pair of sidings, ending in buffer stops at the canal basin.

Archer was having a bad time of it in the six foot, between the two sidings. For Spray to assist him, the truck had to pass onto the right-hand track.

With no conscious thought, an instinctive appreciation of what was needed allied to years of railway experience, Fred set the road and ran on toward the field of battle.

Having desperately struggled to get the wagon moving and then willing it not to leave him behind, Spray was now urging his ponderous transport on. Why was it moving so slowly? The twenty seconds or so it had taken him to get to this point seemed like an eternity.

By the time he'd seriously considered and rejected the alternative of jumping off and running, progress was at a more respectable rate. No, he couldn't quite match the pace on foot. The speed was slowly increasing, but he saw he'd been addressing the wrong problem. The realisation suddenly dawned that by the time he arrived at the joining of the two tracks, at the bottom of the incline, his speed would derail the wagon. It would quite possibly end up in the river, taking him with it.

Ignorance of correct procedure occasionally turns out for the best. So it was here. Failure to have pinned the brake lever in its notch meant that Spray, dangling again from the truck side, was able to dislodge it with his foot as it slid down the guide. He brought his weight to bear by standing on it. It was the best he could do and as he was carried toward the bottom, seemed to have no effect at all. The wind was tearing his hair, the ground was rushing by alarmingly, and then the points were there, under the wheels.

There was a moment of anticlimax as the truck, still on the rails, rumbled across the little bridge. To Spray, the noise was deafening, but it was drowned out by the crashing of the river below. The Christmas snow had all thawed days ago in the valleys, but up on the tops, it had persisted longer. Only now was it melting and rushing down beneath the bridge.

The fight in the yard was in its final stages. Tarp and Archer were now recognisable to the passenger, bucketing headlong on his wagon across the yard. Archer fell and was being brutally kicked by Tarp, who had drawn a revolver.

To Spray, for an agonising moment, it seemed he was too late. Wheels rattled over the first set of points and then, almost as a continuum, over the second. Then he was jumping blindly from the moving wagon and into the fray.

Jarvis Tarp was torn by conflicting emotions. He'd nearly completed his mission: the destruction of a one-time lover who he believed he owned, and the two nobodies who'd stolen him away. But he hadn't quite overcome this interfering busybody. The one who'd had the effrontery to try and prevent the venting of his wrath on the last undeserving nonentity. Another couple of kicks to the head should deal with him. If not, there was always the revolver.

He withdrew the gun from his waistband and fingered it lovingly. Only then did he realise, at last, the danger careering toward him. By the time Spray had launched himself from the rolling wagon, Tarp had half turned in his direction. He was bowled over by the detective's flying body crashing into his shoulder. He hit the ground hard and receiving a heavy blow to the head, was unable to move for a few moments. For his part, Spray was unhurt but winded, having caught Tarp's shoulder straight in his solar plexus.

Fred Maida kept on running and arrived to the accompaniment of a huge crashing and splashing of water. The tearaway truck ran through the buffers and into the canal basin. He found himself viewing a tableau, caught in time, which could have been taken from the last scene of a Jacobean tragedy. The only participant with the education to appreciate the analogy lay semi-conscious on the ground, but was beginning to stir.

Fred knew nothing of theatricals, but he was a man to retain any useful knowledge that came his way. Military training in the service Victor Emmanuel II, of the Kingdom of Sardinia, had preserved his life in the Crimean War – though his skills had provided him little use as a civilian over the intervening twenty years. His instruction in the handling of firearms was to change all that. As Tarp stirred and tried to get to his feet, Fred picked up the revolver knocked from Tarp's hand moments before, and as he had been taught all those years ago, flicked open the chamber to inspect its contents.

The revolver was an effective weapon, at close range at least, for intimidating all those present, with the exception of Jarvis Tarp. Only he would know the chamber was empty. On all fours by now, Tarp was recovering fast. At nearly twelve-inches taller than the little Italian, he was becoming dangerous again. Fred, approaching him from behind, took a firm grip on the gun and smashed it, with a satisfying thud, into the back of Tarp's head. He fell back to the ground; but for how long?

"Meester Archer?"

Archer was also recovering and had just made it onto all fours.

"William?"

He finally focussed, somewhat groggily, on Fred.

"Your cuffs, hand cuffs, where are they?"

Archer made a gesture with one hand in the direction of his coat pocket. It was not a wise move. Requiring support at all four corners, he fell heavily back to the ground. It was enough for Fred though, who dived into Archer's pocket, leaving him to make another attempt to rise on his own.

With the cuffs at the ready, Fred dragged the semi-conscious Tarp toward the nearest rail. With no small difficulty, he managed to drag one of his arms between the underside of the rail and the trackbed below. The other arm he pulled across the top and snapped the handcuffs onto each wrist.

"We got him now." From his tone of voice, Fred could have just landed a particularly choice fish. "You feeling better now, William?"

Archer had finally made it to his feet, but could only mumble a reply. Spray, too, was back on his feet, only winded; he'd caught his breath and was almost back to normal. Surveying the scene, a man dead, his murderer secured, and two policemen in attendance, Fred called it a day.

"My wife worry, I not home on time for my tea. You two alright now?" He was off.

Chapter 26

Spray and Archer were with Superintendent Wayland in his small room on Crewe Station. It was hardly warm, despite the brightly burning fire, which would still singe any pair of trousers that got too close. As a result, Archer was standing by the door, just in line for a good clout had anyone else tried to enter. The other two were sitting.

With Fred's departure, there had been four people remaining in the wharf yard. Riggott was beyond help, his murderer was manacled to a rail, and the other two were trying to regain their bearings as they rose groggily to their feet. None of them were quite clear how things had come to be the way they were. Jarvis Tarp was unconscious at the time of his shackling, and the detectives had not grasped exactly what had happened either.

"We've got a problem here, Sam." To make an arrest in the prescribed manner, Tarp would have to be released from the rail and his hand cuffs reapplied. "He's a nasty piece of work."

Whilst not sure how he came to be restrained, Tarp was certainly angry about it.

"We'll have to remove his hand cuffs and put them on again. If we're not careful, he'll do a runner."

As the adrenalin subsided, dull despair swept over Spray, without him knowing why for a moment. Then it all came back in a rush, taking Lizzie to somewhere safe, the news of her inheritance, the impossibility of... He addressed the matter in hand. It proved simple enough – with a piece of rope judiciously applied to the ankles – to undo one cuff and then snap it shut when the wrist was withdrawn from beneath the rail.

"It's your arrest, William, they're your cuffs." With neither man able to remember much, it was a toss-up.

Spray could see no future for himself in his present mood, and Archer had his whole career ahead of him. Fred's disappearance could only mean that, as a working man, he didn't want to be too closely aligned with authority, particularly as he was a foreigner. So Archer's collar it was.

Wayland was leaning forward attentively. He relished tales of spirited action in the face of the enemy. Unimaginative as he was, memories of his army days could be summoned up vicariously by the prowess of his officers.

"We made it to the yard too late to save Riggott, I'm afraid. Tarp had garrotted him just like the other two. Constable Archer arrived first, but he was having a bad time of it by the time I got to him."

"Ah, yes, Sergeant, you made your entry in fine style, by all accounts." Wayland took a letter from his desk. "This is from the Traffic Department."

Putting on his best disciplinarian's voice he started to read: "It has come to my notice that one of your officers, without permission, moved a wagon in the wharf yard at Whaley Bridge."

Further on, the terms 'reckless', 'dangerous' and 'wanton damage' appeared. Before the end, mention had been made of the cost of retrieving a wagon from the canal.

"I don't think we need to trouble ourselves with that." As Wayland put the letter aside his tone changed, "Now tell me all about it."

Spray had prepared a written report, but it was clear that his senior officer wanted something with a bit more dash than was to be found in the dry prose of an official document.

"Why did he do the first one and then keep on, that's what I want to know?" The last thing Spray wanted to do was to add colour to anything, but he did his best to explain.

"Tarp and Oldroyd had known each other for many years and had a…" there was a pause, "a close relationship. Tarp was a possessive and suspicious man, and I suppose, finally, Oldroyd had enough and ended it."

Wayland asked where the mineral scam came into it.

"Only by accident. Oldroyd ran it quite separately from the rest of his life. Tarp knew nothing of it. When Oldroyd went his own way, Tarp looked round for a reason and uncovered Bardell and Riggott as his associates. He put the wrong construction on the connection."

During interrogation, Tarp had fumed about having what was his taken from him. Spray did his best to give the flavour of what was said. "He kept saying he'd been betrayed by all he held most dear and blamed everyone else for the disintegration of his life. After he'd settled down, he seemed quite pleased with himself. I don't think he believes he's done anything wrong."

A section of the report covered Jones, Markham and where they fitted in.

"Come on, Spray, what about this bounder Jones? You don't seem to have arrested him."

Spray had to admit that although Jones and Markham had intended to kill Oldroyd, they hadn't done him any harm. "If you got them in court, Markham would claim he was coerced by Tarp to help with the disposal of Oldroyd's body, and Jones would deny everything."

"But why did Jones want him dead?" At this point, Spray looked so uncomfortable that Archer broke in.

"Perhaps I can explain, sir. Oldroyd's brother left some, apparently worthless, C&HPR shares to his wife when he died. According to Mrs Oldroyd, Jones, as executor, suggested that he 'dealt' with them and tried to get her to sign a document. She showed it to Oldroyd, who got angry, then broke any connection with Jones."

The rest was only guesswork, but it was likely that Jones had been steadily accumulating shares as the original investors died. He defrauded their beneficiaries by having them assigned to himself. "That was what would have happened to Mrs Oldroyd if her brother-in-law hadn't stepped in."

Spray broke in, "Jones and Oldroyd had wind of a possible buy-out of the shares by the L&NWR. As an act of revenge, Oldroyd was blocking the deal. He had enough influence with Tarp's father, the other big shareholder, to slow things down. I never quite got to the bottom of how that worked, but the gossip has it that Oldroyd was Tarp senior's bastard."

"I see; so Jones and Markham go free?"

Archer answered, "It looks like it, sir. Mrs Oldroyd won't press charges. Although the Sergeant and I were present and witnessed Markham's assault, she made it very clear that she wanted the matter dropped."

Archer received a look of gratitude from Spray. He didn't know why, but he'd seen that anything to do with Lizzie was painful to Sam.

"Very well, let the little scoundrel, Markham, go, but Jones…" Wayland looked thoughtful as he paused. "I think I might do something about him."

Just a week later, Wayland sat in the same chair with two newspapers on the desk in front of him. He found them immensely satisfying in their different ways. The *Derbyshire Times* was not his usual fare, and it rarely strayed beyond the county boundary, but he had gone to some trouble to acquire a copy. An edition dated Saturday 31st December lay open at a page from the middle of the paper. Small snippets and corrections of previous items were to be found. Headed, 'C&HPR acquisition not to proceed', he read it out loud to himself.

"Since our report on the acquisition of the above company by the L&NWR, intelligence has been received by us. The offer to purchase has been withdrawn, based on said intelligence, and we understand the L&NWR have no further interest in the matter."

The main news was a detailed report of the arrest of Tarp for the murder of Oldroyd, Bardell and Riggott. Whilst relishing such gory details as he could get his hands on, the reporter made querulous remarks about the arrest of 'an entirely innocent man'. The article pondered how the 'Railway Constabulary could have made such an error', particularly as 'further murders were committed that might have been avoided, had they got the right man in the first place'.

Wayland harrumphed and turned to his regular reading matter, *The Times of London*. The Peak Railway Murder, as it was headed, was not such a big story in the national paper. Remote Derbyshire was not a place of immediate interest to the majority of its readership. It was full of mines, industry, and wild, untamed hills. Crime and punishment did have a following though, so there was a modest report. Fortunately, the matter of Markham's arrest and subsequent release was not mentioned, but much was made of the garrotting of three victims.

Of greatest satisfaction to Wayland was the final paragraph. 'We must commend the foresight shown by the Directors of the L&NWR in establishing a railway constabulary. This newspaper has published over a number of years, reports of criminal activity on our great railway system, and suggested this remedy as one best suited to restore its tarnished reputation. In particular, we commend Superintendent Charles Wayland, lately Lt Colonel in Her Majesties Corp of Engineers, where he served with distinction in the late war in the Crimea, who led the criminal enquiry which resulted in such an expeditious and satisfactory conclusion.'

All was well with the world.

End Piece

Sometime in the late summer of 1876, a letter arrived at the office of the Railway Constabulary on Crewe Station, addressed to Sergeant Samuel Spray. It was large and stiff, with something embossed on the flap of the envelope.

By now, Sam had more or less managed to restore order to his wayward emotions, and they had been forced back into their restricted little box at the back of his mind. Just occasionally, a chance encounter would cause a break out, but generally everything could be whipped back into its proper place in short order. Without reading what was on the flap, he slit open the envelope to find an invitation card inside.

The gold edge was only a start. An ornate crest with gold leaf and a motto in Latin adorned the top. Below, 'The Chairman and Parish Council of Whaley Bridge' requested the pleasure of 'Sergeant Samuel Spray's company', to help them celebrate the 'Grand Opening' of a newly established 'Reading Room and Library'. The project had been funded from a bequest by 'Mr Isaac Bennett and his daughter Elizabeth' in memory of the late 'Mrs Kezia Bennett'. There was to be a 'Grand Tea' and the guests were to be entertained by the 'Whaley Bridge Silver Band'.

Sam gritted his teeth and tried to keep the lid on his little box. The detective in him couldn't help noting that although the invitation wasn't numbered in the bottom right-hand corner, there had been some rubbing-out which failed to remove an indentation in the soft card. Number 1, in a circle, had once been written there. The card slipped from his fingers and fluttered to the floor, landing face down. He couldn't stop himself reading *Please come, I would value your attendance* Signed: *Elizabeth Oldroyd*

Below *PS It will be Jimmy Allcroft's debut playing cornet alongside his father.* Then a sketch of a face with hands pressed to its ears.

Glossary

Including Derbyshire dialect, Victorian Slang & Railway terminology

Barker	Handgun
Bobby off	Go precipitately, send away
Cloth yer one	Hit you
Chernaya	Crimean War battle
Chink	Money
Cokum	An opportunity
Crow	A lookout
Cuffs	Handcuffs
Cut	Canal
Deadlurk	Empty premises
Down (line or direction of movement on a rail track)	Away from London, or local rail Centre
Drum	House
Dubs	Skeleton keys
Dunnage	Clothes
Ee's never-sweat	He's lazy
Fly	A through train on the C&HPR
Flyman	The guard on a Fly
Gamp	Umbrella
Gretpuddingead	An idiot
Grind	Act of coition
Jack	Detective

Jitty	Alleyway
Kettledrums	Breasts
Kife	Bed
Leg	Dishonest Person
Lush	Heavy drinker
Mandrake	Homosexual man
Mankin abaht	Messing about
Mark	Targeted victim
Paddingken	A tramps doss house
Parliamentary (train)	One cheap train/day imposed on Railway companies in 1844 by Act of Parliament
Peeler	Policeman
Pit	Inside front coat pocket
Reet nesh	Really cold
Roller	Strap to go round a horses girth to keep a rug in place
Scran	Food
Snap	Food
Speeler	Cheat or gambler
Shirkster	Layabout
The four foot	The space between the rails of a rail track
The Knotty	The North Staffordshire Railway
The six foot	The space between two sets of rails
Toff	Stylish Gentleman
Tooler	Pickpocket

Train staff	An object, usually a wooden or brass staff that an engine driver is obliged to carry, or at least see, before he enters a single track section of line.
Up (line or direction of movement on a rail track)	Toward London or local rail Centre.

Historical note and Disclaimer

Opening in 1830, the Cromford & High Peak was one of the earliest lines of the railway era. Its purpose was to carry minerals extracted from the White Peak. Initially, the route was planned as a canal to link with waterways to the east and west of the country. The plan foundered when it was discovered that there was insufficient water on the limestone plateau to supply such a system. Later, the survey work carried out in the 18th century was used as a basis for a thirty-three mile route connecting with the Cromford canal to the south east and the Peak Forest canal at Whaley Bridge.

Where flights of locks were planned, inclined planes were established and traffic was worked up and down by static steam engines winding a continuous cable to which trucks were attached in groups of three. Parallel tracks allowed each movement to be balanced with one group climbing whilst the other descended. The only exception was the incline out of Whaley Bridge wharf where the ground proved too unstable for such a system and a horse driven windlass was installed.

Initially, horses were used to move traffic on the level sections but, slowly, steam engines replaced them. Here again, Whaley Bridge wharf was the exception. As the rail network spread across the country, both ends of the C&HP connected to it. By 1875, it was possible to gain access to the Midland at Cromford and the LNW at Whaley Bridge. In constructing an extension to Buxton, this latter concern crossed the C&HP with such a low bridge that it was impossible for steam traction to access the wharf and only horses were used there.

By 1861, the LNW had taken control of the C&HP and

were responsible for managing its operations, and in 1887 assumed ownership. Any greater detail about the relationship between the two companies to be found in this book is entirely fictitious as indeed are all the characters. The author has endeavoured to adhere to the geography of the area, including some public houses, and the rail system as it existed in 1875, but with one exception: all the events in the book are products of his imagination. The rail accident in the opening chapter is a matter of record and occurred much as he has depicted it. Only one person died, the unfortunate fireman (George Tumington) whilst his driver (William Chappell) suffered a broken thigh. No murdered man was found at the scene.

For anyone interested in the subject *Scenes from the Past: 37 Railways of the High Peak* (parts one and two) by Jones & Bentley published by Foxline is recommended. It provided most of the author's source material. Those with more energy can walk the High Peak Trail which follows the southern half of the original trackbed including Middleton Top where a winding engine is preserved and Sheep Pasture Bottom with its workshops and the canal interchange. The northern section has largely disappeared, but the wharf yard at Whaley Bridge is preserved.

Coming up in the sequel, *Echoes Down the Line*

As the Irish Mail clanked and groaned to a standstill, a watching man stood up. In the crowded compartment he'd benefitted from a degree of anonymity, but as passengers started to step out onto the platform he found himself in a quandary; more exposed now, whilst his quarry dozed on.

The sleeper was supposed to alight at Crewe and the watcher's orders were simple. "Just make sure he gets out at the right station and reports to his superior in the Railway Constabulary." Perhaps not quite that easy, it wouldn't be difficult to check that he went to the right office, but what if the officer in question was absent; the possibility of the sleeping man failing to disembark had not been covered at all.

Two things happened at once. One passenger, who must have been bound for Euston as he had remained seated throughout the melee, reached out and tapped the weary traveller on the knee. "I believe I heard you tell the guard you were for Crewe, sir."

Outside a porter called loudly "Crewe, Crewe Junction, change here for…" before he'd finished his announcement there was an eruption in the compartment's corner seat. A dishevelled man rose explosively and without glancing round stepped into the hustle and bustle of the busy station. His abrupt movement dislodged his hat. It had been pulled low for the whole of the train journey, hiding his face, but standing, he pushed the battered bowler to its accustomed position revealing a black eye and damage to his lip.

Once on the platform he pushed his way through the crowd and the watcher saw him greeting a uniformed man who, despite his limp, retained a military bearing.

"Ah, there you are, Sergeant," was loud enough to be heard at a distance: had the watcher been closer he might have noted the softer tone of, "My God, Sam, what have they done to you."